PLAYING FOR KEEPS

Gabriella turned sharply right and pulled the car into the circular rotunda of the Romana Hotel.

"Would you care for a drink?" Claudon asked.

"No, thank you." She paused. "Pierre, you must make it clear to Hamilton that without those missing triangles our task at Megiddo may be hopeless."

"You've already made that point with him, but I will emphasize it." He smiled. "Well, *bonne chance*."

"You, too." Gabriella waved and drove off.

Claudon unlocked the door of his eighth-floor suite and reached for the light switch. A pair of powerful hands came out of the darkness, pinning his arms. Another man leveled a gun at Claudon. "Take off your clothes!"

The big man released him, and Claudon removed his jacket.

"Quickly! Your socks and shorts."

"But . . . I . . ." Claudon found his voice. "I don't understand. Who are you? I've done nothing."

They shoved him out onto the open balcony and stared at the frightened, naked man a moment. They moved quickly, professionally. One seized his arms; the other, his legs. They swung him out over the balcony in a wide arc and let him go. He screamed a long, piercing scream. . . .

THE DISCOVERY

Steve Shagan

BANTAM BOOKS
TORONTO · NEW YORK · LONDON · SYDNEY · AUCKLAND

THE DISCOVERY
*A Bantam Book / Perigord Book / published in association with
William Morrow and Company, Inc.*

*PRINTING HISTORY
Morrow / Perigord edition published August 1984
A Literary Guild Selection
Bantam / Perigord edition / October 1985
Bantam UK edition / May 1986*

*While this is a work of fiction, the events surrounding the Ebla dig
are based in fact.*

*Grateful acknowledgment is given for permission to reprint from
"Everything Happens to Me" by Matt Dennis and Thomas Adair,
copyright 1941 (renewed) by Dorsey Bros. Music, a division of
Music
Sale Corporation.*

ISBN 0-553-17186-0

Published simultaneously in the United States and Canada

Printed and bound in Great Britain by Hunt Barnard Printing Ltd.

O   0 9 8 7 6 5 4 3 2 1

For my friend Vic Morrow

And I will give thee the treasures of darkness, and hidden riches of secret places. . . .

—ISAIAH 45:3

PROLOGUE

△

The Land of Moab
1260 B.C.

The tall, erect purple-robed figure appeared at the mouth of the cave high up on Mount Nebo. The son of Amram leaned on the wooden staff with which he had performed God's miracles. Moses was one hundred and twenty years old, but his eyes were not dim as he beheld the descendants of Abraham, Isaac, and Jacob.

The tribes of Israel were assembled below: shoulder to shoulder, clan by clan, column by column.

Their number had been swelled by Hebrews summoned from the pagan lands of Ethiopia, Canaan, Philistia, and the ancient kingdom of Ebla. Their black and white goatskin tents stretched eastward across the desert to the sea of salt and south to the crumbling ruins of Sodom and Gomorrah.

Their goats, sheep, donkeys, and herds of cattle darkened the desert landscape. In the deep wadis between the scarred hills, a pack of jackals howled, unnerved by the rising human chant and ominous percussive throb of drums.

It was a ritual chant of sorrow and lamentation, for this was to be the day of the great prophet's death, and never again would there arise in Israel a prophet like Moses. He had led them out of bondage in Egypt to the very edge of the

3

Promised Land. He had given unto them the Lord's covenant and commandments. They would call their God Yahweh, and there would be no other before him.

High upon Mount Nebo, Moses gazed for the last time at the fertile hills and valleys of Canaan—the Promised Land, to which Yahweh had forbidden him entry.

The jackals fell silent. The drums and timbrels did not sound. The chanting priests sang no more. The soldiers of Judah stood rigid, silent, the sun glinting off their spears and shields.

On the scarred mountains and stony desert tableau not a breath of wind stirred. A fierce, perfect silence descended on the assembled tribes; it was the silence of God.

A great, blinding blue light came out of the sun. The Children of Israel cast down their eyes, for they could not look upon that light.

In the front ranks of the tribe of Levi, a young priest trembled, for he alone heard the voice of Yahweh.

"Ithamar, son of Aaron, cast out your fear, go up unto the mountain called Nebo, into the cave of eternity, where you will find my servant, Moses. He will give unto you a sacred task, for I have chosen you to preserve my last word now, and forever into the midnight of time."

And Ithamar gathered his cloak to shield his eyes from the terrible light of Yahweh and picked his way up the stony face of Mount Nebo.

△

Tell Mardikh
Syria

CHAPTER ONE

⚠

The great sandy mound swelled above the desert floor like an immense blister covering 50 acres and rising to a height of 120 feet.

Tell Mardikh had been formed by the accumulated debris of four thousand years of human settlement; beneath its crest lay the residue of mankind's nobility and savagery—layer upon layer, like brick mortared to brick.

Sitting behind the wheel of a dusty jeep, Professor Emilio Sabitini held an umbrella against the merciless Syrian sun and stared off reflectively at the tell.

Sabitini was the director of Middle Eastern studies at Rome University, a master Egyptologist and renowned authority in classical topography.

His fame as an archaeologist was somewhat muted by the fact that he was frequently mistaken for the American film actor Ben Gazzara, to whom he bore a striking resemblance, and with typical Roman humor the professor had signed numerous autographs in the actor's name.

Sabitini's career spanned almost thirty years and countless expeditions, but nothing in his professional experience had prepared him for the astonishing events that were to transpire here in the desert country of northern Syria.

He could scarcely believe that five years had passed since the expedition's first spade turned the dust of Tell Mardikh. In that distant summer, Sabitini and his Syrian colleague Dr. Amin Gamasi had reason to believe they were probing the outer crust of the legendary kingdom of Ebla.

Sumerian tablets inscribed in 3500 B.C. depicted Ebla as a sophisticated society that had achieved extraordinary advances in the arts and sciences. A thousand years later Egyptian scrolls described Ebla as a center of knowledge and learning. The Old Testament had also mentioned Ebla as the birthplace of Eber, for whom the Hebrews were named, but the actual site of the mythical kingdom remained a frustrating, timeless mystery.

The first solid clue to the possible location of Ebla surfaced in typical archaeological fashion—by sheer chance.

In the spring of 1974 a farmer tilling the soil in southern Lebanon near Tyre had uncovered a basalt stone inscribed on both sides with Sumerian cuneiform. The wedgelike script was the first known written language using a form of letters rather than pictures.

Sabitini and his associate, the brilliant epigrapher Dr. Gabriella Bercovici, were summoned by the Lebanese curator of antiquities. They photographed and carbon tested the basalt stone and determined the date of origin to be between 3500 and 3400 B.C.

After returning to Rome, Gabriella began the painstaking task of translating the cuneiform. She was not yet thirty-five but was already acknowledged to be one of four living masters of ancient Middle Eastern idioms.

After weeks of tedious decipherment her efforts were rewarded by a startling revelation. The inscribed text indicated the location of Ebla to be astride the ancient trade routes south of Aleppo and north of Damascus.

Gabriella's initial elation was tempered by Sabitini's

reminder that the area in question was vast and dotted with numerous small tells.

Almost two years were spent surveying the torrid, windblown Syrian desert before Sabitini decided on Tell Mardikh as the possible site of ancient Ebla. The sheer size of the mound, its strategic position on the principal highway to Damascus, and the profusion of Bronze Age potsherds just below its surface were in the end decisive factors.

The choice of Tell Mardikh represented an immense gamble of time and money. An expedition had to be organized, funding secured, Syrian cooperation obtained, and a small army recruited: epigraphers, engineers, draftsmen, architects, and experts trained in the delicate process of handling artifacts. The entire team had to be assembled, transported, and housed.

In the early fall of 1976, with the cooperation of Dr. Gamasi, Syrian permission was finally obtained. The expedition was financed by Rome University, the Syrian Ministry of Culture, and a consortium of private investors called Pyramid International.

A compound was constructed along the lines of a French Foreign Legion fort. Huge concrete walls, painted white, protected an interior square of barracks, workrooms, kitchens, photo labs, and medical facilities.

In July 1977 the Italian-Syrian team sank an east-west trench into the crest of Tell Mardikh. Digging their way through clay, mud, and limestone, they unearthed their first important discovery at a depth of forty feet. A massive bronze gateway appeared at the eastern perimeter of the trench; its sculpted arch had crumbled, but under Sabitini's patient supervision it was meticulously pieced together. The restored carving depicted a ceremonial procession circa 1600 B.C. A column of robed priests, bearded warriors, and Nubian slaves, trailed by sheep, goats, and cattle, stood with bowed heads before the Canaanite god Baal.

The dig continued for several weeks before coming to a halt on the advice of the chief engineer. The balance of that first season was largely devoted to shoring up the trench, stringing lights, and pumping water out of underground chambers.

Toward the conclusion of the expedition's second season a bronze chamber was unearthed containing a wealth of artifacts: a gold statue of a Hittite cat-girl; a basalt statue of a bearded winged lion; twenty-seven terra-cotta figurines; and a hideous bronze statue identified as the Canaanite devil-god Pazuzu.

All objects were photographed, carbon tested for age, catalogued, and sent to the museum at Aleppo.

The dark chambers of Tell Mardikh continued to surrender a steady stream of artifacts, but no stone, no statuary, no object had borne an inscription. The huge mound of earth sitting astride the ancient trade routes of the Middle East maintained its silence. A subtle but growing sense of failure pervaded the efforts of the team, for in archaeology nothing equals the importance of the written word.

Gabriella was particularly disappointed. Her expertise in deciphering cuneiform had not yet been required. She became the expedition's unofficial photojournalist. As she worked in the chambers and tunnels sixty feet below the desert floor, her Nikon camera was never still; the motorized click-whirl and synchronous flash echoed in and illuminated the dark limestone chambers.

Between seasons of the dig, she catalogued hundreds of photographs in special files at the Rome University Library.

She made a photographic blowup of the grotesque Canaanite devil-god Pazuzu and hung it in her office, alongside a blowup of the same godhead discovered on a previous expedition in the ruins of Megiddo in northern Israel. She could not define her interest in the photographs since the pagan deity was common to several Middle Eastern cultures but was nevertheless intrigued by the appearance of the idol in both Syria and Israel.

The expedition's fourth summer belonged principally to the architects and engineers. Tunnels were shored up, additional lights were strung in the dark limestone corridors, and serpentine staircases were constructed to connect the various levels of the dig.

Excavations were resumed the first Monday in July, but a pervasive depression hung over the dig. The vision of Ebla faded with each passing day. The stream of artifacts continued to surface, but the archaeologists would have gladly traded all the gold and statuary for a single inscription.

It was as if the presence of some ancient deity lingered in the underground chambers, tantalizing them with an abundance of clues while withholding the ultimate secret—the identity and culture of its inhabitants. Despite all their science and technology, Ebla remained a myth.

CHAPTER TWO

⚠

Sitting in the jeep, just outside the compound, Professor Sabitini shook his head in dismay at the recall of past events. He stared off at the tell, sensing that the results of this, the fifth season of the dig, would be critical to its continuance.

The private investors of Pyramid International had been complaining about the lack of progress and were threatening to end their financial assistance. The administrator of finance at Rome University and the director of the Syrian Ministry of Culture were fast approaching the limits of their fiscal patience.

Sabitini sighed heavily, thinking that perhaps his choice of Tell Mardikh had been too precipitous, but second guessing was endemic to the profession, for in the last analysis all archaeological wisdom came down to instinct and luck.

A sudden dust devil whirled across the jeep. The grainy bits of sand stung his face and pulled him out of his reverie. He wondered what was keeping Gabriella and checked his watch; it was 2:15 P.M., July 25.

Gripping the umbrella against the sun, Sabitini climbed

out of the jeep and walked slowly back into the compound.

He entered the photo lab tent just as Gabriella emerged from the darkroom. She was barefoot, wearing her customary tight-fitting jeans and a white T-shirt with the blue UCLA imprint "Let's go Bruins." She carried several wet prints and smiled nervously. "I'll be with you in a minute."

"The crew is probably halfway through that tunnel by now."

"I'm sorry, Emilio, but I had trouble with the solution."

She quickly pinned the prints to a dry line, then went over to her cot, sat down, and began to pull her boots on.

Sabitini always marveled at how oblivious she was to her own natural beauty. She had high, well-defined cheekbones that curved gracefully down from her ice blue eyes, past the straight patrician nose, angling off, framing her wide, full mouth. She was tall and slim and carried herself with a purposeful stride.

Gabriella got to her feet, slipped a khaki field jacket over the T-shirt, grabbed her Nikon case, tossed her straight pale hair, and smiled. "Ready."

It was thirty degrees cooler deep inside the tell, where Sabitini supervised a crew of tired laborers digging their way through a tunnel at Stratum VI, Level C.

A foreboding sense of danger permeated the dark tunnel, and the damp air smelled of death and decay. Flickering torchlights cast sinister shadows across the sweating limestone walls, as if phantoms of long-dead pagan gods had risen.

Sabitini was engaged in a hushed conversation with Gabriella when he heard the ringing sound of metal striking metal. He moved quickly to the side of a Bedouin laborer, knelt, and gently scooped the earth from a bronze statue. He held the artifact up to Gabriella, who brushed the dust from its face. The statue was instantly recognizable as the Canaanite devil-god Pazuzu.

"I know what you're thinking," Sabitini said. "The Hebrew connection."

She tossed her damp blond hair, and her eyes flashed. "I never said there was a connection—only that it was curious for this idol to have surfaced in both Syria and Israel."

"Well, let's hope it remains nothing more than curiosity. Our Syrian friends would not be thrilled if we proved the existence of an ancient Hebrew presence in northern Syria."

The digging continued for another hour, and Sabitini was about to call a halt when a sudden shout in Arabic echoed down the corridor. At the tunnel's entrance a Syrian foreman waved his arms frantically, shouting, "*Maktaba! Maktaba!*" The word struck them with the force of a thunderclap—*maktaba* meant "library." They dashed down the tunnel, following the foreman into the adjacent corridor.

The Syrian laborers stood aside as Sabitini and Gabriella moved past them. At the far end of the corridor a square hole had been cut in the earthen walls.

Dr. Gamasi smiled at them. "Have a look."

The sight before them was astonishing. The inner chamber was solid gold, and, lining the walls, in stacked piles along wooden shelves, were thousands of clay tablets inscribed on both sides in cuneiform. Positioned in the center of the chamber was a gold statue of a bearded figure wearing a massive jeweled crown.

It was a discovery beyond conception—a large and magnificently preserved royal library.

The Syrian laborers quickly cut a body-size portal in the outer wall, and one by one they entered the chamber.

Gabriella knelt at the base of the statue and brushed the caked dust from the cuneiform inscription carved into its pedestal. She moved her magnifying glass slowly over the script. Royal surnames were easily translated. The sentence structure and content had not varied since the curious wedge-shaped language first appeared in Sumer in 3800 B.C. Royalty simply stated its name, the names of its parents, and the name of the people over whom they ruled.

Her hand trembled slightly as she moved the glass from character to character.

The silence was excruciating, and the passing minutes seemed interminable before she finally rose.

In a voice choked with emotion she said, "The message reads: 'I have by royal scribe set down here my records. For I am Ibbit-Lim, son of Eber, king of the people of Ebla.' "

Gamasi shouted, *"Allah akbar!"* and joyously embraced his Italian colleagues.

The dig was halted, and all hands were summoned to form a human chain from the mouth of the tell, down the earthen steps, along the descending corridors, into the royal library. The biscuitlike clay tablets were passed hand to hand from their long, dark slumber into the light of the twentieth century. Bedouin laborers placed them in the courtyard, where they were catalogued and photographed.

The thrill of discovery spread through the crew, and a celebration was hastily organized. Tables and chairs were brought out into the compound courtyard. Speakers were hooked up to a stereo set. In the kitchen tents Syrian and Italian cooks had their fires going. The night air was scented with sweet spices and pungent garlic. Strong Syrian arak went down with Sicilian Chianti. Italian love songs alternated with haunting, lyrical Arabic wailing.

A spirit of camaraderie enveloped the entire team. The fulfillment of their five-year search for Ebla touched the very soul of their profession; to be an archaeologist, one had to believe in the possibility of the impossible.

The dancing, singing, and babble of languages rose to a high pitch.

From their numbered places lining the compound walls artifacts of Ebla's four thousand years of civilization shadowed the celebration: idols, devil-gods, and ruby-eyed bronze cobras gazed silently at the revelers.

Gabriella did not hear the gaiety, although her working tent was just off the courtyard. Her eyes burned, and her right hand ached from hours of holding the magnifying glass. A knifelike pain spread through her shoulders, and the musky heat of the tent caused beads of perspiration to run down her cheeks, dampening her khaki shirt. She had been studying the cuneiform script of the Ebla tablets for hours and was both obsessed and distressed. She had deciphered only six words on the large clay tablets bearing the royal seal of King Ibbit-Lim. The cuneiform language of Ebla was not pure.

Gabriella was unaware of Sabitini's presence until his hand touched her shoulder. "Enough," he said. "This is not a night for work."

She placed the magnifying glass down and rubbed her hand over her eyes. "I have to return to Rome."

"Why? We still have six weeks of the season left."

She rose, wearily wiping the perspiration from her forehead. "I have never seen this language before. The adjectives and verbs are traditional Akkadian cuneiform, but the nouns are not decipherable, making the sentences unintelligible."

"But you translated the inscription on the statue without difficulty."

"Those words are nothing more than a royal seal. It simply identifies the king, his father, and the people they ruled. But the tablets concerning their laws, commerce, religion, and history are written in a cuneiform variant I've never encountered."

"But the dig must continue," Sabitini said persistently.

"To what purpose? We already have an abundance of artifacts. If we can read their language, the tablets will dictate precisely what we should seek from here on out."

"You don't think it's possible to crack the problem here?"

She shook her long, straight pale hair. "I need the facilities of the university. We must return, Emilio."

The logic of her request was beyond dispute. The possibility of listening to the voice of ancient Ebla was far more important than continuing the dig.

"All right." He nodded. "I will advise Dr. Gamasi."

CHAPTER THREE

△

Upon their return to Rome, Gabriella and her team of student epigraphers pursued the maddening task of deciphering the elusive idiom of Ebla.

Using a variety of ancient Proto-Semitic dialects, they dropped selected nouns into the incomplete cuneiform sentences, hoping to discover the key that would unlock the Ebla language. Their predicament was not unlike trying to piece together a complex jigsaw puzzle by borrowing related shapes belonging to another puzzle: Nothing fitted.

On an unusually cold October night Gabriella left the language laboratory and returned to her fourth-floor office. She paced for a moment, then walked over to a battered piano and with her forefinger picked out the melody of the Beatles' classic "Michelle." After a moment she sat down and played a Debussy prelude.

As a child she had studied the piano on and off for years but soon realized her musical skills were limited and considered her piano playing an avocation—a soothing and stimulating exercise. She loved the classical compositions but was also fascinated with jazz. She

18

was intrigued by the African-American hybrid music and had acquired an extensive collection of jazz recordings.

After finishing the piece, she poured a steaming cup of mudlike coffee, lit a cigarette, slumped in her chair, and stared up at the twin photographic blowups of Pazuzu. Once again she was struck by the presence of the grotesque idol in both Israel and Syria.

She began to pace, concentrating on two mutually exclusive factors: history and logic. Biblical Canaan had been conquered by Joshua after the death of Moses. The Israelite invasion occurred between 1260 and 1240 B.C. and eventually included Megiddo, which was only 200 kilometers south of Ebla.

Could the Hebrew tribes have traded with and even settled in Ebla? And if so, would not their languages have crossed, mixed, and evolved into a new dialect? The same mysterious idiom contained in the Ebla tablets?

Her pulse quickened for a moment, then slowed as she shook her head. The dates were wrong. The Ebla tablets preceded Israel's occupation of Canaan by two thousand years.

She sighed heavily and stared out the window at the distant glow of St. Peter's.

The answer to the riddle lay just below the surface of her consciousness. It was contained in something she had seen the day they entered the royal library of Ebla. She moved quickly to her desk and rummaged through the pile of eleven-by-fourteen blowups of the tablets.

Her hand trembled as she selected the photograph depicting the statue of King Ibbit-Lim. Her pulse raced and her heart pounded as she studied the inscription carved into its base: "I, Ibbit-Lim, son of Eber . . . "

Eber was mentioned in Genesis as the godfather of all Hebrews, and Hebrew was the one ancient, regional language that had not yet been tested.

A sense of exhilaration surged through her, and despite the late hour, she phoned Sabitini. He listened to her conclusions and with a trace of annoyance replied, "The Bible is legend, and you're accepting it as fact."

"Perhaps, but legend is more durable than fact."

"Ah." His voice warmed. "I love you when you think in Italian."

"I always think in Italian," she replied. "You're just envious of my years at Cambridge."

"It's too late to discuss your misspent Anglo-Saxon education. Now, what is it you want me to do?"

"I want to test biblical Hebrew nouns against the incomplete cuneiform sentences. The expertise of a military cryptographer would be helpful."

"All right." He sighed. "I'll phone General Grimaldi. Go home now. Drink some wine. Get some sleep."

They sat on either side of the intelligence officer who operated a massive computer with an entire Hebrew dictionary in its memory bank.

Sabitini chewed nervously on a dead cigar while Gabriella checked her notes. She had translated a selected group of incomplete cuneiform sentences into biblical Hebrew and augmented them with correlating Hebrew nouns.

The officer fed the data into the computer's cryptographic program, and in less than a minute a flashing green light indicated the information had been absorbed.

"Since I don't understand Hebrew," the officer said, "you'll have to tell me when we begin to approach semantic coherence."

"Of course," she replied tensely.

The officer played his fingers deftly across the keys, asking the computer to arrange possible congruent combinations. The electronic brain whirred; lights flashed. Hebrew words running right to left appeared and disappeared.

The better part of an hour passed before a spill of seven Hebrew words appeared on the display screen. "Does this combination make sense?" the officer inquired.

Gabriella nodded, her eyes riveted to the screen. "It says, 'I engraved for eternity the wisdom of' . . ." She paused. "We're missing one word."

"We'll find it," the officer replied confidently.

Sabitini relit his cigar and watched the officer punch another series into the computer.

The sentence reappeared, displaying a variety of Hebrew nouns, none of which closed the sentence with coherence.

The officer sighed and glanced at Gabriella. "I may have been overly optimistic. We're running out of choices." He took a deep breath, and his fingertips hit a series of buttons. The computer's lights blinked rapidly as he continued to change keys and ciphers. He leaned back, studying the results for a moment, then punched up a final combination.

Gabriella gasped as the display screen flashed the new sentence formation.

חרטתי אחרית דברי יהוה.

The single Hebrew noun that completed the sentence was *Yahweh*—the ancient God name of Israel!

She turned to them, her eyes streaming with the light of revelation. "It says, 'I engraved for eternity the wisdom of Yahweh.'"

Sabitini kissed her and shook the officer's hand, exclaiming, "Bravo! Bravo!"

The young officer stared at them with amused detachment. He did not understand their obsession with secrets of the long past and had no conception of the breakthrough Gabriella had achieved.

It was an archaeological triumph that not only gave voice to a lost civilization but carried present-day political implications which even she did not perceive. The name of Yahweh inscribed on the Ebla tablets created a sound, scientific possibility that modern-day Syrians were descendants of ancient Hebrew tribes who had settled in Syria twenty-five hundred years before the advent of Islam.

Sabitini treated her to a superb lunch in a small family-run trattoria in the Piazza Farnese. The courses of pasta and roast veal were topped off by a dessert of fresh cherries and assorted homemade pastries. Sabitini ordered grappa brandy and double espresso coffees.

Gabriella spoke rapidly and excitedly of her plans to organize a staff to begin translating the Ebla tablets.

Sabitini nodded occasionally, but his eyes seemed clouded by other thoughts.

"What is it?" she asked. "What are you thinking?"

"I was turning over the irony of our situation."

"What irony?"

"That current Middle East politics prevent us from announcing your achievement."

"Perhaps I've had too much wine. I don't understand."

"Think for a moment, Gabriella." He leaned forward. "If this Hebrew connection leaks to the Syrians or the Western press, we would be denied permission to return to Ebla."

"But why?"

"You cannot take away from the Syrian people their culture and heritage," he explained. "Besides, it's conceivable that the Israeli government might use the Ebla tablets as historic proof that ancient Israel included Syria. We can't ignore the fact that Syria and Israel have fought five brutal wars and may well be facing still another conflict."

"But what if the Syrians knew they had been fighting their own brothers?"

Sabitini shook his head and sighed. He admired her dedication, her brilliance, and her beauty. But he was amazed at her political naïveté. "Please believe me. The Syrians are not anxious to learn that they may well be the thirteenth tribe of Israel."

"How do you know that?" she asked angrily. "Are you a political prophet?"

"I know Middle East politics."

"To hell with that!" She glared at him. "I'm fed up with politics and bowing our heads to papier-mâché dictatorships. We're scientists, dammit! And we're denying our own science by withholding this information. Maybe—just maybe—if the Syrians and Israelis were made aware of their ancient blood ties, the killing would stop!"

"I love it." Sabitini smiled.

"Love what?" she asked, perplexed.

"Your occasional displays of anger. They remind me of your noble Italian heritage."

"I hate it when you turn everything into a cheap joke."

"There is no other way to get through life."

"That's your self-serving cynicism."

"No, it's my pragmatism," he replied calmly. "I know I'm asking the impossible of you, but we have no choice." He covered her hand with his own. "There are still thousands of tablets in Ebla to be studied. You must keep this information confidential."

"I can't promise that. Withholding a historic truth goes against everything I believe in."

"Remember, Gabriella, it took four thousand years to unearth Ebla. One mistake will bury it again. You do understand that?"

"Yes." She sighed. "I understand."

In the ensuing month Gabriella focused her energy on the continuing task of deciphering the Ebla tablets. Numerous prophecies surfaced. Some had already come to pass. The dispersal of the Children of Israel from the Promised Land and their return almost two thousand years later were inscribed on a large clay tablet. Other inscriptions defied comprehension. There was mention of Megiddo as the site of a cataclysmic battle in the future world between the armies of Satan and the forces of Yahweh. The outcome was not revealed.

Toward the end of the month on a bright, sunny morning, a student assistant burst into Gabriella's office. The young man had translated a tablet containing the last wills and testaments of prominent Ebla citizens. Their names were indexed by profession—military, commerce, politics—and notable guests of Ebla. Among the latter, there was an astonishing inscription: *"I, Ithamar, son of Aaron, messenger of Moses, guardian of Yahweh's last word, have willed my testament and remains be interred in the royal burial chamber of Ibbit-Lim, king of Ebla."*

The text of the sentence was incredible. It was the first mention of a Hebrew priest at Ebla. It was the first mention of Moses, the great prophet of Israel. But even more astounding was the possibility that a lost word of God lay buried in the ruins of Ebla.

Sabitini glanced up from a bronze Etruscan statue as Gabriella entered his office and placed the translation of the Ithamar text on his desk. "A student working on the tablets brought this to me a few minutes ago."

"Don't you ever wear anything but jeans and sneakers?" Sabitini asked with a wry smile.

"Never mind my wardrobe—just read that, Emilio."

He put his glasses on and studied the single sentence for a long time. "Where did this come from?"

"An index in the royal library pertaining to last wills and testaments," she replied. "What do you think he meant by 'messenger of Moses'?"

Sabitini shrugged his broad shoulders. "The greater question is what does he mean by 'guardian of Yahweh's last word'?"

"The answer is in Ebla," she said. "We must move up the schedule."

"I will try again with Dr. Gamasi."

"What do you mean by 'try again'?"

"I phoned him last week—a routine call to fix the visas for our return in May. He said the entire matter of renewing our permits was under study. When I questioned his remark, he stated that reports alluding to a Hebrew presence in ancient Syria had appeared in the Western press. These articles have embarrassed Gamasi's superiors and placed him in a difficult position." Sabitini rose and peered out the window for a moment. "I warned you not to send any documents to London or New York."

"I sent nothing containing the Hebrew connection. Only texts concerning trade, commerce, and religion—to verify my interpretation."

"But you exposed the use of Hebrew within the Ebla cuneiform."

"But that in itself does not suggest that the Syrians are descendants of Hebrew tribes."

"Not to you perhaps, but any link, however vague, between the Syrians and a hated enemy are grounds enough to deny us permission to return. I understand why you did it. I probably would have done the same thing in your place had I found a startling artifact. The curse of our profession is the terrible need for confirmation from our colleagues." He put his arm around her shoulders. "Well, what's done is done. There may still be a way to effect our return."

"How?"

"Never mind." He walked her to the door and smiled. "Remember, I am a distant relative of that great philosopher Niccolò Machiavelli, who once said, 'Empires and states can be reduced to whoredom if the seduction is properly planned.'"

For Gabriella, the month of March was spent in unbearable suspense. The threat of permanent expulsion from Ebla was crushing. The astonishing content of Ithamar's testament and the location of his tomb seemed destined to remain buried in the dark chambers of Ebla.

She was seated on a marble bench in a small plaza of the university, having just shared some cheese and wine with an engineering professor with whom she had an affair several years ago. The professor's proposal of a renewed relationship was attractive, but his recently acquired wife was a major deterrent. Gabriella could not accommodate the Italian convention of rotating nights between wife and mistress.

She noticed a young student couple seated nearby. The boy had just turned up the volume on a transistor radio playing a popular romantic ballad. He had his arm draped around the girl's shoulders and whispered something in her ear. She laughed sexily, and he pulled her to him.

Watching them, Gabriella felt an overwhelming sense of loneliness and sadly, almost masochistically forced her thoughts back to her own student days at Cambridge, to a long-ago fall semester and an American boy with whom she had fallen hopelessly in love. She vividly recalled the small, cozy pubs and concerts at Albert Hall, and jazz clubs on Carnaby Street, and Shakespeare at the Aldwych, and T. S. Eliot, Sylvia Plath, Purcell, and the Beatles, and long walks on dusky autumn afternoons, and cramming for tutorials, and making love silently, wordlessly. . . .

The semester had ended, and the boy returned home. Their relationship wound down to a diminishing trickle of impersonal letters. But the memory of that season of love remained the singular romantic experience of her life. In the ensuing years she had had several affairs but never again sensed the pure, joyous exhilaration created by the mere presence of another human being.

She sighed, thinking that perhaps the very nature of her work precluded a true and meaningful relationship. The more deeply she penetrated ancient mysteries, the more obscure and irrelevant the present became. She closed her eyes and tilted her face up toward the strong Roman sun. The wine made her feel heady, and the familiar gravellike voice seemed to come out of a dream. "Take care you don't damage that pretty skin."

She opened her eyes in time to see Sabitini pick a shred of tobacco leaf from his lip. "Come, let's walk."

They strolled past students walking arm in arm, engaged in animated conversation.

"A marvelous spring day," Sabitini said. "You can see the seasonal change in the students. The sap is rising."

Gabriella did not respond, and he became instantly aware of her melancholy mood. He had seen these fits of profound sadness before and sometimes forgot that underneath her professional veneer, there was a full-blown woman whose personal life remained unfulfilled.

"What is it?" he asked.

"I was thinking about London and old Beatles songs and a cute boy who reminded me of sunny autumns."

"Ah, the toys of childhood."

"Perhaps, but they held more truth for me than any artifact I've ever seen."

He stopped, took the cigar out of his mouth, and put his hands on her shoulders. "Listen to me, Gabriella. The only truth in life is to survive it. Romance is a luxury that belongs to the very young, who don't know any better, and the very old, who should know better. Romance is an innocent pause—an unguarded moment. Nothing more."

"It's easy for you to say. You've been happily married forever."

"No one is happily married," Sabitini said as they resumed walking. "People are adequately married. Romance is the first victim of marriage and has nothing to do with its duration. Fatigue is the key to lasting marriage; the passing years make it too tiresome to change."

"How do you shut off emotions?"

"Practice." He smiled. "Television. Football matches. Good wine, and now and then perhaps an interlude— something to confess."

"God, that's sad."

"Only for Anglo-Saxons. We're Mediterranean people. We must think in terms of the moment. Romance never lasts because it's not real. It's a seductive but dangerous illusion. History is crowded with the outrages brought upon mankind by romantics."

"Like your distant relative Machiavelli."

"No. He was a pragmatist. Mussolini was a romantic. He confused Romans with Italians, and two hundred thousand boys died chasing imperial dreams in Africa."

They passed the medical building and noticed that its freshly painted ocher walls were already marred by political graffiti.

"This melancholy mood is a transient thing," Sabitini continued. "Eventually you'll forget your English influences and learn to enjoy the moment. Besides, today is a day of triumph, not sadness. I have good news for you." He paused. "We leave for Ebla next week."

Her morose eyes suddenly sparkled, and she threw

her arms around him. "How did you manage it?" she exclaimed.

"By employing a very old method of persuasion—political blackmail. Our Foreign Ministry threatened to withhold delivery of ten Savoia-class missile boats from the Syrian Navy." He chewed the cigar and continued. "This is a classic case of armaments taking precedence over culture. However, the conditions of our return are severely restricted."

"In what way?"

"A skeleton crew; no further digging. Only cataloguing and perusing those artifacts and tablets already uncovered. Nothing may be removed. All photographs will be censored by Gamasi. All objects are to be sent to the museum at Aleppo. The private investors have been advised as well."

"Suppose we locate the burial chamber of Ithamar?"

"That's quite a supposition. But in any case we must take care to abide by Gamasi's rules."

"Rules and politics!" Her eyes blazed with sudden anger. "None of it has anything to do with archaeology!"

"You know better than that. Rules, politics, and money have everything to do with all the sciences. That's the way things are. Now be thankful for small favors. Besides, once we're there"—he shrugged—"perhaps things can be arranged."

An American girl carrying three philosophy books asked Sabitini for his autograph and told him how much she admired his work. Aware that her compliments had nothing to do with archaeology, he signed Ben Gazzara's name with a great flourish.

CHAPTER FOUR

△

Shafts of moonlight broke through low clouds, sending columns of light streaking across the desert floor, and swirling funnels of sand danced through the flashing light like ghostly dervishes.

Standing outside the compound gates, Sabitini watched the sand blowing off the crest of the floodlit tell. The eerie cry of jackals rose from a distant wadi and carried on the wind. Sabitini was a scientist and did not believe in evil spirits or omens, but he knew the desert had a way of telling you things, and its message tonight was ominous.

Two weeks had passed since their return to Ebla, and Gamasi had spoken to them only when it was absolutely necessary. The fraternal relationship they had once shared with their Syrian host had disappeared. Their activities were policed, and their basic requests treated with bureaucratic disdain. Syrian officials flew in daily to confer with Gamasi, and earlier that afternoon Gamasi had boarded a military helicopter without a parting word and left for Damascus.

Sabitini glanced up at the Bedouin sentry standing

29

on the parapet of the compound wall. Before this night
was over, they would require the sentry's goodwill. He
waved to the Bedouin and climbed the worn steps
leading to the parapet.

The sentry's eyes were glazed by hashish, and his
ears were plugged by a headset attached to a Sony
recorder. Sabitini handed him a pack of Italian cigarettes. The sentry smiled, removed the headset, and
placed the plugs against Sabitini's ears. The cassette
played a lively Bruce Springsteen number. Sabitini com-
plimented the sentry on the instrument's fidelity. Then,
in the manner of desert people, he kissed the Bedouin
on both cheeks and descended the courtyard side of
the steps.

The single-story bungalows lining the compound were
dark, and their wooden shutters slammed fitfully against
the stucco walls of vacant dwellings that formerly housed
the Italian team of architects. Sabitini passed a variety
of tagged artifacts as he strolled toward the spill of
light coming from Gabriella's tent.

The paraffin lamps hissed, and the tent's canvas
folds slapped loudly against the wind. Gabriella was
seated at a large wooden table, a dish full of cigarette
stubs and a bottle of strong Syrian arak at her side. She
was physically exhausted but emotionally elated.

For the past week she had been absorbed by an
inscription on a royal tablet, which indicated the existence of a necropolis at Stratum IV. This would account
for the burial site of Ebla's common citizens, but she
was seeking a royal crypt—Ithamar's final resting place.

She moved the magnifying glass slowly over the
royal tablet, rereading the wedged script. The final
translation confirmed all her hopes: "Below the chamber of Baal, I King Ibbit-Lim shall be interred. I will rest
there with my friend who became my brother, who
lived in Ebla for twenty and seven harvests. I speak of
Ithamar, son of Aaron, messenger of Moses."

She placed the magnifying glass down and took a
long swallow of the arak brandy. The chamber of Baal
had been unearthed the previous summer, but they

never suspected that a royal crypt lay beneath its claylike floor.

She slipped her field jacket on, slung the camera over her shoulder, picked up two high-powered flashlights, and went out into the courtyard.

Sabitini was crouched in front of an exquisitely crafted bronze serpent when he heard her boots crunch across the sand and, straightening up, said, "I was on my way to your tent. But I couldn't resist the ruby eyes of this cobra; for a moment it appeared to be alive."

Once again the mournful cry of jackals rose on the night wind and seemed to be closer.

"That's the saddest sound I've ever heard," she said reflectively. "You remember the cries of that jackal the Bedouins trapped?"

"It's a sound one never forgets," he replied softly. "Come, we better get started."

As they walked through the open gates, Sabitini waved to the sentry and shouted a blessing in Arabic. The Sony earplugs prevented the Bedouin from hearing the benediction, but knowing the odd ways of Italians, he assumed the professor and the blond girl were going to make love in some dark chamber of the tell—a ritual of sorts peculiar to that excitable race that ate long strings of soft dough and refused the delicacy of lamb's eyes.

The chamber of Baal was situated at a depth of sixty feet, just inside the western trench of the tell. The limestone walls were painted in vivid colors. The central panel depicted the Canaanite deity Baal and the hideous devil-god Pazuzu seated naked on a throne, presiding over a vast and complicated orgy involving slaves, warriors, gods, and goddesses. The sexual acts were graphic and erotic.

Their flashlights played across the painting. "Magnificent," Sabitini said. "It tops Pompeii."

"We don't have time for voyeurism." She smiled. "The royal crypt is under our feet, not on the walls."

They paced off a center mark and began working their trowels and spades, turning the earth over quickly, expertly. The Bacchanalian figures on the wall stared down at them, and the wind moaned eerily through the labyrinthine chambers and tunnels.

Gabriella dumped a scoopful of claylike earth off to her left, inserted the spade once again, and stopped abruptly as the point struck a solid object.

Sabitini directed the light toward her hands as she cleared away thick clumps of earth concealing cedar struts wired together, forming a six-foot-square cover.

"This place has been visited before," Sabitini said, "and from the smell of the cedar, fairly recently."

"Grave robbers?"

"I doubt it. We've seen no signs of grave robbers at any stratum. It had to be Gamasi or one of his assistants."

Sabitini shoved the cedar planking aside, revealing a set of clay steps curving down to a lower level. Descending slowly, they entered a dark chamber shrouded by a heavy, sweet scent.

"You smell that?" he asked.

"Jasmine." She nodded. "It was used to sweeten the journey of royalty into the afterworld."

Their lights pierced the darkness, bisecting on a three-foot-high oval-shaped headstone embedded in the earth. The stone was engraved with cuneiform, and a curious triangular indentation was carved into its top.

"This triangular space held something," Sabitini murmured.

"Probably a symbol of sorts," Gabriella said as she knelt at the foot of the stone, studying the inscription. After three complete readings she took out a pad and began to write the English translation.

From above and way off, they heard a rapidly approaching percussive sound that echoed down through the strata of the tell.

"Helicopters!" Sabitini rasped.

Gabriella rose and in a trembling voice recited the translated inscription: "For all time I have inscribed on this stone the words of Moses, spoken to me on the day of the great prophet's death. It was he and none other who gave unto me the last words of Yahweh—

which I did place in the chamber at Megiddo. I am Ithamar, son of Aaron, messenger of the great prophet."

The ominous throb of whirling rotor blades suddenly ceased.

"They've landed!" Sabitini exclaimed.

Ignoring his warning, she proceeded to photograph both sides of the headstone, expertly changing exposures and depth of field. The click-whirl, click-whirl set off the automatic flash, illuminating the dark chamber for split seconds.

Footsteps and shouts in Arabic sounded from the level above.

She ran off thirty-six exposures, capturing the full inscription on both sides of the stone along with several close shots of the triangular indentation. She unloaded the film and tucked the exposed roll into her boot, then swiftly threaded a fresh roll of negative and snapped random shots of the crypt.

Six burly Syrian paratroopers, led by a colonel, bounded down the steps. Using the muzzles of their automatic weapons, they pinned Gabriella and Sabitini against the far wall.

Standing at the top of the stairs, Dr. Amin Gamasi smiled enigmatically at his former colleagues and nodded to the paratroop colonel.

The officer pulled the Nikon from Gabriella's hand.

"Maftou!" Gamasi ordered.

The colonel opened the camera's back panel and ripped the roll of negative from its sprockets.

Sabitini strained against his captors but directed his anger at Gamasi. "This business will not end here. I can promise you that, Doctor!"

"You are in no position to promise anything," Gamasi replied calmly. "This is Syria, not Rome. You are agents of Zionist imperialism—and will be treated accordingly."
He then issued a command to the colonel: *"Al-dour al-mala!"*

The soldiers herded them up the steps out of the perfumed crypt.

Two jet-powered Soviet MI-8 helicopters were parked

in the shadow of the tell, their rotor blades revolving slowly.

Gamasi walked through the ring of soldiers surrounding his former colleagues. "You will be flown directly to Damascus International Airport, where you will depart at once for Rome."

Two paratroopers hustled them into the helicopter and thrust them into their seats. The rotor blades whirred, increasing their velocity. The pilot achieved liftoff and gained altitude rapidly.

Gabriella peered down at the curving contour of Tell Mardikh and whispered a silent prayer of gratitude. In their haste the soldiers had neglected to search her. The roll of exposed negative containing the full text of Ithamar's will and testament was safely hidden in her boot.

△

Los Angeles

CHAPTER FIVE

△

The chalky face seemed to be suspended in the cone of concentrated light. The features were spread and puffy; the eyes, bloodshot and glazed, the pupils, reduced to pinheads.

Sergeant Vince Rizzo lounged against the wall. His partner, Lieutenant Jack Raines, had been questioning the sweat-soaked junkie for the past half hour.

"Pepe, tell me about Pancho Villa."

"A shot. Jesus Christ . . . I need a hit."

"Tell me about Pancho, and I'll get you straight."

"I don't know any Pancho. I gotta puke."

Raines sighed and walked over to a grimy window that overlooked the freeway interchange and thought about Captain Louis Cordero's funeral the previous Sunday. He remembered the line of black and whites, their lights flashing like the red eyes of some prehistoric serpent. The priest did his thing. They played taps. Fired rifles. And it was all over for Cordero. His killer, a Cuban dealer nicknamed Pancho Villa, was out there in the barrio, lining up a fresh score.

"Pepe! Pepe! Where are we, Pepe?" Sergeant Rizzo growled at the sweat-stained junkie.

"I dunno . . . I dunno. I'm sick, man."

Rizzo slapped Pepe hard.

The impact flushed the pusher's pale complexion.

"Talk to me, Pepe . . ."

"I need a shot bad. Oh, Jesus, I'm gonna piss."

Again Rizzo's hand crashed into Pepe's face.

Raines moved swiftly, grabbing Rizzo's right arm. "That's enough, Vince."

A dark stain had spread across Pepe's crotch.

Raines spoke softly to the junkie. "What's my name, kid?"

"You're Lieutenant Jack."

"Who's your friend?"

"You. You're my friend, Lieutenant Jack."

"That's right. Now, tell me about Pancho."

The glazed eyes tried to focus. "Pancho . . . Pancho. I don't know nobody called Pancho Villa."

"Sure you do. He cut Captain Cordero's heart out."

Pepe stared at the crimson half-moon scar on Jack's right cheekbone and began to tremble. "Don't hit me no more. Please, Jack. I'm sick. I'm sick, Teniente."

"I never hit you, Pepe."

"Give me a shot."

"Give me Pancho."

"I got a knife in my brain."

Pepe's shoulders shook, and his color went lime. A stream of lumpy vomit burst from his mouth.

Jack jumped back.

"Shit!" Rizzo exclaimed as some of the residue landed on his shoes.

Pepe fell to his knees, retching and convulsing, drooling green bile onto the hardwood floor.

Jack took a grimy towel from the sink and wiped the pusher's face. Pepe's body trembled in the grip of a cold sweat.

"That nark outside?" Jack asked Rizzo.

"Yeah."

"Get him in here."

Jack helped Pepe over to a cracked leather couch.

"You're a prince, Teniente. I'm dying. I'm going cold. I'm crappin' out."

"You'll be fine."

"I pissed in my pants. Someone gave me a bad fix."

"Tell me about Pancho. Where's the drop?"

"I'm pissin' blood . . . for three weeks I'm pissin' blood."

Rizzo came in, followed by a slim, balding narcotics officer carrying a kidney-shaped tray with a vial of methadone and a syringe.

"Look at that needle, Pepe," Jack said.

"Oh, Christ, you're a great man, Lieutenant."

"No shot till you talk to me."

"I'm pissin' blood."

"You're pissing on my friend's grave—Captain Cordero's grave."

"I can't tell you about Pancho. He . . . he'd carve me up. He's a mean Cuban, man." Pepe shuddered, and his teeth chattered uncontrollably.

Jack pulled a chair over to the couch, and his voice grew warm and persuasive. "See that needle, Pepe. You'll feel great in five, ten minutes. You'll feel good enough to join the marines. Tell me about Pancho Villa."

The pusher's glazed eyes darted from Jack to Rizzo to the narcotics officer holding the gleaming syringe.

"You got my life, Teniente. You gotta swear to the Holy Virgin. If I give you Pancho Villa, you'll ice him. No fucking courts because that Cuban fucker ain't real. He's a fucking wolf—a lobo. He'll track me. You gotta ice him. Because if I give him to you, and he makes bail, I'm in sixty pieces. You gotta kill him."

"I can't do that, Pepe. I'm not in the murder business. But you have my word; Pancho won't see daylight for the rest of his life."

"Jesus. That's no good, Lieutenant." Pepe suddenly clutched his stomach. "Oh, Christ, I gotta puke again."

Jack grabbed the junkie's shoulder. "Look at that needle. In a couple of minutes you're straight."

Pepe's black eyes stared at the glittering kidney-shaped dish. His lips moved in slow motion as if they were

forming words for the first time. "The party . . . the
party is to . . . tomorrow night . . ."

"Where?"

"At Gloria's place. You . . . you know, on Holly Ridge,
sometime in the night Pancho drops the coke."

"Who gets the coke?"

"Charlie the Bump."

CHAPTER SIX

⚠

The Doheny-Palms was a tall, terraced apartment building built into the steep curve of a street that angled sharply up from Santa Monica Boulevard to Sunset. Its tenants were a mixture of aging character actors, airline stewardesses, retired eastern mafiosi, and call girls whose prices were negotiable.

Jack parked his restored 1971 GTO convertible in the subterranean garage and noticed the vacant parking space belonging to Linda Jensen. He vaguely remembered having made a dinner date with the pretty Pan Am stewardess, but he was bone-tired, and their dates were frequently broken by her flight schedules.

His relationship with Linda was absurd: she was twenty years younger than he, street-smart and hip. She never confused amusement with emotion. On rare occasions, perhaps out of ego, he suspected she truly liked him, but those moments were almost always triggered by her comments regarding his enduring infatuation with his former wife. And Linda wasn't wrong: He had never gotten over Laura.

Jack walked up to the desk and asked the night clerk

for his messages. The man searched the numbered cubbyholes and shook his head. "Nothing. By the way, I was sorry to read about Captain Cordero's death. Awful when they murder a police officer and get away with it."

Jack nodded almost imperceptibly and walked across the fake marble into the waiting elevator.

He took a TV dinner out of the freezer, put it in the oven, and went into the bathroom. He slipped out of his robe and turned the shower taps on. The rancid odor of Pepe's vomit still lingered, and he poured some mouthwash into a glass, added water, and swished the minty-flavored liquid around before spitting it out.

He stared at his reflected image in the mirror over the sink. The half-moon scar over his right cheekbone was growing progressively livid, and Linda had commented on the purple color of the scar on his left buttock.

He shook his head in dismay. He was not yet forty-five and took reasonable care of his health, working out and limiting his intake of booze and cigarettes. But his hair was going gray, his brown eyes were edged by severe lines, and it was hell itself to keep his weight down.

He stepped into the shower, turned the faucets to the hot side, and tilted his face up to the shower head as if the steamy jets could wash away the mental and physical scars.

But the damage was indelible. It came with the profession. Cops were society's garbagemen, sifting through the remnants of human bestiality, and none of them remained unmarked for very long. Even Rizzo with his pleasant wife, three kids, and paid-up mortgage was on a short fuse. If Jack had not been in the interrogation room, Rizzo would have beaten Pepe to a pulp.

Jack turned, and the hot needlelike spray played across his neck and shoulders. He had tried earlier to phone his daughter, and Laura had answered. They exchanged a few pleasantries, and she told him Jenny was at a friend's but looking forward to Sunday with her father. He replied he'd be picking Jenny up in the morning, but their day together would be shortened by pressing police business.

"Of course," Laura had answered. Her comment was edged with sarcasm, but it made no sense to defend himself; the ensuing dialogue would have inevitably led to a very old conclusion: His police career and obsessive sense of duty had destroyed their marriage.

They had been happy in the early years, when he worked for the CIA. They were young and impressionable and enjoyed the subsidized first-class life-style that went with his career in government service. Under the guise of the State Department diplomatic corps they had traveled to Madrid, Rio, Tel Aviv, and finally Santiago, Chile.

Jenny was born in July 1970 in Santiago, at the British-American hospital. In that same month his career with the CIA came to an abrupt end. He had been a victim of duplicity: used by the agency to effect the assassination of the Chilean finance minister. But in the world of professional secrecy nothing remains secret for very long. One of his fellow agents informed Jack that he had been used as a pawn in a game of geopolitical murder. There were no meetings with his station officer, no lengthy discussions; he simply wrote out his resignation and returned to Los Angeles.

He joined the LAPD in September 1970, and almost from the moment of their return the marriage soured. Laura could not accommodate the empty nights, the broken dinners, the missed birthdays, but more profoundly she grew to believe in the inevitability of a fateful late-night phone call, summoning her to the morgue to identify his body. The tension and pressure she felt diminished their relationship. They were like strangers, condemned to live together, rear a child, and go through all the motions of a marriage that had become devoid of emotion.

They were divorced in the fall of 1978; two years later Laura remarried—and she chose well. Dr. Martin

Sorenson was a leading figure in the field of brain chemistry—a renowned neurophysiologist. The doctor was a multimillionaire and owned a modern medical complex in Westwood just east of the UCLA campus.

The doctor was close to sixty, but the years had not diminished his physicality. Sorenson's entire history spoke of strength and courage. During World War II he had served with valor and distinction in a special unit of the OSS operating behind enemy lines. He was an expert sailor, a licensed pilot, and an amateur archaeologist.

Sorenson was warm and friendly and treated Jenny as if the child were his own daughter. Jack saw the doctor infrequently because his visitation rights were limited to Sunday, the one day Sorenson usually spent on his boat.

Seeing Laura every Sunday was, for Jack, a trip into pain and remorse. Everything about her still got to him: the familiar scent of her perfume, the sparkle in her gray eyes, the almost perfect profile, and the way her dark hair fell across her shoulders as if it just happened that way.

He shut the taps off and sighed; it was madness to carry on a love affair with a woman who was lost to him. But he had shared his soul with her. She was the mother of his child and the only woman he had ever loved.

He stepped out of the shower and began to towel the water off his face when he noticed the crescent scar on his cheek and his thoughts turned to the youth who had knifed him, a nice-looking kid from a solid family. The boy had augmented his generous allowance by dealing cocaine to his fellow high school students. Jack had ignored Captain Cordero's advice and refused to handcuff the sobbing youth, not wanting to humiliate him. Jack offered the boy amnesty if he would name the source of his cocaine. The boy nodded, asked for a handkerchief, then struck with sudden swiftness. The switchblade missed Jack's jugular but caught his cheek, ripping it open to the bone. A uniformed cop brought his blackjack crashing down into the boy's skull.

The boy never recovered from the blow and remained in a coma—a vegetable for life. Had Jack handcuffed the kid—gone by the book—the boy would have received nothing more than a few years in a correctional institution. So the guilt remained, as it did with the assassination of Velásquez in Chile. He should have known the agency had set the finance minister up.

He should have sniffed that one out, and he should have handcuffed the high school kid. He blamed himself, and all the soul-searching and excuses didn't help. Guilt and remorse scarred his conscience. The hell of it was that knowing what was right did not always take precedence; despite training and experience, when a man is placed under extreme stress, his actions are governed by his reflexes.

Jack slipped his robe on, went out into the kitchen, and mixed a vodka and tonic. It would be a long night, and he hoped there would be an old Garfield or Bogart movie on television. He didn't understand the current crop of movies and saw them reluctantly, only at the request of his daughter. He thought snakes in spaceships and teenaged boys who peed through fences and ax murderers with prune faces were a long way from "Here's looking at you, kid."

CHAPTER SEVEN

⚠

Chalon Road wound through the heart of Bel Air. The exclusive section was only minutes from Sunset Boulevard, but it reminded Jack of the hill country north of Madrid. A forest of tall pines fought for space with groves of wild palms shading sprawling Spanish estates. Bel Air reeked of old California money, some of it going all the way back to Spanish land grants.

At the crest of Chalon Road he turned sharply into a private driveway and pulled up to a pair of tall spear-topped wrought-iron gates. He opened his window and pressed a button on a speaker box. After a moment Laura's muffled voice came through the speaker; Jack identified himself, and the gates slowly swung open. He drove up the long, curving driveway for a quarter of a mile before parking near an open garage that sheltered a gray Mercedes sedan and a maroon-colored Rolls-Royce.

Laura greeted him at the door. She was tall and slim, her figure almost boyish. Thick, wavy black hair framed her oval face and patrician features. She wore cashmere slacks, a white silk blouse, and no jewelry except for a simple gold wedding band on her ring finger.

He followed her into the huge Cathedral-ceilinged living room decorated with contemporary Italian furniture enhanced by period antiques. French Impressionist paintings were hung on the walls, and illuminated glass cases displayed a variety of artifacts.

"Jenny will be down in a minute."

"It's okay; I'm in no hurry."

"Some coffee?"

"No, thanks."

"Something stronger?"

"No, I'm fine."

She thought the lines around his eyes were deeper, and there was a sense of tension in the way his dark pupils darted from object to object.

"I guess Martin's out on the boat," he said, trying to make conversation.

"He's out of town."

"That's four Sundays in a row."

"I suppose it is," she replied, smiling nervously. "He's been away so often lately I bought him a Saint Christopher's medal."

"You used to get upset with me for a lot less."

"The difference is Martin's business doesn't involve any danger."

"I suppose that does make a difference." He sighed and stepped down into the sunken portion of the living room.

He walked casually past the African and pre-Columbian displays but stopped abruptly in front of the glass case containing Middle Eastern artifacts and stared at a grotesque bronze idol with leering, bulging eyes. A pair of wings sprouted from its shoulders, and its hands and feet were clawed.

"What the hell is this?"

"A Canaanite devil-god called Pazuzu," Laura replied. "Something Martin acquired from an archaeological dig in northern Syria."

"I'd hate to wake up facing this guy every day."

"You'll think I'm crazy," she said, "but since Martin

brought that home, we've been struck by a series of tragic events."

"Like what?"

"Six months ago, almost to the day that piece arrived, Martin's colleague Dr. Brody committed suicide. And a few months later, around the holidays, the Allisons were killed in a car crash on Pacific Coast Highway. Last week it got closer to home—our maid, Elvia, was mugged. She's at Saint John's in critical condition."

"What's the history of this idol?"

"I don't know. But if I had my way I'd get rid of it."

"What does Martin say?"

"He's amused by my superstition. Besides, you know how he feels about these artifacts."

"Not really. I've never spoken to him about it."

"Maybe I'm making too much of it, but it seems as though what began as an avocation has turned into an obsession."

"How are things with you and the doctor?"

"We've never been happier. Why do you ask?"

"No reason."

"It's been six years, Jack."

"I know. It just seems we ran a better race than we finished."

"You always were a great one for penance. You'd have made a marvelous Catholic."

She took a cigarette out of a ceramic cup. He lit it for her. And their eyes met over the blue flame. She inhaled deeply and said, "I was going to call you about Captain Cordero."

"He was two weeks away from retirement when he decided to go undercover," Jack said. "The Mexican barrio is full of kids strung out on heroin—hooked by a Cuban dealer called Pancho Villa. Cordero made it a one-on-one personal vendetta. Pancho knifed him to death in the toilet of a Main Street bar."

"And you're going to avenge Cordero's death."

"Let's drop it, Laura."

"I can't just drop it. You're still Jenny's father."

"Nothing's going to happen to me."

"And you've got the scars to prove it. For God's sake, why put yourself in that kind of jeopardy?"

"Because Cordero was very kind to me. He was there when I needed him. He sponsored me on the force and kept my career on track. He was a true friend."

"I thought Nolan had forbidden any direct action by his officers."

"He has. He gave me the full speech. 'This is a tactical unit, an intelligence unit. We do not engage in street actions.' I told him he could have my badge if I stepped out of line. He finally agreed to let me supervise the stakeout."

Their attention was drawn to the sound of clattering shoes coming down the staircase. A sandy-haired, pug-nosed girl of fourteen bounded into the room and ran up to Jack. He hugged and kissed her.

"That's a pretty dress, but it doesn't go with the Dodger baseball cap," Laura said.

"I always wear this with Dad. He got it from Steve Garvey."

"Absolutely. Garvey wore that cap in the World Series."

"You've made her a star at school," Laura said. "She's captain of the girl's softball team."

"I can really hit, Dad."

"That's more than I could do." Jack smiled. "What about your ballet class?"

"Not too shabby."

As they started for the door, Jenny asked, "Can I put the top down?"

"Sure. Go ahead," he said, then turned to Laura. "I'll have her home by six."

Laura kissed him on the cheek and whispered, "Have a good time."

She closed the door and went back into the living room and, as if drawn by an unseen force, walked deliberately to the glass display case and stared hypnotically into the grotesque eyes of the devil-god Pazuzu.

CHAPTER EIGHT

⚠

At that same moment it was 8:15 P.M. in Rome.

Gabriella stood at the fourth floor window of the Middle Eastern studies building, staring off at the deserted entrance on the Viale della Università; but there was still no sign of Sabitini's vintage gray Fiat. The professor was thirty-five minutes late.

She walked up to the battered piano and ran some scales and arpeggios, trying to calm herself. She then lit a cigarette and paced, remembering that punctuality was not one of Sabitini's virtues. He had other, more important virtues. He was a superb scholar from whom she had learned a great deal, but more important, he was patient, kind, and totally supportive. Emilio Sabitini was not only her colleague but a true friend.

Gabriella shivered slightly, and a sudden sense of foreboding crept into her consciousness, as if some fateful tragedy would, at the last moment, deny her sharing this triumph with her colleague.

The film of the Ithamar stone she had hidden in her boot had been developed and printed up perfectly, and in the ensuing weeks of painstaking decipherment an incredible text had evolved. Ithamar's last will and testament revealed historical and theological implications that were both thrilling and frightening.

She crushed the cigarette out, pulled the window shades down, and checked the focus on the slide projector.

The door opened suddenly, causing her to jump reflexively.

Sabitini ambled into the room, chewing on his ever-present cigar. "Sorry," he said. "I didn't mean to startle you. I should have called. I fell asleep watching the football finals. Next thing I knew Antonella was shaking me."

"Well, at least you arrived in one piece; with that Fiat of yours one never knows. I have some coffee, but it's six hours old."

"So what? I'm fifty-four years old. Have I lost my flavor?"

"How would I know?" She smiled and poured the thick brew into a paper cup and handed it to him.

He sipped the coffee and smiled. "Any woman who can read cuneiform, play jazz piano, and produce coffee like this would make a superb mistress but a terrible wife."

"Is that an expert opinion?"

"Just a colleague's observation. I'm certainly no expert."

"When it comes to marriage, you are."

"Ah." He shrugged and waved his hands. "You can't call my situation a marriage. Antonella has confused me with Ben Gazzara for twenty years." He swallowed some more coffee, relit the cigar, and blew the smoke toward the ceiling. "Now tell me, what does the Ithamar stone have to say?"

"Everything I hoped for. But the triangular indentation at the top of the stone turns out to be critical."

"How so?"

"You'll see."

He slumped into a chair facing the projection screen. Gabriella doused the overhead lights and walked up to the projector. "I've arranged the sides as you would a record. There is a side one to the stone and a side two.

My translation appears below each line of Eblaite cuneiform."

She clicked the first slide into position, and it appeared instantly on the screen. Clouds of billowing cigar smoke filtered up into the light beam. The room fell silent as they studied the slide.

> *On the day of the great prophet's death in the land of Moab, before the mountain of Nebo, the voice of Yahweh commanded me, "Ithamar, son of Aaron, go up to the cave of eternity. You will find there my servant Moses." And I went up the face of Nebo into that chamber, and the great prophet said unto me, "At the place of the waters, in Meribah-Kadesh, I withheld from the people God's last word, for in my heart I feared they would pervert its meaning. This faithless act did cause Yahweh to judge me unworthy of entry to the Promised Land." So Moses spoke unto me, Ithamar.*

The hum of the projector underscored the silence in the darkened room. After a moment she asked, "Shall I go to side two?"

"Is it possible to hold side one as well?"

She nodded and pushed two buttons on the Kodak projector; side one shifted to the left of the screen, and side two appeared at its center.

> *The great prophet then commanded me, "Take this tablet, Ithamar. Upon it is inscribed the path to the last word of God. It is your sacred mission to place this tablet in the Canaanite city of Megiddo, where it shall be preserved into the midnight of time." And there, in Megiddo, did I place the tablet. And it came to pass, as Moses prophesied, that I departed Megiddo and lived out my time in the ancient kingdom of Ebla. And no man set his hand against me. Upon this stone I have inscribed my will and testament. Whosoever shall come upon it must read the triangles of gold and will know the chamber in Megiddo where lies the tablet of Moses.*
>
>

Ithamar, son of Aaron,
> *priest of the Levi tribe*
>

There was a long moment of silence. Then Sabitini rose and turned to her. "You're certain of this translation?"

She nodded. "Remember, my original translations of Eblaite cuneiform were confirmed by both Delgado in London and Ettinger in New York."

"Well, assuming there are no mistakes, we have edged our way toward the ultimate artifact—an astonishing discovery more profound than the Dead Sea Scrolls. An archaeological time bomb that will destroy theological and historical facts confirmed by generations of scholars."

Sabitini picked up a long wooden pointer and, directing it to a portion of the translation, read, "I withheld from the tribes God's last word, for in my heart I feared the people would pervert its meaning." He turned to her and asked, "What do you make out of his use of the word *pervert*?"

"I suppose I just take it literally."

"How can you treat it literally? The use of this particular word is astounding."

"In what way?"

"Moses was the only man to look upon the face of Yahweh. He was God's servant and scribe from the time of the burning bush, through the Egyptian period of enslavement, all the way to the exodus. It was Moses who received the commandments and liturgical laws. And yet this great prophet, this loyal servant, withheld God's last word out of fear of its message being *perverted*. That means the text of that final word contained something so fateful that this great prophet went against the wishes of Yahweh and took it upon himself to withhold its contents."

"Do you think the words constituted a commandment?"

"Not at all. I suspect it was an admonition or a prophecy and its meaning frightened Moses to the point of disobedience."

Gabriella's hand trembled as she lit a cigarette.

Sabitini took no notice of her nervousness. He was totally absorbed in the text of the Ithamar stone, and

like a brilliant diagnostician analyzing an obscure illness, he warmed to the task. The pointer moved to
side two of the slide. "Look at this line. Again, Ithamar
speaking, 'I departed Megiddo and lived out my time
in the ancient kingdom of Ebla.' Whose ancient kingdom?" Sabitini asked. "We know Ebla was certainly
not Islamic. There is no trace of Arabs in Syria until 650
B.C. Almost eight hundred years after Moses. It's my
guess that this Moses tablet contains written reference
to Ebla's having been a Hebrew kingdom, which will
be the nail in the Syrian cultural coffin."

Gabriella crushed her cigarette out. "What about the
missing golden triangles?"

"Well, your translation is quite clear. Whoever finds
those triangles will know exactly where in Megiddo
Ithamar placed the Moses tablet. Remember, someone
was in that royal crypt at Ebla before we discovered it,
and whoever it was removed three gold triangles from
the Ithamar stone."

"How do you know there were three?"

"I don't know. I think it. The number three plays an
important part in the Mosaic period of biblical Israel.
Moses belonged to the tribe of Levi, which is the third
tribe. He himself was the third child in his family; his
own name in Hebrew consists of three letters; as an
infant he had been concealed for three months.

"And," Sabitini added, "the Hebrews are descendants of three patriarchs: Abraham, Isaac, and Jacob.
Also, the triangle itself has three sides. Therefore, it is
a fair assumption Ithamar would have used three triangles as directional pointers to the Moses tablet."

"You should have been with the carabinieri." She
smiled. "You'd have made a great detective."

"I doubt it; violence makes me nervous," he said,
and crushed his cigar out. "All right, let's review matters. Point one: We have the possible existence of a
tablet inscribed by Moses setting forth the last word of
God. Point two: The text of that tablet may also confirm Ebla as the ancestral home of the Hebrews. And
point three: We require three gold triangles to know

precisely where in the ruins of Megiddo to look for that tablet.''

"I'll phone Tel Aviv and get in touch with General Barzani," she said. "It's been a long time, but we worked together in Megiddo."

"Have you maintained contact with him?"

"Yes. I phone him every so often."

"Well, Barzani is the right place to start. Do you recall the extent of the dig in Megiddo?"

"At a depth of fifty feet we uncovered King Solomon's stables."

"And that's where you stopped?"

"We had no choice. It was October 1973. Israel was attacked by the Syrians and the Egyptians. The entire Israeli archaeological team was called to service. The dig was suspended."

"But the deepest penetration was to the time of Solomon?"

"Yes."

"Moses and Ithamar were three centuries before Solomon," Sabitini said reflectively. "Meaning you would have to go down at least one more stratum. So we're talking about a full-fledged expedition."

"Without question."

"Whom do we get to finance an undertaking of that size?"

"Perhaps the state of Israel?" she suggested.

"I doubt it. Its economy is bankrupt. Sixty percent of its income is spent on armaments. There have been no serious archaeological digs in Israel since Yadin uncovered the Bar Kochba scrolls at Qumran in 1979. Besides, I'm not sure the Orthodox Jewish sects in Jerusalem want to know about the possibility of a Moses tablet, much less a lost word of Yahweh." He paused and scratched the stubble on his cheek. "Who else knows about this translation?"

"No one."

"Good. We must assume that either Gamasi or an associate entered that crypt before we did and by now has translated the Ithamar text."

"What of it?"

"Just this. Damascus is home base for at least five different Palestinian terrorist groups, all of whom are controlled by the Syrians. If Gamasi knew we had acquired this text, it would be a simple matter for Syrian intelligence to dispatch professional assassins to eliminate you or me or anyone else who threatened to disclose their possible Hebrew ancestry. Our only advantage over Gamasi and his superiors is the fact that they cannot enter Israel. We can."

He paced for a moment and continued, "All right, phone General Barzani. Go to Israel. Take the photos and translation with you. Go up to Megiddo. Examine the condition of the ruins. See what will be required. I'll speak with our Ministry of Culture. Perhaps financing can be obtained. I doubt it, but I'll try."

"I can contact the members of Pyramid International," Gabriella suggested. "Perhaps they would underwrite some of the financing."

"It's worth exploring, but in view of the Syrian anger already expressed by Gamasi and his superiors, I doubt that anyone connected with Ebla would be willing to risk his safety."

"It's incredible to think that something inscribed three thousand years ago constitutes a modern political threat."

"Not really. Ancient ethnic hatreds have historically plagued successive generations. The Syrians were enraged at the mere mention of a Hebrew link to their past. Imagine how they'd feel about a Moses tablet the text of which may very well confirm their Hebrew ancestry."

"It's a risk we have to take," she said.

He nodded and sighed. "There's something else to consider. Suppose we find this tablet, and its text is counter to all Judeo-Christian principles. What is our moral responsibility?"

"You've always maintained that we're history's detectives, not its judges."

"Yes, but isn't it curious how we draw these narrow moral lines when it suits our professional interests?"

"Spoken like a failed Catholic." She smiled.

"No. Spoken like a failed scientist." He touched her pale hair. "Call Barzani. I'll arrange your leave and expenses."

CHAPTER NINE

△

Lieutenant Jack Raines and Sergeant Vince Rizzo were in the front seat of a black Buick, their infrared night-seeing binoculars trained on Gloria Penrod's terraced A-frame. The lights of the hillside house blazed, and the throbbing sound of amplified acid rock echoed through the canyons.

Gloria Penrod was a former fashion model who now operated a coast-to-coast call girl ring and provided talent for pornographic films. The vice squad had an extensive file on Miss Penrod, but the attractive flesh peddler had never seen the inside of a cell.

Sergeant Rizzo lowered his glasses. "I've got to take a piss."

"Be careful some coyote doesn't bite it off."

"He'd have to find it first."

The pine forest masked their vantage point on the auxiliary road above Holly Ridge Drive. The secluded spot afforded them a panoramic view of the numerous canyons that snaked through the Hollywood Hills. A backup car of narcotics agents was stationed down the canyon.

Jack picked up the radio speaker. "This is Red Arrow One. Over."

"Red Arrow Two."

"You guys still awake?"

"Fuck you, Raines."

"Just checking, Gilbert. Over."

"Over your ass—and out."

Jack smiled to himself. The narks always felt somewhat superior to all other divisions.

Rizzo was back, zipping up his fly. "Still no sign of Pancho?"

Jack shook his head and handed him a flask. "Have a shot."

"No, thanks. Maybe Pepe threw us a curve."

"I don't think so."

A chilling, baleful cry rose up out of the woods.

"What the hell is that?" Rizzo asked.

"Coyotes—they own these hills. A big male came down Laurel Canyon a week ago, killed a small child, and went after her father."

"I saw something about that on the six o'clock news. I didn't know coyotes went after humans."

"When they're rabid, they'll attack anything. They're like sharks. The smell of blood, or food, or garbage sets them off."

Rizzo got in the front seat and poured a cup of steaming coffee from a thermos. "How was your day with Jenny?"

"Perfect. She's a terrific kid, not only because I'm her father, she just is. Funny, though, as we were coming up the drive in Bel Air, she asked me if I had a lady friend. In all this time she's never asked me that." Jack paused. "Neither has Laura."

"How is Laura?"

"She seemed tense. Frightened. I started to talk about things past. Maybe that upset her."

"Bad business, carrying a torch for yesterday's lady."

"It's not the torch, Vince. I just keep remembering how good it once was and how I screwed it all up."

"You can't blame yourself. There isn't a seasoned

cop I know that hasn't had a rocky marriage. It's the goddamn profession."

"You and Angie have made it work."

"The only reason it works for us is that her sister is married to a fucking bum, and by comparison I look like a saint."

Once again the eerie wail of coyotes carried on the night wind.

"Christ . . ." Rizzo muttered. "That sound goes right through you."

"Let's check Gilbert again," Jack said.

Rizzo leaned out the window and extended the antenna on the walkie-talkie. "This is Red Arrow One. Come in, Red Arrow Two."

There was a crackling sound of static, followed by a male voice that sounded as if it had been programmed by a computer. "This is Red Arrow Two. Ready to receive. Over."

"You guys see anything?"

There was another crackle of static, and a voice came back. "Pancho Villa's in a red Jag, right?"

"According to our informant."

"Well, when we see a goddamn Jag, you'll be the first to know."

"Okay, don't go to sleep, Gilbert."

"Fuck you, Rizzo. Over and out."

Jack had his glasses trained on the A-frame terrace. "Get a load of this, Vince."

They could clearly see a naked girl on her knees in front of a man seated in a deck chair, wearing an open black cloak. His legs were spread, and the girl's head bobbed up and down. Two other girls watched and seemed to be cheering her on.

"Porno auditions," Rizzo said.

"I'd like to bust them up, Vince. I mean, go down there right now and bust them up."

"You'll screw things up. We're here to nail Pancho. Besides, you gave Nolan your word. We supervise the stakeout, but the narks make the pinch."

"I'll bet you a week's salary those girls are my daughter's age."

"Forget it, Jack."

The naked girls on the porch applauded the kneeling girl, who straightened up, wiped her mouth, and took a joint from another girl.

Jack lowered his binoculars. "Let's circle around the back and have a look."

"What for?"

"I want the layout of that place before Pancho shows."

"Shit," Rizzo muttered. "It's against orders. You get directly involved, and Nolan will have your badge."

"If you want out, Vince, it's okay. I understand."

"That's a bullshit thing to say," Rizzo growled, and got out of the car.

They checked their Smith & Wesson .38 revolvers, whirling the chambers and taking the safeties off. Neither man was an expert shot, but the heft of the guns in their shoulder holsters was comforting.

Moving cautiously through the woods, they reached a point just beyond the Penrod house. Grabbing clumps of sagebrush for support, they descended the hill crest and made their way through a grove of lemon trees, toward a large bay window. Kneeling, they peered into the living room through a three-inch crack between the venetian blinds and the sill.

Gloria Penrod sat naked in a high-backed wicker chair. She smoked hashish through a tube connected to a hookah. Below her, spread out over a Persian rug, couples were joined together front and back. A young man wearing red silk panties bent over a coffee table striped with white lines of cocaine. Two very pretty girls were lying on a low bed, smoking joints, and playing with each other. A man wearing a black cape snapped Polaroids of a ponytailed blond girl who was on all fours, working on three men simultaneously.

Standing apart from the writhing bodies, a nattily dressed gray-haired man watched the proceedings with mild interest. He sipped his drink and checked his watch.

"You see what I see?" Jack whispered.

"Charlie the Bump."

"Come on, let's get back."

*   *   *

They reentered the woods, switched on their flash-lights, and groped their way through the thick pines.

"Well, even if Pancho doesn't show"—Rizzo puffed—"we've got the Bump for being in the presence of narcotics and forcible prostitution of minors. You were right, those girls in that circus are under age."

Jack did not respond. His mind concentrated on a single fact: The presence of Charlie Bumpinsello meant Pepe had told them the truth. Sooner or later Pancho Villa would show up.

The path of pine needles narrowed gradually, and a low, ominous growling sound came at them from the darkness up ahead. They drew their guns and moved forward cautiously.

"Jesus Christ," Rizzo murmured.

A pair of malevolent yellow eyes glowed in the beam of Rizzo's flashlight.

The big coyote stood its ground. Unafraid. Its luminous eyes reflecting ancient hatred. Its mouth foamed and its lips were drawn back over its teeth. Its ears were flattened; and white froth oozed from its mouth drooling down to its chest. The coyote howled, then pawed the ground and snarled defiantly, challenging them for a moment before loping off into the woods.

"You see the size of that son of a bitch?" Rizzo asked.

"Yeah . . . come on, let's get out of here."

The walkie-talkie crackled from inside the Buick.

Jack picked it up. "This is Raines—go ahead."

"Where the hell have you guys been? A red Jaguar just passed fifty feet above us!"

"What do you mean, 'above you'? He should have passed your position *on* the road, not above it!"

"We're right here on Holly Ridge Road."

Rizzo shook his head. "Goddamn narks."

Jack shouted angrily into the perforated speaker, "You're in the wrong fucking canyon, Gilbert! We said Holly Ridge *Drive*, not Road."

"Hold your water, Raines. We'll get up there!"

"You've got to go all the way back down to Mariposa. You're talking about twenty minutes."

"We're on the way!"

"There's the Jag!" Rizzo shouted, pointing toward the road leading up to the A-frame.

Jack grabbed the binoculars and trained them on the approaching headlights.

The red Jaguar slowed and parked in front of the Penrod house. A tall, slim man wearing jeans and an army field jacket stepped out of the driver's side.

"It's him!" Jack exclaimed.

Pancho reached inside the Jaguar and removed a large brown grocery bag. He checked the road behind him, then walked quickly past the parked cars and rang the doorbell. The door opened and he disappeared inside.

"Let's nail him," Jack said.

"What about the narks?"

"No time. He'll drop the coke. Bumpinsello will give him the money. Pancho won't be in there more than five minutes." Jack's voice was tense, and his words came in short, staccato bursts. "We'll take the walkie-talkies. You circle around the back. I'll cover the front. When you're at the door, give me the word. Then go. Anyone comes at you, use that thirty-eight."

"Christ, Jack. Nolan swore us to—"

"Listen to me, goddammit!" Jack cut his partner off. "The narks fucked up. We have no choice. The bastard killed Cordero!"

"Okay . . ." Rizzo sighed.

"Let me know when you're in position."

Rizzo nodded and started down the road.

Jack stood silently in the mist rising out of the woods. He waited for two minutes, then quickly moved out of the pines, crossed the road to the Penrod house, and crouched down behind a Toyota parked close to the red Jaguar.

He took a penknife out of his pocket, crawled around the Toyota, moving to the right front tire of the Jaguar.

His breath came in spurts, and his armpits oozed cold sweat.

He jabbed the point of the knife into the soft white outer wall of the tire. There was a high, hissing rush of escaping air as the tire flattened. He then punctured the left front tire.

The walkie-talkie crackled loudly. "Jack . . . you read me?" Rizzo's voice was hushed.

"I read you, Vince."

"Are you set?"

"Yeah."

"Okay. I'm going in."

Rizzo wiped the sweat from his palm and clutched the revolver. He crouched down and peered through the rear door window.

Naked people were sprawled around the room, some sleeping, others sitting up drinking coffee and smoking dope. Charlie Bumpinsello was standing near the front door, putting glassine envelopes of cocaine back into the brown bag. Pancho Villa stood next to him, counting a pile of hundred-dollar bills.

Rizzo exhaled, took a deep breath, straightened up, kicked the door in, and burst into the living room. "Police! No one move!"

The girls screamed and frantically sought blankets and clothing.

The man in the black cape lunged at Rizzo with a bread knife. Rizzo swung the gun butt across the man's temple, dropping him instantly.

Pancho bolted toward the front door. Rizzo fired. The shot went wild, but the report was deafening, causing the revelers to freeze in position like so many statues.

Charlie Bumpinsello's arms were raised, a glassine envelope of cocaine still clutched in his right hand.

Pancho Villa burst out of the house and dashed toward the red Jaguar. He carried an attaché case in his left hand and clutched a German P-38 automatic in his right hand. He spotted the Jaguar's deflated front tires, spun around, and started running down the road.

"Freeze, Pancho!" Jack shouted from behind the Toyota.

The Cuban whirled around, fired twice, and kept going. Holding the .38 with both hands, Jack took careful aim and squeezed off two shots. The bullets exploded harmlessly against the sloping asphalt road.

Pancho left the road and bolted toward the woods.

Jack ran full-out for thirty yards, then climbed the embankment into the moonlit pine forest. Following Pancho's thrashing sounds, Jack kept coming on—crouching, moving from tree to tree.

There was a sharp report, and a piece of bark just above Jack's head blew into pulp. Splinters of wood split the skin on his forehead, and drops of blood seeped into his eyes.

He heard a twig snap off to his left and moved quickly to another tree. A loud report was followed by the whine of a bullet. Jack noticed a wisp of gunsmoke rise from between two boulders.

Hoping the slug would fragment, Jack took dead aim on a rock situated at an angle to the boulders and pulled the trigger.

Pancho screamed and jumped up, blood spurting from his right thigh. He hobbled back into the woods, stumbled, and fell. The attaché case flew out of his hand, struck a rock, and sprung open, spilling packets of hundred-dollar bills onto the pine needles.

Jack moved cautiously toward him. The Cuban dealer was on his back. His face contorted in agony.

"Keep your hands in sight," Jack said hoarsely, his .38 pointed at Pancho's head.

"Go ahead, Raines," the Cuban gasped. "Nobody here. You can avenge that asshole Cordero. Go ahead, you gutless fuck—pull the trigger."

Jack felt a wave of heat rising from his chest to his throat. His finger tightened on the trigger. He wiped the drops of blood from his eyes. His heart pounded. His palms were sweating. The pressure on the trigger was at the point of no return. He had reached the edge of murder.

Pancho's black eyes blinked. He had guessed wrong. This Anglo cop *would* kill him.

The Cuban dealer rolled to his left, grabbed Jack's ankle, and twisted it with surprising force. Jack fell heavily across the wounded man. Pancho pulled a six-inch hunting knife and plunged the blade into Jack's thigh. Jack screamed and cursed as blood gushed from the open wound.

Pancho had the knife raised again when Jack heard the low growl and saw Pancho's eyes widen in terror.

The powerful jaws of the coyote clamped down on Pancho's neck and shoulder. Pancho gasped, his features distorted in agony. Blood spumed from his neck, staining the coyote's fur. The animal emitted low, snarling sounds as its teeth ground into Pancho's flesh.

Weaving unsteadily, as if caught in the slow motion of a nightmare, Jack picked up Pancho's P-38 automatic and, gripping the butt with both hands, fired two shots. The coyote collapsed instantly.

Stoned on adrenaline, Jack staggered, trying desperately to maintain his balance. He pulled the dead animal off the blood-soaked dealer and sat down heavily on Pancho's chest. Jack locked his hands around the Cuban's throat and squeezed.

Pancho's face had turned blue when a pair of powerful arms pulled Jack off the unconscious dealer. Rizzo's voice boomed, "Enough, Jack! Enough!"

The morning light streamed into Gloria Penrod's living room. Jack had just completed his report to an internal security detective. Rizzo was on the phone.

The police doctor gave Jack a small white box. "Take one of these pills every four hours. That's a pretty good slice in your leg. I want to see that in about a week."

"Thanks, Doc."

Rizzo hung up and walked over to Jack. "That was County Medical. Pancho's critical, but stable. The best part of it is that that coyote was rabid. Pancho's gonna have twenty-seven needles shoved into his belly."

"They ought to build a monument to that coyote," Jack replied.

Rizzo glanced out of the bay window. "Oh, shit, here we go—Nolan's coming up the hill."

"Well, I didn't kill that Cuban bastard." Jack sighed.

"No, but you came pretty fucking close."

"You're right. If not for you, Vince, I'd be facing a murder rap."

The sound of tires crushing gravel came through the open door. A door slammed, and seconds later the paunchy gray-faced chief of Tactical entered the room.

Nolan stood in the center of the room, his troubled eyes staring at Jack. He started to say something, changed his mind, and walked quickly over to the wet bar, poured a shot of brandy, and handed the glass to Jack.

"Take this," Nolan ordered.

"Now, John, before you go crazy, let me take you through this thing step by—"

"Knock that drink down," Nolan interrupted.

"Whatever you say."

Jack swallowed the brandy, feeling it warm his stomach.

Nolan cleared his throat. "About an hour ago Laura Sorenson was found shot to death up in the Bel Air house." He paused. "Your daughter is safe—she's at school."

CHAPTER TEN

△

The drive to Bel Air passed in silence. Jack sat next to Rizzo, chain-smoking and hyperventilating. The wound in his thigh ached, but the violent night seemed to be part of a distant nightmare. The news of Laura's death had triggered conflicting emotions of rage and disbelief, and shadowing his consciousness was the dread of having to break the news to Jenny.

Official vehicles with flashing red lights were parked in the circular driveway fronting the house.

A tall, grim-faced man wearing a dark blue suit with a gold captain's badge pinned to his lapel greeted them.

"Lieutenant Raines?"

"Yes."

"I'm Captain John Scanlon, Sheriff's Office, Homicide Division."

Scanlon noticed the cuts and bruises on Jack's forehead and quietly said, "I'm sorry as hell about this."

"Thank you, Captain. This is my partner, Sergeant Vince Rizzo."

Scanlon nodded at Rizzo and said, "We got the call from a deliveryman about eight-twenty A.M. He's upstairs in a guest bedroom—pretty shook up. His name is Sorell, works for a dry cleaner." Scanlon paused. "I've spoken to Nolan. I figured you'd want the case, and I didn't want you to go through a lot of jurisdictional bullshit."

"I appreciate that, Captain. Has anyone checked the guesthouse?"

"I didn't know there was one."

"It's a five-acre estate," Jack explained. "There's a guesthouse down the hill, near that stand of pines. I'd like Sergeant Rizzo to check it out."

Scanlon signaled to a uniformed cop. "Price, get a print man and a photographer and go down the hill with Sergeant Rizzo."

"Yes, sir."

The living room was a beehive of organized confusion: Police photographers' cameras clicked and flashed, fingerprint technicians dusted objects scattered throughout the room, plainclothes detectives moved in and out of alcoves leading to other rooms, and uniformed police clambered up and down the spiral staircase that led to the upper floor.

In the sunken portion of the room Gabriel Torres, chief coroner for the city of Los Angeles, leaned over the corpse of Laura Sorenson. Her left arm was exposed, but the rest of her body was covered by a wool blanket. Torres had just taken a blood sample from her arm and placed a few drops on a glass slide before handing the specimen to his assistant.

"I've got my best people here, Raines," Scanlon said.

"Have you located Dr. Sorenson?"

"We've issued a nationwide APB."

"Anything of value missing?"

"Not that we can determine. Fur coats are in the closet. Silver service in the kitchen. The jewelry seems to be untouched."

Scanlon brushed his gray hair. "Only one curiosity—all the paintings and pictures were taken down."

"Not so curious," Jack said. "Someone was after a wall safe."

"Possible, I suppose."

"Well, what the hell else could it be, Captain?" Jack snapped.

Captain Scanlon's pale cheeks flushed. "Look, Raines, I know you've been up all night. I know what happened up there in the hills. I realize the extent of your personal loss, and I don't want to pull rank, but I'm over my head in six homicides and haven't had a fucking day off in four months. So let's keep it civil."

"Sorry, Captain."

The coroner was a stocky, balding man with broad Mexican features, set off by kind brown eyes. Over the years Torres had worked on a variety of cases with Jack, and they enjoyed a warm professional relationship.

"I'm sorry . . ." Torres murmured.

"I want to see her, Gabby."

"No, you don't. She was hit three times: face, stomach, chest."

Jack ignored the coroner's advice and leaned down to pull the blanket from Laura's face. Torres grabbed Jack's arm. "If it was my wife, I wouldn't want to see her."

"He's giving you good advice, Lieutenant," Scanlon added.

Jack sighed and straightened up. "Was she molested?"

"No." Torres shook his head. "She was fully clothed, no apparent sexual abuse. If it means anything, the first shot killed her."

"How do you know that?"

"No significant blood flow. Her brain ceased functioning instantly."

"What about the weapon?"

"From the size of entry, I'd guess it was a thirty-eight."

"We found no shells," Scanlon said. "It was a revolver, in all probability a Saturday night special."

"Have you determined the time?" Jack asked.

"I'd say she was hit five hours ago," Torres replied. "Her blood is not yet congealed, but I can confirm that tonight."

Two white-clad attendants rolled a low-slung metal

stretcher over and gently lifted Laura's body onto the tray. Jack noticed a bloodstain on the Persian carpet, marking the spot where Laura had fallen.

"I will have my wife light a candle for her tonight," Torres said. "I am very sorry, *amigo*."

"Thank you, Gabby."

The stocky coroner walked quickly out of the room.

Scanlon took out a pack of Camels and offered one to Jack.

"No, thanks."

Lighting his cigarette, Scanlon said, "Looks like she walked in on a couple of professional thieves who panicked. But then professional burglars normally don't kill their victims."

"What do you mean by 'normally'?"

"Well, a professional thief who's a three-time loser might kill to avoid a life sentence."

They walked over to the glass cases containing artifacts. "Now, this is something of a puzzle," Scanlon said. "The African and pre-Columbian cases are undisturbed, but this one . . ." His voice trailed off as he indicated the Middle Eastern case.

The glass had been smashed, and the objects moved off their dust spots and labels. The grotesque statue of Pazuzu was on its back, grinning up at the two detectives.

"Ugly bastard," Scanlon said.

Jack nodded. "The African and pre-Columbian stuff was stone and wood, but as I remember, there were some gold objects in this Middle Eastern case."

"That probably explains why it was the only case they smashed."

"I still think they were looking for a wall safe," Jack said. "A strongbox that contained something more valuable than cash, jewelry, or negotiable securities."

"Like what?"

"I wish I knew, Captain."

As they climbed the stairs, Jack noticed a detective taping an outline around the spot where Laura's body had fallen.

*   *   *

The deliveryman's features were regular, but his for-lorn eyes reminded Jack of aging horseplayers who invariably lost photo finishes.

Scanlon said, "Mr. Sorell, this is Lieutenant Jack Raines. The deceased woman was Lieutenant Raines's former wife."

"Oh, my God—Jesus Christ. I'm sorry."

"Thank you." Jack paused. "I don't want to keep you, Mr. Sorell. This must have been quite a shock for you. Just tell me what you know."

"I deliver the dry cleaning every Monday up here in Bel Air. Dr. Sorenson's house is usually my first stop. I got here a little after eight, the gate was open."

"Was that usual?"

"If Mrs. Sorenson had dropped her daughter off at school, she'd get back here around seven forty-five, and sometimes the gate would be open."

"But not always?"

"No."

"Go ahead, please."

"Well, I drove up, took the clothes out of my van, went to the door, and rang the bell. No one answered. So I tried the door, and it opened."

The sad-looking man sneezed violently and wiped his nose on his sleeve. "Sorry. I'm allergic to pollen."

"What happened once you opened the door?"

"I—I came in. I looked down into the living room." Sorell's face contorted. "My God. I'll never forget it. She was—she looked like—"

Captain Scanlon cut him off. "Just tell the lieutenant what you did."

"I went to the phone by the front door and called the police. Then I waited outside by my van."

"Now think carefully," Jack said. "Get the sight of the body out of your mind. Concentrate on the time you drove up and when you went out to wait for the police. Did you notice anything unusual?"

Sorell rose, walked to the window, and studied the exterior grounds for a moment. "I can't be sure, you understand. I was still in shock. But while I was outside, I thought something moved, down there near the cottage."

"You mean the guesthouse?"

"If that's what it is, yes."

"What was it you saw or thought you saw down there?"

"Well, it was more of a movement than anything else. It could have been the trees—or shadows—maybe a deer—or a human figure. I can't be sure. But something was moving away from that cottage."

Jack glanced at Scanlon. "Can you think of anything else, Captain?"

"Just this," Scanlon said. "Didn't the Sorensons employ a maid?"

"She's in Saint John's," Jack explained. "She was mugged."

"How do you know that?"

"Laura told me yesterday."

"Can I go now?" Sorell asked.

"Do we have your address and phone number?"

Sorell nodded. "I gave the sergeant my work number and home address."

"I appreciate your help," Jack said.

A uniformed cop stuck his head in the door. "Call for you, Captain, on the squad car radio."

Scanlon turned to Jack. "Why don't you look around, Lieutenant? You know the house better than I do."

In the master bedroom a fingerprint technician dusted a framed photograph.

"Anything?" Jack asked.

"Lots of prints, Lieutenant. But they probably belong to the family. We'll be running everything through FBI computers on a rush basis."

Jack walked up to the king-size bed. A Princess phone and a pair of reading glasses rested on the night table.

He opened the top drawer. Inside was a white note pad with "Dr. Martin Sorenson" embossed at the bottom. A single handwritten number appeared on the pad: 202-555-8888.

Jack recognized the Washington, D.C., area code

and punched the number up. The call was immediately answered by a pleasant, officious-sounding female voice. "Number please?"

"I dialed 202-555-8888."

"Your code and number please."

"I'm calling from area code 213-471-27 . . ."

"I require your code and number, sir," the woman's voice interrupted.

The repeated request suddenly struck him with familiar clarity. He had dialed a number belonging to perhaps one of fifteen different intelligence agencies. The woman was asking him for his personal agent's ID code.

"Listen to me carefully," he said with quiet authority. "I'm Lieutenant Jack Raines, Tactical Division, Los Angeles Police. I'm working on a homicide case, and it's imperative that I speak with Dr. Martin Sorenson."

There was a pause, and Jack knew the woman was running a trace.

"Did you hear me, miss? This is official business!" The connection clicked rapidly for a full minute, then went dead.

The living room was quiet. The police technicians had left. A few detectives and one uniformed cop were grouped outside the open door.

Jack stared at the bloodstained carpet for a moment and turned to leave just as Rizzo entered. The swarthy, menacing-looking sergeant carried a large framed photograph under his arm. "Nothing disturbed at the guesthouse," Rizzo said, handing Jack the framed photograph. "I thought you might want to see this."

The photograph depicted a group of people posing in front of a huge sandy mound. There was a very attractive blond woman in the center of an otherwise male group. Dr. Sorenson had his arm around the woman's shoulder. A caption ran across the base of the photograph: "Pyramid International group with Italian and Syrian colleagues. Ebla. May 1981."

"Mean anything?" Rizzo asked.

"That's a question for Sorenson. Any other pictures down there?"

Rizzo nodded. "A shot of Sorenson at some medical convention in New York, and a photograph of Laura, Jenny, and Sorenson on a cabin cruiser at the L.A. marina."

Jack's hand trembled visibly as he lit a fresh cigarillo. "Okay, Vince, make sure everything's sealed. I want cops front and back and down at the guesthouse. Co-ordinate with Scanlon, see that all the data get over to Tactical."

"Any ideas?" Rizzo asked.

"One or two."

Jenny was surprised to see her father in the principal's office. She noticed the scratches on his forehead and asked, "What's wrong, Dad?"

"Come on, Jenny, let's take a walk."

Jack favored his right leg slightly but held her tightly to him. They walked together on the far side of the school's running track.

Fighting back his tears, he told her of Laura's death, gently and simply. The initial shock triggered a flood of questions. He answered them honestly but withheld the details.

Over and over the child asked if there could have been some mistake, if maybe her mother was still alive. He kept shaking his head, telling her there was no mistake. She finally burst into tears and sobbed uncontrollably.

He swept her up in his arms, kissed her tearstained cheeks, and softly said, "We still have each other. We always will."

CHAPTER ELEVEN

△

Gabriella Bercovici and General Zvi Barzani stood atop the ruins that marked the site of ancient Megiddo. The crest of the tell overlooked the green and gold valley of Jezreel. The verdant plain was shadowed by the Golan Heights to the east and Mount Tabor to the west. There was nothing in the peaceful valley to suggest it had once been the site of ferocious and historic battles.

"Hardly the place for Armageddon," Gabriella said.

"Nevertheless," Barzani replied, "the Book of Revelations in the New Testament is quite emphatic. It predicts the world will end here in Megiddo."

"I don't accept legend as fact"—she smiled—"except when it's convenient."

"And now you've come to me with the grandest legend of all."

"We have reason to believe that somewhere below this mound is a tablet containing the final word of your God—Yahweh."

"I'm not so sure that anyone in my country is anxious to hear Yahweh's last words. If Moses was fearful of it, he was probably right."

Two sudden thunderous cracks shocked their ear-drums. "F-sixteens breaking the sound barrier," Barzani explained. "They're on reconnaissance missions over Syrian forces in the Bekaa Valley."

The general's regular features were dominated by large, cold black eyes that were curiously vacant as if they had erased a lifetime of recorded imagery. His black, curly hair was flecked with silver, and his dark skin was crisscrossed by severe lines. Barzani was not yet fifty, but he had already survived five wars. His most recent foray into combat had occurred in Lebanon in June 1982, when he led a crack commando unit up the beach at Sidon behind PLO lines. After a vicious fire fight the guerrillas had broken and the coastal highway was opened to Israeli armored units.

While the general was no stranger to battlefield violence, his personal life had been devastated by an act of senseless murder. His wife and two sons had been killed by a PLO terrorist attack on a bus traveling along the coastal highway from Tel Aviv to Haifa. From that day he had insulated himself from all emotional attachments. Bearing his pain alone, he centered his life on his military career and his abiding interest in archaeology.

The general stared off at the Plain of Jezreel. "Look there, Gabriella." He pointed to a distant field of wheat waving gently in the wind. "From that field Pharaoh Thutmose the Third, riding a golden chariot, attacked the Canaanites in 1500 B.C. And there, in those olive groves, King David smashed the Philistines." He then indicated the gently sloping meadow directly below them. "In that field the Crusaders made their final stand against Saladin. They were massacred to the last man."

Gabriella nodded her appreciation but offered no comment. She knew the general enjoyed reciting the history of his country.

"And here—right here," Barzani continued, "where we stand—on April sixteenth, 1799, the Turks attacked a small French garrison. They were saved by a cavalry troop led by a young officer named Napoleon Bona-parte." He put his big hand on her shoulder. "The

richness of history is before us. And you want to bur-
row under this mound of dirt."

"And so do you." She smiled. "You'd like nothing
better than to be part of a team that discovered a lost
word of God."

As they started down the steep mound, Barzani said,
"Your Ebla expedition created an uproar in ruling Syrian circles. Your old colleague Dr. Gamasi has been
holding press conferences, branding you and Sabitini
as Zionist propagandists."

"But wouldn't it be something," she replied, "if the
Moses tablet proved conclusively that the Syrians and
Israelis were blood brothers."

"Perhaps, but before we acknowledge our common
heritage, I would like one more crack at our Syrian
brothers."

In the shade of the tell two soldiers armed with Galil
automatic rifles lounged against a jeep. Gabriella stared
uneasily at them. Their faces were burned to a coppery
color, and their eyes were hidden behind reflecting
sunglasses. She thought there was an ominous quality
to their impassive, relaxed attitude.

The general spoke to the soldiers in rapid Hebrew,
explaining that he and the woman were going to enter
the tell.

The dark opening had been carved out of the mound
in 1925, and over the decades various expeditions had
cut their way into the tell inch by inch, meter by meter.
Every layer of sand removed signified another chapter
in human history.

Crouching slightly, they moved down a cool tunnel,
dimly lit by a string of naked overhead bulbs. The level
was designated Stratum I and had yielded artifacts
relating to Persian and Babylonian military expeditions.
A winding stone staircase took them to Stratum II.
Vivid paintings on the limestone walls depicted Assyrian
warriors.

Toward the far end of the stone corridor the dank,
musky air turned sharp and rancid. Gabriella gasped as
she saw the decaying maggot-infested carcass of a huge
rat.

They entered a dark, body-size opening, and the general's flashlight played over steep marble steps. "Careful now," he cautioned. "It's been a long time since you were here. The marble is smooth."

"I remember." She paused. "October 1973 was a fateful month."

Their eyes met briefly, and the memory of shared intimacy passed between them.

He took her arm, guiding her down the winding steps.

At the base of the steps he hit a switch, activating a battery of floodlights that illuminated huge mud walls enclosing stone ruins of villas, granaries, and stables. "This is where we found the scroll proclaiming Megiddo as King Solomon's fifth military district," Barzani said.

"Well"—she sighed—"perhaps fifteen or twenty feet below is the Mosaic period, the time of Israel's conquest of Canaan, when Ithamar hid the final word of Yahweh."

"It's not that simple, Gabriella. You're speaking of a full-fledged dig. We would require a thirty-meter north-south trench, support levels, engineers, architects, draftsmen—the works. We'd need a minimum of a quarter of a million dollars. And without Ithamar's legendary gold triangles, how do we find the Moses tablet?"

"The odds are we'll never find it, but Sabitini is certain the triangles are not legend, and there is always the possibility that one of them will turn up."

"You realize that should we discover this tablet, your life will come to an abrupt end. Even I can't protect you."

"You mean the Syrians?"

"No—to hell with them." He smiled. "From the Jews. You will become the greatest prophet of Israel since Moses. You'll be the pope of all the Hebrew tribes. You'll be enshrined in the temple."

"Does that mean I have to join the army?"

"Absolutely. But I'll arrange your assignment."

"I'll bet." She smiled and set the F-stop on the fast Japanese lens. "Are we all right for time?"

"Yes. The old man in Jerusalem will see us only after sundown. I hope you realize he's a self-proclaimed sage. A cabalistic prophet. A man who sees visions, not facts."

"Perhaps, but Sabitini felt there might be something in the cabalist theories concerning a last word of Yahweh."

"You Romans are something. You destroyed our temple, took one of our carpenters, made him your God, killed his followers, and now almost two thousand years later you want to find out what the carpenter's father said."

She laughed. "I don't remember your being so amusing—attractive, even sexy, but never amusing."

"Go ahead, shoot your pictures." He smiled. "Show Professor Sabitini you did some work in the Holy Land."

They parked the jeep at the foot of Mount Zion and walked through the Dung Gate into the old city.

Gabriella always marveled at the harmonious beauty of Jerusalem and the fact that despite all the misery and violence that had befallen the city, it survived with enduring majesty.

Barzani had given her an army beret and a field jacket, which went well with her jeans and sneakers. When she asked about the beret, he explained that women were not permitted to enter the Orthodox Jewish quarter bare-headed.

The two impassive soldiers followed them through the narrow cobblestoned streets.

They passed men wearing long black coats and wide-brimmed black hats, their faces adorned with flowing side curls. Women dressed in shapeless robes hung their wash on clotheslines strung across flat rooftops. Children sat alongside scribes in well-lit open stalls, learning the ancient craft of copying the Scriptures by hand. The sound of Hebrew prayer chants filled the alleys of the ancient quarter.

The general stopped at a small house and knocked loudly on the heavy wooden door. It was opened by a small child, and Barzani motioned Gabriella to enter. The boy led them along a musty corridor, through an alcove to another door and down a flight of worn wooden steps, into the basement.

The room was bathed in a magenta glow cast by huge incense candles encased in red glass. There was a Star of David on three of the four walls. Paintings rendered in vivid colors covered the floor and depicted jackals, lions, the number 3, and a triangle in the center of which stood a nude woman with sightless eyes. Two serpents were curled around her waist. She cupped her breasts in her palms, offering her nipples to the snake heads.

Sitting on the bare floor, ashes smeared across his forehead, an old man wearing a purple robe rocked and chanted in an idiom that Gabriella recognized as Aramaic—the God language of Hebrew. The small boy motioned them to be still and left. The old man continued to pray for a few minutes, then stopped abruptly and made the sign of a triangle.

He rose and turned to them. His skin was the color of coffee, and his eyes were midnight blue and seemed transfixed. He didn't wear the side curls of the Orthodox sect but had flowing silver hair that fell across his shoulders. Barzani guessed the shaman of cabala was either Moroccan or Egyptian by birth.

The old man spoke in a reedy, hollow voice that sounded as if it were being played on an old Victrola. "This is the blind daughter of Baal, sister of Pazuzu," he said, indicating the sightless woman painted inside the triangle. "She is the devil-woman Ishtar. She breathed the power of the sun to Pharaoh Akhenaton one thousand years before Yahweh spoke to Moses. She has the force of the triangle, from which came the pyramid. She was present in Samaria three thousand years before Genesis. She fought for the soul of Moses with the archangel Michael until Yahweh kissed the lips of the great prophet." The old man moved closer to them. His eyes were glazed, and his movements slow and trancelike. The sweet-smelling incense pervaded the room.

"You will find Ishtar in Megiddo. There she sleeps into eternity still possessed with great powers. Only the prophet Elijah can still the satanic hand of Ishtar." The old man suddenly fell silent.

"But what was the transgression of Moses?" Barzani gently asked. "Why was the great prophet forbidden entry to the Promised Land?"

"We see in the book of life, in the midnight of time, that Moses forsook the last words of Yahweh at the place of the waters. I know no more."

The general nodded and pressed some money into the old man's hand.

A ghostly, opaque moon peered out of the black night like a single malevolent eye. A cool wind blew down from the Judean hills, whipping against the red-stone dwellings. Yellow-eyed cats prowled the Via Dolorosa. A Gregorian chant came from the open stained glass windows of the Church of the Holy Sepulcher. And from the Moslem quarter a muezzin wailed, calling the worshipers to prayer.

The general draped his arm around Gabriella's shoulder as they made their way up the Street of Sorrow, passing stations of the cross. The two soldiers followed at a distance, their eyes flickering from windows to doorways, their index fingers curled around the triggers of the Galil automatic rifles; despite the temples, mosques, and synagogues, the old city of David had not yet seen the blessings of peace.

Gabriella shivered slightly.

"Zip your jacket up," Barzani said. "The nights in Jerusalem are always cool."

"It's not the cold. It's that old man."

"Ah, you make too much of him. These prophets of the cabala live only for signs, symbols, and incongruities in the Bible."

"Still, he came close to confirming Ithamar's inscription," she replied. "He said Moses 'forsook' the word of God."

"True, but remember, these cabalistic prophecies are

passed down by generations of storytellers. They have no basis in fact."

"Perhaps, but I believe that old man has prophetic perception—a visionary power." She paused. "What did you think about his mention of Ishtar still present in Megiddo?"

"Ishtar is a satanic Canaanite legend, nothing more."

"Yes, I know, but almost every major archaeological discovery was generated by legend."

"Forget the old man, Gabriella. We have the full text of Ithamar inscribed in his own hand. That's a fact, not a legend. What we require are the funds to dig down two strata to the time of Ithamar. Then with or without those missing triangles we'll do what we can. Everything depends on your ability to raise the money."

"Yes . . ." She sighed. "In the end everything comes down to money."

As they passed through the Dung Gate, the general turned to the soldiers and shouted something in Hebrew to them.

"Why are we going up the hill?" Gabriella asked.

"I keep forgetting you speak Hebrew." He smiled. "I want you to see the old city from Mount Zion."

His arm circled her waist, and the night wind played with the tips of her hair as they climbed the gentle slope of Mount Zion. They reached the pine-covered crest and stared off at the amber glow of domed mosques and church spires, and the floodlit Western Wall of the Second Temple.

"It's truly beautiful."

"It's more than beauty. The force of history is in every stone. When I was very young, I used to come up here and just . . ." His voice trailed off, and he forced a smile. "Ah, well, that was another lifetime."

He turned to her and touched her hair. The wind rose and whispered gently through the pines. "You know, I think often of that long ago October night, of that moment, you and I, with my ears still ringing with the sound of Syrian artillery and the blood of my boys on my uniform." He paused. "Only with the passage of time have I come to understand how kind you were to me that night."

"Making love to you had nothing to do with kindness. It had everything to do with life and treating death as an illusion."

He clasped her hand, and they stood silently in the pale moonlight, high above the old city of King David.

CHAPTER TWELVE

△

"Hail, Holy Queen Mother of Mercy . . . our life, our sweetness and our hope. To Thee we send up our sighs, mournings and weepings. . . ."

Laura's funeral had been held the preceding Thursday, but the words of the priest echoed as Jack steered around the sharp curves of Chalon Road.

Dr. Martin Sorenson had been located in a Maryland suburb of Washington and flew his own Learjet back to Los Angeles in time to attend the funeral.

During the services Jack had tried to divert his daughter's attention from the television crews covering the ceremony. Laura Sorenson's death was an ideal subject for the six o'clock news; the former wife of a police lieutenant and present wife of a prominent physician brutally murdered in her Bel Air estate was a story that captured all the lurid elements that ensured high ratings.

After the funeral Rizzo's wife, Angela, offered to take care of Jenny, and Jack gratefully accepted. The Rizzos had three girls, one of whom was the same age as Jenny; it seemed the perfect temporary haven for his daughter.

Jack turned into the open gates of the Sorenson estate, drove up the curving driveway, and parked beside a Bekins moving van. He walked past four men hefting a huge sofa and entered the house.

Sorenson was a tall, muscular man with austere features that were softened by an ingenuous, seductive smile. His face was permanently tanned by the sea; the coppery color dramatized his dark blue eyes and thick silver hair.

They shook hands, and Sorenson smiled. "I take it this is an official visit."

"As agreed."

"Right. Well, as you can see, I'm putting everything in storage, closing the house. I'll be living on the boat. I can't bear this place—since . . ."

"I understand," Jack said. "Where can we talk?"

"In here."

The study was a large, comfortable room complete with wet bar and billiard table. A bay window overlooked a luxurious rose garden.

"A drink?" Sorenson asked.

"No, thanks."

The doctor poured some brandy into a snifter and swished the gold-colored liquid around. "I'm still shaky. I just can't accept the fact of her death."

"Neither can I."

An unstated tension lay just beneath their surface cordiality. Laura's violent death was in a curious way an indictment of both men—one way or the other they had failed her.

"How is Jenny doing?"

"All right, I suppose."

"It was kind of the Rizzos to take her."

"Yes, it was," Jack replied, and took a folded eight-by-ten photograph out of his pocket. "I had this reproduced from the original Rizzo found down at the guesthouse."

Sorenson glanced at the picture captioned in part "Ebla—May 1981."

"Can you identify the people in this picture?"

Sorenson nodded. "I'll read them off, left to right. This is Dr. Amin Gamasi." He paused. "You want their titles?"

"It would help."

"Gamasi is director of antiquities for the Syrian Ministry of Culture. The man alongside is Professor Emilio Sabitini, dean of Middle Eastern studies at Rome University and one of the foremost archaeologists in the world."

Jack jotted the information down, and Sorenson continued. "This attractive lady is Gabriella Bercovici. She's an associate of Sabitini's and a brilliant epigrapher."

"Which means?"

"A specialist in ancient languages, in her case Western Semitic and Middle Eastern idioms. She's an acknowledged leader in her field—a rare combination of beauty and brains." Sorenson paused. "That's me to her left, and to my left, that portly chap is Lord Anthony Hamilton, to his left, the smallish man is Pierre Claudon, and finally, this is Dr. Howard Emory." Sorenson swallowed some brandy. "The last three— Hamilton, Claudon, and Emory—are part of a consortium I put together called Pyramid International. We finance archaeological expeditions as an avocation and, of course, a tax write-off."

"Is the date on this picture accurate?"

"Yes. It was taken in early May 1981 at the Ebla dig in Syria. The sandy mound behind us is called Tell Mardikh. After six years of excavation the Italian-Syrian team uncovered the ancient kingdom of Ebla."

"When was the dig concluded?"

"Last summer. The Syrian government sealed the site and expelled Sabitini's group."

"Why?"

"A royal library was discovered at Ebla, with thousands of clay tablets written in a heretofore-unknown cuneiform idiom. Miss Bercovici managed to decipher the language. What surfaced was an unmistakable Hebrew presence in northern Syria, two thousand years before any recorded Islamic history.

"The Syrian government believed the Ebla tablets constituted a threat to their culture and an insult to their Arab heritage. In other words, they would suffer an incalculable loss of face in the Islamic world if there existed even the slightest suspicion that Syrians had descended from ancient Hebrew tribes."

"And if we take that one step further," Jack added, "the Syrians might not want anyone around who could prove that Hebrew connection."

"It's a reach, Jack. You're implying that the Syrians might have come after me, and Laura got in the way."

"A reach maybe, but a possibility."

"Not really," Sorenson countered. "The story of the Ebla tablets and the Hebrew connection broke in the world press almost a year ago. Dr. Gamasi dismissed the Ebla findings as Zionist propaganda. It's inconceivable that Syrian political motivations caused this tragedy."

Jack nodded and lit a cigarillo. "Laura told me you've been out of town quite a bit lately."

"That's right."

"Doing what?"

"Business."

"What kind?"

"I can't discuss that with you or anyone else."

"Why not?"

"Let's just say it's not relevant to Laura's death."

Jack took a note out of his pocket. "You recognize this phone number?"

"Yes."

"Who does it belong to?"

"I can't tell you that."

"I called that number," Jack said. "It connects to an intelligence agency in Washington. The operator asked for my agent's ID code. Now, what agency do you work for?"

"What has this got to do with Laura's death?"

"Maybe nothing, but I'd appreciate an answer."

Sorenson brushed his silver hair and sighed. "All right. I'll go this far. I'm involved in a secret government project that has to do with neurophysiology, behavioral research for NASA."

"How much did Laura know?"

"Nothing. I told her my absences were part of a neurological research program at the U.S. Naval Medical Center in Bethesda, Maryland." The doctor paused. "As you know, Laura was used to husbands who said very little about their work."

Jack ignored Sorenson's sarcasm. "You're certain that no secret government agency could have been searching this house for some document or memorandum connected to your research?"

"Absolutely."

"Okay. Now what about other business? You have that medical complex in Westwood—everything from dentists to brain surgery. Any problems with partners, patients, anyone with a grudge, or some psychopathic individual who might have it in for you?"

"Not to my knowledge. But a deranged person seeking revenge for some imagined reason is always a possibility."

"What is that complex worth?"

"Gross value, including real property, I'd say close to twenty million."

"Any unusual recent transactions?"

"Well . . . some months ago I bought out Dr. Emory's interests."

"The same Dr. Emory who was in the Syrian photograph?"

"Yes."

"Everything friendly?"

"The negotiations got a little testy, but that's normal when large sums of money are involved."

"Where do I find Emory?"

"He's retired—lives in Palm Springs."

"I'd like his phone number and address. Also your phone number on the boat and the slip number at the marina."

"Anything else?"

"Do you have a wall safe here in the house or down at the guesthouse?"

"No. Why do you ask?"

"All the paintings had been taken down. Obviously someone expected to find a wall safe."

"Well, they were disappointed." Sorenson paused. "Can we conclude our business now?"

"Another minute or two." Jack crushed the cigarillo out and asked, "Was Laura involved with another man?"

"Not to my knowledge."

"Are you involved with someone else?"

"No, no one else," Sorenson replied quickly, then added, "I'm not a criminologist, but it seems apparent that Laura walked in on a pair of common criminals who panicked and killed her."

"It's possible, but the evidence says otherwise. The coroner reported flash burns on Laura's skin and clothes. She was shot deliberately—almost executed."

Sorenson drained the brandy. "Let me give you those numbers."

The doctor jotted down his personal numbers and added Dr. Emory's Palm Springs phone number and address.

Jack tucked the paper in his pocket and decided to take a parting shot. "Martin, I'm not certain about the Syrian motives one way or the other or your secret agency people. Maybe they're both totally unrelated to this case. Maybe this *is* a street crime. But history tells me that professionals were looking for a specific item. Something small, something that would fit comfortably in a wall safe. I think you know what it is they were after, and if I'm right, you'd better level with me— because they're not going to stop with Laura."

"Good-bye, Jack," Sorenson said quietly.

Sorenson walked quickly back through the hall into the study and noticed the red light blinking on the phone answering machine. He pressed the replay button and a female voice came on. "This is the overseas operator. Rome, Italy. Miss Gabriella Bercovici wishes to speak with Dr. Martin Sorenson. Please call at her office, 514-6037, or home, 591-4876."

CHAPTER THIRTEEN

△

Arthur Benson was nattily dressed in a blue blazer, red vest, gray slacks, and a dark blue bow tie over a light blue shirt. His aquiline nose was marred by a network of purple veins, and he had grown a mustache with fine-pointed ends to detract attention from his blue nose. He reminded Jack of an aging Broadway character actor who had enjoyed a long run in a hazardous profession. Benson's theatrical appearance was the antithesis of what one would expect of a regional FBI director.

He was on the phone, leaning back in his chair, his fingers fine-tuning the pointed ends of his mustache. His eyes flicked nervously around the office, trying to avoid making contact with the two detectives seated opposite him.

"Tell them to turn that file over to Simmons," Benson said. "It's strictly narcotics. Thank you, Mary."

He hung up, opened a drawer, took out a bottle of Gelusil tablets, and popped two in his mouth. "My stomach's become a minefield."

"What about Sorenson's file?" Jack asked.

Benson rose and walked to the water cooler, pulled a paper cup, filled it, drank half of it, tossed the cup in a wastebasket, and returned to his desk.

He cleared his throat. "Needless to say, there is no question of personal intent here. I would move mountains to help you fellows crack this case. The problem is I have no legal basis for issuing this sort of request."

Rizzo glanced at Jack, hoping his partner would not explode. But Jack's voice remained calm. "I'm not asking you to do anything clandestine. I'm officially requesting the federal file on Dr. Martin Sorenson. This is routine procedure. What the hell are you afraid of?"

"You know damn well what I'm afraid of. You said Sorenson's involved in some secret government project."

"It's NASA, for chrissake."

"Maybe so, but you don't know what agency runs the project. It might be CIA, or DIA, or NSA, or even that goddamn supersecret NRO. It's like Beirut back there—no one knows who's on first. This sort of request could have a domino effect in Washington; I could get burned—fatally burned."

Jack walked over to the far wall and glanced at the photograph of Richard Nixon with his arm around Benson's shoulder. He studied the photograph for a long moment, then turned to Benson. "Okay, Arthur, let's cut the bullshit. About two months ago Rizzo and I committed a criminal act on your behalf."

Benson fingered his mustache nervously. "Christ, you're not going to bring that up?"

"You're goddamn right I am!" Jack snapped. "And don't make the mistake of having a short memory. We installed an illegal tap on Counselor Mirell's office phone."

"A tap that's still operative," Rizzo added.

Benson stammered, "Well, fellows, I—I've held you in the highest esteem; I trusted you one hundred percent."

"And we never betrayed that trust," Jack replied. "Now I'm asking you for a small favor, and you give me a lot of bureaucratic double talk."

"Christ, Jack, you worked for the agency; you know that spook world. They can crucify me."

"For what?"

"For surfacing the identity of a secret operative."

"You don't know that Sorenson is an agent. From where you sit, it's just a routine request from Tactical Division. Sorenson's wife was murdered, and he's part of the case."

"I'm sorry. I'll need a written request from Nolan."

"You're fucking me around, Arthur," Jack said menacingly. "You know goddamn well Nolan won't put his name on a requisition for a paper clip. Now, either you handle this favor for me or I let Mirell know there's an active tap on his phone."

"So it's come down to blackmail."

"No, Arthur, it's come down to murder."

Benson stared at them for a moment, then punched the intercom button on the phone console. "Mary, come in and bring your book, please."

The paneled door opened, and a tall, shapeless girl entered. Her large, sad eyes seemed to sense Benson's stress. She stood hesitantly near the door, clutching her steno pad.

"Sit down, Mary," Benson said, indicating the leather sofa. He rubbed his hand wearily over his eyes and leaned back in his chair.

"This is a top priority Telex; use a classified code. From Benson to Mannings—urgently require federal file on Dr. Martin Sorenson, spelled S-O-R-E-N-S-O-N. Origin of request, Lieutenant Jack Raines, spelled R-A-I-N-E-S, Tactical Division, LAPD."

The girl glanced at Benson for a moment, her sad eyes full of sympathy.

"Thank you, Mary."

She walked quickly out of the room.

"Now that wasn't too tough, was it, Arthur?"

"It was dirty pool."

"So was the tap."

"Right," Benson said. "I guess it all balances. The important thing in this life is friendship."

CHAPTER FOURTEEN

△

Gabriella was awakened by the harsh, insistent ring of the phone. She was naked and soaked with perspiration. The air-conditioning unit had never been properly installed and failed with remarkable consistency. The green radial dials of the bedside clock read 5:45 A.M.

"*Pronto?*" she answered in Italian.

"Is this Gabriella Bercovici?"

"Yes, this is she."

"Gabriella, this is Martin Sorenson."

She was suddenly fully awake.

"Forgive the hour, but I didn't know when I'd get another chance to return your call."

"It's all right. Please hold a moment."

She rose quickly and threw open the French windows, letting in a rush of fresh air. She slipped her robe on, thinking it was an absurd reaction, but some subconscious scruple would not allow her to conduct a phone conversation while naked.

She sat down on the edge of the bed and picked up the receiver. "I'm sorry, Martin, go ahead."

"Well, as I said, I'm returning your call."

"Yes, of course," she replied nervously. "I phoned to tell you we discovered a stone at Ebla that I managed to photograph before we were expelled. It contained a cuneiform inscription—a last will and testament of a Hebrew priest named Ithamar. He speaks of a mission that directed him to place a tablet inscribed by Moses in Megiddo."

"I suppose it's possible," Sorenson replied. "There have been countless rumors of a Moses tablet. After all, he was God's scribe."

"This is more than a message. This tablet contains the last words of God—some final edict that Moses withheld from the Hebrews. I've been to Megiddo, and General Barzani will grant us permission to dig below the current fourth stratum."

"I see. . . ."

"There's more to it." Gabriella cradled the phone and reached for a cigarette. "The stone of Ithamar contained an empty triangular space. According to his inscription, gold triangles were embedded in that space, detailing the exact location of the Moses tablet."

"You're saying 'triangles' plural?"

"Yes. Professor Sabitini makes a strong case for three, by virtue of the ancient Hebrew affinity for that number." She paused. "The triangles are missing."

Sorenson could feel his blood rising, but the tone of his voice remained indifferent. "Why do you call me?"

"Barzani estimates we would require at least a quarter of a million dollars to go down to the next level at Megiddo."

"But even if you reach the Mosaic period, how will you find the tablet without the triangles?"

"By fine-combing every chamber, every crypt, every tomb."

"Well, I am, of course, intrigued, but unfortunately I'm in no position to decide anything right now." He paused. "I've suffered a great personal tragedy. My wife died a week ago. She was shot to death."

Gabriella was stunned and for a moment could say nothing. She inhaled deeply on the cigarette and finally sighed. "I'm sorry, Martin. Forgive me, I didn't know."

"It's all right," Sorenson replied. "I appreciate your calling. When my affairs are in order, I'll get back to you."

"Please accept my condolences. I know that I speak for Professor Sabitini as well."

"Thank you, Gabriella."

She hung up and walked to the open window. A very white, timid sun was slowly rising over the domes and spires of the Eternal City.

Sorenson thoughtfully replaced the receiver. He was surprised that Gabriella had so quickly perceived the true value of the triangle. But no harm was done. His conversation with her did not in any way alter his plans.

From the moment he had heard of Laura's death his course of action was clear. They would soon understand that Martin Sorenson was not a man one betrayed with impunity.

Laura's death would be avenged.

CHAPTER FIFTEEN

△

The canvas top of the GTO convertible was up against the fierce desert sun. The silence in the car was broken by the whirring air conditioner and the drone of the all-news station. Jack drove west along a broad palm-lined road, heading toward the immense purple silhouette of Mount San Jacinto.

Palm Springs was not Jack's favorite resort. He thought the proliferation of motels, condominiums, and fast-food chains had destroyed its historic charm. It had become a bizarre refuge for fading movie stars, alcoholic writers, and aging widows, who sat beside tiny swimming pools swilling martinis and sunning themselves into skin cancers. And above it all, high up on Mount San Jacinto, an elite group of millionaires, sequestered behind the walls of opulent villas, played tennis, tossed lavish parties, and dabbled in platinum futures.

The Emory house was tucked into a cul-de-sac off Las Palmas Boulevard. Lush purple bougainvillaea cascaded over its white walls, and tall palms shaded the red-tiled roof. Jack felt a searing rush of heat as he got out of the air-conditioned car and walked up the driveway.

The door was opened by a tall, regal middle-aged woman. Her fine features were remarkably free of lines, and her figure was trim. Only her strong brown eyes, rimmed by dark circles, betrayed fatigue and tension.

He flashed the gold badge pinned to his wallet. "I'm Lieutenant Jack Raines."

"Oh, yes. I'm Helena Emory. Come in, please."

He followed her into a spacious living room that overlooked a swimming pool and patio area. The furniture was French, old and expensive. An impressive collection of contemporary paintings covered the walls, and artifacts, housed in glass cases similar to those at Sorenson's, were prominently displayed. On a concave glass stand stood a bronze statue that caused Jack to shudder—it was unmistakably another representation of the Canaanite devil-god, Pazuzu.

Mrs. Emory rubbed her wrists nervously. "I tried calling you, Mr. Raines, but you had already left." She paused and brushed some invisible lint from her white blouse. "My husband suffered a severe heart attack last night." Her voice wavered. "He's not expected to live. I've just come from the hospital."

Jack cleared his throat and said, "I'm sorry. I had no idea. We can do this another time."

"No, it's all right. I don't mind. I feel bad about your coming all the way down here to see Howard. I know you're in the midst of an important investigation." She took a cigarette out of a silver case. "My husband and I were shocked by Laura's death."

"Are you certain you won't mind answering a few questions?"

"Positive," she said, and lit the cigarette, inhaling deeply. "Would you care for a cold drink?"

"Some ice water would be fine."

She walked over to the wet bar, placed some ice cubes in a glass, opened a bottle of Perrier water, and poured it carefully over the ice. Jack knew that her exterior calm was due to the fatigue of an all-night vigil.

She handed him the glass. "I tried phoning my son in Chicago, but he was on a call. He's a pediatrician, quite successful." She sat down and crossed her legs. "Now, how can I help you, Mr. Raines?"

"I understand your husband and Dr. Sorenson were financial partners in an archaeological expedition."

"Yes, in Syria, with two other men—a Frenchman, Pierre Claudon, and an Englishman, Lord Anthony Hamilton."

Jack indicated the bronze of Pazuzu. "Did that handsome fellow come out of the Syrian expedition?"

"Yes. As a matter of fact, it only recently arrived. Lord Hamilton sent it as a gift. Why do you ask?"

"Nothing special. I saw that same figure at the Sorensons'."

"It's some sort of devil-god, from what my husband told me, quite common to various Middle Eastern cultures."

"Would you say Dr. Emory was heavily involved in the Syrian dig?"

"Not at all. Howard visited the Ebla site one summer, but even that was in the nature of a holiday."

"Did you go with him?"

"No." She smiled. "The wives were not invited."

"So it's fair to say Dr. Emory's involvement was minor."

"Yes. Martin Sorenson got my husband interested in archaeology some years ago. It was simply a hobby."

Jack nodded and sipped the ice water.

"I believe your husband and Dr. Sorenson were also partners in a medical facility in Westwood."

She smiled a small, sad smile. "You seem to know quite a lot, Lieutenant."

"Not enough, or I wouldn't be here. What was the nature of their relationship?"

"It was always amicable, but there was a rift of sorts when Martin bought out my husband's interests in the medical complex."

"But that rift was healed?"

"Oh, yes. Once the negotiations were concluded, they remained courteous and friendly."

"When did you last see Laura Sorenson?"

"Several months ago at a dinner party."

"Where?"

"At the Sorensons'."

"Anything unusual happen that night?"

"I don't know what you mean by 'unusual.' "

"Oh, any arguments or excessive drinking, any problems between Laura and Dr. Sorenson, or any tensions between your husband and Dr. Sorenson?"

"Well, yes, there was something just before dinner. Howard and Martin were in the study; Laura and I were in the living room. We heard their voices grow loud."

"You mean, angry?"

"Yes, but only for a moment. Their conversation was indistinct, but at one point Martin shouted something about a triangle."

"The geometric figure?"

"Yes."

"And how did your husband respond?"

"I can't be certain, but I thought he said, 'We ought to advise Hamilton.' In any case that's what it sounded like."

"Did you take it to mean that your husband was suggesting that they inform Hamilton about the triangle?"

"I didn't take it to mean anything."

"Did you ask your husband about the triangle?"

"No. The atmosphere at dinner was convivial, and I forgot about it."

"What kind of medicine does your husband practice?"

"Howard is a brain surgeon."

Jack sipped the water and said, "Can you describe the circumstances of your husband's heart attack?"

"We were upstairs, watching television. The doorbell rang. Howard had told me he was expecting a business associate."

"Did he identify the associate?"

"No." She hesitated. "I don't think I asked."

"What time was this?"

"I'm not certain. It seemed to me close to midnight."

"Wasn't that late for business?"

"I suppose so. But we've purchased some property down here, and I assumed it was a pressing matter."

"Go ahead, please."

"Howard went downstairs and returned after twenty minutes or so."

"Did you hear anything unusual? Loud voices, anger, scuffling—anything like that?"

She shook her head. "No, nothing. Howard came into the bedroom complaining of a mosquito bite on the back of his thigh. He got undressed and put on his pajamas. We started to watch a movie on the cable station. Ten minutes or so passed when Howard began to suffer severe chest pains and I called the paramedics."

The phone rang, and she stared at the instrument fearfully as if the sound conveyed the inevitability of disaster.

She lifted the receiver and listened for a few seconds before saying, "Yes, this is she."

Jack watched the color slowly drain from her face. She hung up and softly, unemotionally said, "That was Dr. Santoro. My husband is dead." She bit her lower lip and fought for composure.

"Would you like me to try to reach your son in Chicago?"

"No, thank you." She brushed the tears away. "I don't understand. Howard was—was blessed with good health all his life."

"Mrs. Emory, I know this will come as a shock to you, but your husband may have been murdered."

Her brown eyes grew wide with fear and consternation. "I don't understand."

"There's something too convenient about this sudden heart attack. I'm guessing, but experience tells me that your husband's death may be related to Laura Sorenson's murder."

"How?"

"I don't know. But I would like your approval to order an autopsy."

"Do whatever you think is right, Lieutenant."

*   *   *

Jack held the speedometer needle at sixty as he headed back to Los Angeles on the San Bernardino Freeway. His mind raced, and he was oblivious to the passing stream of traffic. He wondered about the identity of Emory's night caller, what they had discussed, and the mosquito bite, and what the word *triangle* meant, and if Emory's medical background in brain surgery connected to Sorenson's secret government activities. The strands of the web spinning out of Laura's murder were widening.

CHAPTER SIXTEEN

△

Gabriella carefully steered her small Fiat down the curving slope of the Viale del Muro and entered the Porto del Popolo. After passing the illuminated Egyptian obelisk, she parked on the far side of the ancient piazza, close to the crumbling church of Santa Maria di Monte.

In her faded jeans, sneakers, and turtleneck sweater, she looked more like a student than a distinguished authority in ancient languages.

Crossing the gaily lit square, she thought about her impending meeting with Pierre Claudon. The thin-faced, dapper antique dealer had been an investor in Pyramid International, and she had had several conversations with him when he visited the Ebla site. Her impression of Claudon was that of a pretentious little man, preoccupied with small deceits.

She had agreed to this dinner date knowing it was a direct result of her phone conversation with Lord Anthony Hamilton; in point of fact, Claudon was Hamilton's errand boy.

* * *

The Trattoria Bolognese was crowded with a mixture of movie people, expensive call girls with their Milanese clients, politicians with wives, businessmen with wives and mistresses, and agents of the Italian secret police trying to look like left-wing radicals.

The maître d' showed Gabriella to her table and advised her that Signor Claudon would be arriving a few minutes late. She thanked him and ordered a bottle of Gavi di Gavi white wine.

The sidewalk terrace was covered by a striped awning and illuminated by small globes of amber light. A romantic ballad sung by Julio Iglesias drifted across the restaurant and filled Gabriella with a recurring sense of inner loneliness.

The smiles and animated conversation of the dining couples only heightened her sadness, and she promised herself that after the dig at Megiddo she would go off somewhere alone and take stock of her life. She could not abide this emotional emptiness much longer.

She glanced up as the maître d' ushered Pierre Claudon to the table.

"Forgive me, Gabriella." Claudon smiled and kissed her hand. "It was impossible to locate a taxi."

"It's all right. I just got here."

He sat down and adjusted the knot in his tie. "How are you, my dear?"

"Fine. And you?"

"Perfect, as always."

"I ordered a Gavi di Gavi. But if you prefer something else . . ."

"No, no. When it comes to Italian wines, I must trust your expertise."

"Well, there really is no such thing as a fine Italian white wine, but Gavi comes close."

"And how is my good friend Professor Sabitini?"

"Busy as usual. He wanted to join us, but he's preparing an exhibit of Etruscan art for the Villa Giulia Museum."

"That's as it should be." Claudon smiled. "After all, art comes first."

The waiter deftly opened the wine bottle and filled their glasses.

Claudon raised his glass. "A toast—to the Megiddo dig."

They touched glasses and sipped the cold wine.

"Tell me, Gabriella, has Sabitini had any success obtaining a grant from your Ministry of Culture?"

"Not yet. But he hasn't given up."

"And the Israelis?"

"General Barzani said there are no government funds available for archaeological exploration."

"A pity—but understandable. After all, they have a huge war machine to maintain." He paused and smiled. "Shall we order?"

"Please. I'm starved."

He signaled for the waiter, then asked Gabriella, "What do you suggest for a main course?"

"The clams here are delicious."

"Good." Claudon turned to the waiter. "We will start with a salad of anchovies and roasted peppers. Then we'll have two orders of clams Posillipo."

The waiter left, and Claudon asked, "Is that Fellini at the table to our right?"

"Yes, the grand maestro."

"The lady with him is breathtaking."

"What is it you wish to discuss with me, Pierre?" Gabriella asked impatiently.

"Ah, yes, the matter at hand." He glanced around quickly and leaned forward. "Lord Hamilton asked me to see you. He is interested in financing the proposed dig at Megiddo but is fearful of the Syrians and was therefore reluctant to appear in person."

"I don't know why everyone is so intimidated," she said. "The events at Ebla appeared in the world press almost a year ago—Gamasi and his superiors dismissed my interpretation of the tablets as Zionist propaganda. The story died, and the Syrians maintain control of all the remaining Ebla tablets. They have not suffered any loss of face with their Arab brothers. Why all this fear?"

"Well . . . you may not be aware, but a small stream

of Ebla tablets have found their way to the British Museum and to the Metropolitan in New York. I've been in touch with Gamasi, and I can tell you, the Syrians are in a dangerous mood."

"But how does this affect our search for the Moses tablet?"

"If that tablet surfaces, and if its text confirms Ebla as the ancient kingdom of Hebrew tribes, you will see a violent Syrian reaction. We must proceed with great care."

The waiter served the anchovies and peppers and poured vinegar and oil over the salad. They wrapped the anchovies around the peppers and washed them down with the strong white wine.

"Marvelous anchovies," Claudon said.

Gabriella sipped some wine, touched the napkin to her lips, and asked, "Don't you find it curious that Lord Hamilton is afraid to meet with me but sends you in his place?"

"I depend on Hamilton for a large measure of my income. If there are attendant risks"—Claudon shrugged—"I must accept them."

"Perhaps there is no risk for you. After all, you were quite close to Gamasi."

"I'm everyone's friend. I'm a dealer. A salesman. I am not obsessed by the need to own ancient artifacts. I have no passion for history." He stared into her blue eyes. "My tastes are simple. I adore money and women."

She ignored his remarks and busied herself with the process of shelling the steaming bowl of clams that had just arrived.

In the center of the piazza, close to the obelisk, two men were discussing the results of an important football match, but they never looked at each other. Their eyes were trained on a sidewalk table in the Trattoria Bolognese where an attractive blond woman dined with Pierre Claudon.

*   *   *

Claudon had become progressively expansive with the food and wine. Gabriella flattered him and kept the wine flowing, thinking that Hamilton's proposal would be more honestly presented if the Frenchman's guard were down.

They ordered espresso coffees and Sambuca. Claudon lit a thin cigar. His face was flushed, and small beads of perspiration appeared on his upper lip. He leaned forward and in a low, conspiratorial voice said, "There is at this moment one hundred thousand dollars deposited to your account at the Banque Genève in Bern, Switzerland."

"I'm afraid that won't be enough."

He shrugged, took a passbook out of his jacket, and handed it to her. "I'm certain you will raise the balance."

"Let's hope so." She sighed, placing the passbook in her purse. "What does Lord Hamilton want in return for his investment?"

"Nothing, until you're certain of the tablet's existence. At that point he is to be summoned to Israel. He wishes to be present at the moment of discovery."

"That's no problem."

"He also requires exhibition and leasing rights to the tablet and that it be placed on a worldwide tour under his name."

"I can't agree to that. We will be operating under Israeli supervision. If we discover the Moses tablet, it belongs to the state of Israel."

"All we ask is the normal leasing arrangements granted to any investor."

"I suppose that's possible."

"Well, I have done my part." He smiled. "The rest is up to you."

Gabriella glanced off at the crowded piazza and noticed the two men standing near the obelisk who seemed to be watching them. But she dismissed the thought, believing her suspicion was stimulated by the wine and the pervasive paranoia surrounding Ebla. She turned to Claudon and said, "It's ironic, but raising the money is often more difficult than finding the artifact. It's incredible that we have to beg for funds to pursue the history of mankind."

Claudon puffed on his cigar and asked, "Why don't you appeal to Sorenson and Emory? If they suspected the possible existence of a Moses tablet, I'm certain they would cofinance the dig under similar leasing arrangements."

"I don't really know Emory, but I have spoken to Sorenson. He's been struck by a terrible tragedy—his wife was murdered a week ago."

Claudon's eyes blinked in surprise. "This crime occurred in Los Angeles?"

"Yes."

"Do you know the details of the murder?"

"No, nothing. But I suppose wealthy people are always targets."

"Yes, that's probably it," he replied nervously. "A common street crime."

He added a generous tip to the bill and signed the American Express voucher with a flourish. "Can I give you a lift?"

She shook her head. "I have my car. I'll drop you at the hotel."

As they strolled across the piazza, Gabriella noticed one of the men she thought had been watching them. He was in a phone booth not fifteen feet from her car. She eyed him warily but said nothing to Claudon.

Driving out of the piazza, she checked the rearview mirror but could not detect a car following. She drove past the ocher-colored Roman walls circling the Villa Borghese gardens, through the archway of the Porta Pinciana, and entered the Via Veneto. At the corner of the Via Ludovisi she turned sharply right and pulled into the circular rotunda of the Romana Hotel.

"Would you care for a drink?" Claudon asked.

"No, thank you." She paused. "Pierre, you must make it clear to Hamilton that without those missing triangles our task at Megiddo may be hopeless."

"You've already made that point with him, but I will emphasize it." He smiled. "Well, *bonne chance.*"

"You, too." Gabriella waved and drove off.

The lobby was nearly deserted as Claudon approached the elderly concierge and smiled. "You know, my friend, I find myself overwhelmed with loneliness."

"The price for first-class company has risen since your last visit," the concierge replied. "It is now two hundred thousand lire."

"A bargain." Claudon grinned, and handed him two 100,000-lire notes and a 50,000-lire tip.

"Have a brandy in the bar," the concierge suggested. "The girl will arrive in a few minutes."

Claudon toyed with a cognac and waited patiently for almost half an hour before a shapely young girl wearing a fashionable evening dress approached him. "You are Signor Claudon?"

"Yes."

"My name is Gina." She smiled. "Am I acceptable?"

"Desirable is the proper word. Shall we go?"

"It's your time."

Claudon unlocked the door of his eighth-floor suite and reached for the light switch. A pair of powerful hands came out of the darkness, pinning his arms, and simultaneously another unseen hand swung the butt of a heavy automatic against the girl's temple. She dropped silently to the floor.

One of the men leveled the gun at Claudon. "Do not make a sound."

The warning was unnecessary; fear had stolen Claudon's voice.

"Take off your clothes!" the short, stocky man ordered.

The big man released him, and Claudon removed his jacket.

"Quickly!" the small man ordered.

Claudon stripped off his shirt, dropped his pants, and kicked off his loafers.

"Your socks and shorts."

The Frenchman obeyed.

The man motioned with the gun. "The terrace."

"But . . . I . . ." Claudon found his voice. "I don't understand. Who are you? I've done nothing."

They shoved him out onto the open balcony and stared at the slight, frightened naked man for a brief moment. "What is it you want of me?" Claudon pleaded. "If it's money, I can—"

They moved quickly, professionally. One seized his arms; the other, his legs. They swung him out over the balcony in a wide arc and let him go.

For a moment Claudon imagined he was caught in a nightmare, floating over the streaming traffic far below. His legs churned as if he were pedaling a bicycle; then gravity pulled him down.

He screamed a long, piercing scream.

The streetlights came rushing up at him.

His scream ended abruptly as his head exploded against the roof of a parked car.

The men went back inside and carried the unconscious prostitute into the bedroom. They stripped her clothes off, and the stocky man took out a switchblade and carved deep slashes into her breasts, belly, and pubic area. The big man then placed his hands around her throat and squeezed until her face turned blue and her tongue protruded.

They left the suite, one of them taking the stairs, the other riding down in the elevator.

CHAPTER SEVENTEEN

△

Fire storms raged in the Santa Monica Mountains. Sirens screamed through the hills. Horses, deer, and coyotes ran madly through canyons. The conflagration was bombarded by aerial tankers dropping chemical suppressants, and an army of weary fire fighters manned a last-ditch firebreak on the Bel Air side of the inferno. Ash and smoke mixed with the usual layer of smog covering the city.

The wall fan groaned, shoving dead air around the small lime-colored office. Jack's eyes smarted as he studied the Ebla press clippings obtained from Tactical's research section.

Rizzo was at the window, peering at the distant smoke. "One of these days the whole fucking city is gonna go up in flames."

"I doubt it. The floods are due any minute." Jack sighed. "Why don't you pour us a shot?"

Rizzo opened the top drawer of a steel cabinet, removed a bottle of Bushmills, and set two glasses down on the desk.

Jack sipped the Irish whiskey, lit a cigarillo, and

concentrated on the photocopied documents. *Time* magazine's banner story read: 4,500-YEAR-OLD TABLETS PLACE NOMADIC HEBREWS IN NORTHERN SYRIA. The article went on to describe the process by which the Italian epigrapher Gabriella Bercovici had broken the Eblaite cuneiform using a mix of biblical Hebrew. The authors of the piece considered the presence of Eber in ancient Ebla significant. Eber was the great-great-great-grandfather of Abraham, the same Eber referred to in Genesis 10. This tended to confirm that Abraham was not only a patriarch of the Jews but the ancestor of modern-day Syrians as well. The tone of the story strongly implied that the Syrians and Israelis were blood brothers.

In rebuttal, Dr. Gamasi, speaking for the Syrian Ministry of Culture, was quoted as saying, "The meaning of the Ebla tablets has been perverted by Professor Sabitini and his colleague Gabriella Bercovici to suit their Zionist political beliefs." The article concluded by saying that politics aside, the discovery of ancient Ebla and its tablets represented the third great modern archaeological breakthrough following the Rosetta stone and the Dead Sea Scrolls.

The *Times* of London headline read: HEBREW PATRIARCH LINK TO ANCIENT SYRIA DISCOVERED.

The *New York Times* headlined: EBLA DISCOVERY INDICATES HEBREW PRESENCE IN SYRIA 2,500 YEARS BEFORE ISLAMIC INFLUENCE.

The *Los Angeles Times* carried a similar banner: WAS ANCIENT SYRIA BIRTHPLACE OF NOMADIC HEBREW TRIBES?

The Los Angeles piece quoted a Harvard professor of Middle Eastern studies who dodged the political implications of the Ebla tablets but stated, "Theologically speaking, one can only be thankful the tablets did not reveal an eleventh commandment."

Jack leaned back, rubbed his hand over his eyes, and swallowed some whiskey. "These articles make a hell of a case for the Syrians to take out everyone connected with Ebla."

"I don't know," Rizzo said. "Those stories are almost a year old. Why would the Syrians act now?"

"You're thinking like an American, not a Syrian. The

Israelis understand the Syrian mentality. I should try to contact General Barzani."

"Who's he?"

"Barzani was the Israeli liaison officer assigned to the CIA in Tel Aviv. During the time I was stationed there we became good friends." Jack crushed the cigarillo out. "Wonder where Torres is?"

"His secretary said the Emory autopsy was completed at six A.M. this morning. Torres went home to get some sleep. He should be here any minute."

The phone rang, and Rizzo picked it up. "He's right here." Rizzo handed the phone to Jack. "Benson for you."

Jack could see Arthur Benson seated at his gleaming desk, stroking the waxed points of his mustache. "How are you, Arthur?"

"Considering our fair city is surrounded by flames, I'm fine."

"What have you got?"

"The reply on Sorenson's federal file just came in." Benson paused dramatically. "It's coded Black."

"Christ . . ." Jack murmured. "What about Dr. Emory?"

"I've just received Nolan's authorization to make that request. I'm putting it on the wire to D.C. right now."

"Thanks, Arthur."

"Anytime."

Jack hung up and glanced at Rizzo. "Sorenson's file is coded Black."

"Meaning what?"

"No information is released to anyone except on direct request of the commander in chief."

"I think I'll have another shot," Rizzo said.

"Help yourself." Jack rose and paced for a moment. "The behavioral research and space program is Sorenson's cover. No way that would rate a black code. He's into heavy traffic."

"The son of a bitch lied to you."

"Technically you're right, Vince. But professionally he followed orders. Every agent is given a cover story, and if pressed, he reveals the cover—in Sorenson's case, the NASA program."

"What about the Emory file?"

"Benson's requesting it now. But if Emory was connected to Sorenson's intelligence activities, we'll get the same result."

There was a sharp knock at the door, and Gabriel Torres entered the office. The coroner's eyes were ringed by circles of fatigue, and his broad shoulders were slightly stooped. He carried a manila envelope and chewed on a dead cigar. "The air in here is as bad as the air out there. This is cancer weather. That fire-smoke mixed with the smog is unfit for human consumption."

"Tell it to the city fathers," Rizzo said.

Torres sank into a green Naugahyde chair with white stuffing protruding through an old rip. "Are you fellows going to offer me a drink?"

Jack handed him a glass and poured a shot.

"*Salud*," Torres said, tossed it off, and grimaced. "Christ, did you make this yourself?"

Rizzo nodded. "We bought a jug of cat piss and let it sit for a week."

"Wakes you up—I'll say that." Torres relit the cigar. "Well, *amigos*, I worked all night for you. And in my view—my forensic view—you have another homicide on your hands." He handed the manila envelope to Jack. "It's all there. But I'll save you reading the Latin. We found significant traces of propranolol hydrochloride in Emory's blood. I would say close to eight hundred milligrams."

"What the hell is propranolol?" Jack asked.

"It's a chemical blocking agent used to treat angina pectoris or abnormal heart rhythms, easily obtainable under the trade name Inderal."

"How does it kill?"

"If induced orally or intravenously in amounts exceeding five hundred milligrams, it produces classic angina symptoms: shortness of breath, chest pains, and finally heart stoppage."

"You were right, Jack," Rizzo said. "They hit him in back of the thigh with some kind of needle."

"No." Torres shook his head. "The inflammation behind the thigh was actually a mosquito bite. We found no traces of needle marks. Besides, if someone had injected eight hundred milligrams into Emory, he never would have made it back upstairs."

"So it was orally induced?" Jack asked.

"No question, either by pills—they're highly soluble—or, more likely, by a vial of liquid propranolol slipped into a drink. The chemical is tasteless and colorless. We also found eight percent alcohol in Emory's blood samples."

"I expected something more exotic," Jack said.

"Like what?"

"Curare."

"Ah." Torres smiled. "Curare is a favorite of spooks, especially the KGB—difficult to trace. It produces severe abdominal pains, like animal venom. I had a case of curare during the Tylenol arsenic scare. A woman used curare on a cheating husband, blamed it on Tylenol, but I spotted the curare in his lower bowel—one of my small victories." Torres rose. "Well, *amigos*, thanks for the drink."

Jack walked the stocky coroner to the door. "I appreciate your handling this, Gabby."

"It was no big thing. The Palm Springs coroner would have found it. Once you suspect the heart attack and work the blood, you'd find the chemical. How did you know Emory wasn't a heart attack victim?"

"I didn't. It was a stab."

"Jack's a contemporary Sherlock Holmes," Rizzo said.

"Well"—Torres smiled—"don't get hooked on cocaine. That drug was ninety percent of Holmes's genius. He got higher than a kite as a case progressed." The coroner reached the door and glanced at Jack. "How's your daughter?"

"She's doing fine."

Torres nodded and left.

Jack glanced at the official autopsy reports. "Emory's killer was cute, but he gave a lot away."

"Like what?"

"Well, Emory knew him or knew who sent him. He

wasn't afraid of the meeting. It was all very civilized. They had drinks—no noise, no argument, no torture. The killer wasn't looking for anything—just Emory."

Jack walked up to the case diagram and studied it for a moment.

He chalked an X alongside Dr. Emory's name—the symbol for "deceased" that appeared next to Laura's name.

"Did we ever get a line on that deliveryman?" Jack asked.

"Sorell?"

"Yeah."

"I gave it to you a week ago."

"I must have missed it."

"He was clean. Korean vet, honorable discharge, married, four kids. One arrest for drunk driving coming out of Santa Anita."

Jack picked up his jacket and draped it over his arm. "I'm going out to the marina."

"Want company?"

"No. Sorenson's edgy enough; a stranger would really throw him. Listen, Vince, go up to communications and send a top priority request to Interpol. Try to get a current line and location on Pierre Claudon."

"That might be a common name."

"His business address and number are in my case file."

"Should I include Lord Hamilton in the same request?"

"No. I'd rather have Nolan phone Scotland Yard intelligence on that one."

"You coming out to the house tonight?"

"I don't think so. I'll phone Jenny from Sorenson's boat."

Jack walked through the warren of glassed-in cubicles. Phones rang, typewriter keys hammered out their staccato messages, and the smell of stale cigarette smoke and sweat hung over the men and women protecting the citizens of Los Angeles.

CHAPTER EIGHTEEN

⚠

A quartet of screaming sea gulls glided over the moored boats, and the Pacific breeze smelled of salt and fish bait.

Jack reached the end of the slip and saw the painted gold letters *Shooting Star* on the stern of Sorenson's eighty-five-foot-long yacht. Its chromium fixtures gleamed in bold relief against a dark mahogany superstructure. The sleek craft was topped by antennas, radar, and high-tech electronic dishes.

Jack thought it was the ultimate in adult toys, the kind of boat used in TV commercials on which luscious bikini-clad girls sold suntan creams that came in six delicious flavors.

Jack masked his surprise at the change in Sorenson's appearance. The doctor had grown a beard, and his silver hair was long and unkempt. His dark blue eyes were sunken and bloodshot. He wore a pair of oil-smeared jeans and a faded chambray shirt.

They shook hands at the gangway, and Sorenson said, "Come on, I'll fix you a drink."

The afterdeck salon was tastefully appointed with

contemporary Italian chairs and sofas. An Oriental rug covered the floor, and several winter scenes painted by Sisley hung on the dark oak walls. A Shang dynasty porcelain horse stood imperiously on a round table.

The doctor poured himself a brandy. "What would you like, Jack?"

"A Scotch and soda."

"According to the radio," Sorenson said, "they've got the fire under control."

A tall, thin man wearing blue coveralls stuck his head in the doorway and called out to Sorenson, "Engines are all set."

"Loran and SAT-NAV check out?"

"In the green."

"Thanks, Pete. Why don't you disconnect the shore power and water?"

"Right."

Sorenson handed Jack the glass. "You haven't been on the boat for quite a while."

"A couple of years ago."

"You were seasick as I remember."

"I've never been much of a sailor." Jack sipped the Scotch. "Looks like you're getting ready for a trip."

"Thought I might go down to Baja—fish and rest, clear my head." The doctor's hand trembled slightly as he lit a fresh cigarette. "Since Emory's death I can't seem to get myself together. Hell of a shock. He was a textbook specimen of good health. But"—Sorenson sighed—"sudden heart attacks are not that unusual."

"This one was," Jack replied softly. "Emory was murdered."

Sorenson blanched, and his jaw muscles jumped reflexively. He swallowed some brandy and in a strained voice said, "You phoned me from the Springs and said it was a heart attack."

"The autopsy says otherwise. You ever hear of the chemical propranolol hydrochloride?"

"Of course, it's quite common, used in the treatment of angina."

"What happens when eight hundred milligrams are

slipped into a drink and swallowed by a healthy individual?"

"My God . . ." Sorenson whispered. "You're certain? I mean, there's no mistake."

"I can show you the coroner's report. There's no mistake. Last Tuesday night Emory entertained a visitor—someone he knew, felt secure with. They chatted and had drinks. The visitor left. Emory went back upstairs and complained of chest pains. He was dead by morning." Jack paused. "Can you account for your time last Tuesday evening?"

The doctor shook his head in disbelief. "You don't suspect me?"

"It's a question I have to ask. You and Emory had broken up a long partnership, you both were involved in the Ebla dig, and the method used to kill Emory indicates some prior medical knowledge."

Sorenson sighed disconsolately. "What's the time frame in question?"

"Mrs. Emory wasn't precise, but I'd say between eleven and midnight."

"I was up at the Bel Air house and oddly enough placed a call to Rome close to that time."

"Who did you speak to?"

"Gabriella Bercovici. I'll give you the number. You can check it out."

"What did you talk to her about?"

"Enough." Sorenson held up his hand. "I'll answer relevant questions—period."

"*Everything* in this case is relevant!" Jack replied angrily. "A team of professional killers is going down a hit list. I don't give a fuck if they take out the entire medical profession, but they killed Laura, and if Jenny had been home, they'd have hit her." Jack paused and lowered his voice. "Now I may be able to keep you alive if you level with me. But don't give me any more crap about relevance."

Sorenson glared at him for a moment, then sighed wearily. "I was returning Miss Bercovici's call. She wanted to know if I'd be interested in financing a dig at Megiddo."

"You mean, in Israel?"

"Yes."

"Is this dig related in any way to Ebla?"

"It might be. The inscription on a stone found at Ebla indicated the possible existence of some final word of God inscribed by Moses. The tablet is presumably hidden somewhere in the ruins of Megiddo." Sorenson did not mention the missing triangles.

"What was your response?"

"I told her about Laura's death and that I couldn't deal with anything else at this time."

"Do you know if Miss Bercovici spoke with Emory?"

"No."

Jack walked to an open porthole and watched the dying sun brush its scarlet hue into the Pacific. The opulent salon fell silent except for the exterior cries of sea gulls.

"I can't understand it," Sorenson said. "Why would anyone want Emory dead?"

Jack decided it was time to take his best shot. "Maybe it was the triangle."

"What triangle?"

"You tell me, Martin. You and Emory argued over a triangle. Mrs. Emory heard you."

"Where did this alleged argument take place?"

"At a dinner party, up at your house."

"Well, she's mistaken. I never argued with Emory over anything but business. The only meaning I attach to the word *triangle* is in the classic sense, as a geometric pattern."

"Why would Mrs. Emory lie about that?"

"I said she was mistaken."

"So Emory was murdered without any apparent motive—same as Laura."

"I'm sorry, Jack. I wish I could help you."

"So do I. Was Emory connected in any way to your intelligence activities?"

"I can't discuss that."

"Why is your federal file coded Black?"

Sorenson seemed surprised by the question, but his

voice was flat and devoid of emotion. "I can't tell you that either."

"I'll find out eventually, Martin. The question is how many people have to die in the interim."

Sorenson refilled his glass and sighed. "Emory was obliquely involved in my government project."

"Tell me about the project. I'm not a KGB agent. Your secret will die with me."

Sorenson sat on the arm of the sofa and looked forlornly at Jack. "I'm taking one hell of a chance, but I'm going to trust you." He drained the brandy, got to his feet, and flexed his hands nervously.

"It's taken mankind thousands of years to realize that the center of all thought, emotion, sensation, and bodily control lies somewhere in the skull. The adult human brain is a moist, pulsing, jellylike tissue weighing almost three pounds. It contains more than ten billion nerve cells or neurons. When you hold the brain in your hands, you almost expect to see pinpoints of lights and ideas crackling across its surface. It is the most complex electrochemical organism known to man. The brain performs miracles with dazzling speed: sight, sound, memory, coordination, anger, sensuality, creativity, hunger, thirst. Everything. Some years ago I was approached by a government agency to organize a task force of my colleagues. Our goal was to determine the answer to a single question: 'Can acquired characteristics be transmitted?' "

"Genetically?" Jack asked.

"No. Genetics is another science. I'm talking about chemically injecting principal character traits into the unborn."

"You mean, implant a character virtue or fault into a fetus?"

"That's close enough. We've taken rats, nocturnal creatures afraid of light, and subjected them to torture in the dark and pleasure in the light, and since we have not yet determined which part of the brain controls fear, we slaughter the rats and pulverize their brains in a blender. We inject this solution into rat fetuses. The next generation of rats fears the dark and enjoys the light. In theory we could keep a teenage human awake for eighteen hours a day for, say, ten years, make soup out of his brain, shoot the residue into a fetus, and produce a child requiring little or no sleep." Sorenson poured himself another brandy.

"Using similar techniques, we could create an astronaut immune to fatigue, or a spy impervious to the normal seductions of money, sex, or drugs, or the perfect soldier immune to fear of death. In other words, we can program a species of soulless, robotlike people."

"Have you experimented on humans?"

"That's one question I simply can't answer." He paused. "I know it's hideous, but the Soviets are working on it as well."

"And you actually believe this project is in the national interest?"

"Obviously I did."

"How much did Laura know?"

"Nothing."

"What was Dr. Emory's role in this project?"

"Purely technical. He was a surgeon and took no part in direct research."

"What agency controls this project?"

"Strategic Operational Deployment."

"Never heard of that one."

"Few people have. Only a select group know it by the initials SOD. The CIA recruits and shields SOD, but the agency operatives are distanced from the actual work."

"Does this project have a code name?"

"Is that relevant?"

"Look, Martin, I don't know if any of this connects to Laura's murder. But I do know the spook world. It's a house of mirrors where anything is possible. Now, I've given you my word. I'll protect what you've told me."

"The project is code named Rosemark."

"Have you done anything to upset your project officer?"

"Not that I know of."

"You've taken no action that would have caused a team of spooks to comb through the Bel Air house?"

"Absolutely not."

"Well, I appreciate your leveling with me, Martin." Jack drained the last of the Scotch. "Can I use your phone?"

The wheelhouse was a study in high-tech instrumentation: sonar, loran, a navigational computer, sophisticated radar, TV scanners, and a powerful ham radio console.

"Pretty fancy stuff," Jack commented.

"All necessary on long cruises," Sorenson replied, and indicated a green push-button phone. "You can use that."

Jack dialed, and Angela Rizzo answered. They exchanged a few words, and he asked for Jenny.

Jack stared out the bridge window. The sun had disappeared over the horizon line, and the sky had turned a deep indigo.

"Hello, Dad."

"Hi, Jenny. Listen, I won't be coming out tonight, but I'll see you tomorrow."

"It's okay. I've got a ton of homework."

"Good. We'll catch up tomorrow night and spend the weekend together."

"Can we go to the Dodger game?"

"Sure. I'll get some tickets."

"And, Dad . . ."

"Yes?"

"Don't forget Friday night I'm in the school play."

"I haven't forgotten. I'll be front-row center."

"Well, I have to get back to my homework now."

"Okay. See you Friday."

"Bye, Dad."

The VHF radio suddenly crackled with voices speaking rapidly in a Slavic language.

"What the hell is that?" Jack asked.

"Soviet trawlers about twenty-five miles out," Sorenson replied.

"You understand Russian?"

"More or less."

"What are they saying?"

"At the moment they're talking about tuna and yellow-tail catches, but their real purpose is to monitor naval units of the Seventh Fleet moving from San Diego to Pearl Harbor."

"They don't miss a trick."

"I'm certain we do the same. The peace of the world is stabilized by eavesdropping." Sorenson paused. "I'll walk you to the gangway."

The gulls dipped low over the boats, searching for scraps of discarded bait. Jack glanced at the city; a thin pall of smoke hung over the Santa Monica Mountains.

"Looks as though they've licked the fire," Sorenson remarked.

"Look, Martin, if you want me to, I can arrange police protection."

"No. I don't want anyone shadowing my life. I have weapons on board, and I know how to use them."

"Are you definitely sailing to Baja?"

"I'm not sure. We might just go over to Catalina."

"You're really quite a paradox."

"How so?"

"You're manipulating human behavior in a way that borders on science fiction and at the same time you're interested in events that go back thousands of years."

"All my life I've been obsessed with the history of mankind."

"You really think there's a lost word of God in the ruins of Megiddo?"

"It's possible. There have been constant rumors of a Moses tablet."

"Well, take care, Martin. And if you get any fresh ideas, let me know."

"You can count on it."

They shook hands, and Jack left.

Sorenson walked forward and went down the ladder into the engine room. "How's it look, Pete?"

"These goddamn Vosper stabilizers are questionable."

"Well, let it go. According to the Coast Guard, there's only a two-foot sea running. Everything else check out?"

The engineer nodded. "We're topped off. We can run for eighty hours."

"Listen, Pete, take my car keys, go up to the liquor store, and get a case of Scotch."

"Sure thing."

Once the engineer had disappeared down the wharf, Sorenson pulled the boarding ramp onto the deck. He then walked quickly into the bridge and concentrated on the soft green lights of the control console. It required considerable skill to sail a yacht of this size alone. But he had planned the trip meticulously. Painstakingly. And there was no turning back. This was a rendezvous that had to be kept. He took a deep breath and studied the checkoff starting list.

He hit the switches activating the blower system, bilge pumps, and battery charger. He checked the oil pressure gauges before turning the ignition keys on both engines. The yacht shuddered slightly as the screws turned over. He watched the automatic synchronizer equalize the port and starboard RPMs. He then activated the water-cooling system, went out on deck, and released the bow and fantail lines. The big craft drifted slightly away from the dock, and Sorenson dashed back into the bridge. He set the rudder in dead neutral and gently depressed the reverse gear.

The eighty-five-foot yacht slowly backed out of the slip into the main channel. Sorenson eased the forward gear ahead, and the craft began to turn. He placed the radar on standby, turned the running lights on, and set the speed at five knots. People on moored boats waved to the large vessel as it slid majestically out to sea.

CHAPTER NINETEEN

△

Jack stared in terror as the fog-shrouded phantoms came out of the pine forest. The coyote's malevolent yellow eyes glittered. The devil-god's clawed wings were extended, and its puffed lips grimaced hideously. Laura glared at him out of eyes that floated in a gory syrup of blood and bone. Jenny walked beside her, crying blood tears. Pancho Villa, smiling menacingly, carried a straight razor in one hand and Captain Cordero's head in the other. A huge rat sniffed the air and moved cautiously forward. Martin Sorenson had his arm draped around the bare shoulders of Gabriella Bercovici.

A black-cloaked apparition appeared, carrying a huge hypodermic needle. The faceless, shrouded figure plunged the needle into the rat and drew the blood into the syringe.

The phantom figure turned to Jack, the needleful of rat blood clutched in its bleached skeletal fingers.

Gasping for breath, Jack screamed and bolted upright in bed, his heart racing, his body chilled by a cold sweat.

There was an unidentifiable shape at the foot of his

bed. Unable to separate nightmare from reality, he peered at the figure, listening to his own breath coming in spurts. He grabbed the .38 revolver on the night table and, clutching it with both hands, pointed the quivering muzzle at the apparition.

"Jack! Don't! It's me! Linda!"

His hand trembled, and his sweat-soaked body shivered. The girl's familiar voice penetrated the lingering horror of the nightmare. He slowly lowered the gun and switched the bedside lamp on.

The pretty stewardess Linda Jensen stood immobilized at the foot of the bed, her innocent brown eyes wide in terror.

"Christ"—Jack sighed—"don't ever do that again."

"I'm sorry," she gasped. "But . . . this . . ." Her voice wavered. "Well, it isn't the first time. You gave me the key, remember? I've just come in from Panama. I heard about Laura."

"Why didn't you call?"

"The night clerk said you weren't taking any calls, and I had to see you. I'm flying out again in the morning." She paused. "My God, those screams—what is it?"

"A nightmare. I haven't had one of those in years, since Chile." He wiped the cold beads of sweat from his forehead. "There's a bottle of Bushmills behind the bar. Pour me a shot, and fix yourself a drink."

He rose and walked unsteadily into the bathroom and stared at his chalky image in the mirror. He turned the cold-water tap on, ducked his head under the faucet, and let the cool water run for a long time—until the horror of the nightmare receded.

Jack drained the strong Irish whiskey, refilled his glass, and lit a cigarillo. "Where the hell have you been?"

She tossed her ash blond hair. "Flying back and forth from Panama to Rio." She smiled. "I missed you."

"I'll bet."

She came around the bar and kissed him softly on the mouth. "I know you think I sleep around, but the truth is I'm practically celibate."

He stared at her freckles and wide, lazy eyes, thinking how close he had come to pulling the trigger. "Let's get some air."

They walked out onto the terrace. The city lights twinkled all the way to the Pacific and a sultry Santa Ana breeze stirred the leaves on the potted ficus trees. A siren wailed in the distance, and a Sinatra tune floated up from the apartment below.

"It's been hell," Jack said. "You were right. I never stopped loving her."

They watched the dancing lights for a moment.

"Would you like me to stay?" she asked softly.

He shook his head. "I'll take a rain check."

"With all due respect, Jack, you haven't slept with Laura in years."

"It isn't that."

"What is it?"

"I'd be using you."

"It's a two-way street. I've never asked you for any commitments. If it is a wash, okay; I've been rejected before. I'm a waitress at thirty thousand feet—that's about as high as I get."

His arm circled her waist. "It's got nothing to do with you. It's this goddamn case. Christ knows I've seen enough horror for five lifetimes. But certain facts that have surfaced are so grotesque I can't even talk about them."

"You don't have to. The nightmare says it all." She paused, and her voice brightened. "Listen, I'll be back early Sunday evening. What do you say we go out?"

"It's a date. We'll have dinner at Orlando-Orsini's, eat some pasta, drink some wine, and see what happens."

He walked her to the door, kissed her cheek, and smiled. "You realize that key to my apartment could have been lethal."

"That would've made you the star of the six o'clock news for a month."

"A week anyway," he said. "They'd have called it a crime of passion."

"They would have been wrong," she murmured, and stared at him for a moment. "You're sure about Sunday night?"

"Absolutely."

Jack leaned back against the pillows and, using the remote TV clicker, impatiently searched the channels for something to watch: A car salesman rode by on an elephant; a monster surfaced in Tokyo Bay; a government spokesman explained the need for a new fleet of nuclear submarines; an Egyptian mummy stalked Abbott and Costello; a vampire sank his fangs into the smooth neck of a sleeping girl.

Jack clicked again.

Edward G. Robinson sat in a bathtub, puffing on a long cigar, a drink in one hand, his face turned into the breeze of a small fan. Jack sighed gratefully. The film was *Key Largo*, one of his all-time favorites.

CHAPTER TWENTY

⚠

The Coast Guard cutter's bow knifed through the glassy sea, and its yellow sodium searchlights swept the rising mists, trying to pierce the fog. A seaman stood in the eyes of the bow, peering through infrared binoculars. High above the mast the radar scanner revolved on an emergency speed cycle, and in the pilothouse men sipped hot coffee and bent to their tasks.

The helmsman maintained a gyrocompass course of 286 degrees and a speed of eighteen knots. The radio operator repeated the message he'd been sending intermittently for the past two hours: "This is U.S. Coast Guard *Point Bridge* calling Whiskey, Union, Zebra two-four-two-eight. Come in, yacht *Shooting Star*—over."

The radar technician peered into the hooded shield. The green sweeping finger rotated across the screen, illuminating a flowing dot that grew brighter with each sweep.

The commander, Captain Jameson, was on the radio mike, calling the Coast Guard air-sea rescue helicopter. "*Point Bridge* calling Eagle four-two—over."

There was a crackle of static followed by the pilot's response. "This is Eagle four-two—over."

"Jameson, on *Point Bridge*. We have positive radar contact with craft bearing your ID. We are proceeding to intercept *Shooting Star* due west Point Dume at eighteen knots—gyro reading two-eight-six—over."

"Read you, *Point Bridge*. You're on dead reckon course. I am in hover position above *Shooting Star*; vessel appears to be abandoned—over."

"Do you sight debris, smoke, or indications of water seepage? Over."

"Negative—all counts. Over."

"Right, Eagle four-two. Please hold your position until we establish visual contact with *Shooting Star*—over."

"Roger, *Point Bridge*."

Commander Jameson left the bridge and walked up to a seaman standing watch at the bow. "Anything?"

"I can make out running lights, sir."

"Let me have a look."

Jameson trained the powerful binoculars due north and depressed the infrared button. The sleek outline of the *Shooting Star*'s superstructure emerged ghostlike in the pale light.

He handed the glasses back to the sailor. "Keep her in sight."

Jameson went back up to the pilothouse and stood over the radarman's shoulder. "What have you got?"

"She's about eighty feet, Captain. And motionless. We should have visual by now."

"We do." Jameson then picked up the ship-to-air radio mike.

"*Point Bridge* to Eagle four-two—over." There was a crackling pause before the helicopter pilot responded, "This is Eagle four-two—over."

"We have established visual contact with *Shooting Star*. You can go in."

"Roger, *Point Bridge*. Returning to base."

The *Shooting Star* bobbed gently in the flat sea, the American flag hanging limply from its fantail.

The cutter pulled alongside, turning parallel to the drifting yacht. Jameson switched on the amplified speakers, and his voice boomed across the narrow gap between the two boats.

"Ahoy, *Shooting Star!*" He paused and called again. "Hello, aboard *Shooting Star!*"

Jameson then turned to his chief petty officer. "Prepare a boarding party."

"Weapons?"

"Sidearms."

A bosun hit some switches, and a bank of powerful floodlights illuminated the *Shooting Star*.

The helmsman manipulated the wheel, dexterously bringing the cutter dangerously close to the *Shooting Star*. Bumper guards were thrown over the side. The hulls brushed, and seamen hooked the railing of the *Shooting Star* with long, pronged poles. The boarding party, led by Jameson, jumped from the cutter's gunwale down onto the deck of the yacht.

Jameson issued a stream of orders. "Webb, Martinson, go below. Staterooms first, then engine rooms, storage lockers, galley, bilges, and ballast quarters. Keep your sidearms at the ready with safeties on."

Accompanied by his chief petty officer, Jameson entered the *Shooting Star*'s bridge and conducted a swift inspection of all systems. The engines and VHF and UHF radios had been turned off, but the bilge pumps, fathometer, cooling system, SAT-NAV and loran-C systems were in perfect operational order.

"Peculiar," the petty officer said. "No charts, no maps. No destination indicated, yet fuel load is capacity."

"Stand by," Jameson said, and walked out onto the forward deck.

His flashlight played across the wooden decking; at a point near the prow he noticed a dark red stain. He knelt and touched the substance. It was sticky and odorless. He was about to rise when he saw a small, shiny object rolling back and forth. He picked it up and turned it over in his palm; it was a shell casing of undetermined caliber. He walked quickly back into the bridge.

"Look at this," he said to the petty officer.

The chief examined the shell casing. "Either a nine millimeter or a thirty-eight."

"There are bloodstains on the foredeck," Jameson added.

The bosun stuck his head in the door. "Captain!"

"Yes?"

"Not a trace of anyone, and nothing disturbed."

"All right. Have the men stand by."

"Yes, sir!"

Jameson walked up to the control console and switched the ignition key on the starboard engine. The screw turned over instantly. He repeated the process in the port engine; it kicked in, and the big yacht shuddered slightly. He glanced at the card displaying the *Shooting Star*'s call letters and picked up the radio mike.

"KOU. KOU. This is Commander Jameson aboard yacht *Shooting Star*—Whiskey, Union, Zebra two-four-two-eight—over."

There was a momentary pause, and he repeated the message. The radio crackled with static for a brief moment. "I read you, *Shooting Star*, this is Coast Guard, San Pedro—over."

"We have boarded *Shooting Star*. Find it abandoned. All systems functional. There are indications of foul play. Notify Sheriff's Office. I'm bringing her in on her own power—over."

"Roger. Am here with engineer of *Shooting Star*, Pete Carr, who originated search request. He advises that owner of craft, Dr. Martin Sorenson, was interviewed by a Lieutenant Jack Raines of LAPD Tactical Division shortly before Sorenson departed—over."

"Okay, San Pedro. Notify Raines as well as the Sheriff's Office—over."

"Roger—and out."

The sun had broken through the dawn cloud cover, and the sea was up, causing the moored boats to pitch slightly. The *Shooting Star* was tied up just aft of the cutter at the Coast Guard slip.

Sergeant Rizzo had gone below. Uniformed police of the sheriff's squad were sawing a piece of bloodstained planking out of the foredeck.

The spent cartridge was in an envelope in Jack's pocket. He was tense and tired but pleasantly surprised by the professionalism of the young Coast Guard commander.

Jack knew very little about technical marine matters and was totally dependent on Jameson for answers.

"Besides the obvious signs of foul play," Jack asked, "is there anything else that strikes you as unusual?"

"The absence of maps indicating a destination is irregular."

"Why? I mean, suppose he was simply cruising outside the channel."

"You would not take on a capacity fuel load for a few hours of aimless cruising."

"But it's possible?"

Jameson smiled. "When it comes to civilian sailors, anything's possible."

"Would a boat of this size normally be operated by one man?"

"No, sir. It's extremely hazardous, and the return docking would be impossible without total disregard of safety regulations."

"Would you then conclude that Dr. Sorenson wasn't planning to return?"

"Not necessarily. He could have returned, entered the main channel, geared into neutral, then called for a tow."

Jack sipped some coffee. "What can you tell me about Russian fishing trawlers operating off our coast?"

"We know they're out there monitoring movements of the Seventh Fleet."

"Could Sorenson have been picked up by a Soviet trawler?"

"I doubt it. They almost never enter our territorial waters."

"Why is that?"

"Our air-sea patrol units would have them on radar in a matter of minutes."

"Suppose they dispatched a small motor launch and boarded the *Shooting Star*."

"They'd be taking one hell of a chance. It would have required extremely precise navigation to have located the *Shooting Star* in that fog. Do you have reason to suspect a Soviet involvement?"

"It's a remote possibility," Jack said. "Do you have any ideas, Captain?"

"It appears to me that Sorenson deliberately sent his engineer on an errand and set sail alone to keep a secret rendezvous. Either that or someone came aboard and forced him to sail while the engineer was gone."

"My partner, Sergeant Rizzo, questioned the people at the adjacent slip; they confirmed Sorenson sailed out alone almost at the minute his engineer left."

Rizzo entered the bridge and motioned to Jack. "Excuse me, Captain," Jack said, and followed the puffy-eyed sergeant outside.

Rizzo took a small memorandum book out of his pocket. "I found this in the top drawer of a night table in the master bedroom."

Jack saw the word *Rosemark* on the first page. The balance of the pages was covered with handwritten chemical formulas. "Anyone see you take this?"

"No one."

Jack slipped it into his pocket.

"What the hell is it?"

"Rat soup."

"Christ. You mean Sorenson stole that out of SOD files?"

"Looks that way," Jack said, noticing the stocky figure of Gabriel Torres coming aboard.

The coroner carried a container of coffee and walked as if lead weights were attached to his feet. "Don't you fellows ever handle cases that break at decent hours?"

"Stop complaining." Rizzo smiled. "You can be deported to Tijuana at any moment."

"No, not to Tijuana. I'll follow you back to Palermo,

the garden spot of the Western world," Torres replied. "Want some coffee?"

"Thanks." Rizzo took the container.

"What have you got, Jack?"

"Bloodstained decking. They're cutting a piece of it for you now. And this . . ." Jack handed him the shell casing.

The coroner turned the spent cartridge over. "Probably nine millimeter—unusual crimp, right there. Might be foreign."

Torres moved forward to where the uniformed cops were cutting into the decking.

"Where the hell are the print men?" Jack asked.

"On the way," Rizzo said. "What do you make of Sorenson's engineer, this guy Pete Carr?"

"Absolutely clean. He came back with a case of Scotch, saw the boat missing, and went straight to the Coast Guard."

"Where the fuck was Sorenson going?"

"Looks as though he had a prearranged meeting with someone he knew and probably trusted. Whoever it was came aboard, shot him, and dumped him into the sea."

"What about suicide? You said he looked seedy and despondent."

"Why the slug? Why not simply jump overboard?"

"Drowning is a tough death."

"Doesn't work, Vince. If Sorenson shot himself, someone had to throw him overboard."

A tall, broad-shouldered, thin-faced man wearing a quiet blue suit came around the bridge and walked up to them. "Lieutenant Raines?"

"That's right. . . ."

"My name is Frank Piersall."

The man flashed a wallet with a CIA identification card in the glassine window. "I'm agency director for Southern California. The Coast Guard had Sorenson under surveillance at our request. I was notified a few hours ago."

"What can I do for you?"

"I'm officially advising you that all evidence is to be turned over to me. We'll take the case from here."

"You will?" Jack asked incredulously.

"That's right."

"Mr. Piersall, let's talk privately."

They reached a quiet spot on the fantail.

"Since when did the agency acquire jurisdiction in domestic criminal investigations?" Jack asked testily.

"I assure you my authority has been cleared with Police Commissioner Harris. Now, I demand any evidence of any kind you may have discovered on this boat be remanded to my custody."

"Have you spoken to John Nolan at Tactical?"

"I repeat. My authority has been cleared with the commissioner."

Rizzo noticed the half-moon scar on Jack's cheek turning scarlet.

"You have no authority here," Jack said quietly.

"I know all about you, Raines. You're one of those former Santiago crybabies."

"Mr. Piersall," Rizzo said calmly, "you better get off this boat while your asshole is still in its proper place."

Piersall shoved Rizzo aside and started past him.

Jack grabbed Piersall, spun him around, and whistled a left hook into his solar plexus. The big man staggered back. Jack threw a right cross that landed high up on Piersall's cheek and toppled him over the low railing into the murky, oil-slicked water.

Piersall broke the surface, treaded water, and shouted up at them, "You have me and Washington on your case, Raines!"

The Santa Monica Freeway streamed with heavy early morning traffic.

Rizzo drove, and Jack examined the chemical formulations in the Rosemark notebook. "I wish I understood this stuff."

"I wonder why he left it unprotected in the top drawer of that night table."

"Maybe he wanted it to be found."

"Why?"

"Beats me." Jack shrugged and slipped the small memo book into Rizzo's jacket. "Stick that in an old suit at home. The kind you don't wear anymore. If I ever need it, I'll say something about sending the suit to the dry cleaner's."

"You realize we're withholding evidence."

"Who from?"

"CIA, for starters, and this secret agency in charge of Rosemark—SOD."

"Strategic Operational Deployment," Jack replied. "Has a nice ring to it. Fancy way of saying 'rat soup.' "

"It's still evidence. If Sorenson took those chemical formulas out of SOD files, the whole spook world will be looking down our throats."

"Fuck 'em. You know something? In the early days when I was with the agency, the guys were pros, solid, stand-up guys. There was a sense of purpose, of cama-raderie. Now they're bloodless bureaucrats pissing in the wind. Their intelligence stinks. Maybe the best of it ended with Nixon and Kissinger on their knees in the Oval Office praying to the gods of Watergate. Batman and Robin. They took everything right into the toilet. The world's going up in smoke, and the agency is worried about rat soup."

"They may be a bunch of bums," Rizzo said, "but they have clout. Why screw around? Why not give them the goddamn Rosemark notes?"

"We may need a trade-off down the line."

They were approaching the Harbor Freeway inter-change.

"Where're we going?" Rizzo asked.

"Get off at Los Angeles Street. We'll go to Chico's, have some breakfast, then fill Nolan in."

Rizzo edged the car over to the extreme right lane. "You shouldn't have belted that guy."

"You're right. My hand is killing me. That bastard's cheekbone was made out of concrete. I should have arrested him for obstructing justice."

"You'd be booked on a federal rap for revealing the identity of an agent."

"That's why I belted him," Jack said, and turned the radio on. The weatherman predicted a new Santa Ana condition would blow its hot breath into the city by nightfall.

CHAPTER TWENTY-ONE

⚠

Seated opposite Sabitini and Gabriella was Antonio Anjulo, special investigator for the Office of the Procuratore della Repubblica. He was a thin, wiry man in his mid-forties with patrician features and penetrating black eyes. Anjulo assiduously avoided publicity, but the sensational nature of the cases assigned to him carried an irresistible attraction for the press, and despite all his efforts to maintain anonymity, he had reluctantly become a celebrity.

They watched him expectantly as he studied the documents detailing Gabriella's previous testimony concerning the death of Pierre Claudon.

Gabriella was annoyed by Anjulo's request for this meeting; several days ago she had spent an entire morning answering questions put to her by detectives from the local Polizia Criminale. She was also distressed by the continuing media coverage of the tragedy. The newspaper articles graphically described the gory details of the prostitute's mutilation by an agonized French pervert, who, after committing the atrocity, leaped naked to his death.

Gabriella smoked and swung her leg up and down impatiently, waiting for Anjulo to begin. The silence in Sabitini's office was underscored by the ticking wall clock.

Anjulo finally closed the file and addressed Gabriella. "This is an unpleasant task for me, signorina. I'm aware that you have already been questioned by the local police, but I must ask your indulgence."

"Can we be frank?" she asked.

"Of course."

"Has this interview been prompted by media pressure?"

"Hardly," Anjulo replied coolly. "The Office of the Procuratore is not influenced by so-called journalists who pander to the basest elements of our society. This case has assumed certain international aspects and was officially remanded to federal authority."

"But surely you do not doubt Signorina Bercovici's previous testimony?" Sabitini inquired.

"Let us say I am not completely satisfied with the quality of her interrogation," Anjulo replied adroitly.

"What did you mean by 'international aspects'?" Gabriella asked.

"We received an official inquiry from Interpol concerning Pierre Claudon's death. This request was initiated by a Los Angeles police officer named Jack Raines."

"Why would an American police officer be interested in Claudon?"

"I'm hoping you can answer that question, signorina."

"But you have my testimony," she replied testily. "I spent an entire morning telling your associates all I know."

"The local police are not my associates." Anjulo rose and came around the desk. "You may be unaware of the fact that my European and American colleagues consider our Italian investigatory methods primitive by their standards. That means my final report to Interpol transcends this particular case. The quality of my response is now a matter of national honor."

"I understand your position, Commendatore," Gabriella said, using Anjulo's formal title. "But I've already given my testimony, and frankly my work is at a standstill. I must raise funds for this Megiddo expedition. As a matter of fact, I'm at the moment preparing to leave for New York."

"I know the mystery of past civilizations awaits your expertise." Anjulo smiled ingenuously. "But those secrets have remained hidden for thousands of years. A few more minutes can hardly matter." He paused, and the smile vanished. "I gather from your testimony that Claudon acted as an emissary for Lord Hamilton."

"Yes."

"So Claudon was simply a middleman?"

"More or less. Although he was a partner in Pyramid International and quite friendly with Dr. Gamasi."

"Therefore, we can safely characterize the late Mr. Claudon as an emissary of some importance."

"Yes."

"According to your testimony, you had dinner with Claudon at the Bolognese restaurant in the Piazza del Popolo, at which time he gave you the Swiss passbook with a deposit totaling one hundred thousand dollars."

Gabriella nodded. "I have already transferred those funds from the Banque Genève to Bank Hapoalim in Tel Aviv."

"So that you can commence the Megiddo dig?"

"Yes," she replied impatiently. "An Israeli general named Barzani has organized a team to prepare the dig."

"What did Lord Hamilton ask in return for his investment?"

"Only to be present when and if we discovered a certain tablet. And, of course, the usual leasing and exhibition rights."

Anjulo directed his next question to Sabitini. "Professor, as a matter of curiosity, how would the university benefit from the use of Signorina Bercovici's time?"

"You mean, by granting her a leave to pursue the Megiddo dig?"

"Yes."

"It is not unlike your present task, Commendatore. It is a matter of national pride. If we succeeded at

Megiddo, the attendant worldwide recognition for Rome University would have incalculable benefits. Unfortunately the university cannot finance this expedition, so we are forced to deal with individual financiers. Archaeology is not a pristine science. More often than not we are thrust into a world of nefarious collectors, dealers, thieves, forgers, and receivers of stolen artifacts."

"That appears to be the case with Claudon," Anjulo said. "The French Sûreté suspected him of receiving and selling stolen artifacts."

Anjulo returned to the documents and for a moment studied a particular section of Gabriella's testimony. "Signorina, I noticed that you asked Claudon why Hamilton had not come to see you personally."

"Well . . . yes. I was frankly puzzled by Hamilton's absence."

"And what was Claudon's response?"

"He said Hamilton was frightened."

"Of whom?"

"The Syrians."

"Why?"

"Claudon said that a small but continuing flow of Ebla tablets had found their way into Western museums, and this illicit traffic had caused profound anxiety at the highest levels of Syrian government."

"It's my understanding that once you were expelled from Ebla, the dig was sealed and placed under tight Syrian security."

"That's true—"

"Can we then assume that someone within the Syrian hierarchy sold these tablets through Claudon?"

"It's possible."

"Now, in your opinion, who would this Syrian supplier be?"

"The only one in a position to sell those tablets would be Dr. Gamasi."

"Have you had any contact with him lately?"

"No."

"What about you, Professor?"

"We speak from time to time."

"Has Gamasi ever mentioned these stolen artifacts?"

"Not to me."

Anjulo sat on the edge of the desk and brushed a piece of lint from his superbly tailored jacket. "Now, signorina, describe for me Claudon's attitude at dinner. Not what he said, but his demeanor."

"Warm. Friendly. Businesslike."

"Did he make any advances or romantic suggestions?"

"He was flattering and flirtatious but not offensive."

"So you finished dinner, dropped him at the hotel, and at two-fifteen A.M. you were awakened by the police, who had found your name in Claudon's appointment book. They informed you of Claudon's death and the mutilation of this unfortunate prostitute."

"Yes."

"And once you heard the details of this grisly crime, were you not frightened?"

"I was shocked."

"Yes, but didn't the thought cross your mind that you had been dining that very night with a homicidal maniac and that only by the grace of God you were spared the same fate that befell the poor prostitute?"

"No, that never occurred to me."

"Which means that you could not consciously conceive of Claudon as a demented killer. Isn't that a fair conclusion?"

"I—I suppose that's true."

"You stated in your previous testimony that you had contacted this American, Dr. Sorenson, for financing."

"He was the first member of Pyramid International I called."

"And Sorenson declined?"

"Yes."

"Why?"

"He had suffered a personal tragedy."

"What was the nature of that tragedy?"

"His wife had been murdered."

"In Los Angeles?"

"Yes."

"Why didn't you tell this to the detectives when they questioned you?"

"No one asked."

"And you did not volunteer?"

"It didn't seem relevant. What did Dr. Sorenson's tragedy have to do with Claudon?"

"Yes. What indeed? Yet the fact remains: Two brutal homicides strike two members of Pyramid International on opposite sides of the world."

"I never made any connection between them."

"Apparently this American detective, Raines, makes a connection, and I tend to agree with him."

"Why is that?" Sabitini asked.

"The French dossier on Pierre Claudon contains no history of violent sexual aberrations. And even if we assume Claudon maintained a secret, perverse side to his life, why would he come to Rome to find a victim? After all, there is no shortage of prostitutes in Paris. Now I am going to ask you to forget the subject of your dinner with Claudon. Forget about Syria and Megiddo, and stolen tablets, and what you said and what he said." He paused, and his hard black eyes narrowed. "Concentrate on the piazza itself."

"I don't understand."

"Come, come, you are a gifted woman who can look at carvings on a limestone wall and decipher the entire history of a lost civilization. Surely you can re-create what that piazza looked like the night of your dinner. The people, the cars, the food, the weather, anything that comes to mind."

She rose and paced nervously. "I parked near the church. Two men were arguing over a parking space. I walked across the piazza to the restaurant. Claudon was late. I ordered wine. Federico Fellini was seated nearby. He was with a beautiful woman. The piazza was crowded. The restaurant was full. Claudon arrived."

"The piazza," Anjulo interrupted. "Think only of the piazza."

"There were very few tourists." She stopped pacing. "Across the piazza the walls of the Villa Borghese were illuminated and . . ." She suddenly fell silent. Her blue eyes widened with revelation. "The obelisk . . . at the center of the piazza."

"What about it?"

"I wasn't certain at the time because of the distance, but there were two men standing at the obelisk who seemed to be watching our table."

"What did they look like?"

"Well-dressed typical Romans. When we left, I noticed one of them in the phone booth near my car."

"You mean the public booth near the church?"

"Yes. Santa Maria di Monte."

Anjulo smiled with satisfaction and glanced at Sabitini. "You see, Professor, same witness, same events, yet we have new information."

"It's the quality of the questions, Commendatore."

"You're being kind, Professor. But isn't it remarkable that a woman like Signorina Bercovici steeped, reared, and nurtured in the history of ancient civilization would forget to mention an Egyptian obelisk?"

"Obelisks are common in Rome," Gabriella replied.

"Yes. To you they are part of the scenery, but a tourist would have remembered." He picked up his briefcase and placed the blue file inside. "Do you know the history of that obelisk?"

"Vaguely," she said. "I think Pope Sixtus moved the obelisk to the Piazza del Popolo in the late sixteenth century."

"He was always re-dressing Rome," Sabitini added.

Anjulo snapped his briefcase shut. "You're quite right, Professor. Pope Sixtus also had a plan to turn the Colosseum into a wool factory. But the College of Cardinals suggested that the Colosseum had seen enough animals in its day. Pope Sixtus mercifully abandoned the idea."

"Are you a student of Roman history, Commendatore?"

"To a degree. After all, I am a product of Roman history." He smiled. "Well, thank you for your courtesy, signorina. We will not bother you again."

"I'm sorry if I was short-tempered."

"Perhaps it's the pollution—it tends to aggravate the nicest of people."

"What is your final opinion of the case?" Sabitini asked.

"In my view, Pierre Claudon and the unlucky prostitute were murdered by professional assassins acting on orders."

"Whose orders?"

"That's a question for the American detective Raines to pursue. I am finished with this matter. I can now relay the facts to Interpol with enough detail and theory to preserve the national honor."

CHAPTER TWENTY-TWO

⚠

The Los Angeles Dodgers still had a chance to make the play-offs, and the outcome of this game was critical to their chances. The Mets were going nowhere, but their ace relief pitcher, Jesse Orosco, was performing brilliantly.

Pedro Guerrero stepped out of the batter's box and checked signals with the third-base coach. The count was three and one. It was the bottom of the seventh, and the Dodgers had men on second and first. The Mets were ahead by one run, and the way Orosco was pitching, the one run loomed very large. The base-runners had resulted from a walk and a fielding error.

Jack's left arm circled the back of Jenny's chair. She was eating her third bag of peanuts and was totally absorbed in the game.

"What do you think, Dad—hit or take?"

"He'll swing if he gets his pitch."

The runners led off. Orosco peered intently toward home plate. He nodded at the catcher, stretched, checked the runner leading off second, reared back, and threw a hard slider that broke down and away from Guerrero, catching the outside corner for a strike. The crowd groaned.

"You said he'd swing, Dad," Jenny said.

"I guess he was looking for a fast ball."

It was three and two. Two out. Orosco checked again, came to a stop, and fired a high, fast ball. Guerrero swung, and the crack of the bat against the ball was solid and resonant.

The baserunners took off. The crowd were on their feet, roaring. The ball curved into deep right center, fell between the outfielders, and rolled to the wall. The runner from second scored easily. The runner from first, digging hard, came home standing up. The relay throw from deep center was cut off, and Guerrero slipped under the tag at second base.

"He's great!" Jenny exclaimed.

"That's called clutch hitting, sweetheart."

The Mets' manager went out to the mound to talk to Orosco. The crowd was still buzzing. The Dodgers now had a one-run lead.

"How about another hot dog?" Jack asked.

"Peanuts."

"Okay."

He waited in line at the food stand and looked anxiously at the field. The Mets' manager had decided to stay with Orosco. Jack slipped the peanuts in his pocket, sipped the beer, and lit a cigarillo.

Orosco got the next batter out on a pop fly, and the teams changed sides. Jack watched Fernando Valenzuela take his warm-up pitches and tried to focus on the colorful Mexican pitching ace, but his mind drifted back to the case.

He was puzzled by Interpol's lack of response to his request regarding Pierre Claudon. He wondered what was behind Sorenson's sudden departure and disappearance and the significance of the bloodstained deck and the nine-millimeter shell casing. He pondered the importance of the Rosemark note pad and the mystifying use of the word *triangle*.

The crowd roared their approval as Valenzuela struck out the first Met batter. Jack sighed heavily and thought, the hell with the case. It was a beautiful Sunday, an exciting ball game, and he was with his daughter.

He went back to his seat and handed Jenny the peanuts. "The guy at the counter wants to know how many more peanuts you plan to eat so they can stock up."

Jenny smiled and cracked a peanut. "You've been smoking."

"Cross my heart."

"Come on, Dad. I can smell it. You promised to stop."

"I will. I've got it down to five a day."

"That's five too many."

"Okay, okay. Let's watch the game."

"How about a sip of beer?"

"It's against the law."

"Just one."

"Well, for an actress of your stature I'll make an exception."

"I was pretty good in the play, wasn't I?"

Before Jack could answer, Jenny was on her feet with forty thousand other fans. The Mets' third baseman had cracked a towering drive off the left-field wall, missing a home run by inches, and the speedy runner cruised into second with a stand-up double.

"Looks bad," Jack said.

"Uhh-uhh," Jenny replied. "Fernando will get them out. He gets stronger as the game goes on."

"I wish I did." Jack smiled.

"What do you mean?"

"Nothing, honey."

CHAPTER TWENTY-THREE

△

Thirty-five miles west of Dodger Stadium the *Camilla Two* rolled easily in the Pacific swells off Point Vicente. The deep-draft fishing boat specialized in shark catches and supplied a portion of the shark steaks that had begun to appear on menus of pretentious West Hollywood restaurants.

The *Camilla Two* had been lucky this Sunday. Two dozen sand sharks and five large basking sharks had been pulled from the sea, cleaned, stripped, cut into steaks, and placed in portable freezers. The windburned fishermen had packed their gear and were relaxing with very dry martinis, provided by the captain as a bonus to his regular customers.

On the starboard side near the bow, Edmund Sperling still desperately sought his first catch. He picked up a bucket of fish blood and bits of shrimp and dumped the contents into the water surrounding his line. Fishing was not simply a sport to the famous screenwriter; it was a matter of survival: The fish markets were closed on Sunday, and without the evidence of at least one fish, Sperling's fifth wife would have suspected an afternoon of adultery—a crime the consequences of which he could no longer afford, his capital having evaporated in the marital battlefield of the Santa Monica Superior Court.

"You're not gonna catch anything but a fucking sunburn."

Sperling glanced at a gin-soaked red-faced man seated to his right. "How do you know that, Charlie?"

The man sipped some of his martini. "It's too late. The sharks are gone. Pack it in. Have a drink."

"I suppose you're right."

"Sperling!" a voice suddenly shouted from the bridge. "Your line!"

Whirling around, Sperling grabbed the rod, which was already arcing under the weight of the catch.

Using his full weight, Sperling reeled in the line, straining against the catch, and, with a final mighty heave, he raised what appeared to be a gigantic blue jellyfish. The carcass landed on the deck with a sickening thud.

It was a mutilated, bloated corpse. The gas-filled male torso hissed, and a foul-smelling stench assaulted their senses. Sea worms, looking like maggots, filled the eyeless sockets. The hands and feet had been consumed by predators, leaving only shredded stumps. Crabs, mollusks, and starfish swarmed over the swollen torso. The face was a skeletal mask, with layers of desiccated flesh still clinging to the shattered skull. A gold medallion dangled tenaciously around the neck and glinted in the sunlight.

Sperling and his companion raced to the starboard side and vomited. The ship began to list as the overwhelming stench drove the other fishermen frantically to the leeward side.

On the bridge the grim-faced captain was already on the ship-to-shore phone with the Long Beach Coast Guard station.

CHAPTER TWENTY-FOUR

⚠

Linda murmured softly in her sleep, and Jack studied the hollow of her flat stomach, the curve of her hips, the fine angular line of her cheekbones, and the splash of ash blond hair splayed across the pillow. He sighed heavily, swung his legs over the bed, slipped on his robe, and went out into the living room.

He poured a ginger ale over ice and walked out to the terrace. The lights of the city winked back at him, and the warm Santa Ana breeze played across his face.

All in all, it had been a fine day. The Dodgers and Valenzuela held on to their one-run lead. Jack smiled, remembering how Jenny had squealed with delight when the last Met hitter flied out.

On the ride back to Rizzo's house their conversation ranged from baseball to ballet. Only at the moment of his departure did Jenny ask him about the case. He told her it would all be okay and not to think about it. They made plans for the following week, and Jenny kissed him good-bye.

His dinner date with Linda had been casual and lighthearted. She had made him laugh with her acerbic

comments on his apartment's state of disrepair. She suggested he either hire an interior decorator or set the place on fire.

After dinner they returned to his apartment. He put a stack of Sinatra records on the stereo while Linda poured Courvoisier over ice and lit a Panamanian joint she had smuggled through customs. And under the influence of brandy and grass, Jack's demons slowly slipped away. They made love for a long time, but he found himself mentally transforming Linda into the shape, face, and being of the dead woman he still desired.

He swirled the ice in his glass and thought sooner or later he would have to relegate Laura's memory to that part of his consciousness uninhabited by ghosts—a place of remembered beauty.

The phone rang, sharply snapping his reverie. He walked quickly back into the living room, picked up the receiver, and cleared his throat. "Hello?"

"This is Torres. Sorry to wake you."

"What's up, Gabby?"

"You had instructed the Coast Guard to call Tactical if a John Doe floater showed up."

"Right."

"Well, there was a bureaucratic foul-up with the Long Beach Sheriff's office. They finally got to Fitzsimmons, and Fitz called me. Some guy fished a torso out of the water at Point Vicente."

Jack felt a cold foreboding invade his chest. "When?"

"Late this afternoon."

"No ID?"

"There's a Saint Christopher medal around the floater's neck. The inscription reads: 'To Martin with love, Laura, 8/'83.' "

"Christ . . ." Jack murmured.

"They just brought the remains in," Torres continued. "Gomez called me from the morgue. It's badly chewed up. No hands, no feet. Just a torso and shattered skull. There's a bullet entry behind the left ear. I'm on the way down."

"When will you have something?"

"I would say close to eleven—make it eleven-thirty. And, Jack . . ."

"Yeah?"

"Don't put yourself on the cross. You offered Sorenson protection."

CHAPTER TWENTY-FIVE

⚠

Jack and Rizzo walked down the harshly lit corridor, passing white-clad morgue attendants, plainclothes detectives, uniformed police, and weeping relatives of the numbered cadavers that lay in refrigerated compartments on the lower level. A public address system sporadically paged private citizens and police officers.

The coroner's office was sparsely furnished with an uncluttered desk, three chairs, and two steel file cabinets. The windows facing Spring Street were shielded from the sun by dusty venetian blinds. The one incongruity was a movie poster on the rear wall featuring Raquel Welch in *Kansas City Bomber*.

Gabriel Torres was seated behind his desk. Dark blue circles rimmed his eyes. He sifted through reports labeled "Pathology," "Toxology," "Forensic Dentistry," and "Medical History." Each folder was stamped with the Sorenson case number.

Torres sipped some coffee and belched loudly.

"Good morning to you, too," Rizzo said.

"Excuse me, *señores*, but I've been drinking this machine-made coffee all night." He paused and pointedly added, "While you were sleeping."

Torres shuffled some documents. "I'll start with the torso: 'Right thigh: disarticulated at knee joint, no foot present. Left thigh: disarticulated at hip, no foot present. Left arm: humerus disarticulated at elbow, no hand present. Right arm: disarticulated at wrist, no hand present.' "

He glanced up from the reports. "You have to understand, *disarticulated* loosely means 'separated.' But the quality of those separations are interesting. They're fairly clean considering the body had been immersed in seawater for over one hundred hours."

"For chrissake, get to the point," Jack said with annoyance.

"That's the problem. There is no definite point, only theory. The separations could very well be shark bites, sea lions, or other sharp-toothed predators, but the clean angle of severance suggests the possibility that the body could have been intentionally dismembered."

"Why would anyone shoot Sorenson, then take the time to dismember his corpse?"

"It precludes checking fingerprints and footprints," Rizzo said.

"That doesn't work," Jack replied. "They left the goddamn Saint Christopher medal around his neck."

"Hold it," Torres said. "I don't want to throw you fellows off. The odds are the dismemberment *was* caused by predators. Intentional severance is a possibility, nothing more." Torres paused and belched again. "Can I continue?"

"Go ahead."

"We found abrasions and canvas fibers from bindings used to weight the body."

"What happened to the weights?" Rizzo asked.

"Body tissue shrivels in seawater. Weights slip off after fifty, sixty hours. What was left of Sorenson wasn't pretty. Ears, cheeks, buttocks, genitals, torn and shredded." He glanced across at the two detectives. "These mutilations are unmistakably fish bites. The blood type

AB we found on the decking matches Sorenson's. The tissue age equates—late fifties or thereabouts.

"Size of torso, thighs, and ankles measures one hundred and seventy centimeters, indicating a body height of six feet. Skull outline matches: nose size, jawline, and cheekbone. Sea worms chewed the eyes pretty good, but color is blue, same as Sorenson."

Jack felt a sickening horror as he listened to the clinical descriptions of a man's mutilated and fragmented corpse, a man whose personal elegance and grace he had grudgingly admired.

"Bullet was a nine-millimeter," Torres continued. "Ballistics confirmed it was fired from a Soviet Makarov SL automatic. Entry wound behind left ear. The slug ripped through the brain, destroyed mastoids, obliterated seven lower-jaw teeth, damaged trachea and larynx. The skull, orbital margins, vertical scope, and superciliary arches ruptured. The shot was fired from less than two feet."

"Did the shot kill him?" Jack asked.

"I doubt it. His lungs were full of water. But more significantly there was an absence of leukocyte infiltration."

"Keep it in English, Gabby."

"Sorry. There was no evidence of white cells converging on the wound."

"Which indicates he was drowned, then shot?"

"Nothing's a thousand percent, Jack, but I'd go to court with that conclusion."

Torres rose and flipped a switch, illuminating sets of dental X rays. The skull with gaping teeth grinned at them hideously.

"These X rays were shot from the cadaver's mouth," Torres explained, and pointed to an adjacent light panel. "They match these X rays sent down by Sorenson's dentist, a Dr. Vogel. You can see the upper-left first molar has an MOD gold inlay, and lower-right first bicuspid has porcelain fused to a semiprecious metal crown. There's an upper bridge, tooth number six through number eleven, porcelain fused to precious metal. He has, and this is unusual at his age, retained all wisdom teeth in occlusion, fully erupted, in harmony with the rest of his teeth. The balance of the lower front teeth, as I told you, are fragmented. But the forensic odontologist confirms the match of the surviving teeth."

Torres went back to his desk, opened the top drawer, and handed Jack the gold Saint Christopher medal.

Jack turned it over and saw the engraved inscription: "To Martin with love, Laura—8/83."

Torres emitted a long, growling belch and grabbed his stomach. "Sorry. This goddamn case—nothing happens in normal hours. I haven't taken a crap in two days."

"Have we got it all now?"

"*Sí, señor, todo.*"

"Thanks, Gabby."

"Before you go, there's something else you should be aware of. Again, it's probably irrelevant. But for a corpse immersed that length of time, the tissues are well preserved."

"Meaning what?"

"I don't know." Torres shrugged. "It's unusual. But then again the temperature of the sea may have acted to preserve the tissues."

"What are you getting at, Gabby?"

"Nothing, compadre. I know this case is very personal, and I don't want to miss anything."

"You're a regular Jack Klugman," Rizzo said.

"I wish." Torres sighed. "Quincy's the only coroner who never misses."

"Why don't you just give me your conclusions?" Jack said with obvious impatience.

"Sorenson was drowned, then shot, maybe dismembered, weighted, and dumped."

"And the dental charts match?"

"Absolutely."

"The tissue preservation in no way changes your basic conclusions?"

"No, *señor.*"

"Go home." Jack smiled. "Get some sleep."

*   *   *

They walked out of the gloomy building into the bright sunlight. Jack flipped the official police visor up as he got behind the wheel of the GTO convertible. Rizzo waved to a pretty meter maid ticketing civilian cars the owners of which were inside the morgue identifying the remains of loved ones.

CHAPTER TWENTY-SIX

△

They stood on either side of the communications officer who operated the Telex and watched expectantly
as the receiving keys printed bursts of unintelligible
words. The tattoo of the keys sputtered briefly and fell
silent.

"Problems?" Rizzo asked the operator.

"Maybe. I sent them a 'ready to receive,' but nothing's come back."

"Send it again," Jack said.

The operator punched the keys, and they hammered
the message across the cylindrical roll of yellow paper:

LAPD—TACTICAL—LA—TELEX #167432 TO PARIS INTERPOL—
#333878: RECEIVED YOUR STAND-BY AND ACKNOWLEDGE.
ADVISE IF LINE OPERATIVE.

The return keys suddenly flew across the paper.

INTER—PARIS TO #167432 LAPD—TACTICAL—READY NOW.
ACKNOWLEDGE.

The officer sent "LA #167432 READY TO RECEIVE."

The whirring sound of electric current was drowned by a sudden hail of clicking and a furious battering of keys pounding out the message from Paris:

YOUR REQUEST FRENCH CITIZEN PIERRE CLAUDON DELAYED BY CONFUSED REPORTS FROM ITALIAN AUTHORITIES. CLAUDON KILLED IN ROME NIGHT OF 9/8. POLIZIA CRIMINALE INITIALLY REPORTED MUTILATION AND STRANGULATION OF PROSTITUTE BY CLAUDON FOLLOWED BY HIS SUICIDE. CLAUDON PRESUMED TO HAVE JUMPED FROM EIGHTH-FLOOR TERRACE OF ROMANA HOTEL. REQUESTED MORE SPECIFIC DETAILS FROM OFFICE OF PROCURATORE DELLA REPUBBLICA. COMMENDATORE ANTONIO ANJULO ASSUMED INVESTIGATION. AFTER SUBSEQUENT ANALYSIS OF EVIDENCE AND FURTHER INTERROGATION OF WITNESS (ITALIAN CITIZEN GABRIELLA BERCOVICI) ANJULO CONCLUDES CLAUDON POSSIBLE MURDER VICTIM. PROSTITUTE STRANGLED AND MUTILATED TO CREATE FALSE MOTIVATION FOR SUICIDE. ANJULO'S FULL REPORT FOLLOWS. ACKNOWLEDGE.

The operator glanced up at Jack. "Anything else, Lieutenant?"

"Give me a minute."

The murder of Claudon was a thunderbolt. Jack paced nervously, his thoughts pressured by the tenuous electronic link to Paris. He finally tapped the operator's shoulder and said, "Ask them for an ID on Gabriella Bercovici."

The operator punched the request and waited. A few seconds passed, and the receiving keys slammed across the cylindrical roll: "GABRIELLA BERCOVICI, COCHAIRS MIDDLE EAST LANGUAGE DEPARTMENT, UNIVERSITY OF ROME."

"Ask them for a brief account of Bercovici's connection to Claudon's death," Jack said.

The operator punched up the message. A few minutes of silence passed before the receiving keys resumed their rapid-fire movement: "G. BERCOVICI DINED WITH CLAUDON NIGHT OF KILLINGS. ANJULO REPORTS G. BERCOVICI ABOVE SUSPICION AND COMPLICITY. ACKNOWLEDGE. STANDING BY."

"Ask them for their own data on Claudon."

The operator sent the message, and seconds later the receiving keys hit the paper: "FOLLOWING FROM OUR DEUXIEME BUREAU: CLAUDON UNDER SURVEILLANCE SUSPECTED OF RECEIVING AND SELLING STOLEN ARTIFACTS. NO PRIOR CRIMINAL RECORD. ACKNOWLEDGE."

The keys fell silent, and Jack said, "That's it. Thank them."

The operator hit the keys exchanging salutations with his counterpart six thousand miles away.

Back in his office, Jack chalked an X alongside the name of Pierre Claudon and stepped back to examine the case diagram.

"That leaves one Indian," Rizzo stated. "Lord Hamilton, the last surviving member of the Pyramid group."

"Come on, let's go see Nolan," Jack said.

John Nolan was seated on an air-filled cushion, smoking a long panatela. His usual gray pallor was obscured by the cigar smoke. A homely middle-aged woman poured stiff shots of Scotch for the two detectives and a glass of buttermilk for Nolan.

"Thank you, Elizabeth," Nolan said, and swallowed some buttermilk. "Between the goddamn hemorrhoids and the ulcer, I'll never make retirement."

"They'll have to shoot you, John." Jack smiled. "You'll outlive us all."

"I certainly hope so." Nolan sighed. "The heat is starting to come down. Commissioner Harris called me. 'What we're doing about the Sorenson-Emory murders? And do we, for chrissake, have anything at all he can go to the press with?' Harris also received a formal complaint from the CIA concerning that altercation you had with—what was that agent's name?"

"Piersall."

"Yeah. It might be a conciliatory gesture to bring Piersall up-to-date on the case."

"Not from where I sit," Jack replied. "Besides, you're

the one who says let's keep our distance from the feds."

"True. But those agency spooks are going to be climbing the walls—two key brain scientists working on a secret project murdered within weeks of each other. They'll also have a lot of fun with the fact that Sorenson was shot with a Soviet automatic."

"There's that and Sorenson's habit of tuning in on those Russian trawlers," Jack replied. "They'll have to consider the possibility that Sorenson was dealing information to the Russians."

"Well, maybe he was an agent," Rizzo remarked.

"I don't think so," Jack replied. "It's professionally unsound to murder a double agent. A dead agent has no market value. It makes more sense to run him or trade him off."

"Didn't this Piersall fellow tell you the agency had Sorenson under surveillance?" Nolan asked.

"That's right."

"Did he say why?"

"He didn't have to. Any operation coded Black would call for automatic surveillance."

"Wait a minute!" Rizzo said with sudden excitement. "Suppose Emory knew Sorenson was dealing to the Russians."

"Not bad . . ." Nolan murmured. "The drug used to kill Emory required some medical knowledge."

"It doesn't stand up," Jack responded. "If Emory had any suspicions regarding Sorenson's loyalty, he'd have taken them straight to Rosemark's project officer."

"Suppose he was blackmailing Sorenson?" Nolan asked.

"What for? Emory was a multimillionaire."

"It didn't have to be money. Emory could have been blackmailing Sorenson for possession of the triangle."

"That's one hell of a reach, Vince."

"Wait a minute, Jack," Nolan said with rising interest. "It's a theory that has some merit."

"It doesn't work."

"Why not?"

"Because it's conjecture riddled with conjecture. In

the first place we don't know what the hell *triangle* stands for."

"It might be a code word."

"It might be anything, John, but for the moment it's just a goddamn word that Mrs. Emory picked up. Besides, for a blackmail theory to work, we have to assume Sorenson *was* a Soviet agent, which I don't buy. The whole history of the man says otherwise. Remember, Sorenson served in the OSS during World War Two. He operated for three years behind enemy lines. He was a tough case. Decorated for heroism. In order to pursue this theory, we'd have to ignore his patriotism and assume that suddenly late in life he became a Soviet agent. And," Jack emphasized, "an ineffectual Soviet agent."

"Why ineffectual?"

"Sorenson was seasoned. Professional. If he had become a Soviet agent, an amateur like Emory would not have noticed anything irregular. Sorenson may have been many things, but he wasn't stupid. But even if we tossed logic to the winds, we'd have to assume further that Emory risked his life to blackmail Sorenson for some mythical triangle. It doesn't work."

"What about that phone call?" Nolan asked.

"What phone call?"

"The one Sorenson made to Rome the night Emory was killed."

"I checked it. He called Rome a little after ten P.M., but that doesn't tell us much. Mrs. Emory wasn't precise as to the exact time her husband went down to meet whoever it was he was expecting. She thought it was close to midnight."

"Still, it does place Sorenson in Bel Air that night," Rizzo said.

"Christ, everything's a blind alley." Nolan sighed. "Now this goddamn Frenchman gets clipped in Rome, and the Bercovici girl suddenly weaves her way into the case."

"She was always in the case," Jack replied. "She played a key role in the Ebla discovery."

"Wonder why Claudon went to Rome to see her?" Rizzo asked.

"It's probably in Anjulo's report," Jack said. "But I would guess she was pressing Claudon to finance the Megiddo dig. She called Sorenson for the same reason."

"What the hell is she after?" Nolan asked.

"Something to do with a biblical tablet."

"Fucking mysteries . . ." Nolan murmured, and got to his feet. "The question is, where do we go from here."

"I'll check with Sorenson's attorney," Jack said. "There may be something in his will. Some beneficiary out of his past. It's not much, but it's a shot."

CHAPTER TWENTY-SEVEN

⚠

Jack steered the classic GTO convertible into the line of cars moving up the freeway on ramp. The black Ford was still behind him, moving leisurely, five car lengths back. Almost from the moment Jack exited Tactical's garage the innocuous-looking sedan had maintained its following position.

Jack flicked his left-turn blinker and gained the free-way entry lane. He then floored the accelerator, kicked the turbo charger, and propelled the yellow convertible into the adjacent lane. The rush-hour traffic had thinned, and the westbound flow cruised at sixty-five miles an hour, heading directly into the last rays of a scarlet sunset.

He checked his side-view mirror: The black Ford was positioned precisely five cars back.

Taking a deep breath, he accelerated, spun the wheel, and veered dangerously across three lanes. The black Ford changed lanes with perfect precision, holding the yellow GTO five car lengths ahead.

A police traffic helicopter zoomed in low over the

freeway, the pilot noting and reporting the erratic lane changes of both vehicles.

Jack hit the right-turn blinker, swung the wheel, and swerved abruptly into the fast lane. The black Ford stayed with him.

Jack wiped the beads of cold sweat from his forehead and decided to gamble. It was dangerous and fallible, but one way or another he would smoke out the intentions of the tailing car.

His palms sweated against the steering wheel. His eyes flicked at the rearview mirror. The tailing Ford had moved up three car lengths. He glanced at the streaming line of traffic to his right, kicked the turbo charger in, spun the wheel, and darted between two tightly spaced cars. Ignoring the angry blare of their horns, he cut into the exit lane and sped down the Crenshaw off ramp.

Surprised by this unexpected maneuver, the driver of the Ford could do nothing but maintain his position on the freeway.

Jack caught the four-way traffic light just as the cycle changed from green to amber. The GTO roared across the wide boulevard against the traffic and shot up the westbound Crenshaw on ramp. Back on the freeway, he spotted the black Ford eight car lengths ahead, cruising at sixty. He now had the tail in front of him.

He heard the distant wail of a siren as he passed a line of cars, swerved sharply into the adjacent lane, and came up directly behind the Ford. A cloud of black smoke blew out of the Ford's tailpipes as it accelerated.

Jack floored the gas pedal.

They raced in tandem, veering wildly across lanes as the Ford desperately tried to shake the GTO. Jack's knuckles turned white; beads of perspiration leaked out of his armpits and snaked down his rib cage. The wail of sirens was closer.

The Ford cut across three lanes and angled into the exit lane heading for the Robertson off ramp.

Jack stayed with him.

The red taillights of the Ford glowed as it braked behind exiting traffic. Jack swung parallel to the Ford, spun the wheel, and smashed his right fender into the left front grille of the Ford.

The Ford careened off the low concrete rail, becoming airborne for an instant before bouncing to a halt on the grassy slope.

Jack leaped out of the right-side door, clutching his .38 revolver. A tall, youthful male stepped out of the Ford.

"Freeze!" Jack shouted.

The man turned and raised his hands. He was blond and wiry and wore reflective sunglasses that glared in the beams of the GTO's headlights.

Jack approached him slowly. "Get over against my car. Put your hands on the hood."

The youth started to turn, then suddenly whirled around. Jack saw the blur of the foot too late.

A knifelike pain exploded in his groin. He dropped the gun and fell to his knees. The perfectly aimed judo kick had caught him full force.

The man was on him. Grappling for position, they rolled down the slope, slamming into the base of the concrete divider.

Jack jammed his forearm into the man's Adam's apple. "Who sent you?" he screamed. "Syrians? CIA? KGB? Answer me, you bastard!"

The reflective glasses slipped onto the bridge of the youth's nose, and he gasped. "You're crazy!"

An amplified voice suddenly boomed at them. "On your feet. Hands raised!"

Two black and white highway patrol cars were parked at the ramp. A patrolman in each car manned the radio. Their partners had twenty-gauge shotguns trained on Jack and the youth.

The shotgun-wielding patrolman prodded them up against a prowl car. "Turn around and spread your legs."

"Listen, fellows, I'm Lieutenant—"

"Shut up. Don't say another word!"

Jack felt the cold steel of the handcuffs snap shut around his wrists.

"Turn around."

The patrolman took Jack's wallet out of his torn jacket. The blond youth received the same treatment.

A police helicopter hovered above. The red lights of the motorcycles and prowl cars flashed. Traffic was backed up as motorists gawked at the scene.

The patrolman's eyes widened with surprise when he saw the gold badge pinned to the flap of Jack's wallet. "Look at this," he said, passing it to his partner.

The officer checked it and said, "You Raines?"

"That's right. I'm working a classified case out of Tactical. This guy was tailing me." Jack started to move toward the cops.

"Just hold it until we get an ID on your plate."

"You'll find my thirty-eight police special up there," Jack said. His cheek was cut, his jacket torn, and a dull pain spread from his groin up to his belly.

The blond youth glared sullenly at the cops.

After a moment an officer got out of the prowl car and came over. "Central confirms GTO is registered to Jack Raines, Doheny-Palms, blue starred, lieutenant with Tactical."

"Take off the cuffs," the cop ordered.

The patrolman came down the slope and handed Jack his revolver. "What the hell's going on, Lieutenant?"

"He was tailing me."

"Bullshit," the youth said. "The fucking guy is nuts!"

The radio officer indicated the youth. "His name is Arnold Ferris. Got a yellow sheet on him as long as the freeway. He's a car thief out on parole."

"A car thief?" Jack repeated incredulously.

"According to his sheet, one of the best," the officer replied.

Jack studied the handcuffed youth. "Why the hell were you tailing me?"

"Your car is a '71 classic GTO convertible. I've been watching it for weeks. I had the fucking thing sold for eight grand to a customer in Bridgeport, Connecticut. My luck—I had to pick a cop."

"You want to press charges here, Lieutenant?" the patrolman asked.

"If you need a report, I'll give you one."

Jack walked slowly back to his car, noticing the crushed right fender.

The cops surrounded the youth, who shook his head in disbelief. "That guy is crazy. Yelling about Syrians, KGB, and CIA—a goddamn nut case."

Two officers herded the car thief into the rear seat of a patrol car. The remaining patrolmen stared at the GTO's disappearing taillights.

The big cop muttered, "That kid isn't wrong. Those Tactical guys are well-known flakes."

CHAPTER TWENTY-EIGHT

△

Gabriella folded and packed her wool coat for the third time before deciding to carry her light silk raincoat. She did not suffer from fashion fatigue and disliked taking two coats, but late fall in New York could be cool, and London on the way back made rain a certainty.

She zipped the suitcase closed, then snapped the latches shut on her attaché case. She was elated at the thought of the forthcoming trip. The dig at Megiddo was already under way, and she was hopeful of securing the additional financing from either the Metropolitan or the British Museum. She stood for a moment in the soft sunlight streaming through the open windows.

Her apartment was in the Villa Balestra, atop Monte Parioli, and offered a splendid view of the ancient city. She had purchased it with a small inheritance she received after her mother's death. Her mother was a woman of grace and strength—a Florentine beauty who had displayed tremendous courage in the face of a terminal illness.

During that time Gabriella and her father had lovingly supported each other. She adored her father and traveled often to Milan to see him perform at La Scala. He was a fine cellist, but Gabriella believed he had never fully exploited his talent. She had encouraged him to pursue a career as a soloist, but the old man had merely smiled. "You, my daughter, were blessed with a certain courage I lacked. Nothing daunts you. Everything is attainable. But even when I was your age, I accepted limitations. And now I'm like an old racehorse trying to reach the finish line with some dignity."

She knew he was proud of her achievements, and when she received worldwide acclaim for cracking the Ebla cuneiform, he sent her a telegram that simply said "Brava!"

He teased her occasionally that her preoccupation with the past was robbing him of grandchildren.

She would smile and say, "Don't give up yet, Papa."

In the bathroom mirror she checked the mascara on the long curling lashes that framed her vivid blue eyes. She rarely paid much attention to her hair; it was a gift from her mother—long, straight, and pale, "the color of champagne," her father had said.

She switched off the bathroom light and went back into the living room. She thought about phoning General Barzani, but decided it would make better sense to wait until after her meeting with Dr. Ettinger in New York.

Barzani's team had already sunk a new north-south trench, reaching a depth twenty-five feet below the stratum of King Solomon's time. There was good reason to be encouraged. A huge bronze gate had been uncovered bearing the image of Reshef, the Canaanite war god. They were clearly approaching the time of Israel's conquest of Canaan—the time of Ithamar. Gabriella longed to be there, but without the additional funds the Megiddo dig would come to an abrupt halt.

The phone rang, jarring her thoughts. She picked up the receiver. *"Pronto?"*

"Is that you, Gabriella?" The voice was reedy, old, and unmistakably British.

"Yes. Who's calling?"

"Anthony Hamilton here. I trust you haven't forgotten me."

"Not at all," she said. "I tried phoning you after Claudon's death, but your London number had been disconnected. I wanted to thank you for the advance."

She heard some rustling noise, and Hamilton said, "Hold on just a moment."

Lord Anthony Hamilton was seated in a thronelike, high-backed chair. Behind him were shelves of artifacts. The dark walls of the medieval-looking den were decorated with mounted heads of lions and elephants— murdered souvenirs of Hamilton's African hunts.

A butler entered, carrying a glass of sherry on a sterling silver tray. Hamilton's bald head shone under the lights of the vaulted ceiling, and his birdlike eyes flicked from the crystal glass to the butler. "Thank you, Henry."

Hamilton shifted his bulk in the chair, sipped the Spanish sherry, and lifted the receiver.

"Forgive me, Gabriella. Sabitini tells me you're off to New York and London."

"That's right."

"Yes. Well, I thought you might have some word from Megiddo."

"The dig is proceeding on schedule," she replied. "Barzani's team is very close to the period in question."

"Ah. That is good news indeed. We all can use some encouragement at this point"—he paused—"after the cruel fate that befell our colleague the late Mr. Claudon."

"It was a terrible shock."

"Yes, but in a sense predictable. You know I liked the man, but he had this irresistible penchant for selling artifacts that were, well, to be kind, not his to sell."

"You don't relate Claudon's murder to Ebla or the Syrians?"

"No. Pierre was a victim of his own greed. He obviously offended some dealer or collector. I warned him repeatedly."

"Did you know Martin Sorenson's wife was murdered in Los Angeles?" she asked.

"I read something about it in the *International Tribune*. A great tragedy. But I don't connect her death to our former Syrian colleagues."

"Sabatini thinks we all may be in jeopardy."

"I disagree," Hamilton replied. "But in any case I am more determined than ever to pursue the Moses tablet. I wish I could have provided all the required funding, but it was simply not possible."

"You realize," she said, "we are fighting long odds without those triangles."

"I understand, but disappointments are part of the process of discovery. Win or lose, I have without pause or regret placed my faith in your expertise."

"I appreciate your trust, and I assure you we'll do our best."

"I'm certain you will."

Hamilton's huge belly heaved as he rose and looked out the open stained-glass windows at the rolling green slopes and wooded hills of his vast estate. "You must forget Ebla, the Syrians, and Claudon," he said. "Concentrate your efforts on Megiddo. We are engaged in a glorious quest. For whatever reason, it has fallen to us to uncover the last word of God. And you, my dear, are in a sense exactly where Ithamar was thirty-two hundred years ago. You are, by fate, by skill, by chance itself, the modern-day messenger of Moses."

She smiled at Hamilton's melodramatic cheerleading. "Well, at least the great prophet of the Hebrews had the good sense to choose an Italian girl."

"Ah. You see. That's the Gabriella I'm counting on. I'm positive your trip will be fruitful and I look forward to seeing you on your return from New York."

"Thank you, Anthony."

Gabriella hung up and rubbed her arm nervously, instinctively sensing something sinister behind Hamilton's jovial demeanor. She recalled the summer of 1981, when Hamilton had visited Ebla. They had uncovered a magnificent gold ruby-eyed cobra. Hamilton had clutched the serpentine artifact to his immense belly, his small, piercing eyes gleaming with the madness of possession.

The speaker on the wall suddenly buzzed. She walked to the mesh box and depressed the button. "Yes?"

"It's Ben Gazzara," Sabatini said. "I'm here to take you to the airport."

CHAPTER TWENTY-NINE

△

Jack parked in the D level, deep in the bowels of the Century City skyscraper. After he had cut the ignition, the battered GTO bucked and growled for twenty seconds.

He flipped the side-view mirror up and checked the swollen cut on his right cheek—a visible reminder of last night's fracas on the freeway.

He crossed the huge subterranean lot, smiling involuntarily, remembering the expression on Linda's face when he had appeared at her door—his suit torn, blood spots on his shirt, his right cheek cut. Before she uttered a word, he had raised his hands and said, "Don't ask. You won't believe it. Just fix me a drink and run a bath."

They had spent the night together, and somewhere in the small hours she confessed a growing need for him.

He pulled her close, telling her that she was important to him. He cared about her and would be there if she needed him but was unable to offer anything more than friendship. He simply couldn't handle any more responsibility. His daughter's welfare was all that mattered now.

Linda kissed him and said, "It's okay, Jack. I'm a big girl. I fly in, and I fly out. Let's see what happens."

He got off the elevator on the twenty-third floor and walked down a carpeted hallway, stopping at a pair of walnut doors embossed with gold letters: "ARNOLD, MESNICK, GARDNER, AND ASSOCIATES." And just below the firm name, In small letters: "A PROFESSIONAL CORPORATION."

Harry Arnold stood at the big window, staring down at the insectlike activity twenty-three floors below. The office afforded a panoramic view of the Los Angeles Country Club, the Twentieth Century-Fox Studios, the Beverly Hills High School, and beyond, all the way to the gunmetal Pacific, shimmering into infinity.

Jack sipped some coffee and studied the final page of Dr. Martin Sorenson's last will and testament. After a moment he closed the file and slid the blue folder back across the desk. "Is that it?"

The handsome, tanned attorney nodded. "A fairly simple document. Aside from the special bequests, everything went to Laura. I called Martin after Laura's death and asked him if he wanted to make any changes, but he never got back to me."

Arnold sat down and picked up a gold golf ball ornament. "The grants go to Columbia-Presbyterian Medical Center, the John Wayne Cancer Clinic at UCLA, the Scripps Clinic and Research Foundation at La Jolla, and a lifetime trust endowment for your daughter. As you can see, there are no surprises in the will, no strange bequests, no odd parties named, no illegitimate children, no skeletons, no secrets."

"Except for Sorenson's government activities."

"I wouldn't know anything about that."

"He never mentioned Rosemark to you?"

"No. Besides, I didn't see him that often. The last time was that Easter Sunday brunch. I think you were there."

"Isn't that curious? I mean, you handled all his business but hadn't seen him in six months."

"We spoke on a fairly regular basis but rarely saw each other. Nothing unusual about that."

"What about the buy-out of Dr. Emory?"

"What about it?"

"Martin told me the negotiations got a little testy."

"I suppose they did, but in the end it was an equitable settlement. Emory walked away with six and a half million." Arnold paused. "God, it's tough to believe they're both gone."

"Not just gone, Harry—murdered."

"I know. I just can't get myself to use that word."

"Did Sorenson ever mention a triangle?"

"You mean the geometric figure?"

"Yes, but it might have had a totally different connotation."

"Martin never mentioned anything about a triangle to me."

Arnold leaned back in his chair and juggled the gold golf ball. "What happened to your cheek?"

"Cut it shaving. Tell me something, did you manage all of Sorenson's business affairs?"

"Yes."

"Meaning you paid the bills—"

"And prepared the taxes."

"I'd like to see the checks, bills, invoices, accounts due, that kind of thing."

"Personal or corporate?"

"Personal."

"How far back?"

"Say, six months."

"What do you expect to find?"

Jack shrugged. "Any unusual expenses, incurred by the doctor or Laura. A one-time payment to some third party. I don't really know—I'm scraping the barrel."

Arnold pressed a button on a green console. "Betty?"

"Yes."

"Would you come in, please?"

A tall, slim brunette with big eyes and a friendly mouth entered the office. "You rang?"

"Yes, Betty, I rang," Arnold replied with a trace of amusement. "Take Lieutenant Raines to the file room and run the computer disks for the Sorensons' personal checking accounts."

"Household?"

"All noncorporate payments for the last six months. Anything else, Jack?"

"No."

Arnold rose, and they shook hands. "You ought to treat yourself to a new razor."

"I'm considering it. By the way, how come you have 'A Professional Corporation' written on the door?"

"It's just reassuring."

"To the clients?"

"No, to us."

Arnold's secretary sat alongside Jack, watching the display of checks flash across the IBM scanner.

The months changed, but the checks maintained a routine continuity: utility bills, landscaping service, interior plant service, dry cleaner, Marconda's Meat Market, California Animal Hospital, American Express, Jurgensen's Market, Neiman-Marcus, Bullock's, Union Oil. . . .

"Should we keep going?" the secretary asked.

"Please."

The checks followed a similar pattern. The girl pressed a button, and a new column of checks appeared. She glanced surreptitiously at Jack and wondered about the welt on his cheek so close to the crescent-shaped scar. She thought his soft brown eyes did not go with his profession, but then her only involvement with the police was an occasional traffic ticket.

Jack was unaware of the girl's attention. He had spotted something toward the bottom of the green column.

"Can you center this line of checks?"

"Sure."

She hit a key, raising the lower half to the center of the display screen.

"There. Between that Neiman-Marcus and Beverly Hills Auto Repair."

"You mean, Rockwell Contractors?"

"Yes."

"What about it?"

"Thirty-seven thousand five hundred and twenty-eight dollars . . ."

"And twenty-three cents," she added.

"Isn't that a hell of a lot of money?"

"I thought so, too. As a matter of fact, I recall checking with Laura Sorenson before issuing the check."

"Do you remember what she said?"

"That it was for some excavation work up at the house."

"Can you find the original bill?"

"Do you mind if I ask you why?"

"I visited the house almost every Sunday and never saw any excavation work."

"I'll be right back," she said.

He wondered if Laura had hidden some secret expense under the guise of a fictitious contracting company, but he shook it off, refusing to accept unfounded suspicions. But then how could he have missed seeing thirty-seven thousand dollars' worth of excavation; that much money would have produced one hell of a hole.

The door opened, and the secretary came in, carrying a bulky file in both hands. She placed it on the desk and quickly leafed through the invoices. "Here it is."

Rockwell Contractors was located on Pico Boulevard in West Los Angeles. The invoice was itemized under three principal categories: bulldozing, earth removal, and construction. There were detailed individual sums for lumber, electricity, lighting, installation, and labor. The period from commencement to completion covered ten weeks. The estimator's name on the invoice was Robert O'Neil.

"It's all there, Lieutenant."

"Thank you."

"Anything else?"

"Would you call my office and leave word for Sergeant Vince Rizzo to meet me up at Sorenson's Bel Air estate at twelve-thirty."

"Is that it?"

"Almost." He smiled. "How do I get an outside line?"

"Just dial nine."

"Thanks again. You've been very helpful."

He dialed the number and asked for Robert O'Neil. After a moment a gruff voice came on the line.

"O'Neil speaking."

"Robert O'Neil?"

"Yeah. Who's calling?"

"Lieutenant Jack Raines, Tactical Division, LAPD."

There was a pause before O'Neil said, "What can I do for you?"

"I'm working on a homicide case concerning the murder of Laura Sorenson and her husband, Dr. Martin Sorenson."

"I read about it. I didn't know them too good, but it's a goddamn shame."

"You did some work for the Sorensons in March of this year up at Chalon Road in Bel Air."

"That's right."

"Thirty-seven thousand dollars' worth."

"Yeah, something like that. It was last spring. What about it?"

"I visited that house almost every Sunday, and I never saw any construction work going on. So I'm curious about this bill."

"Well, the work was done down at the bottom of the hill, at the guesthouse."

"What was the nature of the work?"

"Hey, wait a minute, how do I know you're a cop?"

"You have a pencil, Mr. O'Neil?"

"Yeah, I got a pencil."

"Here's my badge number oh-six-six-four-three-one. Now call 555-6600—that's Tactical Division. Ask for personnel supervisor Charles Fitzsimmons. I'll call you back in five minutes."

"I got my hands full of work. What the hell do you mean, 'five minutes'?"

"Listen carefully, Mr. O'Neil," Jack said in a calm, measured cadence. "You call that number this minute, or I'll have the Sheriff's Office serve you with a summons, and I promise, you won't be digging any fucking holes for a few days."

"Hey, Lieutenant, there's no need for abusive language."

"You're absolutely right. I apologize. Now, call the fucking number."

There was a pause, followed by an audible sigh. "What did you say your name was?"

"Raines." Jack spelled it. "R-A-I-N-E-S."

"Okay, I'll take your word for it. Now, what can I do for you?"

"I'd like to know what you built at the guesthouse."

"Hold on. I'll get the file."

Jack waited and tormented himself over whether to light another cigarillo. Habit won over caution. He lit the brown Sherman, inhaling the strong smoke and promising himself he'd quit when the case was over.

"Raines. You there?"

"Yeah."

"I have the file. We built a subcellar."

"Under the guesthouse?"

"That's usually where you'd put a subcellar."

Jack ignored the sarcasm. "What kind of room did you build?"

"A private study."

"You have a key to that room?"

"Yeah . . ."

"I'd like you to meet me up there."

"When?"

"Well, it's eleven-fifteen right now—say, twelve-thirty."

"Okay. I guess I'd better bring the combination."

"What combination?"

"To the wall safe."

CHAPTER THIRTY

△

O'Neil's square head was too large for his narrow shoulders, and his thick arms swung far below his slim waist, giving him the appearance of a gorilla that had been on an extended diet.

Jack walked down the winding grassy slope beside the red-faced contractor, half listening to O'Neil's litany of complaints. "Jesus. Now that I'm out here, it all comes back. What a bitch of a job. We took two tons of earth from under that cottage without screwing up the water and gas lines." He pointed toward a line of ficus trees shading the guesthouse. "Mrs. Sorenson wouldn't let us touch those trees—had to work the Caterpillar around them."

"Is that right?"

"Yeah. Even the specifications were brutal. I mean, if we were a hair off some goddamn molding, the doctor made us do it over."

"I guess brain scientists have a thing about precision," Jack replied sarcastically, annoyed with O'Neil's complaints about his murdered clients.

The guesthouse was a one-story bungalow with ocher-colored walls and a red Spanish-tiled roof. O'Neil took out a large key ring, checked the ID tape on the key, inserted it in the lock, and opened the door.

The room was simply furnished: a desk, a sofa, two modern Swedish chairs, curtained windows, and a steel file cabinet. Several photographs on the wall depicted Dr. Sorenson at the sites of various archaeological expeditions; the single exception was a black-and-white photographic blowup of eight men and one woman posed in front of a building on Fifth Avenue. The caption read: "Fifth International Interdisciplinary Conference on the Future of Brain Sciences—New York Academy of Medicine, June 1974."

O'Neil waited for Jack to complete his cursory examination of the room before asking, "You ready?"

Jack nodded.

The contractor kicked a Navaho throw rug aside, bent down, grabbed a recessed iron ring embedded in the wooden planking, and pulled a four-foot-square section upright. The hinged section folded over, revealing a staircase. O'Neil hit a light switch. "Follow me, Lieutenant, and watch your step."

The subcellar den had the quiet elegance of a fine art gallery; soft, indirect lights played across framed paintings by Cézanne, Manet, Sisley, and Pissarro. A thick white rug covered the floor, the walls were lined with beige velvet, and a stained glass ceiling atrium, illuminated from within, cast soft glowing colors across the antique furniture.

"Pretty fancy, huh?" O'Neil commented.

"Yeah, pretty fancy."

O'Neil pressed a button on an electronic panel, and the lilting sounds of a Bach prelude, played with superb fidelity, filled the room.

"You ever hear purer sound?"

Jack ignored the question and asked, "Did Mrs. Sorenson come down here often?"

"When we first started, she'd look in to make sure we didn't do any damage to her trees, but once we got through with the excavation, she didn't come down anymore. At least not while I was here."

"What about the doctor?"

"Sometimes he'd be on our case every minute. Then weeks would pass and we wouldn't see him at all. I once asked him why he kept these terrific paintings down here under the ground, where no one could see them. He looked kind of funny at me and said, 'I can see them, Mr. O'Neil.' "

"Collectors are like that."

"Yeah. I once built a secret room for a millionaire insurance guy. You know what he kept in that room?"

"No, Mr. O'Neil, I don't know."

"Fish tanks. Wall-to-wall fish tanks. He'd go in that room and stare at those pretty little fish for hours. I think important money makes people nuts."

Jack looked around the den, thinking that despite the priceless paintings, the elegant antique furniture, and classical music, there was indeed a fine madness here. He checked his watch, wondering where Rizzo was. He wanted Vince to be present when they opened the safe, but his own curiosity precluded any further delay.

"Okay, let's see the wall safe."

O'Neil removed a Sisley snow scene from its place on the wall and pressed a small button. A square panel swung open, revealing a dull gray cylindrical safe with a numbered combination.

O'Neil took out a piece of paper and handed it to Jack. "Read off the numbers. I'll work the knob."

"Who else has this combination?"

"As far as I know, the doctor and us."

"You mean, your company?"

"Yeah. On special jobs like this we keep the combinations locked up with the job folder."

"Anyone else at Rockwell have access to this?"

"Only me and my son, who works with me. Mr. Rockwell's retired." O'Neil frowned. "Hey, Lieutenant, my company's bonded. We'd surrender this combination only on direct request of the owner or an official emergency like this. I've built maybe fifty, sixty of these private safes in Beverly Hills alone. It's a big part of my business, especially since all these fucking

Chinks and Iranians came over here with hot money. You don't think I would screw around with a client's private safe?"

"It's just a routine question, Mr. O'Neil. Now, let's open it."

O'Neil placed his right hand on the knob. "Go."

"Two full turns past zero to twelve."

Jack waited for the ticking clicks as O'Neil rotated the knob.

"Left past zero to thirty-three."

O'Neil turned the knob carefully. "Okay."

"Two full turns right, past zero to sixteen."

The clicks sounded and stopped. "Now watch it," Jack cautioned. "You're going to move it only two digits. Left to fourteen."

There were two distinct clicks. O'Neil gripped the handle and pulled down. The cylindrical door opened.

Jack moved to the safe and said, "Bring that desk lamp over here."

O'Neil unplugged the small lamp and connected it to an adjacent floor socket. Jack switched the light on and tilted the lamp, directing a shaft of light into the safe's interior. Crouching slightly, he noticed an obscure dark shape toward the rear of the vault.

He straightened up and glanced at O'Neil. "I want you to bear witness."

"To what?"

"To any object I remove from this safe."

"Whatever you say, Lieutenant."

Jack reached into the safe. His fingers closed around a velvet cloth that held a metallic object inside its folds. He withdrew his arm and tentatively unfolded the wrapping.

A gold triangle inscribed in cuneiform glittered in his open palm.

CHAPTER THIRTY-ONE

△

Dr. Lawrence Ettinger was the director of Middle Eastern antiquities at the Metropolitan Museum of Art in New York. He was a tall, spare, balding man whose fine, regular features were in startling contrast with his misshapen cauliflower ears. He had been a middleweight boxing star in college and for a while afterward had supported himself by fighting professionally at small boxing clubs in and around New York.

Besides his athletic prowess, Ettinger had been blessed with scholarly talents. He received his master's degree in the history of art at Columbia University and a doctorate in archaeology at Oxford. He was an acknowledged expert in the translation of Sumerian and Akkadian cuneiform and spoke fluent Hebrew and Arabic. He had also written a definitive biography of the great English Orientalist and epigrapher Sir Henry Creswicke Rawlinson.

Ettinger was a bit of an eccentric; although past sixty, he ran six miles every day through Central Park, wistfully hoping for a mugger to assault him so he could test his old boxing skills.

He admired Gabriella and accorded her the respect reserved for an elite circle of professional colleagues. He had awaited her arrival with great expectancy; the possible existence of a Moses tablet dominated his thoughts.

They were seated on either side of the slide projector in the darkened workroom, staring at the screen, oblivious to the shrill, staccato sound of a jackhammer echoing through the labyrinthine corridors connecting the underground network of offices, restorations rooms, and storage areas.

Ettinger puffed thoughtfully on his pipe as he studied the slide displaying the first section of Ithamar's last will and testament.

On the day of the great prophet's death in the land of Moab, before the mountain of Nebo, the voice of Yahweh commanded me, "Ithamar, son of Aaron, go up to the cave of eternity. There you will find my servant Moses." And I went up the face of Nebo into that chamber, and the great prophet said unto me, "At the place of the waters, in Meribah-Kadesh, I withheld from the people God's last word, for in my heart I feared they would pervert its meaning. This faithless act did cause Yahweh to judge me unworthy of entry to the Promised Land." So Moses did speak unto me, Ithamar.

The doctor uncrossed his long legs and turned to Gabriella. "I agree with Sabitini. The use of the word *pervert* is critical. Moses used that word on only one other recorded occasion—in Deuteronomy 16:19 addressing the priests, he warned them, 'A gift doth blind the eyes of the wise and pervert the words of the righteous.' "

Gabriella drew her jacket tightly around her shoulders. She felt chilled and fatigued from jet lag and lack of sleep. She tossed her pale hair and cleared her throat. "The Ithamar stone certainly makes a strong case for Moses' denial of entry to the Promised Land."

Ettinger nodded. "For Moses to commit an act of such awesome defiance he must have regarded God's word as nothing less than cataclysmic."

"There is another factor that lends credibility to the Ithamar text," Gabriella said. "According to the Old Testament, Moses violated Yahweh's trust at the place of the waters, but if you read Deuteronomy carefully, he did precisely what God ordered him to do. He struck the rock and brought forth water."

"There are countless theories as to why God so severely punished Moses," Ettinger replied. "It's confounded theologians for centuries. Every theory I've ever heard is ambiguous, but this text singularly reveals a clear and willful act of defiance by Moses."

Gabriella pressed a button on the projector, and the slide changed, displaying side two of the Ithamar stone.

The great prophet then commanded me, "Take this tablet, Ithamar. Upon it is inscribed the path to the last word of God. It is your sacred mission to place this tablet in the Canaanite city of Megiddo, where it shall be preserved into the midnight of time." And there, in Megiddo, did I place the tablet. And it came to pass, as Moses prophesied, that I departed Megiddo and lived out my time in the ancient kingdom of Ebla. And no man set his hand against me. Upon this stone I have inscribed my will and testament. Whosoever shall come upon it must read the triangles of gold and will know the chamber in Megiddo where lies the tablet of Moses.

Ithamar, son of Aaron,
priest of the Levi tribe

Ettinger walked to the projection screen and traced the triangular indentation at the top of the Ithamar stone.

"You've scaled this triangle to three inches on all sides?"

"Yes."

"And Sabatini believes there were three?"

She nodded. "Based on the thickness of the indentation and the historic importance of the number three to the ancient Hebrews."

"Without those triangles you'll have hell's own time. Megiddo was a powerful Canaanite stronghold. It did not fall to the Israelites until two centuries after Joshua had crossed into Canaan, and it probably covered an area of several hundred acres. You'll have to sift tons of earth, comb every crypt chamber and courtyard. You may be talking about a thirty-year dig."

"Well"—she smiled—"it took three thousand years to find the tomb of King Tut. Thirty years is a pause in archaeology."

"True. But I have to make a case to the board of governors to grant you a hundred and fifty thousand dollars. I can't tell them it's a thirty-year undertaking."

Gabriella rose and removed the slides. "But that's not an outrageous sum for a possible discovery of this magnitude. The last words of God inscribed on a tablet by the great prophet would be an archaeological treasure without parallel."

"Did Sabitini offer any opinion as to the content of those words?" Ettinger asked.

"Only that they might be an admonition or a prophecy rather than a commandment."

"I tend to agree, but it's all speculation. By the way, have you seen this?"

He handed her a copy of a wire story carried by the *New York Times*. The piece was headlined: MOSES' ALTAR BELIEVED FOUND. The article described the discovery of a twenty-seven-foot-high stone slab atop a mountain on the West Bank. The stone was inscribed in biblical Hebrew. The inscription on the altar bore the three Hebrew letters for "MSM," the biblical spelling of Moses. The Israeli archaeologists declared it the altar that Moses had commanded the biblical Israelites to build on Mount Ebal thirty-two centuries ago.

"When you consider the Ithamar text, the timing of this new Moses discovery is rather ironic," Ettinger remarked.

Gabriella nodded and shivered involuntarily.

"What is it?"

"Just a chill."

"Come. We'll get you some hot tea."

*   *   *

They got off the elevator and stepped into the vaulted rotunda with its soaring stone arches, stately Grecian columns, and fresh floral arrangements. They walked through a marble hall, passing imposing statues of Assyrian kings before entering the large, harshly lit public cafeteria.

The crowd had thinned, and they found a quiet table at the rear.

"Would you like some pastry?" Ettinger asked.

"No, thank you. The tea will be fine."

Gabriella studied the animated faces of the visitors and understood their excitement and shared their enthusiasm. She considered the Metropolitan the finest museum in the world. While she had other favorites like the Pergamum in East Berlin with its magnificent altar of Zeus and the Egyptian collection in the British Museum, none held the variety and grandeur of the Metropolitan.

Ettinger returned and placed a tray on the table. He refilled his pipe and glanced at a group of children enjoying milk shakes and ice cream, but his thoughts were centered on the Ithamar stone. He would have given a year's salary to be a part of the Megiddo expedition.

Gabriella sipped the tea and said, "You seem troubled."

"No, I was only daydreaming. I miss not being in the field. What a moment that must have been when you discovered the royal library at Ebla."

"Fortunately we managed to photograph and read hundreds of tablets before the Syrians sealed the dig."

Ettinger nodded. "We've got to exert international pressure on the Syrians to reveal the contents of those remaining tablets."

"It won't help. Gamasi will interpret them to suit Syrian political ideology."

"Well, on the basis of the existing tablets there's still a strong case to be made that Ebla was indeed the ancestral home of the Hebrews."

"Sabitini believes the Moses tablet will confirm that."

"Perhaps. But when I address the board of governors, I won't allude to the Syrians' being related to the

Hebrews. The museum operates in a global arena. I want to avoid current Middle East politics."

The voice on the loudspeaker announced that the museum would be closing in fifteen minutes.

"What do you think the chances are of obtaining a grant?" she asked.

"The Ithamar stone speaks for itself, and the possible existence of a lost edict or commandment is entirely plausible. In 1835 Rawlinson discovered one hundred and thirty commandments carved into a cliff face in southern Iraq. They included the legendary ten—not in the same precise language, but close enough. They were inscribed by Sumerian priests in 3800 B.C., more than two thousand years before Moses brought the tablets from Sinai."

Ettinger poured some tea and continued. "This fresh discovery of an inscribed Moses altar will help us with the board of governors."

"How?"

"It adds credibility to the possible existence of a tablet inscribed by Moses. The overriding factor, of course, is what's written on that tablet. A lost word of God is indeed the ultimate artifact and is bound to excite the board's interest. That's why I'm optimistic about securing the grant." He paused. "Still and all, asking for one hundred and fifty thousand dollars will take some persuading."

"I understand." She smiled and touched his hand. "Win or lose, I appreciate all your efforts."

"Don't thank me yet. Just keep a good thought. In any event without those triangles you may be a very old woman still poking around the crypts and chambers of Megiddo."

The loudspeaker paged Ettinger. "Excuse me," he said, and walked quickly to a wall phone at the far side of the cafeteria.

Gabriella suddenly felt depressed and wondered if it all wasn't hopeless. Besides the riddle of the quest itself, there was the lingering threat of physical danger. She recalled Sabitini's warning on the ride to the Rome airport: "Inspector Anjulo is certain that Claudon's murder is directly related to Pyramid International and Ebla. You may be in jeopardy." She had responded by relating her conversation with Lord Hamilton—that in Hamilton's view, Claudon's death bore no relationship to Ebla. Sabitini said no more, but at the gate he had kissed her and whispered, "Take care, and be alert. If there is the slightest suspicion you are being followed, go straight to the police."

She lit a cigarette, remembering the burly, florid-faced Englishman who had sat beside her on the plane and during the course of the flight asked numerous personal questions. At the time she thought he was flirting, but there was a moment when his eyes seemed to take on a penetrating menace—or was it simply imagined? Was she beginning to see assassins and killers in ordinary businessmen? She sighed and thought it would be a challenge all the way, a contest of knowledge and will against fear and suspicion.

Ettinger returned to the table. His face was flushed, and his eyes were curiously bright.

"That was a colleague of mine, a Professor Setlowe. He chairs the Middle East language department at UCLA. A Los Angeles detective named Raines brought a gold triangle to Setlowe's office. The triangle is three inches on all sides and inscribed in what Setlowe believes to be Eblaite cuneiform. A photostat of the triangle is being air-expressed. We'll have it tomorrow morning."

Gabriella was speechless, overwhelmed by a joyous rush of excitement.

"These are the small miracles that keep us going," Ettinger said exuberantly. "But let's not get too excited. This detective may have stumbled onto an artifact totally unrelated to the Ithamar stone."

Gabriella nodded, but a detail out of the recent past suddenly flashed in her consciousness. "What was that detective's name again?" she asked.

"Raines," Ettinger said, then spelled it. "R-A-I-N-E-S. Why do you ask?"

"That was the name of the Los Angeles police officer who was investigating the murder of Laura Sorenson."

She paused. "I wonder how he came across that triangle."

"What's the difference? The important thing is we'll have a copy of it in our hands by tomorrow morning."

"You know, America always amazes me." Gabriella smiled. "I've spent a lot of time here, but I never get over it."

"Get over what?"

"How a letter can travel three thousand miles overnight."

"Well, it's actually a special service," Ettinger said.

"Special or not, in Italy it takes three weeks for a postcard to get from Naples to Rome."

CHAPTER THIRTY-TWO

△

John Nolan swallowed some buttermilk, belched loudly, rubbed his stomach, and said, "You're asking me to authorize a trip to New York and London on the basis of nothing more than a goddamn artifact."

"The triangle is more than an artifact," Jack replied. "It happens to be a major clue to the location of the Moses tablet; collectors have killed for a lot less."

"You think some lunatic private collector is behind it all?"

"It's possible. It's also possible that the CIA or KGB had a hand in things, but the Syrians have the obvious motives."

"How do you figure that?"

"Everything that came out of Ebla constituted a political and cultural threat to the Syrians."

Nolan bit the end of a cigar. "I can go down the list of victims and give you a totally different theory."

"Go ahead."

"All right. Laura walked in on three-time losers, trigger-happy street thieves. Sorenson and Emory engaged in a top secret government project and were hit by the CIA or KGB. Claudon was killed by his own hand after mutilating a prostitute."

"It's a reach, John. It's all too convenient."

"Maybe, but there's also a flaw in your Syrian theory," Nolan said. "If the Syrians are eliminating the Pyramid group, why is the Bercovici girl still alive?"

"I'm sure she's on their list, but my guess is they started with the members of Pyramid."

"There's no motive. The Pyramid people were strictly financiers, invited and welcomed by the Syrians."

"You're operating out of an American logic—a Western logic that's totally alien to the Syrian mentality. Trust me, John, the Syrians will hit anyone who threatens their Islamic heritage."

Nolan lit the cigar and spoke through a cloud of smoke. "Well, you worked for the agency in that part of the world, so I have to give you an edge on that score. Have you got a line on this Bercovici girl?"

"According to Anjulo's report, she's a dedicated scientist. More degrees than a thermometer. Considered an authority in her field. She's cochaired the Middle East language department at Rome University for the past ten years."

"What about her personal life?"

"Single. Never married. Lives alone. Mother deceased. Her father is a cellist at La Scala in Milan."

"And she's in New York at the moment?"

Jack nodded. "The timing is perfect, John. I can question her and go on from there to London. Hamilton is the sole survivor of Pyramid. He's both a suspect and a possible victim."

"Why a suspect?"

"He may have made a deal with the Syrians."

"What kind of deal?"

"To get his hands on the Moses tablet and promise the Syrians to eradicate anything on it that alludes to their being descendants of Hebrews."

"Why would the Syrians need Hamilton?"

"He can get into Israel—to Megiddo. They can't."

"Have you protected that triangle?"

"I sent a photostat to Ettinger in New York and

placed two copies in the Tactical safe. Your secretary has a copy. Professor Setlowe at UCLA has a copy. I have two in my vault at City National, and Rizzo's got one. The original is in my wallet."

Nolan opened his desk drawer and handed Jack a copy of a document.

"What's this?"

"Hamilton's file—came in from an Inspector Ian Hiller, Scotland Yard Intelligence Division."

Jack studied the gray-smudged page:

> Lord Anthony Hamilton: Born October 18, 1912. Son of William George Hamilton, descendant of Earl of Spencer. Attended Oxford University, B.A. in the history of art. Served with Montgomery in Africa, intelligence officer with Eighth Army. Awarded Victoria Cross and Distinguished Service Order for bravery. Heir to a family estate, Melton Mowbray, Leicestershire. Won a seat in Parliament in 1960, served for fifteen years. Hamilton was created a viscount in 1962 by Queen Elizabeth II. Retired from Parliament in 1975. Lives in seclusion at family estate but is active in archaeological expeditions and is a director emeritus of the British Museum.

"Pretty impressive," Jack said.

"Inspector Hiller offered Hamilton protection, but he refused."

"Why?"

"You may get a chance to ask Hamilton personally—if he stays alive long enough." Nolan sighed with the weight of decision. "Draw expenses from Fitzsimmons; report everything through Rizzo."

"Thanks, John."

"Save it," Nolan replied, and got to his feet. "I'll level with you, Jack. This is a self-serving authorization. I can advise Commissioner Harris the case has assumed international aspects and our only chance to achieve a solution requires the services of a crack investigator to pursue the case abroad. I can also give Harris

enough eyewash for him to conduct a press conference." Nolan managed a smile. "Hell, Syrians, CIA,
KGB, and a Moses tablet ought to sell some newspa-
pers. It's a good feature piece for some enterprising
journalist. Keep the heat off everyone for a few weeks."

"You know something, John, you could make a small
fortune guest lecturing on the fine art of bureaucratic
survival."

"Call it whatever you like. I've always done my best
to protect the integrity of the department. Now I'm
trusting you not to make a horse's ass out of me.
Remember, you can't carry a weapon. You have no
official authority in New York or anywhere else. You
go by the book."

"You know me, John."

Nolan came around the desk and, using the cigar as
a pointer, said, "You're damn right I do. You're going
to have to control that temper. No freeway crap. No
assaults like the Pancho Villa business. You have a hell
of a mix here: CIA, maybe KGB, Syrians, and a bunch
of crazy collectors. You can be hit at any time, and you
won't know where the hell it's coming from."

Nolan's line buzzed, and he picked up the receiver.
"Yeah?" He listened for a moment and glanced at Jack.
"Harry Arnold for you."

"Sorenson's attorney," Jack explained as he came
around the desk and took the phone. "Hello, Harry."
He listened for a moment, then said, "You're sure of
that figure? Okay. Thanks. I appreciate it."

He hung up and turned to Nolan. "Arnold found an
invoice in Sorenson's corporate account. The doctor
paid two hundred and fifty thousand dollars to Pierre
Claudon for that gold triangle. The money was transferred to Claudon's account at the Credit Lyonnais in
Paris, three months ago."

"What does that tell us?"

"Three things. One: Sorenson had the triangle months
before Laura was killed. Two: Claudon knew Sorenson
had it. And three: They're both dead."

Nolan shook his head in dismay and murmured,
"Fucking mysteries."

They started toward the door, and Nolan said, "By the way, I had a visit from this fellow Piersall—the CIA man you assaulted. The agency believes you have something that belongs to them."

"Like what?"

"A code book called *Rosemark*. Piersall said the recovery of that book is a matter of national security."

"I don't know what he's talking about."

"That's what I told him. I said Jack Raines is a man of honor, a patriot."

"Absolutely true. Any country that protects its whales has my undying loyalty."

"Don't get cute, Jack; those guys play hard ball."

"I know. I used to play on their court."

"Then why fuck around?"

"Because as long as they think I have *Rosemark*, they'll try to keep me alive."

"So you're holding *Rosemark* as an insurance policy?"

"No comment."

"All right . . . just remember, anything happens to you, and Jenny is alone." They shook hands, and Nolan said, "You get in a jam, call me direct. And, Jack, if you don't come up with anything, invent something. I want this case closed."

CHAPTER THIRTY-THREE

⚠

"I'd like two scoops of maple walnut in a sugar cone," Jenny said.

"Anything for you, mister?"

"One scoop of chocolate chip," Jack replied.

"Cup or cone?" the boy behind the counter asked.

"Cone, please."

They were in Baskin-Robbins on Ventura Boulevard. Jack had had dinner at the Rizzos' and afterward suggested an ice cream dessert to Jenny. The Rizzo girls wanted to come along, but Vince chased them into their bedroom. He knew Jack needed some time alone with his daughter.

They came out of the ice cream parlor, licking their cones, and walked past garish neon signs that advertised pizzas, hamburgers, porno cassettes, records, and motels that had hourly rates.

"Pretty tacky," Jenny said.

"It's a long way from Bel Air."

"The thing is, Dad, the valley doesn't even look like California. It reminds me of pictures I've seen of highways in Oklahoma."

"When I was a little boy, the whole valley was one big orange grove. You could smell the orange blossoms as soon as you came over Coldwater Canyon."

"I guess it was beautiful," she said. "But it's hard to imagine."

"It was the Garden of Eden. Well, that was before fast food, fast music, and fast sex."

"Some boys in my class have sex pictures."

"Did you see them?"

She looked at him and touched the napkin to her lips and smiled coyly. "I don't think I'll answer that one."

"Just an innocent question."

"I'm fourteen, Dad."

"Practically a senior citizen."

"How do they get the girls to pose for those pictures?"

"Money."

"Maybe they like it."

"Can we change the subject?" He smiled.

"One of these days we're going to have to talk about it."

"About what?"

"Sex."

"Sure. Maybe I'll learn something."

"Come on, Dad. I mean it."

"Okay."

"Promise?"

"Scout's honor."

She took his hand, and he remembered that when she was a toddler, she'd put one finger in his hand and they'd walk up Doheny to Sunset and have chocolate cakes at Pupi's café. It seemed now to be part of another lifetime.

They turned the corner and strolled toward a tree-lined playground. The small park was well lit. Groups of teenagers were playing soccer, and a few old men were engaged in chess matches.

Jenny led him to a pair of swings. They sat on the wooden seats, swinging gently, eating their ice cream cones.

"Dad."

"Yes?"

"Can we go ice skating Sunday at the rink in Santa Monica?"

He sighed and chewed the last of his cone.

"Can we?" she pressed.

"I don't think so."

"Why not?"

"Come on, let's walk."

They started around the perimeter of the park, and he said, "I've got to leave town for a while."

She looked up at him. "For how long?"

"A few weeks."

"What's a few?"

"Three, four at the outside."

"That's a whole month."

"Maybe less."

"Why do you have to go?"

"The trip has to do with the case."

"You mean Mom's death?"

"That's right."

She stopped and turned to him. "But why? I don't understand."

"Because whoever killed Mom must be caught and punished."

"But nothing you do can bring her back."

He put his arm around her. "I know that. And I know it's hard for you to understand, but I can't help it, Jenny. It's something I have to do—not for Mom, for myself."

"Where are you going?"

"First to New York, then to Europe."

A soccer ball bounced up onto the walk. Jenny grabbed it and kicked it back toward the boys.

"Pretty good reflexes, kiddo."

"I need new track shoes, Dad."

"Okay. I'll tell Angela Rizzo."

"She's been swell to me. But I've never ever eaten so much spaghetti in my life."

"Well, it's good for you."

"When do you leave?"

"Tomorrow."

"Don't go. Please."

He placed his hands on her shoulders.

"I'll phone you every night if I can. You'll know where I am and how I'm doing and when I'm coming home. Okay?"

She nodded, and they walked silently out of the park, turned the corner, and started up the tree-lined street toward the Rizzo house.

"You know what?" he said.

"What?"

"When I get back, we'll start looking for a house."

"For you and me?"

"Who else?"

"Well, you might meet someone."

"I suppose that's possible, but the house will be ours."

"Can I help decorate it?"

"That depends how rich your tastes are."

"Oh, we can get nice stuff that isn't expensive. Angela took us all to Sears, Roebuck and got us new jeans. And we looked through the furniture part and it's not—" Her voice suddenly broke, and she burst into tears, sobbing, "Don't go, Daddy . . . don't go!"

He swept her up in his arms, hugged her, and whispered in her ear, "You just be a good girl. I'll be home before you know it." He kissed her cheek. "As a matter of fact, you can start picking out some furniture."

"Please don't go, Daddy."

"I have to, sweetheart. I just have to . . ."

CHAPTER THIRTY-FOUR

⚠

Pagan godheads stood atop tall cabinets like silent senti-
nels, guarding the artifacts scattered about Dr. Ettinger's
workroom. Gabriella concentrated on the magnified cuneiform inscription carved into the gold triangle. Her
straight pale hair fell across her shoulders, and the
scent of her perfume sweetened the musky air.

Jack watched her in fascination as she reduced the
cuneiform script into biblical Hebrew before finally translating the Hebrew words into English sentences. From
time to time her fingertips moved across the triangle's
wedged indentations with the same deft touch the blind
displayed reading Braille.

Ettinger had introduced them earlier that morning
before taking Jack on a guided tour of the museum.
After a light lunch Jack took a long walk through Central Park, trying to shake off the L.A. to New York jet
lag. He returned to the workroom and told Gabriella to
ignore his presence. She thanked him for his understanding and immediately turned her attention back to
the triangle.

She had assumed an almost ethereal presence in his

mind: a fantasy figure, a blond prophetess out of another time. He could feel himself being inexorably drawn into her arcane world of dead civilizations and mythical treasures. He thought her ability to translate the Eblaite cuneiform was nothing short of miraculous, but he wondered if she would survive her own expertise and whether she would be permitted to stay alive beyond the moment of discovery.

Gabriella felt as though a mystical force had risen from the triangle. The very spirit of Ithamar seemed to radiate from its glittering surface. She could barely contain her excitement as word after word fell into its logical place. An early mention of the goddess Ishtar was both thrilling and critical; it not only narrowed the area of search but also confirmed the period in question.

"Almost through." She smiled and proceeded to jot down a few Hebrew letters, matching them with the cuneiform wedges. She paused. Concentrated. Erased. Rewrote. Corrected.

She continued the exacting process of refinement for another twenty minutes before she snapped the magnifying light off and rotated her head from side to side, relieving the tension in her neck muscles. "You can't imagine what a difference it makes working from the original triangle."

"Original or copy"—Jack smiled—"it's amazing to see letters and words come out of those wedged lines."

"It looks more complex than it actually is. Once you know the key, it's just a matter of patience and tenacity."

The door opened, and Ettinger strode into the room. "Well"—he grinned—"I see you two are still talking."

"We haven't been doing much talking," Jack said.

"He was very patient," Gabriella acknowledged. "Actually I finished hours ago. I've been checking my translation. The message is remarkably clear."

She returned to her desk, sat down, and began to assemble her notes. A fateful silence enveloped the room as she pored over her notes.

After a moment she cleared her throat and in measured cadence read her translation aloud: " 'Ishtar, mistress of war. Queen of joy. Cobra of dread. Vigilant goddess of the temple. I follow your eyes. Forty cubits below the altar. Close to the east wall is the entrance to Reshef's tomb, and there is the passage . . .'

"That's where it ends," she said, "and I hope where the second triangle begins—if we find it."

"That remains in the hands of the fates, but we have to count our blessings," Ettinger replied. "The mention of Ishtar confirms the time period."

"You know, it's curious," Gabriella said. "A prophet of the cabala in Jerusalem said that Ishtar still resided in Megiddo—still possessed of great powers."

"Forgive my ignorance, but who is Ishtar?" Jack asked.

"A Canaanite goddess," Gabriella explained. "Half woman, half serpent. The sister of a rather hideous devil-god called Pazuzu."

"I've met him. He was on display at Sorenson's and Emory's. Laura mentioned that from the moment Pazuzu arrived a series of tragic events hit their friends and seemed to be moving closer."

"Closer to whom?"

"The Sorensons."

"Well, I for one place no stock at all in legends and myths," Ettinger said. "The fact is we have the Ithamar triangle, and for that we are forever in your debt, Lieutenant."

"It's a two-way street, Doctor. I have a very personal stake in all this."

"With that in mind"—Ettinger smiled—"I'd appreciate it if you would let me borrow the triangle for this evening. Its physical presence will be more persuasive with the board than anything I can say."

"It's yours," Jack replied. "By the way, what do you estimate its value to be?"

"You mean, if sold to a collector?"

"Yes."

"That would depend on whether the buyer understood the cuneiform message carved into its face."

"How does that affect its value?"

"If you merely accepted it as an artifact circa 1260 B.C., I would guess perhaps a hundred thousand dollars, but if you were aware that its message could lead to a tablet containing the last word of God"—Ettinger shrugged—"there is no price. Why do you ask?"

"Because Sorenson paid a quarter of a million for it."

"Well, if he knew its ultimate value, I'd say it was a bargain; on the other hand, if he assumed it was simply an artifact, he paid too much. In any case, this triangle could make you a very rich man, Lieutenant."

"There's only one problem with that. The triangle belongs to the Sorenson estate."

"I suppose that's true," Ettinger replied, and glanced at Gabriella. "What time is your London flight tomorrow?"

"We're booked on the three P.M. Pan American."

"Who's we?"

"Lieutenant Raines is going with me."

"I'm hoping to see Lord Hamilton," Jack explained.

"I see." Ettinger nodded. "Well, I've got to lock up here and go straight to the board meeting. Why don't you two have some dinner? Charge it to the museum."

"Won't you be needing Gabriella at the board meeting?" Jack inquired.

"She's met the board. I had a party in her honor at my house. The entire directorate was present. She showed up in jeans and sneakers, sat down at the piano, and proceeded to play hard rock blues."

"It wasn't quite that way—and you know it."

Ettinger kissed her cheek. "You're just too Italian for the board. Now go on, relax, enjoy the Big Apple. I'll phone you at the hotel the moment I have an answer."

CHAPTER THIRTY-FIVE

△

They strolled along the grooved stones bordering the park side of Fifth Avenue. It was late October, but an Indian summer had settled over the eastern seaboard, and the night air was warm and sultry. The last leaves of autumn stirred as the breeze murmured through the park. Old-fashioned lamps bordering the serpentine walkways glowed softly like long, curving amber necklaces.

On Fifth Avenue, buses hissed and gasped, horns sounded, yellow taxis darted in and out of the heavy traffic, distant sirens wailed, and rock music blared from ghetto blasters. The pedestrians were impervious to the cacophony and strolled at a leisurely pace, enjoying this last magical echo of summer.

Jack and Gabriella exchanged small talk, each of them somewhat reserved. He thought she looked younger and more vibrant than she had in the museum. The unseasonably warm night, the crowds, the traffic, and the pungent lingering smell of African animals coming from the park seemed to have elevated her spirits. She was radiant, striding along, her topcoat swinging open, her hair dancing in the night wind, her blue eyes wide with excitement.

"I know a fairly good Italian restaurant on Lexington not far from here," Jack said.

"Does it have to be Italian?" She smiled. "I really get my share of pasta."

"It's your night. Just name the place."

"The Green Dragon. I had dinner there with Ettinger and his wife. It was quite good." She paused. "Unless, of course, you don't like Chinese food."

"Me—not like Chinese food?" He put his hand on her shoulder. "I've been in hospitals, intensive care, critical condition, the priest about to give me last rites, and I say, 'Forget absolution, Father, get me some mushu pork.' " She laughed, and he continued. "Now, where's the Green Dragon?"

"Seventy-second and Third Avenue."

They crossed Fifth Avenue and continued east.

Gabriella said, "I understand we have a mutual friend in General Barzani."

"How do you know that?"

"When I spoke to him this morning, I mentioned your name."

"We were pretty close years ago."

"Barzani's in charge of the Megiddo expedition."

"Doesn't surprise me. There were more artifacts on his lawn than in the Jerusalem museum."

"When did you last speak with him?"

"It's been years."

"The general is not the same man you once knew." She paused and hesitantly said, "His . . . that is, Barzani's wife and two sons were killed on a bus in a terrorist attack."

Jack stood stock-still as a taxi screeched around him, the driver cursing magnificently. "Christ almighty . . ." Jack sighed. "I had no idea. I vaguely remember the children, but I knew his wife, Narda. A terrific girl. They met in the army." Jack resumed walking. "She was blond, blue-eyed—like you. She had that sabra quality, tough, unafraid, and a marvelous sense of humor. God, what a loss."

"I don't know how any man deals with that kind of tragedy," she said sadly.

"I can empathize with Barzani to a degree." Jack paused. "Laura Sorenson was my former wife."

The Green Dragon was a large L-shaped room with framed panels of Chinese snow scenes on the walls. Small candles flickered on the tables, and huge tufted lanterns decorated with green dragons were suspended from the ceiling.

They were seated in a dark corner close to the long ebony bar. Gabriella studied Jack's face as if he were one of her artifacts. She thought his tired brown eyes, bent nose, and warm, friendly mouth were like disparate features, randomly selected, but pieced together with an attractive harmony.

Their drinks arrived, and she raised her glass. "Cheers."

"Cheers."

She lit a cigarette, leaned back, and said, "Can you tell me how you came to find the triangle?"

"That's a long story."

"We have time."

"On one condition. I would like you to tell me everything you know about this case, starting with Ebla."

"It's a deal."

Outside, the sky had gone from indigo to black, and the balmy night continued to attract a heavy flow of pedestrians. Window shoppers, dog walkers, joggers, lovers, and muggers mingled and swirled along Third Avenue. No one paid particular attention to the blue Lincoln parked in a red zone across the street from the Green Dragon.

The wan-faced, slightly built driver chain-smoked nervously, the tips of his fingers orange with nicotine. The burly, florid-faced Englishman seated alongside picked up a CB high-frequency microphone. "This is Lincoln calling Havana. Over."

There was a static-filled pause. Then a voice came on in heavily accented English. "This is Havana. Over."

"We have them inside the Green Dragon. Third and Seventy-second. Over."

The Cuban parked in a black Buick on Sixtieth and Fifth Avenue replied, "I'm on station. Over."

"Stand by. We'll be back to you when they leave. Over."

"Havana reads, and out."

The Cuban assassin lit a cigarette and took a photograph of Jack Raines out of the glove compartment.

Across town, the thin-faced driver of the Lincoln sipped some brandy and turned to his burly companion. "I respect the fact you're running this bloody operation, Charlie, but I don't fancy that bloody Cuban."

"Not to worry," the big man replied with quiet authority. "Mendoza has superb credentials."

The hot, spicy Hunan dishes had come and gone along with the better part of two bottles of wine.

Jack had recited the chronology of the case from that Sunday at Laura's through the murders of Emory and Sorenson, including the possible involvement of the CIA and KGB in Sorenson's death and the fact that both doctors had been employed by the supersecret SOD agency. He spared her nothing, telling her in clinical detail the evolving Rosemark research and the injecting of brain soup into unborn rat fetuses.

Gabriella winced at the rat soup details, wondering if man's relentless misuse of science was not inexorably leading civilization toward that final abyss.

She lit a fresh cigarette, cleared her throat, and unemotionally related the events surrounding the Ebla expedition. She mentioned Sabitini's theory that the Moses tablet might confirm the Hebrew ancestry of the Syrians and perhaps establish a historic territorial claim by Israel to present-day Syria. She concluded by telling him the details of her phone conversations with Lord Hamilton.

Jack refilled their wineglasses and casually asked, "What kind of man is Hamilton?"

"He's always been supportive and generous. But." She shrugged.

"But what?"

"When he holds an artifact in his hand, a metamorphosis takes place. You can almost see his features change, as if some sinister force has taken hold of him."

"Isn't that mad, possessive quality endemic to all collectors?"

"I suppose so—in varying degrees."

"I thought I detected a little of that with Ettinger when I handed him the triangle."

"Well, that triangle is a very impressive artifact."

"How much help was it to you?"

"Quite a bit. It narrows the search at Megiddo. We can now concentrate our efforts on locating the temple of Ishtar. Of course, those two missing triangles are critical."

"Suppose they never turn up?"

"We do the best we can. Keep looking. Turning spades. Dusting. Sifting. Searching. It may take decades."

The pretty waitress took the check and disappeared. "What can you tell me about Dr. Amin Gamasi?" Jack asked.

She shrugged and criss-crossed the hot end of her cigarette across the glass surface of the ashtray. "We enjoyed a true fraternal relationship—until the Hebrew connection surfaced. Then he turned grim and formal. I suppose, too, this clandestine trickle of Ebla tablets finding their way to different museums has caused the Syrian officials some anguish."

"How are these tablets getting out of Syria?"

"Obviously some Syrian official is selling them."

"Gamasi?"

"It's possible. But he didn't seem like the kind of man who would steal artifacts from his own government."

"What does a man like Gamasi earn?"

"In Western terms it would not be very substantial."

"The Syrian penalty for stealing national treasures is pretty substantial," Jack replied with authority. "The theft of cultural objects would call for a public hanging in Martyrs' Square, in downtown Damascus."

"How do you know about Syrian criminal codes?"

"I was stationed in Tel Aviv with the CIA. We used to exchange political data on Syria with Israeli intelligence. That's how I met Zvi Barzani."

The warm October breeze enveloped them as they came out of the air-conditioned restaurant. Across the street the beefy Englishman held a sennheisir super directional sound gun out of the Lincoln's window, directing it toward the entrance of the Green Dragon.

"Do you feel the wine, or is it just me?" Gabriella asked.

"I feel it." Jack smiled. "Why don't we walk back to the hotel?"

"Fine with me. I feel as though I've put on five pounds."

The red-faced Englishman in the Lincoln spoke into the CB microphone. "This is Lincoln. Come in, Havana."

"This is Havana. Read you. Go ahead."

"They're on their way back to the Plaza. We'll rendezvous there. Over."

"Havana reads—and out."

They strolled past window displays of pumpkins and witches in black costumes flying broomsticks to yellow moons. The Halloween decorations seemed incongruous against the warm Indian summer night. Jack's thoughts turned to Jenny and he remembered taking her trick-or-treating years ago.

"Jack?" Gabriella asked softly.

"Yes?"

"What will you do if it turns out the Syrians are actually behind these killings?"

"What do you mean?"

"You can't achieve vengeance on an entire nation."

"Well, there are a lot of ifs, but I still hope to find the individual who ordered Laura's death, and if it turns out to be the Syrians, and if you discover the Moses tablet, and if its contents prove the Syrians are descendants of ancient Hebrews, I can make damn sure that information becomes public knowledge. That would tend to even the score a little. In the Arab world face is everything." He paused, and his voice was hard and tense. "I can't bring Laura back, but I may be able to give the Syrians something to remember her by."

They crossed Madison and walked south past small, expensive boutiques.

"When were you divorced?" Gabriella asked.

"Six years ago."

"That's a long time."

"Yes, it is."

"And yet you seem to feel responsible for her death."

"I feel a lot of things."

His brown eyes glittered dangerously, and she realized there were demons behind his calm demeanor. He was obsessed with vengeance and tormented by the past.

On the southeast corner of Fifty-eighth and Fifth the man in the jogging suit walked his motorbike into the alcove of the F.A.O. Schwarz store and looked north toward Fifty-ninth Street. He watched the Cuban get out of the black Buick and enter the rear seat of the double-parked Lincoln. He knew the Lincoln was the control car. The Cuban would do the killing.

The Lincoln was perfectly positioned opposite the Plaza fountain. The beefy Englishman aimed the sound gun at Jack and Gabriella as they crossed Fifty-ninth and Fifth.

Gabriella stopped to admire a gleaming horse-drawn

hansom cab stationed at the curb beside the Plaza fountain. She glanced at the driver, who wore a tuxedo complete with tails and top hat.

"Perfect night for a ride, lady," the driver suggested.

She turned to Jack. "You know, I've seen these carriages in American films and always wanted to take one through the park."

"Let's do it."

"Right now?"

"Why not?" He smiled and asked the driver, "How much for your best ride?"

"That would be a round trip—the scenic route, Park Drive North to Ninetieth and Fifth, thirty-five bucks."

"Okay."

They climbed up and leaned back in the soft leather seat. The driver clicked at the roan mare, and the carriage wheeled around, heading west on Fifty-ninth toward the Sixth Avenue park entrance.

Inside the Lincoln the burly Englishman turned to the Cuban. "There's a fork at West Seventy-second. They'll follow a serpentine route around a small hill. It's dark and wooded. We'll drop you and park on the other side of the S curve. You stay in contact. After the hit just walk down the far side of the slope. We'll be waiting."

The driver gunned the Lincoln, and the big car shot past the hansom cab. The professional assassins did not notice the single following light of a small motorbike.

Gabriella felt heady from the wine, and the soft park lights and rhythmic clip-clop of the horse's hooves added to her euphoria.

They noticed the glow coming from a jazz concert on the mall; a trumpet solo carried on the wind and sounded startlingly pure and magical. The warm breeze played against the last leaves of autumn and overhead a jet wheeled in low, streaking toward La Guardia.

"It's lovely," she said.

"Just like the movies." He smiled.

*   *   *

The Lincoln pulled over and stopped on the curb side of the east-west park drive. The driver placed the hood up and peered into the engine as if the motor had failed. His partner moved to the curb, turned his back to the traffic, and spoke into the walkie-talkie. "This is Lincoln calling Havana. Over."

"This is Havana. Read you. Over."

"They should be coming into view in a few minutes."

"I'm set."

"Remember, the girl is your primary target. Raines is icing."

"Relax, *amigo*."

The Cuban placed the walkie-talkie down and lay prone in the tall shrubs. He checked the M-16 carbine: safety off; starlight scope battery on; range two hundred yards; flat trajectory. He aimed up ahead at the fork in the roadway where for five seconds the carriage would approach almost head-on. He pressed the button on the night scope, and the roadway was bathed in a pale green light.

Satisfied, he set the rifle down and flexed the fingers of his right hand. He took a few deep breaths and glanced off at the towering skyscrapers bordering the park; their lights were like a maze of yellow eyes staring impassively down at the great park.

The Cuban wiped the beads of perspiration from his forehead and cradled the M-16. Once again he checked the firing systems and took dead aim at the fork. Several cars came around the curve, blurring past the black crosshairs projected on the starlight scope.

The Cuban's pulse raced as he saw the approaching side lanterns of the carriage.

He held the carbine steady.

The crosshairs bisected over the girl's right eye.

The Cuban's finger curled around the trigger. He squeezed it gently, increasing the pressure with the studied perfection of a marksman who knew precisely the centimeter of no return.

*   *   *

The man in the jogging suit slid the gleaming blade of the bayonet across the Cuban's jugular, pulling hard, pressing his knee into the assassin's back for leverage. A gurgling sound came from the gaping hole in the Cuban's throat. The decapitated head rolled a few feet from the body, the lips still moving, the eyes wide, staring. The man in the jogging suit thrust the bayonet into the Cuban's back all the way to the hilt, then moved quickly into the brush and righted his motorbike. He removed a nine-shot, .25 caliber Beretta automatic from the saddlebag, slipped it into his jacket, and walked the motorbike down the far slope of the hill.

The thin-faced, surly driver still peered under the hood of the Lincoln while his beefy companion spoke anxiously into the walkie-talkie. "Come in, Havana. Over."

He waited and repeated the message, but the only response was a thin crackle of static.

"The bloody carriage had to pass that bloody Cuban," the driver growled angrily.

The big man's attention was diverted by a single, small light coming directly toward them. "What the hell is that?"

"A bloody cyclist," the driver replied.

The motorbike sputtered to a halt just in front of the Lincoln's upraised hood. The man in the jogging suit asked, "Anything I can do to help?"

"No." The driver shook his head. "Just overheated."

There was a sharp report.

The big man's face exploded; a geyser of dark blood spurted out of his mouth and splashed across the engine block. He slumped over the fender.

Two more gunshots followed.

The stunned driver clutched his ruptured belly and fell backward, his skull cracking open against the sidewalk. The Lincoln shielded his body so that it could not be seen from the roadway.

*   *   *

The man in the jogging suit slipped the warm automatic back into his running jacket, wheeled the bike around, and moved into the darkness of the shrubs.

From his seat in the hansom cab, Jack saw the raised hood of the Lincoln and a big man sprawled across the fender apparently staring at the engine block.

The man in the jogging suit waited for the carriage to pass before emerging from the shadows. He climbed up on his bike, kicked the engine over, and drove off at a leisurely pace.

A blue-shaded desk lamp cast its cyan light into the deep circles under Bensinger's eyes. The CIA operative was seated at his desk high up in the Chrysler Building. Heavy drapes were drawn around the office windows. It was close to midnight, and Bensinger was edgy. The operation was out of control.

He had just come from the Bellevue police morgue. The two bullet-riddled bodies were bad enough, but the image of the decapitated Latino made Bensinger's hand tremble as he reached for a cigarette. A frozen grin creased the face of the severed head, as if the brain had registered something humorous at the very second of decapitation.

Bensinger took a deep drag of the cigarette, pulling the smoke way down into his lungs. He slid the bottom drawer open, removed a bottle of bourbon, and took a long swallow from the mouth of the bottle. He opened his shirt at the neck and loosened his tie. A muffled ring came from inside the desk. He opened the left drawer, removed a clear Lucite phone, and picked up the receiver. "Bensinger here."

"Piersall," the voice replied. "Go ahead."

"We lost Raines and the girl."

"How?"

"They unexpectedly hired a hansom cab and took a ride through the park. The agent who tailed them from the restaurant had trouble with his walkie-talkie. He finally established contact with one of our vehicles, but it was too late. When we swept the park, the police were all over the place. At a spot close to the traverse road the cops found the bodies of two men. They were blown away by hollow-head slugs from a twenty-five automatic. Their bodies were adjacent to a blue Lincoln with a raised hood. The police uncovered a cache of small arms in the trunk and a sophisticated sound gun in the front seat. The car was equipped with a high-frequency two-way CB unit. A couple of hundred yards away, on the reverse side of an S curve, they found the decapitated body of a Latino, an M-sixteen with a starlight scope alongside, and a VHF walkie-talkie." Bensinger paused. "There was no ID of any kind on the victims."

"Have the police identified the weapon used on the Latino?"

"A World War Two Wehrmacht bayonet. It was stuck in his back up to the hilt."

"Christ . . ." Piersall murmured.

"Inspector Konicky, Mid-Manhattan intelligence unit, has requested fingerprint ID's from Interpol."

"Why Interpol?"

"Dorchester Hotel matchbooks, five-pound British notes, and a two-day-old London *Times* were found in the Lincoln. The Latino had a pack of Cuban cigarettes in his shirt pocket."

"Do you connect the killings with Raines?"

"I do, yes. The carriage with Raines and the Bercovici girl passed right by that spot. It's my guess that a team of assassins staked out to hit Raines were themselves taken out." Bensinger sighed. "We're obviously not the only government agency concerned with the recovery of *Rosemark*."

"No other agency is responsible for the recovery of *Rosemark*," Piersall replied curtly.

"I'd still feel better if you called Ducca. This kind of double coverage has happened before."

"All right, I'll check it out." Piersall paused and asked, "Wonder why the killer used a bayonet on the Latino and a twenty-five automatic on the others."

"Confuse the cops, make it look like the usual freaky Central Park homicides. I don't know, Frank. But for chrissake, make sure no other agency is involved. We don't want to be shooting our own people."

"I'll speak with Ducca."

"When?"

"Now. Are you in position to stay with Raines and the girl?"

"We have taps on their hotel rooms. They're booked Pan Am to London, three P.M. tomorrow."

"Get on the flight."

"Okay." Bensinger paused. "You know, Frank, they may not have intended to hit Raines. They might have been trying to waste the girl."

"I'll call you back in five minutes," Piersall replied.

Bensinger hung up and leaned back in the chair. His mind shifted through the details of the triple homicide, but the killings defied explanation. His desk phone buzzed. It was the local safe number used by his wiretap squad stationed in the basement of the Plaza Hotel.

"This is Coleman."

"Go ahead, Lew."

"Raines and the girl have gone up."

"Who's on the tap?"

"Blank and Minardos."

"Okay. Rotate the crew at three A.M."

"Right."

Bensinger hung up and lit a fresh cigarette. He rose and walked to the drapes, pulled them apart, and stared at the multicolored fantasy of lights that traveled across Manhattan, all the way to the cliffs of Jersey.

The Lucite phone buzzed.

He walked quickly back to the desk and picked up the receiver. "Bensinger here."

"This is Piersall. I just hung up with Ducca. He assures me there is no other agency involved in recovering *Rosemark*."

"Then who took those guys out?"

"Probably some lunatic prowling the park." Piersall paused. "Just stay with Raines. We've got to keep him alive until he's ready to deal."

CHAPTER THIRTY-SIX

⚠

Jack woke up with a ravenous appetite and ordered a large breakfast for two. He got to his feet, stretched, and in a triumph of will forced himself to do twenty-five push-ups, followed by a few minutes of sit-ups. He sat on the green rug, puffing for a moment, and glanced at the television set.

A handsome blond woman who coanchored the network news reported a new Soviet threat to deploy a significant number of SS-22 missiles to counter NATO's installation of the Cruise missile. Despite the anchorwoman's vivacious style, her delivery seemed forced as if she were bored with the subject matter. Jack wondered how much money it took to get her out of bed at daybreak, grab a cab, have coffee, make up, and act seductive while describing Soviet doomsday missiles.

He slipped his robe on, stretched out on the bed, and dialed Gabriella's room. The phone rang for a long time, and he thought she had forgotten their breakfast date. On the eighth or ninth ring a breathless "Hello" came on the line.

"Did I wake you?"

"I was in the shower."

"Have you had coffee?"

"No. I'm starved."

"Breakfast is on the way. Throw something on and come over."

"I'll bring a bottle of champagne."

"It's only seven-thirty."

"We have to celebrate. Ettinger phoned late last night. The board of governors approved the grant."

"That's great news. Congratulations."

"I've already spoken to General Barzani. They've uncovered a marble column with plaques of Baal and Ishtar."

There was a loud knocking at the door.

"Tell me about it when you get here," Jack replied. "Our breakfast has arrived."

Gabriella spoke rapidly between mouthfuls of food, explaining the terms of the grant, the clause regarding exhibition rights and a bonus for Rome University's Middle East studies department. Her cheeks were flushed with excitement, and her eyes sparkled. Her pale hair was backlit by the sunlight and shimmered with the movements of her head. Jack made an occasional comment, his attention divided between the rush of Gabriella's words, the food, and the television set. She poured some more coffee and began to discuss the progress of the Megiddo dig.

Jack noticed something on the television and waved his hand. "Hold it."

"What is it?"

"Listen."

The local newscaster reported the events surrounding a triple homicide occurring late the previous night in Central Park. His commentary continued over a videotape of a fleet of police cars drawn up on the traverse road, their red lights flashing. A battery of night-lights illuminated an area on a hill where a blanket-covered body lay. A burly detective holding an M-16 with an attached scope and a walkie-talkie was being interviewed by a reporter. The detective stated the carbine and walkie-talkie had been found alongside the decapitated body. He continued to describe the shooting deaths of two other men on the far side of the slope. The time of all three murders had been loosely fixed at between 10:30 P.M. and midnight.

The reporter queried the detective on the disparate weapons used, a bayonet in the case of the sniper and a .25 caliber automatic on the other victims. The detective politely stated he had nothing more to say at this time.

Jack switched the set off and ran his fingers through his hair. "We passed that place probably minutes before the killings. You remember the Lincoln with the hood up?"

"Yes. There was a man peering into the engine."

"Right. Which means we had already passed the spot where this would-be sniper was found. We were probably in the crosshairs of his night scope."

"Well, then he obviously wasn't concerned with us."

"I guess so."

Jack poured some coffee, started to light a cigarillo, then stopped and blew the match out.

"No. That doesn't stand up. The sniper may have been killed before he had a chance to fire."

"But why do you relate this to us? From what I've read about Central Park these senseless killings are not uncommon."

"But a random killer wouldn't leave an M-sixteen with a starlight scope and walkie-talkies. That's expensive equipment."

"Still, it has nothing to do with us."

"How do you know that?"

"No one knew we'd be going into the park. *We* didn't know. It was a thing of the moment."

She rose and, using her palms, rubbed the champagne bottle so it swirled in the ice bucket. She then removed the bottle and began to unravel the gold foil cap.

Her blue eyes were smiling at him now. She was like a chameleon with many colors: by turns tough and determined, mysterious, childlike, and flirtatious. He wondered whether she consciously orchestrated her attitudes to suit the moment or if it was simply a reflex and he was creating a mystique around her to suit his own illusions.

She struggled with the cork.

"Here, I'll do that," he said, and took the bottle from her. "I suppose you're right. I'm beginning to see assassins everywhere—on freeways, in parks, and even in bed."

"In bed?"

"A few weeks ago I woke up out of a nightmare and almost killed a very sweet young lady. Hand me the glasses."

He held the cork and twisted the bottle. There was a loud pop. The pale foam rose up, and he quickly poured the champagne.

The phone rang, and he picked up the receiver. "This is Jack Raines." There was a pause. "Yes. Put him on."

He cupped the receiver and glanced at Gabriella. "It's London. Inspector Hiller, Scotland Yard."

Jack listened for a long moment, and Gabriella watched disappointment slowly cloud his eyes.

"I understand . . ." he said disconsolately. "If there is no legal recourse, I suppose we're stymied." He paused. "No, no. I appreciate your position."

"What's wrong?" she asked.

"Just a moment, Inspector." He cupped the receiver. "Lord Hamilton has refused to meet with me."

"Let me speak to the inspector."

"Why?"

"Please, Jack. Listen to me."

He uncupped the phone and said, "A Miss Bercovici is here with me now. She's a principal in this case and would like to speak with you."

He handed Gabriella the receiver.

"Inspector, can you relay a message to Lord Hamilton?" She paused. "Please tell him that Mr. Raines is coming with me. And that we will be bringing with us a triangle—a gold triangle." She listened while the inspector repeated the message.

"That's right . . . a gold triangle. No, there's no need to phone back. Thank you."

The CIA agents stationed in the hotel's basement removed their headphones. Their long vigil had proved disappointing; neither Raines nor the Bercovici woman had mentioned anything relating to Rosemark.

CHAPTER THIRTY-SEVEN

△

They hired a taxi at Nottingham Station and traveled along the single-lane asphalt road through the village of Melton Mowbray out into the countryside. Brilliant rays of sunshine knifed through low, scudding clouds, casting dark and light patches across rolling green meadows. Flocks of sheep grazed serenely in the timeless pastoral setting.

"Look," Gabriella said, pointing skyward toward a covey of birds flying high and fast in a straight arrow formation.

Jack watched them until the arrow dissolved into a formless cloud vanishing over the distant hill.

"Lovely, isn't it?" she said.

"Like a painting."

But for Jack the specter of faceless assassins lingered, and though it was sheer speculation, he believed the killings in Central Park were directly related to their ride in the hansom cab. The M-16 with night scope, walkie-talkies, and placement of the stakeout indicated a professional hit team. And if he was right, a maddening question remained unanswered—the identity of the man or men who had taken out the trio of assassins.

The only logical answer pointed to CIA operatives assigned to protect him until he struck a deal with the agency for the return of *Rosemark*. He took some satisfaction in the thought that the small code book with its baffling chemical formulations was already acting as an insurance policy.

The Austin taxi slowed and turned off the main road at a signpost that read HAMILTON HALL. The private road wound its way through a thick stand of pine trees before sloping down into a wide valley dotted with grazing cattle. They drove slowly, climbing gradually for five more miles before catching their first glimpse of the sprawling Tudor manor house.

Lord Anthony Hamilton greeted them in the spacious eighteenth-century salon. Medieval tapestries depicting hunting scenes hung from the walls, and antique furniture rested on a magnificent Oriental carpet. Floor-to-ceiling French windows opened onto a wide terrace overlooking immaculately tended gardens.

Hamilton kissed Gabriella's cheek and shook hands with Jack. "You've had a pleasant trip, I trust," he said, and flashed a broad smile. "Sit down, sit down." He indicated a silk embroidered love seat. "Now, what can I fix you to drink?"

"A Scotch over ice," Jack said.

"And you, my dear?"

"A sherry, please."

Hamilton's belly heaved against the constraints of his velvet smoking jacket, but despite his bulk, he moved with surprising agility, his shoulders straight, his bearing almost military.

He fixed the drinks and spoke in a thin, reedy voice that betrayed his advanced years. "You know King Edward the Seventh used to shoot birds on this estate. Yes, these grounds have been the scene of many a royal hunt. Now we have these so-called conservationists opposed to the blood sports. But, of course, in the end tradition will prevail. It is, after all, England's past that has caused her to endure."

Hamilton crossed the rug and handed them their drinks. "I think Ogilvie said it best. 'This heritage none can take—this spirit time cannot break.' "

He raised his glass. "To the dig at Megiddo."

He sipped the sherry and sat down opposite Jack. "I hope you understand my reluctance to meet with you, Mr. Raines," Hamilton said apologetically. "It was nothing personal. I simply cannot tolerate intrusions in my private life over matters I can neither change nor control."

"I understand," Jack replied. "But you're the sole surviving member of the Pyramid group, and I was hoping you might be able to clarify certain aspects of this case."

"I'm afraid not."

"That's too bad"—Jack paused—"because the history of this case tells me that you're in mortal danger."

"I'm not questioning your professional acumen, Mr. Raines, but your opinion is based on nothing more than instinct and speculation."

"That may be true, but if I were you, I would reconsider Inspector Hiller's offer of protection."

"You may very well be right, but at my age the only thing left to fear is senility. That is not to say I don't respect danger. On the contrary." He sipped his sherry and continued. "As a young man I faced death many times, and, believe me, Mr. Raines, I understand fear, but it's too late and too tiresome to worry about phantoms and assassins."

"But, like it or not, you are part of a complex case that directly concerns my own safety and Miss Bercovici's safety—and that bothers me."

"And well it should, my boy," Hamilton agreed. "I understand your position, and I'll be pleased to answer any questions you care to put to me."

"Thank you."

Jack rose, paced for a moment, and asked, "In your

opinion, could Sorenson and Emory have been murdered by a team of assassins hired by Syrians?"

"Absolutely not. It is inconceivable that Syrian officials would dispatch killer squads to Los Angeles."

"What about Rome?"

"Ah, you're referring to my late friend Pierre Claudon. As I told Gabriella, Pierre was cheating people. Dangerous people. He sold illegal and forged artifacts. In my view, his violent demise is totally unrelated to the California killings."

"Could Claudon have been selling Ebla tablets for Gamasi?"

"Anything is possible, Mr. Raines. But knowing Dr. Gamasi's dedication to his profession and his respect for the cultural integrity of his country, I would say that it was highly unlikely." Hamilton paused and turned to Gabriella. "By the way, my dear, congratulations on your success in New York."

"We really owe everything to Mr. Raines," she said. "Once Ettinger showed that triangle to the board of governors, we had our grant."

"And from what you told me, on our terms," Hamilton added. "Equal exhibition time and my name credited on all U.S. exhibits."

"*If* we find the Moses tablet," she said softly.

"But we now have the primary clue—the triangle."

"Only one of three."

"Yes, one of three." He sighed.

The sounds of chirping birds and the distant bark of a dog echoed into the high-ceilinged salon. Hamilton's eyes suddenly narrowed to slits, and his pale cheeks flushed. "May I see the triangle, sir?"

Jack nodded and slowly unwrapped the velvet cloth. "Go ahead, take it."

"You're very kind, Mr. Raines."

Hamilton's hand trembled as he grasped the triangle. They watched him as he scrutinized the artifact from a variety of angles like an expert jeweler examining a diamond to determine its purity.

He then crossed to the desk and picked up a leather-handled magnifying glass and studied the cuneiform inscription, first one side and then the other.

"Can you tell me how you came by this?" he asked.

"I found it in a vault belonging to Dr. Martin Sorenson."

"And where did Sorenson get it?"

"He bought it from Claudon for a quarter of a million dollars."

Hamilton's eyes blinked in surprise. "A quarter of a million . . ." he murmured. "You're certain?"

"Absolutely."

"How did Claudon acquire the triangle?"

"I was hoping you could tell me."

"I, sir?" Hamilton asked incredulously. "I'm afraid not. I can, however, offer an educated guess."

"Go ahead, please," Jack said.

"We know this triangle was taken from the Ithamar stone in the crypt at Ebla. It is therefore logical to assume it was initially appropriated by a Syrian official."

"If we take that one step farther, would Gamasi have been that official?"

"No, no, not at all," Hamilton replied quickly. "One of his underlings perhaps, but not Gamasi. As I said before, he's too honorable a man to stoop to petty thievery."

"The sum involved was not petty."

"True enough," Hamilton agreed. "There are people who would sell Damascus for a quarter of a million dollars."

"But would Gamasi?" Jack pressed.

"You'll have to ask him yourself."

"How?"

"I suggest you speak with Professor Sabitini. He and Gamasi were quite close."

"They still are," Gabriella added.

"Well, then, Mr. Raines, it appears you will have to go to Rome."

"I suppose so." Jack paused. "You know, there's a business aspect to all this that puzzles me. As I understand it, you've advanced one hundred thousand dollars to help finance the Megiddo dig. Why? I mean, the odds of finding a Moses tablet are not too terrific."

"Risks are simply part of the hunt. I've always been something of a gambler—if the stakes are high enough."

"But even if this tablet surfaces, the best you get is exhibition rights."

"My dear man, if our brilliant lady here is successful, I will, even if for only a moment, hold in my hand the last word of God. You can't possibly understand what that means to me."

"I have a vague idea." Jack smiled. "I'm sort of hooked myself."

"Well, is there something else, Mr. Raines?"

"Just a few routine questions."

"Yes?"

"When did you last speak to Sorenson?"

"Some months ago. We discussed the possibility of a dig in Peru. Sorenson was not interested. He seemed preoccupied. Troubled. And nothing came of it."

"What about Emory?"

"I haven't seen or spoken to him since the conclusion of the Ebla expedition."

"When did you last speak with Dr. Gamasi?"

"I would say during the late summer of 1980."

Jack nodded. "Thank you. I appreciate your time and hospitality."

"A pleasure. Do you have transportation back to the station?"

"Our taxi is waiting."

"I would have had my chauffeur meet you, but the Bentley is undergoing repairs. There was a time when I maintained several touring cars but now the Bentley suffices. You see, I seldom leave the house."

He ushered them into the marble foyer and kissed Gabriella's cheek. "Remember, my dear, keep this old boy informed."

"Every step of the way."

"I will join you at the precise moment of discovery."

"Nothing would please me more." She smiled.

Hamilton shook Jack's hand. "A distinct pleasure to

meet you, Mr. Raines. I hope you succeed in your quest."

"Thank you." Jack paused and said, "Now I'd like to have that triangle back."

Hamilton smiled broadly. "How could I have forgotten? Forgive me. The excitement, you know."

He reached into his pocket. "Here we are."

"You know something." Jack smiled. "I wouldn't want to play poker with you. Chess maybe, but never poker."

Hamilton roared with laughter and waved good-bye.

He watched the taxi disappear, then closed the door, walked quickly into the study, picked up the telephone receiver, and dialed Dr. Amin Gamasi at the Ministry of Culture in Damascus.

CHAPTER THIRTY-EIGHT

△

The restaurant's walls were made of brick and decorated with long tendrils of real ivy. The stereo sounds of a jazz trio were lost in the noisy din of high-pitched chatter and clattering dishes. The small, square dining room was crowded with well-dressed Londoners who seemed to be enjoying themselves. The pungent aromas of garlic, perfume, and tobacco mingled and drifted across the room.

Jack and Gabriella sat at a table close to the open kitchen. They were working on their second bottle of a Sancerre but ate their linguine and clams with a disappointed reluctance. The pasta was overcooked, and the clams were tough.

Gabriella wore a colorful Saint Laurent silk blouse and a matching challis skirt; a large scarf was draped casually over her shoulders.

Jack chewed on a particularly tough clam and finally gave up, placing the residue into the folds of a napkin. "These clams taste like sugarless gum."

"I warned you," Gabriella said. "The English have problems grilling lamb chops. I'll never understand why you insisted on an Italian restaurant when we're leaving for Rome in the morning."

Jack swallowed some wine and shrugged. "I had this terrible craving for pasta."

"Sudden cravings can be dangerous." She said it simply, but her attitude carried an unmistakable seductive quality.

"You know something?" He smiled.

"What?"

"You ought to wear dresses more often."

"I happen to own quite a few dresses—expensive dresses. A pretty dress lifts my spirits. I simply don't have occasion to use them." She hesitated. "Or anyone to wear them for."

The waiter emptied the last of the wine into their glasses. "Will there be anything else, sir?"

"How about a Sambuca?" Jack asked Gabriella.

She nodded. "And a double espresso."

"Two Sambucas and two double espressos."

"Would you care to see the dessert tray?"

"No, thanks. Just the coffee, Sambuca, and a check."

The waiter left, and Jack lit a cigarillo. "Tell me something, did you actually show up at that party in sneakers and jeans?"

"What party?"

"The one Dr. Ettinger gave in your honor. When you met the museum's board of governors."

She tossed her hair and smiled. "It wasn't like that at all. Ettinger said it was casual. I wore designer jeans, an expensive Armani blouse, and leather boots."

"And then you went to the piano and played hard rock."

"Not quite. First I played a very romantic Chopin nocturne. Then I followed it with 'Piney Brown,' a classic Kansas City stride blues."

The waiter served their Sambuca and coffee.

Jack sipped the liqueur and shook his head. "You're more of a mystery than those artifacts you go after."

"Not at all. I couldn't be less complicated."

"How do you know about American jazz?"

"I've always been fascinated with jazz. After Cambridge, I went to New York and studied anthropology at Columbia. I had quite a few friends, and we used to go to the jazz clubs on Fifty-second Street and the Village. I collected records and read everything I could get my hands on about the history of jazz."

"So you became something of a connoisseur."

"Not really. I guess you'd call me a student of jazz. I once had the good luck to see Oscar Peterson at a small club out on the Island," she said wistfully, and looked toward the center of the dining room. Her eyes were wide and penetrating as if she were staring into another time and place. "Peterson was really something," she murmured, then turned to Jack. "He did a guest solo that night. I'll never forget it. He walked between the tables, those big black hands dangling in front of him. He sat down in a blue spotlight and played something out of a Debussy prelude. But it was jazz. Complex. Full of ideas and technically astonishing. I wanted to speak with him, but I didn't have the courage."

Her eyes suddenly seemed clouded by broken dreams. He touched her wrist and smiled. "Who the hell are you?"

"You know all about me."

"Okay. Who were you?"

"No different from any other girl you've met. I had all the childish fantasies. I wanted to act, paint, sculpt, be a ballerina, and fall desperately in love with a Russian poet."

"Sounds like my daughter; only you'd have to add baseball and lose the Russian poet."

"What's her name?"

"Jenny."

"How old is she?"

"Fourteen."

"You're going to have to be very patient. She's moving into a difficult age."

"I've been getting those signals."

The waiter picked up the check along with Jack's American Express card.

Gabriella took out a cigarette and used the table candle to light it. She exhaled, leaned back, and stared

at him. Her fixed gaze was disconcerting, and he asked,
"What is it? Am I drooling?"

"I'm sorry." She smiled. "I was just wondering about
something."

"What?"

She shook her head. "No, it's too personal."

"Go ahead, say it. I promise not to be offended."

"I was wondering about your motives for pursuing
this case. I'm not playing Freud, but it occurred to me
that by seeking vengeance, you may subconsciously be
trying to reclaim the memory of a woman you lost a
long time ago."

"No. Not a chance. What you're suggesting is the
ultimate macho trip. I've got a lot of flaws, but ego isn't
one of them."

"That was a very Latin question I asked. Italian men
never accept the loss of a woman they once loved. Not
after divorce, not even after death. I'm sorry. I shouldn't
have asked. Your personal reasons are none of my
business."

"It's okay. I tried to explain all this to my daughter.
She didn't understand, and you probably won't either.
I don't know if it's genetic or what the hell it is, but
ever since I can remember, if someone shows me love,
kindness, or loyalty and gets hurt—I mean, willfully
damaged—I have to even the score. It isn't so much for
the victim as it is for me, and it has nothing to do with
possession or ego."

"But in this particular case, given the set of circumstances with your daughter alone, the risk hardly seems
worth it."

"In a pragmatic sense you're right, but if I walked
away, I'd be risking everything. Nothing would matter. I might as well be dead."

The waiter brought the check, and Jack signed the
voucher.

"Was everything satisfactory?" the waiter asked.

"The pasta was memorable," Jack replied. "Give the
chef my compliments."

"Thank you, sir."

"That's one way to make sure the quality never improves." Jack smiled. "I mean, why break tradition?"

She smiled and brushed the hot end of her cigarette lightly across the surface of the ashtray and asked, "What did you think about Hamilton?"

"He revealed himself only once—when I explained how Sorenson acquired the triangle."

"You mean that Claudon was the sales agent?"

"No, that didn't get a big reaction. The amount Sorenson paid for the triangle surprised Hamilton. He blinked when I said it was a quarter of a million. I have a feeling that Claudon offered the same triangle to Hamilton at a different price."

"Perhaps Claudon offered Hamilton a second triangle."

"It's possible. But I still think the prices were different."

"Is there any significance to that?"

"I'm not sure," he said, and drained the last of the Sambuca. "Ready to go?"

"I was ready to leave after the first bite of linguine." She smiled.

"My fault," he said as he rose and pulled her chair out. "We should have had a sandwich at the hotel."

"No. It was fun to get out. At least the wine was good."

"And the company?"

She flashed a smile. "Well, well, the hard-boiled detective is fishing for compliments."

"It's my Anglo-Saxon insecurity."

The night sky was starry, and the brisk wind refreshing. They strolled through a maze of narrow cobblestoned streets before cutting across Berkeley Square. The tall plane trees in the famous park were almost bare, and the fallen leaves swirled around their feet. The walkway was softly lit by turn-of-the-century lamps, and lovers sitting on benches embraced without regard to the stares of passersby.

"I love this city," Gabriella said. "The best time in my life was spent here."

"That has the ring of an old but passionate love affair."

"It was more romantic than passionate. We both were very young. He was American, a medical student."

"What happened?"

She put the collar up on her topcoat. "He went home after the semester. His older brother was called to service in Vietnam, and his parents asked him to continue his studies at home. He never returned to Cambridge."

"Well, be glad you had the moment."

"You sound remarkably like Sabitini," she said. "That's his philosophy. Take the moment."

A gust of wind played with her hair, and the scent of her perfume drifted toward him. She walked under the streetlamp, and its light suddenly sculpted her face out of the darkness, the arc of her cheekbones illumined, the hollows dark. Her eyes were radiant and midnight blue.

He put his hand on her shoulder, turning her toward the light.

"What is it?"

"There are times when the light paints your cheekbones and eyes in a very perfect way."

She stared at him a moment, then impulsively kissed him on the cheek. "That's a wonderfully sweet thing to say."

They picked up their keys at the desk and rode up the elevator to the fifth floor. Two robed Arab sheikhs, surrounded by three black-suited Africans, passed them in the hallway.

"Those guys looked deadly," Jack said.

"You mean the Africans?"

He nodded. "I've never seen skin color like that; it was blue—and those scars."

"They're Sudanese. The scars are carved into their faces almost at birth; it's a tribal ritual."

"How do you know that?"

"I told you, in between jazz nights I studied anthropology."

"I keep forgetting."

"Well, you'd better get used to it." She smiled. "I'm a genius."

"I won't hold it against you."

They stopped at her door, and she said, "I suppose this is where I ask you in for a drink."

"Only in bad American movies."

"Well, what do you say?"

"It's four P.M. in Los Angeles. I want to phone Jenny, and we've got to get up at the crack of dawn."

She nodded. "I'll meet you in the lobby at seven-thirty."

"Right."

They stood for a moment in an awkward silence. Then he took her face in his hands and kissed her softly on the mouth.

"Good night, genius," he whispered.

CHAPTER THIRTY-NINE

△

The chatter of passing students echoed through the open window of Sabitini's office. Jack watched the professor, hunched over a magnifying glass, studying the triangle.

After a moment Sabitini got to his feet. "An astonishing piece of history."

"Astonishing enough to motivate four murders?"

"Unfortunately the answer is yes. There are collectors who would kill for this, especially when one considers what it may lead to."

"Ettinger called the Moses tablet the ultimate artifact."

"Without question." Sabitini nodded. "Come, let me show you something."

He strolled past display cases lining the walls of his office. "You see this gold scepter, it belonged to Rameses the Second, thirty-three hundred years ago. The hieroglyphic inscriptions speak of the great temple at Karnak. And here"—he picked up a bronze scarab—"this froglike fellow carries an inscribed message concerning fig plantations in Thebes."

He moved to a glass case containing a row of wax

objects shaped like bars of soap. "Carnelian seals belonging to Cleopatra, the queen of queens."

Sabitini gently lifted a leather parchment covered in familiar cuneiform wedges. "This scroll was written by an engineer in four thousand B.C. It describes an irrigation system in Sumer, southern Iraq, and is remarkably similar to systems still in use.

"I could take you down to our own exhibition hall and show you absolute wonders of ancient creativity in all the arts and sciences. But nothing here or in any university, museum, or private collection would equal a discovery that brought to light the last word of God inscribed by his great prophet Moses. Its value historically, scientifically, and theologically is beyond conception. Think for a moment. What did God say? What do those words portend? Why was Moses fearful of relaying its contents to the Hebrew tribes? Will those words destroy the very fabric of the Judeo-Christian religious precepts? If it is a prophecy rather than a commandment, does it contain a warning to man? Does it alter our perception of the one Almighty God? And, finally, does it confirm the Hebrews as ancestors of the Syrians?" He paused. "If its text addresses any of these questions, it is indeed the ultimate artifact."

"What would you say the odds are of finding that tablet?"

"It depends on two factors: whether the directions on the first triangle are accurate, and, if they are, whether the other triangles turn up."

"Let's assume they don't."

"In that case there are no odds; without the remaining directions the search could stretch over decades. Then again, sometimes we succeed by pure chance."

"That's hard to believe."

"It's true. The greatest archaeological discovery in modern times was found by chance. In 1799 a corporal in Napoleon's infantry was making love to an Egyptian girl in a marsh, alongside the Nile. He saw his officer approaching and pulled up his pants and ran for a few meters before falling flat on his face. You know what that amorous French soldier tripped over?"

"Not a clue."

"The Rosetta stone. And that legendary basalt slab gave the great epigrapher Champollion the key that unlocked the four-thousand-year-old mystery of Egyptian hieroglyphics." Sabitini relit the cigar. "So, you see, in archaeology luck almost always wins out over intelligence."

"Like police work." Jack smiled.

"More or less."

Jack glanced at Cleopatra's carnelian seals for a moment, then turned to Sabitini. "I understand you're on speaking terms with Gamasi."

"Yes. He's made a genuine effort to restore our relationship."

"Why?"

"We archaeologists share a very strong professional bond." Sabitini shrugged. "Perhaps that bond transcends political differences."

"Can you arrange a meeting for me with Gamasi?"

"You realize Damascus is a haven for the most violent terrorist organizations in the world, and Americans are not exactly welcome in Syria these days."

"Maybe Gabriella could go with me. After all, she knows Gamasi and speaks Arabic."

"That would be impossible. She leaves for Megiddo tomorrow." Sabitini paused. "You're certain you need a meeting with Gamasi?"

"Absolutely. He's been a critical part of this case from the very beginning."

"What makes you think he'll agree to see you?"

"I have to depend on your persuasiveness."

"You're putting me on the spot."

"No choice."

"It's a dangerous trip."

"I understand."

"All right." Sabitini sighed. "I'll speak with Gamasi, but first you must obtain a visa to enter Syria."

He quickly scribbled a note and handed it to Jack. "The address of the Syrian embassy, Piazza Coelli, number one. It's fifteen minutes by taxi. Ask for Vice-Consul Hamidi. I'll phone him. He's a friend of mine. Perhaps he can expedite your visa."

*   *   *

"Religion?"

"Protestant."

Hamidi jotted the answer down on the triplicate form. The red, white, and black striped Syrian flag with two green stars hung limply behind the embassy official, and a large portrait of Hafez al-Assad, the somber-faced Syrian president, peered down at them from its place on the wall.

"Profession?"

"Police officer."

The dark, thin-faced diplomat glanced up at Jack. "Rank?"

"Lieutenant."

"What branch?"

"Tactical Division, Los Angeles."

"Purpose of your visit?"

"Business."

"The nature of your business?"

"I hope to have a meeting with Dr. Amin Gamasi of your Ministry of Culture."

"Regarding what, Mr. Raines?"

"I have reason to believe that Dr. Gamasi can provide some information concerning a series of homicides that have occurred in Los Angeles."

"Is this matter in any way connected to the discoveries at Ebla?"

"Yes. The victims constituted a group that partially financed the Ebla expedition."

"Passport, please."

Jack handed him the small blue passport.

Hamidi scrutinized each page. There was a West German entry stamp in May 1981, then nothing until the recent British and Italian entries.

Hamidi noted the passport number and place of issue.

"Have you ever visited the Zionist state in occupied Palestine?"

Jack felt his stomach muscles tighten but managed a small smile. "You mean, Israel?"

"Yes."

"No, I've never been there."

"Have you had any contact with Zionist officials?"

"No."

"Do you have any Zionist acquaintances?"

"You mean, Jews?"

"No . . . no," Hamidi said with annoyance. "I speak of the racist political movement known as Zionism."

"To the best of my knowledge, I've never met a Zionist."

"What is your personal view of American support of the Zionist state?"

"I have no view, Mr. Hamidi. I'm a professional police officer, not a politician."

"So you have no personal opinion of current Middle East politics."

"I'm just a tax-paying citizen."

Hamidi nodded and rose. "All right, Mr. Raines, we'll process your visa application."

"How long will it take?"

"Two weeks, more or less."

"I haven't got two weeks."

"I'm sorry, but I must observe protocol. We have very strict regulations regarding tourism."

"I'm not visiting your country as a tourist. This is official business."

"Well, perhaps you can secure a letter to that effect from the American embassy. Under those conditions I might be able to expedite matters. But without such a document, your visa will be processed on a normal priority basis."

CHAPTER FORTY

⚠

The taxi moved along the Via Veneto, passing the sidewalk cafés of *Dolce Vita* fame crowded with patrons sipping Campari and basking in the warm October sun. Turning sharply, the driver pulled into the rotunda of the Excelsior Hotel. Jack paid the fare and handed the change to the uniformed doorman, who saluted him.

He crossed the marble lobby, through a gaggle of Japanese businessmen, and went up to the desk. "Number four-five-three please."

The elderly concierge reached into a cubicle and handed him the key. "A moment, Mr. Raines."

The concierge walked to the message board and returned with two pink slips. "For you."

The message from Sabitini read: "Gamasi will see you—I must advise him of your travel plans." The second note was from Gabriella, confirming their dinner date.

He rode up the elevator, wondering whether to contact the American ambassador on the long chance of expediting his Syrian visa. But having spent years in

government service, he knew no diplomat worth his
stripes would involve himself in a police matter unless
ordered to do so by Washington.

He reached his door at the far end of the corridor,
inserted the key, and entered the room.

His clothes were scattered across the room. His suitcase had been cut open and torn apart. His jackets and
pants were turned inside out; the linings of the jackets
sliced open. The papers in his attaché case were strewn
around the floor. The pillowcases and mattress had
been slashed; the white cotton stuffing protruded like
tufts of snow.

He walked cautiously to the bathroom, took a deep
breath, kicked the shower curtain back and stared at
the gleaming white tile.

His mind raced as he walked back into the bedroom:
Was it the triangle they were after? Or *Rosemark*? He
realized the vulnerability of his position and remembered Nolan's final admonition: "Anything happens to
you, and Jenny is alone."

The phone rang sharply. "Yes?"

"Is this Jack Raines?"

"Speaking."

"My name is Bensinger. I was asked to contact you
by a mutual friend. His name is Frank Piersall."

Jack felt somewhat relieved. The CIA was familiar
territory. "What do you want?"

"Can you come down to the bar?"

"When?"

"Now, if it's convenient. I'm wearing a beige linen
suit, blue shirt, maroon tie."

"What did you say your name was?"

"Bensinger."

The long mahogany bar might as well have been in
Tokyo. The omnipresent Japanese businessmen occupied most of the barstools and tables; with the exception of the bartender, Bensinger was the only Caucasian
in the room.

Jack stood beside the stocky CIA man and ordered a
Scotch on the rocks.

Bensinger sipped his beer and indicated the Japanese. "A few more years, and they'll have the whole world computerized."

"The Japanese can be handled," Jack replied.

"How?"

"Some cold Sunday in December let's drop an H-bomb on the little bastards."

"I guess I walked into that one." Bensinger smiled and placed a white envelope on the bar. "Five thousand in one-hundred-dollar bills."

"What for?"

"New shoes, suitcases, general wardrobe damage. Sorry about the mess in your room."

"You know something, Bensinger, I'm right at the edge of my patience. For two cents I'd shove that envelope right down your throat and throw you through that fucking window."

"They told me you were a tough customer."

"Oh, yeah, couple of more push-ups and I can do a Budweiser commercial. But right now it would be a good idea not to play any games with me."

"I understand your anger, Raines, but I just work here—and for the record, I didn't authorize that break-in. As a matter of fact, I was opposed to it."

Jack fingered the envelope and took his time lighting a cigarillo. "Suppose you had found *Rosemark*, would you have reimbursed me for the damage?"

"I don't think so."

"You're never going to last, Bensinger. You're too honest."

"I have my moments. Listen, if the five grand doesn't cover the damage, let me know."

"It's fine. I buy all my clothes off the rack at Ohrbach's." Jack sipped his Scotch. "In a curious way I'm relieved it was your guys who broke in. For a while I thought it might have been someone dangerous."

"What happened upstairs was as much a warning as a search," Bensinger replied. "We figured you wouldn't be carrying *Rosemark* around with you."

"But if you were wrong and found it, you're ahead of the game."

"More or less."

Jack drained the Scotch and sighed. "I take it you're here to deal."

"Anything within reason."

"Get me a visa to Damascus by noon tomorrow, and *Rosemark* will be delivered to Piersall in L.A."

"That's difficult."

"But not impossible."

Bensinger shook his head. "No, not impossible. We managed to obtain an overnight visa to Damascus fairly recently."

"For a U.S. citizen?"

"Yes. As a matter of fact, I believe you knew the gentleman." Bensinger paused and turned to Jack. "The late Dr. Sorenson."

"When was this?"

"About three months ago. Sometime in July. Sorenson went to his Rosemark project officer and requested help in obtaining a visa to Syria. The SOD people came to us, and we wired Damascus. The visa was approved by no less an authority than the deputy director of Syrian intelligence."

"How long was Sorenson in Damascus?"

"Not more than two days. He was back in Washington that same week."

"But you're certain he was in Damascus in July?"

"Positive. Well, I'd better get started on your visa; but let's make it three P.M."

"Three P.M. it is." Jack then lowered his voice. "If you can't answer this, I'll understand. But I would sure as hell like to know why this rat soup project is so goddamned vital."

"I just work here." Bensinger sighed and dropped two ten-thousand-lire notes on the bar. "See you at three."

"Right."

Bensinger started to leave, hesitated, and said, "By the way, I would advise you not to take any more romantic carriage rides; you damn near bought it in that park."

"I suppose I owe you one."

"No. We lost you. We didn't take those guys out."

"Who did?"

"If you find out, let us know."

"Maybe you've picked up some company on this case."

"Washington says no other agency was assigned to Rosemark."

"Don't bet on it."

Bensinger stared at him for a moment, then smiled. "Listen, Raines, do me a favor, a personal favor . . . "

"Sure."

"Try to stay alive until tomorrow afternoon."

Jack ordered another drink and stared thoughtfully at the amber veins of Scotch circling the ice. The disparate facts of recent disclosures whirled through his brain like raw data fed into a computer. The answers made no sense, but the questions flashed relentlessly. Sorenson had purchased the triangle in June; Hamilton had been surprised at the amount Sorenson paid. *Why?* Sorenson had made a fast trip to Damascus in July. *Why?* Sorenson's visa had been approved by Syrian intelligence rather than through normal diplomatic channels. *Why?* And behind it all, looming like an ominous specter, was the question of who had eliminated the hit team in the park. He sipped the Scotch and thought, one man had the key to most, if not all, of the answers—Dr. Amin Gamasi.

CHAPTER FORTY-ONE

⚠

Sandrone sul Tevere was tucked into the curve of a small piazza close to the Tiber. Its obscure location and its owner's fanatical avoidance of publicity had immunized the fifty-year-old trattoria from tourists. Sandrone's patrons were Romans.

The restaurant's tall iron lamps cast specks of light that darted like fireflies across the black surface of the river. In a corner of the canopied terrace a pianist played "Don't Cry for Me, Argentina."

Gabriella wore a simple black dress that dramatized her pale hair and ice blue eyes. A single strand of coral beads circled her throat.

The breeze shifted slightly, and the briny odor coming off the river wafted across the terrace.

"That river could use a little vacuuming," Jack said.

"It isn't pollution." She smiled. "The Tiber carries the aroma of two thousand years of Roman corruption."

"That's pure chauvinism. The river stinks; it has nothing to do with political corruption."

"I'm only repeating a legend. After all, Nero used to swim naked in that river."

"Nero's exhibitionism notwithstanding, the Romans didn't invent corruption. It was corruption that caused the downfall of those ancient civilizations you poke around in."

She sipped the wine and shook her head. "You're wrong. In almost every instance they were doomed by their scientific achievements, which were used for military conquests. Their resources were wasted in endless wars. In the end they died of exhaustion, victims of their own technology."

"Maybe that explains Moses' withholding God's words."

She seemed startled by his comment. "What do you mean?"

"Those last words might have been a warning, a threat of our ultimate extinction."

"I doubt it. That sort of admonition would not have been regarded as unusual. The Old Testament is laced with Yahweh's dire threats. And Moses never hesitated to relay them to the Hebrew tribes. No, it had to be something else."

"Well, there goes that theory."

"All we can do is theorize. Without those missing triangles we'll probably never know."

"I've got to believe Gamasi knows what happened to those triangles."

"It's possible, I suppose," she said, "but don't take Sabitini's advice lightly: Damascus is a nest of terrorist organizations; they may know you've spent some time in Israel."

"How would they know that?"

"This fellow Bensinger is CIA. He's certainly aware of your past service with the agency in Israel."

"But why would Bensinger tip off the Syrians? We made a deal. He gives me the visa to Damascus, and Rizzo returns *Rosemark*."

"How can you be sure that Bensinger won't trade you off to the Syrians?"

"What's his motive?"

"Since when do they require a motive?"

Jack smiled. "You sure that way back in your family line there isn't a distant relative named Machiavelli?"

"No." She smiled. "Actually it's Sabitini who's related to Machiavelli."

"Well, I was close."

Gabriella glanced off toward the piano player. "God, that's a sad song," she said. " 'Don't Cry for Me, Argentina' ought to be their anthem. It always reminds me of those boys who died in the Falkland Islands."

"Well, the stakes were high. Six thousand goats."

"Sheep."

"Right. That makes it even more profound."

He signaled the waiter and ordered coffee.

"What time do you leave tomorrow?" he asked.

"Two P.M. on El Al. I have to check in at noon. Israeli security is incredible. They go through everything, including the toothpaste."

"With good reason," he added.

The lush romantic melody of "These Foolish Things" floated across the terrace.

A Gypsy woman approached the terrace tables, selling roses. Jack bought one and handed it to Gabriella. "Compliments of the LAPD."

"What's that?"

"Los Angeles Police Department."

"My thanks to that noble organization."

"Don't get carried away. We've been accused of a lot of things, but never nobility."

She smiled and sniffed the rose, then gently fondled its petals. "I guess I won't be seeing you for a while."

"I'll be in Damascus only for a day or two."

"You hope," she replied.

"Will you cut that out? You're ruining my dinner."

"Why don't you pay the check?"

"What's the rush? Where are we going?"

"A special place. A great view of Rome and a superb saloon piano player."

"I take it you've made a reservation."

"I didn't have to. I'm well known at this particular place."

*   *   *

They stood on the small balcony of Gabriella's apartment sipping cold grappa wine and staring at the lights of Rome. Sinatra on stereo sang "I Wanna Be Around." The night air was cold and edged with the promise of winter.

"Hard to believe Rome was the world," she murmured.

"I can make a better case for it than for Pittsburgh."

She smiled and said, "When our subway was constructed, the engineers were constantly forced to detour; they kept uncovering bits and pieces of imperial Rome."

"They're supposed to build a subway in Los Angeles, and I can guarantee no detours. I mean, what's there to find? Rin Tin Tin's collar?"

"Who's Rin Tin Tin?"

"A Chinese dog. A big star in his day."

He turned his back to the view and leaned against the terrace wall. "Pretty cute, telling me we were going to a private club."

"I never said it was a club."

"It's a terrific apartment."

"I bought it with some money my mother left me."

"I've got to find a place when I get back. My daughter's living with some friends. She needs her own home."

"Children are stronger than we think. I was about Jenny's age when my mother died."

The Sinatra song ended, and a sudden silence invaded the terrace.

"I'd better turn those records over," she said.

Gabriella attended to the stereo while Jack studied a photographic portrait of a striking woman. "Is this your mother?"

Gabriella nodded. "She was a true Florentine beauty."

He swallowed the last of the grappa. "Christ, this stuff is strong."

"It's made from the residue of grape left in the vat."

"In America they'd call this moonshine."

"Would you like another?"

"I don't think so. I'm half-loaded now."

"What does it matter?"

"I've got a hell of a lot to do tomorrow, and you've got to leave for Israel."

She walked slowly up to him and said, "That's ten hours away."

He traced the high curve of her cheekbone with his finger. "We wouldn't make much sense, you and I."

"Why not?"

"Too many ghosts."

"We all have them," she said. "We fall in love with the loss of love—and we're haunted by its absence."

Jack stared at her for a moment. "I think I'll have that refill."

She took his glass and crossed to the bar.

"Is Sabitini one of your lost loves?" he asked.

"That's absurd."

"Why? He's attractive, and you share the same interests."

"We could never be lovers. There's no tension between us."

"That's too Italian for me."

She handed him the iced grappa. "You're right. It's very Italian."

He sat on the arm of the sofa, loosened his tie, and opened the two top buttons of his shirt. "Tell me something. How did you get interested in archaeology?"

"When I was quite young, my parents took me to Egypt. The La Scala Opera Company had been invited to perform in Cairo. After the engagement we toured and sailed the Nile. I saw the Valley of the Kings, the Sphinx and pyramids, the temples at Abu-Simbel, and those fantastic forty-foot-high pharaonic faces carved into red limestone walls, and in that moment I knew one day I would have to understand the mystery of it all."

"How old were you?"

"Oh, I don't know. Thirteen, fourteen. Why are you so inquisitive?"

"Because I'm slightly drunk, and I think I'm falling

for you, and I can't separate the mystery of what you do from the reality of who you are."

"Well, I don't know if it helps but Camus said, 'We are what we do.' "

"That may be too French for me." He smiled and got to his feet. "I thought you said there was a saloon piano player in this club."

"I thought you'd never ask."

She turned the stereo off and sat down at a gleaming piano. She raised the lid and asked, "Classical, jazz, or a saloon song?"

"Saloon song . . ."

"Anything special?"

"Yeah, but you probably won't know it. This particular song was composed by a famous saloon pianist who wrote a lot of songs. The one I have in mind is classic but seldom played."

"Just give me his name—not the tune."

"Matt Dennis."

"And the song is 'Everything Happens to Me.' "

He looked at her with genuine surprise. "How do you know that?"

"When I was in New York, there were three great saloon pianists: Joe Bushkin, Billy Taylor, and Matt Dennis."

She started to play the romantic, lilting melody. He sipped the grappa and watched her slender fingers caress the keys. The light rippled across her pale hair, and her eyes were half-closed as she whispered the lyric. She came up to the bridge big and full, then softly segued back into the melodic line and sang the last words of the lyric: "I guess I'll go through life catching colds and missing trains—everything happens to me." She finished with a flourish, and he applauded.

"Now, how about a fresh drink for the piano player?"

He gently closed the piano lid and pulled her to her feet. "I'm sorry, but the bar just closed."

Their eyes met and held.

His arms went around her, folding her into him. He soaked up her perfume and felt the hot flush of her cheek against his own and the softness of her breasts

against his chest. They clung together in a desperate
embrace, fueled by a sensual rush that had a life of its
own. He kissed her eyes, her cheeks, her throat, and
then lightly brushed his lips across hers. Once. Twice.
She pressed her mouth against his. Their lips fused,
and all their inhibitions vanished.

Surreal stripes of moonlight played across their spent
bodies. He cradled her head in his arm, and she brushed
her lips against his ear and whispered, "What are you
thinking?"

"In what order?"

"It doesn't matter."

He kissed her softly. "I was thinking about how
right I was for all the wrong reasons."

She raised herself, crooked her elbow, and propped
her chin against her hand.

"That requires an explanation."

"I said we didn't make any sense. I was wrong. We
make too much sense, and that's pretty damn sad
because it can't go anywhere."

"In London you said something about being glad for
the moment."

"Did I say that?" He smiled.

She rose, slipped into a robe, and smiled. "Don't go
away."

He lit a cigarillo and leaned against the headboard. A
ray of moonlight illuminated the hollow impression her
body had made in the bed.

He took a deep drag of the cigarillo and shook his
head sadly. He knew she belonged to another world—an
arcane world of dark secrets. But they had shared the
intimacy of this night, and in the rapid pulse of time
the future was irrelevant. The ghost of Laura had been
exorcised.

Linda Ronstadt's voice drifted in from the living room.
She sang a lush romantic arrangement of the classic
ballad "What's New?"

Gabriella came into the bedroom, carrying two drinks.
"Is the music too loud?"

"It's perfect."

She sat on the edge of the bed. They touched glasses and sipped the iced Scotch.

"Let me have a puff," she said.

He held the cigarillo to her lips, and its hot end glowed as she inhaled.

"Don't you ever play Italian music?" he asked.

"Not if I can help it. They're all the same. One of the lovers is married, and well, you know."

"Yeah, I know."

The moonlight highlighted her pale hair and cast her profile in silhouette. She seemed lost in some distant thought. The room was silent except for the music.

After a moment she turned to him and asked, "Do you ever take holidays?"

"You mean, a vacation?"

"Yes. We call them holidays."

"I haven't in years."

"Would your daughter be upset if you went on a holiday without her?"

"The next time Jenny blows out the candles she'll be fifteen, probably be glad to get rid of me for a while." He crushed the cigarillo out. "Why do you ask?"

"Because I want to propose a pact." Her eyes shone with a curious merriment that reminded him of a child about to play a trick. She sipped the Scotch and said, "This would be a sacred pact. A covenant that cannot be broken under any circumstances. So think carefully before you answer."

"Okay."

"Have you ever been to Venice in winter?"

"No. I was there once—a thousand summers ago. It was incredibly beautiful but hot, dirty, and full of Japanese taking pictures of Germans feeding pigeons."

"Venice is not like that in the winter. There are no tourists. It's cold and misty. The tides are high, and the water crests up to the piazzas and palaces. You can hear the Adriatic booming from beyond the Lido, like the cry of some sea demon trying to reclaim the city. Every street, every canal is quiet and mysterious. You can have a drink in the Piazza San Marco, and the musicians play just for you. Harry's Bar is warm and lively, and the bartender makes a brilliant martini. You can take a motor launch to the Lido and walk on the beach in cold sunsets. There is no place as romantic and mysterious as Venice in winter."

"What's the pact?"

"We agree to meet in Venice the last Monday in February."

He stared at her thoughtfully and said, "Suppose we come out of this thing hating each other."

"In that case, we imagine that we're strangers without any history who met in Venice by chance."

He tugged at her waist, and she leaned over him, her hair spilling down the sides of his face.

"What do you say?" she asked.

He pulled her down and whispered in her ear, "How can anyone resist a brilliant martini?"

CHAPTER FORTY-TWO

⚠

The first light of dawn leaked out of a slate-colored sky, and a brisk wind caused the rising mists to swirl like columns of spectral dancers. Cradling his shotgun, Lord Anthony Hamilton strode through the thicket of tall reeds. His Spanish boots splashed through the marsh, and his favorite Labrador retriever nipped playfully at his heels.

It was market day, and the butler and cook had gone into the village to shop. Hamilton enjoyed these mornings alone; the solitude seemed to enhance the majesty and tranquillity of the great estate.

He reached the camouflaged duck blind, hunkered down, and clicked at the smiling dog. "Go on, Admiral," he urged. "Make them fly. Go on, boy!"

The chestnut-colored dog splashed off through the marsh. Hamilton released the wooden decoys and watched the current draw them slowly out toward the center of the lake. The wind moaned through the tall reeds, and a brilliant shaft of sunlight pierced the gray cloud cover, lighting up the lake.

Hamilton checked the safety mechanism on his hand-made Beretta shotgun, then took a silver flask out of his field jacket and swallowed some brandy. While capping the flask, he noticed a few birds circling high above the lake. The birds descended in wide, tentative circles before skimming the surface of the lake, passing close to the decoys. Hamilton smiled with satisfaction. The decoys had done their job.

The barking of the dog echoed from the far side of the marsh. Hamilton gripped the rifle and assumed a firing position.

It began like a vast whisper that grew in intensity as the throbbing sound of snapping wings overwhelmed the morning stillness. The birds rose from the marsh like a dark ascending cloud. They gained altitude and with astonishing precision assumed a perfect arrow formation, then wheeled around and came in high and fast over the lake.

Hamilton sighted on the leaders and tracked them expertly before squeezing the trigger in rapid succession. Two birds exploded in dark smudges as if a sudden puff of wind had blown their feathers away. The flock disappeared over the far shore of the lake.

Hamilton opened the smoking breech and inserted two fresh shells. He had some time to relax before the covey made another high pass over the lake. He removed some dog biscuits from his rucksack, ready to reward his Labrador, by now returning with the dead birds.

He placed his collar up against the chill wind and took another pull of brandy. It warmed him, adding to his euphoria. He thought the gods had indeed smiled on him. Life was rich and exciting. He enjoyed perfect health and the respect of his peers. Moreover, at age seventy-two he had not retreated from life's challenges. The Megiddo dig was well under way.

He had become a key player in a deadly scenario the first act of which had been written thirty-two hundred years ago in the Judean desert. And now the final act was almost at hand. The Bercovici girl and Raines would serve their purpose and be eliminated. The civilized world would acknowledge that Lord Hamilton had singularly brought to light the last word of God.

He bit off the tip of a cigar and was about to strike the match when he froze.

Coming directly toward him through the swirling mist was a tall, spare man wearing a tweed jacket and felt hat. The man carried a wicked-looking Browning automatic hunting rifle.

Hamilton stood up and called out to the approaching hunter, "This is a private lake, sir! You are trespassing on my property!"

The hunter smiled but maintained his pace.

"I must insist, sir, you leave at once!"

The hunter listened to the sound of his own boots sloshing through the shallow water. He slipped the safety off the rifle. The distance between them narrowed. He could clearly see the fear in Hamilton's eyes as he pulled the trigger. He pulled both triggers simultaneously.

The charge lifted Hamilton off the ground, propelling him backward. He stared blankly up at the sky. Strands of steaming red and yellow intestines oozed from the gaping hole in his belly. His lips moved but issued no sound.

The hunter removed a large key ring from Hamilton's jacket and walked calmly toward the long hill that led up to the manor house.

Hamilton gasped for breath. His eyes opened and closed, trying desperately to define the frightening blur hovering close to his face. The image came slowly into focus. The Labrador retriever was looking down at him. His tail wagging. The dead birds clenched in his mouth.

CHAPTER FORTY-THREE

△

The vintage Mercedes inched its way along the narrow, noisy street, barely squeezing through huge Corinthian columns before entering the great Suq of Damascus. Jack sat next to the paunchy gray-haired driver. The morning air came through the open windows, carrying the scents of diesel fuel and cooking oil and the sweet, pungent aroma of roasting coffee.

Cries of street hawkers selling fish, dates, and plates of hot rice and macaroni assaulted the browsing pedestrians. Radios blared reedy, melancholy Arabic songs. Butcher shops displayed bloody chunks of meat and neat rows of sheep heads. Potbellied children ran up to the stalled cars, begging for coins. Teenaged girls wearing Western jeans jostled their way past veiled women dressed in traditional black jellabas. Old men wearing dark suits and red fezzes played backgammon in sidewalk coffeehouses.

They passed the Ummayad Mosque with its graceful minarets and made a sharp turn into a lightly traveled side road. The driver accelerated and grunted, "Soon come to highway for Ebla."

The twisted, scorched remnants of an armored personnel carrier complete with bronze memorial plaque marked the beginning of the highway north to Aleppo.

As they passed the wreckage, the driver explained, "Israeli jets, October '73."

Jack nodded but did not respond.

"Next war we take Haifa." The driver continued. "Now Russians come. Bring new tanks. Missiles. Wait. You see."

The sun blazed down from a crystal blue sky, interrupted by a single, towering cumulus cloud. The asphalt highway knifed through the parched desert landscape like a black ribbon stretching into a mirage of shimmering heat waves. The only signs of life were gray-black vultures feasting on roadside carrion.

A dry wind moaned through the open car vents and green bottle flies buzzed their way up the inside windshield. The radio played a wailing Arab song. Jack's thoughts drifted to Gabriella. Her perfume still lingered in his senses. He missed her. And that hadn't happened in a long time. He shook his head, thinking how life always managed to turn that one last trick you thought you were immune to.

The driver's raspy voice interrupted his thoughts.

"Look there!" he said, pointing to a distant wadi at the base of a sloping hill.

Under a vast camouflage netting, their long guns gleaming in the sun, were neat rows of the latest model Soviet T-72 tanks. Atop the hill, poised on mobile launchers, were batteries of SAM-5 missiles. Jack could discern the antlike shapes of technicians manning the electronic control consoles.

"Russians here, next war finish Israelis," the driver said with satisfaction.

He added something else, but his words were lost in the scream of a diving MIG-25. The jet fighters came in one by one, peeling out of formation, taking separate runs at the swiftly moving Mercedes.

The driver grinned, exposing three gold teeth. "Make practice on cars. Good pilots. Our boys. Best pilots.

You see tanks. You see missiles. You see planes. Inside
mountains more tanks. Next war we go to Haifa."

Jack closed his eyes and leaned back. He thought of
those long dusty columns of Israeli tanks. The refitted
American M-60s. The retooled captured Soviet T-62s.
And the men inside those steel coffins. Men like General Zvi Barzani. Men who had been bred by warriors
to be warriors. Their resolve had been baked into their
genes by the ovens at Auschwitz and the burning sands
of the Sinai. Blood was the wine of combat, and cordite
the aroma of victory. The violent death of youth was a
price each generation paid—a common occurrence in a
place where funerals had replaced birthday parties.

Toward the end of his assignment in Tel Aviv Jack
realized that the Promised Land had become Sparta.
The fierce God of the Hebrews had tested them too
long; his chosen people, the people of the Book, had
become warriors. The Syrians would visit Haifa only in
dreams induced by hashish.

The driver pumped the brakes as the asphalt highway ended abruptly, dissolving into a series of goat
trails. They bumped along in low gear trailing columns
of dust, passing through villages of mud huts shaped
like beehives.

"Look, Ebla!" the driver exclaimed.

Looming up beyond the last village was the huge
mound of Tell Mardikh. Its surface contours reminded
Jack of a slumbering elephant. Standing atop the tell,
silhouetted in the backlight, were Syrian soldiers. A
fleet of jeeps, trucks, and two helicopters were parked
in the shade. A hundred yards away were the bleached
walls of the compound housing the technicians.

The Mercedes bounced to a halt at a roadblock close
to the tell. A tall, muscular red-bereted paratrooper
leaned into the car and politely asked for their papers.
The driver presented his identity card and Jack's passport. The paratrooper examined the documents briefly,
then handed them back and directed them to a parking
space inside the compound.

"You go to food place," the driver said, pointing to a
dining area shielded from the sun by a striped awning.

Jack crossed the compound, wondering why the ancient Eblaites had chosen this desolate, forbidding place.

A slim, wiry man wearing a tailored safari outfit stepped out of the kitchen tent into the sunlight. A warm, ingenuous smile complemented his pleasant features.

"I'm Dr. Amin Gamasi. Welcome to Ebla, Mr. Raines."

"I'm pleased to meet you, Doctor."

They shook hands, and Gamasi said, "Nasty trip from Damascus?"

"Not exactly a freeway." Jack smiled.

Gamasi nodded. "Come. You must be thirsty."

They entered the tent, and Jack asked, "Is there a bathroom?"

"Of sorts . . ." Gamasi said. "Through the kitchen. You'll see a door with a male organ in erection painted on it." He shrugged. "One of those small jokes soldiers make."

Jack stood in front of a grimy receptacle that exuded an overpowering stench of urine. He relieved himself, taking care not to come in contact with the rusted, stained metal. He washed in the lukewarm sink water and used the sleeve of his field jacket as a towel.

Two bottles of cold Italian beer were on the table, along with dishes of cheese, olives, and sliced onions and loaves of pita bread. Jack took a long slug of beer from the mouth of the bottle.

"Have some goat cheese," Gamasi said. "It's quite good."

"No, thanks. The beer's fine."

Gamasi motioned to an old woman, who came quickly over and removed the food.

"Cigarette?" Gamasi offered. "French. Very strong."

Jack took one of the oval cigarettes out of the gold cigarette case. Gamasi started to say something, but his attention was diverted by the approach of a junior-grade Syrian officer. The sweat-streaked soldier leaned down and whispered something to Gamasi.

"Will you excuse me, Mr. Raines? I won't be a moment."

Gamasi walked toward a table at the opposite side of

the tent where a paratroop colonel shared a bottle of Scotch with a singularly beautiful woman. Gamasi kissed the woman's hand and spoke briefly to the colonel. They laughed over something, and Gamasi nodded to the woman and made his way back to the table.

He sat down opposite Jack, poured a cold beer, watched it foam up, and said, "That woman is one of our famous film actresses."

"She's quite a beauty."

"Unfortunately she cares only for women. Well, Mr. Raines, I'm afraid you've come a long way on a rather dubious premise."

"The very nature of police work is dubious. We rarely solve any crimes. Most cases are broken on information received. Someone has second thoughts and comes forward"—Jack paused—"and we plodding cops suddenly become gifted sleuths."

Gamasi's eyes twinkled with amusement. "I appreciate your honesty, but I know nothing of these"—he hesitated—"unfortunate acts that have befallen the Pyramid group. Actually I agreed to see you only as a favor to my old colleague Professor Sabitini."

"I understand. But I am here. And I would like to ask you a few questions."

Gamasi leaned back and stretched his arms. "I'm willing to listen."

"How well did you know Pierre Claudon?"

"Not well at all. I rarely spoke to him. He flitted about Europe and the Middle East like a gadfly. I believe he was quite close to Lord Hamilton."

"Were you aware that Claudon was selling stolen artifacts?"

"No. As I said, I barely knew the man."

"What about Dr. Sorenson?"

"He visited this site one summer. We had dinner and reviewed the progress of our expedition. I thanked him for his financial assistance, and he departed a day or two later."

"And Dr. Howard Emory?"

"I remember posing for a group photograph with him. Nothing more. He seemed a quiet man, self-contained."

A sudden dust devil whirled through the tent, and both men shielded their eyes from the blowing sand. The wind died as suddenly as it came up.

"What can you tell me about Lord Hamilton?" Jack asked.

"A strange man. Totally obsessed with archaeology but somewhat schizophrenic. His moods changed swiftly. I'm not a psychiatrist, but it seemed to me he was touched with madness."

"In what way?"

"The manner in which he would hold an artifact. The intensity of his desire to possess an object of some antiquity, as if his own mortality were somehow bound up in the object itself." Gamasi glanced at his watch. "I don't mean to be abrupt, but I must return to the dig. I have an entire crew waiting for me."

"Tell me, Doctor, how does a gold triangle travel from a crypt in that tell all the way to a safe in Sorenson's Los Angeles home?"

"I have no idea."

"Can you explain the steady stream of Ebla tablets finding their way to museums in London and New York?"

"There's nothing very mysterious about that. No dig is totally secure. Obviously some member of my team, an assistant, a laborer, a watchman, or a prowling Bedouin, appropriated them. The very nature of an archaeological excavation makes it impossible to police."

"You're saying someone inside the Syrian staff sold Ebla artifacts."

"That's my opinion. After all, art and culture are not immune to corruption. I would hazard a guess that you have known some fellow police officers who have succumbed to bribes. There is very little sacred in this tired world."

"No argument on that score."

They got to their feet, and Gamasi said, "I feel bad that you've come all this way in vain. It's little consolation, but I can save you that tedious ride back to Damascus. One of those helicopters is about to return to the city. You're welcome to it. You will be back in your hotel within the hour."

"That's very kind of you."

They shook hands, and Gamasi's eyes darted quickly from the paratroop colonel to Jack.

"Are you staying the night in Damascus?" he asked.

"Yes. I'm leaving on an early-morning flight to Cyprus."

"Why Cyprus?"

"It's the quickest way from Damascus to Tel Aviv."

"I see. So you, too, are a victim of the Megiddo fever. The search for the Moses tablet."

"I guess I am."

"Interesting. I would have thought professional policemen were immune to legends." He paused. "Give my best wishes to Miss Bercovici. *Salam alakum*, Mr. Raines."

CHAPTER FORTY-FOUR

△

The sun vanished without a trace, instantly replaced by a full and lustrous moon swelling in the eastern sky. The night sounds of Damascus were distinctly different from those of the day. The blaring horns, wailing sirens, and reedy Arab music were defined; their dissonance reminded Jack of a symphony orchestra tuning up before the concert.

He stood on a small balcony, feeling refreshed but frustrated. Gamasi had not exaggerated; the helicopter flight from Ebla to Damascus had taken less than an hour. He had showered, eaten lightly, and chain-smoked, trying to make sense out of his meeting with Gamasi.

Every instinct told him that Gamasi's polite indifference was a cover. The Syrian director of antiquities had obviously been inhibited by the presence of the paratroop colonel. But then again, Gamasi might have agreed to the meeting simply out of courtesy to Sabitini. In any case, Damascus had proved to be a dead end, and the enigmatic Gamasi another player in a riddle that defied solution.

He tossed the dead cigarillo over the balcony and walked back into the sitting room, stretched out on the sofa, and thought about Gabriella. He could see her now in some dark Megiddo chamber alongside Barzani, following the directions of the triangle, sifting through the debris, trying to close in on the last words of Yahweh.

He jumped as the phone rang.

"Mr. Raines?" the cultured voice inquired.

"Yes, speaking."

"This is the concierge. A gentleman waits for you in the coffee shop just around the corner from the hotel. He said he has information concerning a triangle."

"A triangle?"

"Yes. He waits for you at the counter."

The garishly lit café was crowded with young soldiers, some of whom were absorbed in an old John Wayne movie playing on a television set above the counter. Jack was working on his second espresso when a short man wearing a shiny blue suit sidled up to him.

The dapper man's bright black eyes darted nervously around the café, and in a low, confidential voice he said, "For fifty American dollars I can provide for you two very young, very clean boys."

Jack stared at him in consternation. It was a bizarre opening line for a contact man.

"Ah, sir. I have perhaps offended you. Forgive me." The little man glanced furtively at the other customers before continuing. "For the same price a fifteen-year-old German schoolgirl, a blond child, soft, round, full-breasted, lightly used but gifted. This child will satisfy any request."

Jack's puzzlement vanished. The man projected the ugly intimacy common to all pimps. A quirk of fate had placed him in the café before the actual contact man revealed himself. The Syrian soldiers laughed and applauded as John Wayne tossed two gunslingers through a plate glass window.

The man placed his lips close to Jack's ear.

"For one hundred American dollars, French twins. Only twenty, very special, fine apartment in elegant section. Hashish. Champagne. They are truly magnificent, sir."

"I'm interested in triangles," Jack said quietly.

"Triangles?" the man repeated with puzzlement. "I suppose a combination of sorts can be arranged to accommodate that geometric—"

The pimp's words died abruptly, and the light in his nervous eyes went out. He had seen something that frightened him, and he quickly slithered off, making his way through the soldiers.

Jack had only seconds to register his own bewilderment before feeling the jolting pain of metal thrust against his kidney.

"Pay for the coffee, and walk slowly to the curb," a harsh voice behind him commanded.

Jack paid the bill, thinking he had behaved like a rank amateur; he had fallen for a very old dodge: an anonymous message with just enough bait to hook him. It was the kind of critical mistake professionals never make. He grimaced in pain as the muzzle shifted to the base of his spine.

The pressure of the gun moved him toward the street. The lights of a black Buick flashed in his eyes as it squealed to a stop at the curbside. The rear door flew open, and the gunman shoved him inside. There were two men up front and a Sudanese with blue-black skin in the rear. A pair of powerful hands thrust him down onto the floor. A heavy boot pressed his face against a floor carpet that smelled of dried vomit. The cold muzzle of the gun penetrated his upturned ear.

"No move. No talk," the Sudanese commanded.

Jack felt a numbing, icy chill spreading into his chest. His palms sweated. His heartbeat accelerated. The gun against his ear, held by unseen hands, was terrifying. He knew the triggerman was a professional acting on orders. But whose orders? Had Gamasi set him up? Or had Gabriella's warning been prophetic? Had Bensinger revealed his CIA background to the Syrians? If so, they would know he had once been stationed in Tel Aviv. But why? Jack instantly answered his own question: a trade-off to Syrian intelligence. The agency played those games. But Tel Aviv was a long time ago. He hadn't had any contact with Israeli officials for more than a decade. None of it added up, but none of it could be dismissed. All he could do now was practice absolute obedience. His lungs ached for air, and the rancid odor coming from the carpet was nauseating.

They drove for almost half an hour before Jack felt the pull of gravity as the Buick groaned up a steep incline. At the crest of the hill they made a wide, curving sweep and slowed to a crawl before bouncing over what felt like a speed bump.

The car doors opened, and the boot pressing his face to the floor was withdrawn.

"Up!" the voice commanded.

Jack crawled out backward and straightened up. The muzzle of the gun jammed against the base of his spine. He walked unsteadily between the gunmen through a spotless garage toward a rear alcove.

They climbed a narrow spiral staircase to an upper floor and proceeded down the length of a dimly lit corridor. The Sudanese stopped at a magnificently carved wooden door and took a wicked-looking heavy-caliber automatic out of a shoulder holster and trained the muzzle at Jack.

"Inside," he ordered.

The room was like a set out of *The Arabian Nights*. The walls were powder blue and concave. Low sofas were strewn with tasseled pillows, and a fine antique Oriental carpet covered the floor. A pierced brass lamp suspended from the ceiling emitted a rose-colored light. A smattering of artifacts displayed in a glass case included the grotesque, grinning head of Pazuzu.

The Sudanese indicated one of the sofas. "Sit! No move!"

Jack sat down on the low sofa, and the Sudanese left, closing the heavy wooden door behind him. The room was silent except for the chirping sounds of night birds coming through the open shutters.

Jack noticed a well-stocked portable bar in a dimly lit corner of the room; he ached for a drink but remained seated.

He glanced at the hideous head of Pazuzu. The Canaanite devil-god had shadowed the case from that very first Sunday up at Laura's, and now its swollen eyes seemed to be mocking him.

The doorknob turned slowly, and Dr. Amin Gamasi, wearing a white linen suit and red fez, entered the room. He closed the door and placed his forefinger to his lips, cautioning silence. He turned the radio on and fiddled with the dial before settling on a percussive Arabic chant. He raised the volume slightly, then walked over to Jack and opened his gold cigarette case.

"French. Very strong."

"Yeah . . . I remember."

Jack took one, and Gamasi struck the lighter. "Forgive me, Mr. Raines. These tactics are abhorrent to me, but . . ." He shrugged.

"Just give me a goddamn drink."

"Of course. What do you prefer?"

"Scotch over ice."

"Again, my apologies," Gamasi said. "But there was no choice. I cannot afford to be seen with you."

"What about our meeting this afternoon?"

"That was officially sanctioned, and as you probably noticed, we were under surveillance every moment. These gentlemen who brought you here are members of a terrorist group known as al-Asiqa. I have, by money and circumstance, ingratiated myself with them. They afford me temporary protection"—he paused and smiled—"until I can no longer afford to pay tribute."

He handed the drink to Jack and raised his own glass. "Cheers."

Jack took a long swallow, and Gamasi sat on the edge of an ornate desk.

"I am going to be frank with you, Mr. Raines. Ironically, by virtue of my own expertise I am a marked man. I have read a considerable number of Ebla tablets. There is incontrovertible proof that nomadic Hebrew tribes settled in ancient Ebla twenty-five hundred years before the emergence of any Arab culture. The language, laws, and customs of Ebla parallel the Hebrew codes that surfaced in the time of Moses. There is not a shadow of doubt that today's Syrians are descendants of ancient Hebrews, more specifically of the tribe of Naphtali, which occupied southern Syria.

"I have seen Ebla tablets that prophesy the advent of Moses—the great prophet who would be punished for withholding Yahweh's last word—and on the day of his death would inscribe those words for posterity." He crushed his cigarette out and instantly lit another. "So there you have it. The Ithamar text is confirmed. The Moses tablet is no myth."

Jack rose and paced for a moment before asking, "Why has this knowledge placed you in jeopardy?"

"I am, after all, a man whose professional intercourse places him in touch with Western journalists and academics. It is the view of Syrian intelligence that my background and knowledge make me a potential enemy of the state. My tenuous contact with al-Asiqa has so far given me time to maneuver. But I understand Syrian political realities. I'm on borrowed time." He paused and lowered his voice. "Therefore, in the interest of self-preservation I have taken certain calculated risks."

"What risks?"

"I disposed of two triangles through Pierre Claudon."

Jack stared at him with growing interest. A vague structure of past events was beginning to take shape.

"Why?"

"Money."

"What did Claudon do with the triangles?"

"He sold one to Sorenson and the other to Hamilton."

"Do you know how much he charged them?"

"One hundred thousand dollars for each."

"What was your cut of the sale?"

"Fifty percent."

"Would it surprise you to know that Sorenson paid Claudon a quarter of a million for his triangle?"

Gamasi sighed and smiled a small, sad smile. "No, it doesn't surprise me. The late Mr. Claudon was not famous for his honesty."

"But you're certain that Hamilton paid one hundred thousand?"

Gamasi nodded. "Hamilton personally told me. He phoned me in early June when the sale was effected. The actual purpose of his call was to determine the significance of the cuneiform inscription. I told him nothing. I denied all knowledge of the triangles." He paused and crushed his cigarette out. "You see, I never trusted Hamilton."

Jack paced for a moment, then asked, "Was Sorenson a knowledgeable collector?"

"For an amateur. Yes, I would say so."

"Then why would he pay more than twice what Hamilton paid for essentially the same artifact?"

"I can only speculate that Claudon knew Sorenson was a man of great wealth and charged him accordingly. One must also bear in mind that Claudon worked very closely with Hamilton and would not be inclined to gouge his principal client."

Jack drained the Scotch. "So you don't place any special significance in the variance of the price?"

"None at all." Gamasi smiled. "Let me freshen your drink."

He took the glass and walked up to the portable bar. "Perhaps I can be more informative if you explain exactly what it is you're seeking."

"I'm trying to determine when Hamilton and Sorenson first became aware of the true value of those triangles."

"I have no way of knowing that," Gamasi said, handing Jack the glass.

"When was the last time you spoke to Hamilton?"

"Several days ago. He told me that you and Miss Bercovici had visited him, that you had somehow acquired Sorenson's triangle and were coming to see me."

"Why would he tell you that?"

"He wanted me to ask if you were inclined to sell the triangle."

"What did you tell him?"

"Nothing. I was curt and practically hung up on him."

Jack glanced for a second at the head of Pazuzu. "When was the last time you spoke to Sorenson?"

Gamasi sat on the edge of the ornate desk. "I believe it was in early July. He came to Damascus and asked me to arrange a meeting for him with our intelligence people, and I did."

"What took place at that meeting?"

"I did not personally attend, but I had dinner with Sorenson that evening. He told me he had urged my superiors to reopen the Ebla dig in the name of history and scientific enlightenment. He said the meeting ended inconclusively. We had a pleasant dinner, and he departed the following morning."

"I don't suppose you know what happened to the third triangle?"

Gamasi reached into his pocket and removed a small velvet holder. He turned it over and slipped a gold triangle out of its folds.

Jack picked it up and examined it carefully. It appeared identical to Sorenson's, bearing the same stress lines and cuneiform script.

"I assure you it's genuine," Gamasi said. "I personally removed all three from the Ithamar stone months before my Italian colleagues discovered the burial crypt."

Jack handed the triangle back to Gamasi. "Let me understand this. You discovered the crypt of Baal, removed the triangles from Ithamar's headstone, retained one, and sold the other two through Claudon."

"Precisely." Gamasi rose. "I also managed to move some Ebla tablets through Claudon to various Western colleagues."

"For money?"

"Yes, of course, for money," he replied impatiently. "When I was ordered to expel my Italian colleagues, I made a pragmatic decision. I could no longer live in this police state. I therefore required money, important money, enough to place in a numbered Swiss account.

"I wish to live in a free society in an academic atmosphere, perhaps as a professor at a great Western university. I earn eight hundred dollars a month while my superiors engage in corrupt activities that produce millions in hidden accounts. There comes a time when personal salvation takes precedence over misguided patriotism. I hope you don't think too harshly of me."

"I don't judge anybody. It's just interesting how you draw that fine line between pragmatism and honor."

"Now, now, Mr. Raines. Our time is too short to engage in a philosophical discourse on the mathematics of morality. I have business to conduct with you."

"Before we get down to business, I have a few more questions."

"Make them brief, please."

"Why was Dr. Sorenson murdered?"

"I can only speculate that someone wanted that triangle, someone who knew he had it."

"Claudon?"

"Possibly. More likely Hamilton."

"What about your superiors?"

"If they knew. Yes. They would have strong motives to retrieve those artifacts."

"What about Emory?"

"I have no idea. I met him only once."

"Why was Claudon killed?"

"I had him killed," Gamasi replied with stunning frankness. "He attempted to blackmail me. No amount of pleading, no amount of money satisfied him. He insisted I keep furnishing him with Ebla tablets. He placed me in an untenable position."

"Did Gabriella play a part in any of this?"

Gamasi shook his head. "She is totally dedicated to her science. Money is irrelevant to people like Miss Bercovici."

The door opened suddenly, and the Sudanese asked, "Al-an?"

Gamasi glanced at his watch and replied, "Ihda ahar." The Sudanese nodded and closed the door.

"We must now get to the business at hand. My proposal is simple. You have strong connections with some important Israeli officials—in particular, General Zvi Barzani. I will give you the triangle in return for political asylum in Israel."

"Israel?" Jack repeated incredulously. "You must be joking."

"On the contrary. I am not the first, nor will I be the last, Arab official to seek safety in the enemy camp. Israel is the only country where I will be immune to Syrian assassination squads. After a passage of time perhaps I can migrate to Zurich or Paris. General Barzani is in a unique position to arrange this. This triangle, along with the one already in your possession, will greatly narrow the search in Megiddo." Gamasi paused, and his dark, intelligent eyes were penetrating. "So there you have it. My safe passage for the last words of Yahweh. Put that proposition to Barzani."

Jack crushed the cigarette out and weighed Gamasi's words. There was little to lose. The value of a second triangle was incalculable; it would greatly accelerate their efforts, placing them within striking distance of the Moses tablet. And if Syrian collusion in Laura's murder became a fact, the tablet's text might be the nail in the Syrian coffin. The Syrians would forever be disgraced in the eyes of their Islamic brothers, and his own vengeance would be achieved.

"You understand I can't speak for Barzani or the Israeli government."

"Of course. I am willing to take that chance." Gamasi paused. "What hotel will you be staying at in Israel?"

"The Dan in Tiberias."

"I will phone you Friday morning from Beirut."

"Beirut?"

"Yes. We are restoring part of a museum containing Syrian artifacts. I will leave a number for you at your hotel. If Barzani agrees, phone me and I'll give you the exact details of my"—he hesitated—"travel plans."

"You want me to take you out of Lebanon into Israel?"

"Yes. By sea from Sidon."

"How do I know you'll deliver?"

"You have all the cards. If I fail to produce the triangle, you send me back—and I'm a dead man."

They stared at each other for a moment.

"Do we have a deal?"

"We have a deal." Jack nodded. "That is, if Barzani agrees and if I can get out of here in one piece."

"My friends will see you safely back to the hotel."

Gamasi smiled. "In a more civilized manner than you arrived."

They started for the door, and Gamasi said, "By the way, have you read today's edition of the *International Herald Tribune*?"

"No."

"It seems Lord Hamilton was killed in a hunting accident on his estate."

Jack felt a sudden chill, and his voice grew hoarse. "Christ," he whispered. "The last Indian."

"No, Mr. Raines. The last triangle."

CHAPTER FORTY-FIVE

△

General Zvi Barzani sipped a beer while he waited for Jack in the deserted hotel bar. The general's bodyguards were seated at a rear table, their Galil automatic rifles slung over the backs of their chairs.

Barzani had met Jack at Ben Gurion International Airport and whisked him through customs. During the drive north to Tiberias their conversation was confined to irrelevant pleasantries, each man reluctant to mention the personal loss of the other.

Barzani's fingers drummed impatiently on the leather-topped bar; he was anxious to get back to the dig.

The Yemenite bartender asked Barzani about the tense situation on the Golan Heights, where Syrian and Israeli armor faced each other across a small no-man's-land policed by UN truce teams. The general shrugged his big shoulders. "It goes like it goes."

The bartender then inquired about the long-delayed shipment of American F-16 fighter bombers.

"What is your reserve unit?" Barzani asked coolly.

"Artillery."

"Then worry about howitzers."

The dark-skinned bartender walked abruptly to the far end of the bar and began to polish glasses.

Jack entered the bar, wearing jeans and an Israeli military field jacket supplied by Barzani.

The general turned to him and smiled. "The jacket suits you. Perhaps you'll enlist."

"Not a chance."

"I don't blame you. What will you drink?"

"A cognac on the rocks."

Barzani translated in rapid Hebrew, and the bartender poured a Hennessy over ice.

Jack thought the general's once-lively black eyes had become dangerously vacant. He sipped the brandy and said, "Gabriella told me about Narda and the boys. I couldn't believe it—I—I'm sorry, Zvi. I don't know what the hell to say."

Barzani nodded and sprinkled some salt in his beer, causing it to foam. "My condolences to you as well. Laura's death is, in a way, more tragic than my loss. My wife and children were casualties in a war. Yours . . ." He shrugged. "A vicious, empty waste."

"Well, maybe I can balance the scales."

"I know you want vengeance, and that's something I understand. But you still have the little girl. You must take care. With me, it's different. I have nothing more to lose." The general turned to the soldiers. *"Anachnu hochim."*

The stone-faced, impassive soldiers picked up their weapons and left.

"Drink up, Jack, and we'll go see our Italian beauty."

A cool breeze had risen from the Sea of Galilee, and off to the east the sun's rays refracted off the crest of the Golan Heights. The jeep sped along the curving drive traversing the biblical waters.

"Look there, where the sea thrashes," Barzani said.

Jack gazed at the shimmering water and noticed miniature waves breaking against a submerged sandbar.

"That's the place where Christ walked on water."

"How do you know that?"

"There is no other explanation. He walked there on
that sandbar and came to shore. And over there"
—Barzani pointed to a clearing in an olive grove—"in
that grove is Capernaum. We excavated a synagogue of
perhaps 60 B.C. Christ preached his first sermon there.
And in those hills above Capernaum is Nazareth."

"How do you know so much about Jesus?"

"He was probably our greatest rabbi."

Jack smiled. "How does the dig go?"

"Well. Very well. We're following the directions of
the triangle, seeking the temple of Ishtar. Gabriella and
my boys are at a sixth stratum forty feet below the
Solomon stables, digging in a westerly direction. We've
uncovered a stream of artifacts: Roman coins, bronze
remnants of Egyptian chariots, Solomon's seals, and
Canaanite jewelry." He paused, and for the first time a
trace of light showed in his dead black eyes. "I think if
we turn up another triangle, the Moses tablet is
achievable."

The jeep hugged the single lane road that curved
around the base of Mount Tabor.

"I can get you the second triangle," Jack said.

Barzani stared at him in surprise. "How?"

Jack outlined Gamasi's proposal. He did not explain
nor did the general inquire how Gamasi had obtained
the triangle.

"When must I let you know?"

"Gamasi will phone me tomorrow morning."

"Political asylum is complicated, but I'll have an answer for you tonight."

"What are the chances?"

"We need the triangle. I'll do what I can. Now, tell
me about Syria."

"They're planning to visit Haifa."

"Ah, that's interesting."

"Don't take it lightly. I saw columns of brand-new
Soviet T-72 tanks, attack helicopters, SAM-5 missiles
batteries, and swarms of M-25's."

"Where did you see this arsenal?"

"A wadi, flush to a volcanic hill, north of Damascus."

"On the highway to Aleppo?"

"Yeah . . . maybe twenty-five miles south of the Ebla site."

The general puffed on his thin cigar, and the wind grabbed the gray smoke. "So they're coming to Haifa," he said. "Good. We'll have a parade for them."

They swerved left, following a thin ribbon of asphalt around the shade side of Mount Tabor.

"Ah, Jack, Jack"—Barzani shook his head in mock dismay—"you're passing the site of a great battle, and you don't even look."

"Look where?"

"Here. Mount Tabor. Three thousand years ago Deborah, a prophetess from the hill country of Samaria, summoned all the tribes of Israel. She spoke to them like General Patton. She cursed them. She challenged their manhood. She invoked their ancient covenant with Yahweh. She rallied them and united them, and they followed her up that mountain and won a resounding victory. That twenty-three-year-old girl employed complex infantry tactics and guerrilla warfare that did not become fashionable until Mao Zedong swept across China."

The jeep swung sharply around the western base of the mountain, causing them to wince against the emerging sunlight.

"That battle"—the general continued—"was Israel's last fight against the Canaanites. The memory of that victory kept the nation together for five generations."

"And then?"

Barzani shrugged. "Civil war. Israel split apart. The conquerors came: Babylonians, Assyrians, Romans, and finally banishment. The Promised Land was lost for twenty centuries."

"Well, take care, my friend. History has a way of repeating itself."

"True. But now, fortunately, we have the Arabs. They always manage to take care of our divisiveness."

"But how many wars can any nation tolerate?"

"As many as are necessary."

They swung onto a dirt road that climbed gradually toward a crest marked by two granite mounds of rubble.

"Megiddo," Barzani said. "Once a great city-state. Now a pile of broken stones. The prophet Jeremiah said it best: 'Her town has been turned to desert, parched land, a wilderness. No one lives there. No man goes that way.' "

They stood at ground level near the dark entrance of the tell. The activity at the site reminded Jack of a film crew on location: a mobile kitchen, a DC generator, banks of Sun Gun lights, people shouting orders in English and Hebrew, some actively working, down on all fours with straw brushes, dusting ceramic pottery shards, others lounging, talking, sipping coffee.

Two men came over and saluted the general. They spoke briefly in Hebrew. One of them handed Barzani a powerful flashlight. "Come, Jack, let's find our girl," the general said.

The air was dank but cool as they descended the uneven earthen steps down to the fourth stratum. Barzani trained his flashlight on fallen sections of bronze columns that were six feet in circumference. "Pieces of King Solomon's gates. Beyond that lateral tunnel is the courtyard of his summer palace."

They squeezed through a narrow alcove supported by wooden beams.

"Take care now," Barzani said, and directed the flashlight onto a set of steep, freshly carved steps. "This is the beginning of a severe level change. There are thirty-two steps. You go foot by foot. Slow motion."

They managed without a mishap and found themselves standing in a large oblong limestone chamber. A team of carpenters was hammering floor-to-ceiling support slats, and electricians were setting up lights.

Jack noticed a sealed coffin with a beatific face carved on its lid. Close to the coffin, a group of bronze deities were huddled, an expression of trepidation on their faces as if they were somehow aware they were about to emerge into the light of the twentieth century.

"When we reach the next chamber, stay close to the wall," Barzani cautioned. "The stratum is dangerous.

The floor is a thin crust over underground wells. I warned Gabriella, but she goes her own way."

Barzani's flashlight played against the sweating walls, and they followed the winding corridor into a dark, cavernous chamber. Two battery-charged Sun Guns cast a bluish light over the earthen walls. The air was cold and damp and smelled strangely sweet, as if a clump of jasmine lay hidden somewhere in the chamber. The sound of bubbling, rushing water rose from below, causing the floor to tremble.

Jack spotted Gabriella on the far side of the chamber. She was on all fours, dusting the base of an exquisitely carved bronze altar. A royal figure made of gold and wearing a conical crown was seated on the altar. Gabriella rose and dusted the face of the royal figure. After a moment she stepped back and asked an assistant to bring some additional lights.

There was a sudden hissing sound, and a rush of sand cascaded down from the level above, sending up a dense cloud of silt, obscuring the lights, turning the chamber into a dark cell of choking dust and debris. The hissing sound was followed by an ominous rumble, and the ground under Gabriella's feet yawned open. She screamed and fell out of sight.

Jack bolted toward the open pit.

Barzani dashed after him and, angling his body sideways, hurtled through the air and knocked Jack to the ground. "Don't move!" he ordered.

They lay prone in fearful silence, both men straining for some sound of life from the newly formed pit at the far side of the chamber.

The sand and debris slowly settled, and the lights took hold again. The sound of gurgling underground water filled the cavern. "Now!" Barzani said.

They rose and moved cautiously to the far side of the chamber. Barzani directed the flashlight down into the pit.

Gabriella was waist-deep in a pool of thick, bubbling mud. "I'm all right!" she shouted. "Get that light out of my eyes!"

Barzani shifted the light and shouted in Hebrew to the other men, *"Chevel sulam!"* Two khaki-clad men bolted out of the chamber.

Gabriella noticed Jack standing alongside Barzani. "Oh . . ." she said sheepishly. "It's you. How about getting me out of here before I drown?"

"You won't drown," Barzani said. "You were born lucky. Not only did you fall into mud, but you managed to remain in the Bronze Age. If not for the mud, you would have fallen into the Stone Age."

Barzani's men were back with a coiled rope ladder and dropped the end down to Gabriella.

Barzani shouted to her, "Hold on to the rung. We're going to pull you up."

Struggling against the tug of rising mud, she managed to grasp the bone handle of the rope ladder. The men pulled her up, and, as she neared the surface, they gripped her wrists and with a final heave set her down on the chamber floor.

She looked like a child whose face had been dipped in chocolate icing.

"I warned you," Barzani said.

She brushed some mud from her face. "I didn't get hurt, so let's drop it." She got to her feet and indicated the small royal statue resting on the altar. "Thank God, we didn't lose this. Look. Mixed sexual organs."

The statue had male genitalia and female breasts.

"That's what I would call a classic case of indecision." Jack smiled.

She glared at them out of her mud-rimmed eyes. "This happens to be the single most important artifact we've found. It's a symbolic tribute to Ishtar and her devil brother Pazuzu, the two great Canaanite deities. We're very close to that temple described on the triangle."

"Perhaps," Barzani said. "But in which direction do we dig? East? West? Or down there?"

She wiped her face with the sleeve of her shirt but succeeded only in streaking the muddy residue on her cheek. "We need at least one more triangle, but I have a feeling we should tunnel east, toward the sunrise. The Canaanites worshiped the sun."

"Enough guessing for one day," Barzani said. "Besides, our American friend here may have succeeded in getting us that second triangle."

Her eyes widened with consternation. "How?"

"I'll explain later," Jack replied.

"This whole floor can give way at any moment," Barzani cautioned. "And since I have no desire to end my life in a sea of Canaanite mud, why don't we just get the hell out of here?"

"After you, General," she said.

CHAPTER FORTY-SIX

△

The red sun suspended itself over the horizon line as if reluctant to continue its descent. A fiery light radiated from its core, casting a magenta glow over the restless Mediterranean. On the beach a group of blond Swedish girls wearing brief bikinis stirred themselves, stretching sexily, brushing the sand from their tanned bodies. A few surfers rode the breakers, and joggers ran along the foaming shoreline.

Jack and Gabriella were seated at a table overlooking the beach. Barzani had dropped them off at the seaside café before continuing to Tel Aviv. Once the general had departed, Jack told her about his meetings with Gamasi and concluded with the news of Hamilton's death.

She seemed strangely detached and glanced at a group of Israeli paratroopers seated nearby. The soldiers wore camouflage uniforms and red berets. Their Uzi automatic weapons were slung over the backs of their chairs. They were in a boisterous mood, commenting loudly in Hebrew about the Swedish girls on the beach below.

Jack was puzzled by Gabriella's lack of response and touched her wrist. "Well, what do you make of it?"

"I—I don't know what to say." She hesitated. "I've been trying to absorb the fact that a refined, cultured man like Gamasi, a man I admired, would steal his own country's artifacts and order the death of another human being."

"Gamasi needed money. Claudon was blackmailing him, and murder is the traditional defense of blackmail victims."

"Do you realize what you're saying?" she asked incredulously. "You're condoning murder."

"I don't condone any violent act. But I've been a cop for a long time, and I've seen rational, mature, successful people, men and women, driven to the edge of sanity by blackmailers. Claudon pushed Gamasi too far."

"That may be true, but whatever Claudon was, he deserved a better fate, not to mention that innocent girl who died with him."

"Well, we can go another yard. And I can tell you that a prostitute risks her life every time she knocks on a door."

"It's no good, Jack. You can't rationalize murder."

"I'm not trying to," he replied with a trace of anger. "Claudon set in motion a chain of events that triggered his own death. We can't change that. The reality is that Gamasi has something we need, and I made a deal with him."

"I understand your motives." She sighed. "Because the truth is I want that arrangement to work as much as you do. Perhaps more so—and that frightens me."

"Well, I can't be your conscience. That's a problem you have to resolve yourself."

"I've already resolved it, and that's what bothers me. There's a selfish streak in me that I don't like." She paused. "This isn't the first time I've experienced it."

"If you're looking for sainthood, you're in the wrong profession. Come on now, forget it."

She glanced again at the paratroopers. They were

flirting in sign language and broken English with the Swedish girls who had come up from the beach.

Hidden speakers played a ballad by Charles Aznavour.

"I'd like a cigarette, please," Gabriella said.

Jack took one out of a pack and, cupping his hands against the wind, lit it and handed it to her. She inhaled deeply and stared at him curiously.

"What is it?" he asked.

"Oh, I—I don't know. I suppose I was half wishing that Barzani gets turned down. There is no more dangerous place at the moment than Lebanon. You may be walking into a trap."

"Anything happens to me and Gamasi is finished, too."

"That won't help you."

"Look, I know there are risks, but we're talking about a very clever, pragmatic man. After all these years of planning, why would Gamasi place himself in jeopardy?"

"Gamasi himself may be duped," she said. "From what you tell me, Syrian intelligence has him under surveillance."

"Let's cross that one when we get to it. We don't even know if Gamasi will be granted asylum."

"I wonder why Hamilton gave me the funds to begin the dig but withheld the triangle," she said.

"Maybe he thought it was a life insurance policy, or maybe he planned to ride to the rescue at the eleventh hour. Who knows?" He refilled their wineglasses and said, "You realize, with Hamilton gone, the Metropolitan has exclusive rights to the Moses tablet; that should make Ettinger happy."

"Do you think the Syrians murdered Hamilton?"

"I'm not sure he was murdered. It could have been a hunting accident."

"You don't really believe that."

"No. But I can't discount it either. Sometimes in complex cases you tend to look for exotic motives when the actual resolution turns out to be excruciatingly simple. It just takes one misread piece of evidence to throw you off."

Two sudden earsplitting cracks thundered out of the sky. The paratroopers pointed skyward, showing the Swedish girls the white vapor trails crisscrossing the cobalt sky.

"Jets cracking the sound barrier," Jack said. "Probably a reconnaissance mission over Lebanon."

"It's incredible." Gabriella sighed. "They never stop fighting."

There was another booming crack, and they glanced up at the sky, following the sound as it rolled and peeled toward the horizon.

"F-sixteens." Barzani's commanding voice startled them. "They make a different sound from the F-fours."

The general came up behind them and placed his big hand on Jack's shoulder. "It's all arranged. The state of Israel has granted political asylum to Dr. Gamasi. You can bring him out." Barzani poured himself some wine and glanced at Gabriella. "And you, beauty, you'll have a second triangle—two thirds of the puzzle."

The music changed to a heartbreakingly sad Hebrew ballad. Jack noticed that even the boisterous paratroopers had grown suddenly quiet and reflective.

"What does that lyric mean?" Jack asked.

"It's a love song," Gabriella replied.

"Only technically," Barzani said. "You speak textbook Hebrew, Gabriella. You miss the idiomatic meaning. The song is political. It's called 'Madua' and is a huge hit among our youth. It describes a last meeting between lovers. The boy is killed on patrol in Lebanon and she asks, 'Madua,' which means 'Why?' "

They listened to the song in silence. The night sky had swallowed the last traces of crimson, and the amber lights along the sweeping curve of coastline suddenly blinked on.

After a moment Gabriella said, "Italian songs are never political. The lyrics always sentimentalize the end of a hopeless affair."

"I wish ours did." Barzani smiled. "Cheap sentiment is a sign of a nation at peace with itself. That reminds me: You've never invited me to Rome."

"That's not true. Two summers ago Sabitini extended an official invitation to you."

"That doesn't count. We were at war that summer."

"You're always at war," she replied sadly.

Jack noticed a flash of melancholy understanding pass between them. It was the unmistakable look of a shared experience.

The general laughed nervously. "Ah, to hell with all that. Look at the sea. The Swedish girls. My boys over there. You remember this café, Gabriella?"

She nodded. "We came here to celebrate. It was the week we discovered King Solomon's stables at Megiddo. Only that sunset the girls on the beach were German and the music was American."

Once again Jack caught the nerve ends of nostalgia pass between them.

A full white moon peered out of the black night like a sinister Cyclopean eye. The Sea of Galilee shimmered in the pale moonlight, and a cold wind blew down from the distant Golan Heights, carrying with it an eerie wailing sound.

"Listen," Gabriella whispered. "Do you hear that?"

They were standing on the balcony of Gabriella's suite.

The baying, mournful sound seemed closer.

"What is it?" Jack asked.

"Jackals. They hunt at night. They used to prowl close to our camp at Ebla. The Bedouin sentries set traps for them. One night they caught one, a steel bar clamped fast to his paw. The animal was mad-eyed, ears back, still cunning but pathetic, foaming at the mouth. He began to bite down on his paw, trying to amputate it with his teeth to free himself. And for hours we could hear the cries of the pack. They came up over the rim of the wadi, and we saw them—tribal, shuffling, circling with rage. I couldn't bear it. I went up to the Bedouin and pleaded with him to shoot the animal, put it out of its misery. He refused."

"Why?"

"He said the death of the jackal had no importance unless it suffered."

She shivered slightly against the cold night wind and said, "Let's go inside."

She fiddled with the bedside radio dial before selecting a classical music station. "How's that?" she asked.

"It's okay."

"I can change it if you like."

"I said it's okay!" he snapped.

"What's wrong?"

"Nothing—nothing's wrong."

She knew what was troubling him and decided to get it over with. "I'll tell you about Barzani and me."

"It's none of my business."

"Before Rome it wasn't, but it is now. In October 1973, on the Jewish Day of Atonement, the Syrians and Egyptians attacked Israel. The dig at Megiddo was halted. We Italians were sent back to this hotel. The general left for the Golan front. He was in the vanguard of the Israeli forces that stopped the Syrian advance. On the second night of the battle he came to my room. It was very late. He smelled of death and gunpowder. His uniform was smeared with blood. We made love. We were . . . at least I felt we were"—she hesitated—"cheating death. It was sad and terribly empty. Like the death of the jackal, it had no importance."

His arms went around her, and he whispered, "I'm sorry. I'm sorry for both of you."

CHAPTER FORTY-SEVEN

⚠

It was 7:35 A.M. when Jack walked down the dimly lit corridor toward his room. He had reached the door and was about to insert the key when he heard a sound coming from inside. It was faint. Indistinct. He placed his ear to the door and listened for a moment, but the sound was gone.

He entered the room and blinked against the brilliant shafts of sunlight coming through the open drapes. He tossed his jacket onto the bed, glanced around, *and froze*. An icy rush of adrenaline flooded his chest. He gasped for air. His pulse accelerated. His scalp tingled, and goose bumps pimpled their way up his arms.

Seated in a deep leather chair, one leg dangling casually over the arm, an enigmatic smile playing on his lips, was Dr. Martin Sorenson.

"Hello, Jack." Sorenson swung his leg off the chair arm and got to his feet. "Don't let this dark hair throw you. It's me. I didn't mean to shock you, but I couldn't very well walk up to you in a crowded lobby."

Jack remained speechless. His eyes were riveted on Sorenson.

"As you can see, I'm no ghost." The doctor continued. "Circumstances forced me to stage my death in order to remain alive. Actually it wasn't all that complicated. By virtue of the Rosemark project, I had easy access to cadavers."

Sorenson paced, and his hands flexed spasmodically. "I chose a specimen whose physical characteristics bore a resemblance to my own—that is to say, with respect to size, age, hair color, eye color, skin tissue, and so on. I stored the cadaver in the cold locker on my boat."

Sorenson paused, and his eyes grew reflective as if he were transporting himself back in time.

"The dentist's office was located in my medical complex. My regular dentist had retired some time ago. I waited for the opportune moment and switched the cadaver's dental charts for my own."

Sorenson nodded imperceptibly as if acknowledging his own brilliance to himself. "After you left the slip in the late afternoon, I sailed out alone and dropped anchor just north of Point Dume."

He paused again and searched his pockets for a cigarette. Jack watched him with dread and fascination as though he were trapped in a tight space with a coiled cobra. Sorenson inhaled deeply on the English cigarette and the rush of nicotine seemed to accelerate the cadence of his speech.

"It was a light sea. The air was balmy. I brought the cadaver on deck. I fired a single shot behind the ear, making certain the angle of entry caused significant damage to the lower teeth." Sorenson smiled a small, arrogant smile. "A touch of insurance. I left the shell casing, hoping ballistics would make the match to the Soviet Makarov automatic, the use of which strengthened the possibility of KGB involvement in my 'murder.' I then dismembered the corpse and placed the Saint Christopher medal Laura had given me around its neck. I weighted the torso and dumped it overboard. I made a slight incision in my leg and stained the decking with my blood. I raised the anchor and inflated a rubber dinghy equipped with an outboard motor and ran it into the beach. I went into hiding and

followed the newspaper reports, waiting patiently until
the coroner . . ." He paused. "What's his name?"

"Torres," Jack replied.

"Yes. Torres. Until he officially confirmed my demise."

"For whatever it's worth," Jack said caustically,
"Torres never bought your death one hundred percent."

"Is that so?"

"Yeah. And I may have helped you. Torres had been
up all night doing the autopsy. He was bone tired, and
I rushed him that morning. He raised some points,
some doubts, but I pushed him."

"What points?"

"He suggested the corpse could have been dismembered surgically rather than by predators, but decom-
position and genuine shark bites prevented a definitive
conclusion. He also said the tissues were remarkably
well preserved for having been submerged that long.
But when I pressed him, he couldn't explain its significance. He thought the salt and the temperature of the
sea might have contributed to tissue preservation."

"Not bad," Sorenson acknowledged. "By the way,
you wouldn't happen to have something to drink?"

"Top drawer in that bureau."

Sorenson poured a generous amount of Scotch into
his glass. "How about you?"

"No, thanks."

"It's not like you to refuse a drink."

"Let's cut the chummy bullshit!" Jack snapped. "You
lied to me right from the top. And I want some goddamn answers, and I want them now!"

"Now, now, Jack. I know it's been a shock, but
we're six thousand miles out of your jurisdiction. You're
in no position to demand anything. But since we share
certain common interests, I'll be pleased to enlighten
you. Where would you like to begin?"

"Let's start with Laura."

"She was murdered by professional hit men hired by
Hamilton in collusion with Syrian intelligence. They
were after the triangle, and Laura got in the way."
Sorenson sat on the edge of a desk and methodically
stubbed out his cigarette. "Once Hamilton understood

the triangle's importance, he struck a deal with the
Syrian authorities. In essence, he agreed to become
their agent."

"Agent?"

"A figure of speech but accurate."

"What makes you so sure of the Hamilton-Syrian
connection?"

"Laura's murder."

Jack stared quizzically into the doctor's hard blue
eyes. "You lost me."

"Shortly after I had acquired the triangle, I showed it
to Emory. He was fascinated by the inscribed cuneiform and insisted on notifying Hamilton. He said that
it might be incredibly valuable and that Hamilton had
maintained strong connections with Gamasi, and perhaps we could form another enterprise. I was surprised
by his interest and asked him exactly what he knew
about the triangle. He became very guarded. I suppose
that was the night Mrs. Emory heard us arguing over
the triangle. At any rate—weeks passed—I was com-
muting from L.A. to Washington, and I forgot the
incident. But once Laura was murdered, I knew Emory
had betrayed me."

"How?"

"He knew I had a wall safe somewhere in the house.
You see we both used the same contractor. Emory had
a similar safe built in his Palm Springs house. Laura's
killers were unquestionably guided by Emory's information and were obviously looking for a wall safe.
Laura walked in on them, and they killed her."

"Why didn't you level with me when I first questioned you?"

"I had no legal proof. I was out of time. Marked. I
had only one recourse: to stage my own death and
avenge Laura."

Jack nodded. "So, the night of Emory's murder you
phoned Gabriella in Rome, a little after ten. But you
made that call from the Santa Monica airport, charged
it to your Bel Air number, and flew your own jet down
to Palm Springs. It's only a twenty-minute flight."

"Not bad, Jack." Sorenson smiled.

"You met with Emory close to midnight, told him you had reconsidered and were willing to discuss a partnership with him and Hamilton. It was all very casual and friendly, and at the opportune time you slipped the Inderal in his drink and killed him."

"To avenge Laura's death."

"Of course," Jack replied sarcastically. "You blew Hamilton away, too, didn't you?"

"He had it coming," Sorenson replied calmly. "Besides being responsible for Laura's murder, his hired assassins tried to hit you in the park. I took them out. All three of them. You surprised me, Jack. I never thought of you as a romantic. That was pretty careless, taking a carriage ride. You owe me, my friend."

Jack remembered the newspaper description of the savagery with which the men in the park had been murdered.

"I should have known," Jack said. "That German bayonet was a souvenir of your World War Two OSS activities."

"I thought that was a kind of nice touch."

"How did you track me to New York?"

"During my 'disappearance' I phoned Sabitini and told him I was over my bereavement and wanted to contact Gabriella regarding the possibility of investing in the Megiddo dig. The professor informed me that Gabriella had just left for New York and was staying at the Plaza. I planned to contact her when you showed up, and it worked just fine. You delivered the triangle and became my surrogate."

"How did you know I had the triangle?"

"The day before I left for New York I went up to the Bel Air house to get it and found the safe empty. The only one who knew the exact location of the safe was the contractor. I called O'Neil and said I was the attorney for Dr. Sorenson's estate and certain documents indicated an important artifact had been locked in that secret wall safe, and I was shocked to find it empty. O'Neil proceeded to tell me everything."

Jack crossed to the table and poured some Scotch into a coffee mug. He took a sip and tried to compose his thoughts. The shock of seeing Sorenson was still profound and gave the doctor a decided advantage. He may have been mad, even clinically insane, but he had all the right answers.

"Tell me," Jack said, "what did Hamilton have to offer the Syrians?"

"I should think that would be fairly obvious."

"Well, humor me, Martin, for old times' sake."

"Hamilton gave them everything. The game and the players. That three triangles stolen from the Ebla site were directional clues to a tablet inscribed by Moses, the text of which could brand the Syrians as Hebrew descendants, a cultural and political loss of face more devastating than any military defeat." Sorenson swirled his Scotch. "The tablet was known to be in the ruins of Megiddo, in Israel, a place that is inaccessible to the Syrians. Hamilton told them who had the triangles and offered them his services. He represented a control factor—an inside man, so to speak."

"Why didn't the Syrians just take everyone out?"

"Not that simple. Remember, neither Gamasi nor Hamilton nor I were walking around with those triangles. How could Syrian intelligence be certain that if one of us met a violent death, our attorneys wouldn't have been instructed to turn them over to the state of Israel? Besides, even with all of us out of the picture, there was always the chance some Israeli archaeologist would stumble across that tablet five or even ten years from now. It's happened before. No. It made a lot more sense to make the deal with Hamilton. He was a cheap insurance policy for the Syrians. All they had to do was furnish him with some money and professional assassins."

"What was in it for Hamilton?"

"Syrian approval to pursue the Moses tablet. Hamilton would cofinance the dig, acquiring exhibition rights. Once he had the tablet, he would eliminate any portion of the text relating to the Syrians' Hebrew ancestry. Hamilton would then be left in sole possession of the last words of God—the ultimate artifact."

Sorenson walked to the terrace window, his profile

silhouetted in the backlight. "Hamilton would have kept that tablet in his cellar with all the other illicit artifacts he'd collected over the years. A private room where he could visit God's words. Touch them. Hold them. Upon Hamilton's death his estate would place the tablet on exhibition with duly noted credit: the last word of God brought to mankind by Lord Anthony Hamilton. That's about as close as you can get to immortality."

"What about Gamasi?"

"He's irrelevant. He's frozen in Damascus. The Syrians can deal with him at their leisure." Sorenson turned to Jack. "So you see, once Hamilton had made his arrangement with the Syrians, I was the only threat."

"And Hamilton concluded this deal some time in June?"

Sorenson nodded. "I would say a week or so after we acquired the triangles."

"Is that why you made that quick trip to Damascus last July?"

"Absolutely not. I had no knowledge of the Syrian-Hamilton alliance at that time."

"Then why the trip?"

"Nothing very profound. I appealed to the Syrian officials to reopen the Ebla dig in the name of science. They listened, and I left."

"You also paid a quarter of a million to Claudon for the triangle."

"You've really been doing your homework."

"Would it surprise you to know that Hamilton paid only a hundred thousand for essentially the same artifact?"

"Not at all. Claudon got what the traffic would bear. I thought the triangle was a bargain at anything less than half a million." Sorenson paused and smiled. "What else troubles you, Jack?"

"Nothing. Nothing at all."

"Good." Sorenson reached into his pocket and placed a gold triangle on the table. "Hamilton won't be needing this anymore. I suggest you notify Gabriella; she ought to start deciphering this as soon as possible." He paused, and his voice assumed a messianic tone. "You can't possibly understand what this quest means to me. The discovery of a Moses tablet and the revelation of God's word would be the crowning achievement of my life."

"It's curious," Jack said. "But Hamilton said almost the very same thing to me."

The phone rang sharply. Jack crossed to the night table and lifted the receiver. "Yes?"

"Mr. Raines?"

"Yes. Speaking."

"This is the operator. I have an international call for you from a Dr. Gamasi."

CHAPTER FORTY-EIGHT

△

The Huey helicopter soared over the crest of Mount Carmel, revealing a stunning view of Haifa. Pastel stone dwellings clung to tree-lined hills that sloped gracefully down toward the sea. The lights of the city were just beginning to sparkle against the slowly gathering dusk.

"Looks like San Francisco!" Jack shouted over the roar of the rotor blades.

"You mean San Francisco looks like Haifa!" the general replied.

The pilot issued a final response to ground control and pulled gently back on the gain lever, depressed the left pedal, and the aircraft tilted sharply west, angling toward the port. They skimmed over the camouflaged refineries, homing in on a cement slab at the edge of water where a circle of green lights outlined a landing pad. The pilot set the helicopter down in the center of the circle and warned them to exit forward. Ducking reflexively, Barzani and Jack dashed to the pier.

A stern-faced naval officer saluted Barzani and exchanged a brief formal greeting in Hebrew. He then shook hands with Jack and escorted them down the

long wharf. The sea lapped against the moored war-
ships, and the air smelled of brine and diesel fuel. A
flock of sea gulls screamed for food, and a mangy dog
on the deck of a submarine barked at a pelican perched
atop a piling. They passed sleek, mean-looking ships
bristling with missiles and sophisticated electronic gear.

The officer directed them to a covered pier, which
sheltered an aging nondescript fishing boat. The paint
on its hull and stack was peeled and blistered. Fishing
nets were draped over its side, and the name *Galia* was
painted below the bow. The elaborate gold and white
flag of Cyprus flew from its fantail, and heavy tarpaulins covered the unmistakable outlines of gun emplace-
ments forward and aft. Jack noticed multiple sets of
webbed radar high above the mast.

A bearded, stocky man on the bow waved to the
naval officer and relayed some final instructions to a
deckhand before coming down the small gangway.

Barzani greeted the man, then turned to Jack. "This
fisherman is Mattiyahu. You can call him Matty. His
English is good, and his seamanship is superb. Behind
those jeans, sneakers, and dirty sweater is a commander
in the Israeli Navy."

"Pleased to meet you, Mr. Raines," the stocky captain said pleasantly. They shook hands, and the captain addressed the naval officer. "We're ready."

The officer wished them good luck and left abruptly.
The skipper of the fishing boat stroked his beard and
spoke to Barzani. "The tide is right. We had better
shove off. See you aboard, Mr. Raines."

Barzani put his arm around Jack's shoulder. "This
fishing boat is not interested in anything that swims.
It's designed for surveillance and clandestine opera-
tions. It's powered by twin diesel Mercedes engines
and armed with dual-purpose radar-controlled quad
fifties. Now, officially, you are an American tourist
who has hired this vessel for deep-sea fishing. You
never heard of me. Anything goes wrong, you obey
Matty's orders. He's the boss. Understood?"

"Understood."

"It's now seven P.M. You should return at approximately one A.M. I'll be waiting."

"Listen, Zvi, be certain that your men keep a close watch on Gabriella. I don't want her left alone with Sorenson."

"I have two men stationed outside her room. They will remain with her while she deciphers the triangle."

They reached the gangway, and Barzani said, "What do I tell the Americans if you don't come back?"

"Say that I was swallowed by a whale." Jack smiled. "What the hell, it worked for Jonah."

Splashes of phosphorus glowed against the prow as it cut through the heavy sea. The sky had darkened with the gradual precision of theater lights coming down before the curtain rise. From his position on the flying bridge Jack watched the forward gun crew remove the tarpaulins from the wicked-looking quad fifties. The cold night air, the rolling sea, and the impending action gave him a fleeting sense of exhilaration, but his thoughts quickly returned to Sorenson's reappearance.

The doctor's clinical description of freezing, then mutilating an anonymous corpse in order to stage his own death and the chilling arrogance with which he admitted to and justified killing five people reminded Jack of the cunning amorality associated with mass murderers. Yet there was an almost perfect logic to Sorenson's explanation of Emory's betrayal and the subsequent Hamilton-Syrian alliance.

Jack cupped his hands around a match against the wind and lit a cigarette. He inhaled deeply and shook his head in dismay. A nagging suspicion gnawed at his consciousness. There was an elusive, critical flaw in Sorenson's story. Jack cursed himself. He couldn't define it, but instinct told him that somewhere along the line he had missed a vital clue upon which the entire case pivoted.

"Mr. Raines!"

Jack was startled by the captain's voice and whirled around.

The stocky skipper stood in the doorway of the bridge. "Come in, please. We're approaching the Palmyra Cove."

The wheelhouse was not designed for comfort; most of the available space was crammed with state-of-the-art electronic gear. The helmsman was on his feet, eyes glued to the gyrocompass. The radar- and sonarmen were belted into leather bucket seats, their faces bathed in a green glow radiating from their respective display screens.

"We have little room," the captain said. "But somehow we manage not to get on each other's nerves. Come, look here."

They stood behind the radarman and watched the green line rotate around the scope; a large mass of irregular green dots were briefly illuminated in its wake.

"Those dots indicate the coast near Sidon," the captain explained. "We are running in and slightly parallel to it."

"How far offshore are we?"

"Roughly two and a half nautical miles. Can you read marine charts?"

"I have trouble with traffic signs."

The captain smiled. "Come, I'll explain our tactical position."

The navigator's glassine trace covered a detailed relief map of the Lebanese coastline.

"We are here," the captain said, and picked up a red filter pen and drew a connecting line on the trace. "According to what you've told me, Gamasi will signal us from the Palmyra Cove, which is here. I know the place well." The captain continued. "We took five platoons of paratroopers onto that beach in June '82. It's secluded, shrouded by palm groves and Phoenician ruins."

He took two sets of powerful infrared binoculars

from a cubicle, put the collar up on his parka, and said, "Let's have a look from the flying bridge."

The captain scanned the coastline with meticulous precision, then turned to Jack. "What time do you have?"

"Ten forty-three."

"And the rendezvous signal will be given in approximately ten minutes?"

"According to Gamasi."

"And it will be Morse flashes for SOS?"

"Right."

"I'll bring us to within five hundred yards of shore, stop the engines, and wait. Our danger is from Syrian picketboats coming down the coast from Tripoli."

He picked up the speaker tube and issued a stream of orders in Hebrew. The gun crews fore and aft test fired the quad fifties. White spouts of water stitched their way across the surface of the sea. Jack felt the concussion rings of the multiple-barrel guns as they rippled against the superstructure. The gunners immediately reloaded with orange-colored canisters.

"Tracers," the captain explained.

"Just how dangerous is this operation?" Jack asked.

The captain stroked his beard and shrugged. "As I said, there are fast Soviet-built picketships manned by Syrians that come down the Lebanese coast from Tripoli. From what you told me, it's possible Gamasi is being followed or perhaps has betrayed you to his own people. These are unknowns. We must prepare for the worst."

He glanced toward the shoreline and issued an order to the engine room. Seconds later the deck shuddered under the full thrust of the twin screws.

The two men gripped the railing of the flying bridge as the ship heeled abruptly to starboard. Icy drops of sea spray stung their cheeks, and their hair blew wildly in the cold wind. The bow knifed through the surging sea at flank speed.

The captain again scanned the shoreline. "The Palmyra Cove—have a look."

Jack trained his binoculars toward the shoreline and, in the infrared glow, saw the palm-lined cove.

The captain ordered the helmsman to alter course and reduce speed to five knots. The throb of the engines subsided, and the green running lights went out. The ship rolled and pitched in the deep swells. Fast-moving clouds suddenly obscured the moonlight, and the night turned black.

"Let's hope nature continues to cooperate," the captain said quietly. "The darker, the better."

They stood side by side on the swaying flying bridge, their binoculars trained on the cove. The agreed time for Gamasi's recognition light had passed. The minutes crawled by. Their arms ached from the fixed position of the raised binoculars. Once again the moonlight sliced through the cloud cover, its sudden illumination alarmingly bright. The captain cursed in Hebrew, lowered his glasses, and checked the green radials of his watch.

"Eleven-five. Where is your Syrian?"

"He's only fifteen minutes late."

"In a clandestine operation fifteen minutes can be a lifetime. I'll wait another five minutes. Then we return to Haifa."

"You're the boss, Matty."

"I'm sorry, but this is a—"

"Look!" Jack shouted.

The captain retrained his binoculars on the cove. A red light from the Palmyra beach blinked at them in long and short bursts of threes. The captain moved quickly to a signal light, switched the power on, and flipped the shutter handles in answering sequences of threes. The red light from the cove responded. The captain grabbed the speaker tube and issued a stream of orders. The engines roared into life, and the ship quivered as it headed toward the cove at flank speed.

Dr. Amin Gamasi stood in the prow of an open boat. A Lebanese seaman was seated at the till. The outboard motor groaned as it thrust the small craft through the surging sea, toward the large Israeli ship.

Gamasi ran a final mental check over his preparations. The triangle was in his jacket pocket along with his passport. The key to his Swiss account was tucked in his wallet. Around his waist he wore a money belt containing fifty thousand dollars.

The distance between the open boat and the Israeli ship narrowed. The Israeli captain ordered a decrease in speed and instructed the sailor at the gunwale to toss a Jacob's ladder over the starboard side.

Low, scudding clouds once again obscured the moonlight.

"Perhaps the fates are with us, Mr. Raines," the captain said.

Jack watched the tiny red lights of the open boat growing larger and coming into focus.

The bridge door burst open, and the radarman shouted something in Hebrew. The captain hurried into the wheelhouse.

Jack remained on the flying bridge and in the red glow of his binoculars could now clearly discern the faces of Gamasi and the Lebanese seaman.

The captain was back, his binoculars trained north into the darkness.

"What is it?" Jack asked.

"Radar has picked up a fast-moving surface vessel closing on us, perhaps six hundred yards off."

He lowered the glasses and barked orders at the gunners, who set range and direction according to radar control's fix on the unseen craft.

"Go down on deck!" the captain ordered. "The moment we hook that open boat, pull Gamasi up. If we are fired upon, let him go and lie flat on the deck. No heroics!"

Jack went down the stairwell to the main deck and stood alongside a sailor holding a long grappling hook. The red lights of the open boat were less than a hundred yards off.

Jack thought he heard a muffled rumble like distant thunder coming out of the darkness to the north.

The young Israeli sailor shouted, "Engines. Big. Powerful. Syrian picketship."

The open boat chugged slowly toward them, only sixty feet of surging sea now separating them.

"Gamasi!" Jack called out.

The tall figure at the prow of the small boat waved. "I'm here, Raines!" Gamasi answered. "Somewhat late! But here!"

The ominous throb of unseen engines was closer.

The Israeli sailor holding the grappling hook motioned to the Lebanese manning the tiller of the small boat. The seaman waved his acknowledgment and brought the boat parallel to the starboard side of the Israeli ship.

A sudden blinding shaft of light came out of the blackness, bathing them in a brilliant hot white cone. The forward Israeli gun crew opened up, and a shower of tracers streaked toward the intruding ship's searchlight.

The captain hurtled down the ladder to the main deck and handed Jack a steel helmet. "Put this on!"

The sailor hooked the railing of the open boat, pulling it flush to the side of the Israeli ship.

The racket of the multibarrel guns was deafening. The helmsman burst out of the wheelhouse, shouting at the captain in Hebrew.

"They're having trouble with the aft gun," the captain explained to Jack. "Remember my orders!" he snapped, and dashed toward the fantail.

The guns on the Syrian warship opened fire. The crisscrossing tracers flashed between the two vessels like streaking pieces of neon. Jack's eyes teared from the acrid bite of cordite, and his face burned with the heat of concussion rings.

The seaman alongside Jack flinched against the incoming tracers but held the hooking pole fast to the small boat. Jack leaned over the gunwale, trying to grasp Gamasi's shoulders.

Yellow gun flashes from Syrian deck guns were followed by tracer hits spraying the Israeli vessel in a crossing pattern. Shards of glass and wooden splinters screamed across the deck.

The Israeli seaman shouted to Jack, "Get down! Get down!"

Ignoring the sailor's command, Jack hooked his hands under Gamasi's shoulders and raised the terrified Syrian up to the gunwale. The aft gun crew on the Israeli

ship finally went into action, directing its fire at the
Syrians' searchlight.

Jack had pulled Gamasi level with the gunwale.

The Lebanese seaman gunned the outboard motor
and turned the small craft toward shore. Suddenly a
hail of smoking tracers stitched their way across the
boat and shredded his chest.

The glowing pattern of tracers lit up the sea and the
racket of the guns drowned the seaman's screams. A
thunderous explosion was instantly followed by a brilliant orange ball that rose from the aft section of the
Syrian vessel.

Bravely ignoring their imminent danger, the forward
Syrian gun crew continued to fire.

Jack had Gamasi firmly in his arms when a stream of
blood spurted from the Syrian's right eye. Jack eased
Gamasi's body onto the deck and hunkered down be
side him. He gulped the sea air, trying to lose the foul
odor rising from Gamasi's body. His heart pounded,
and his eardrums were clogged with the concussion of
the guns. He crouched beside the dying man for a long
time before the sound of the guns diminished.

Cautiously Jack raised his head and peered over the
gunwale. The Syrian ship was ablaze, its stern underwater, its bow raised vertically. The stricken vessel
seemed to freeze for a long moment before it slipped
under the black waters.

The Israeli captain came forward, barking orders
through a megaphone, and the quad fifties ceased firing. The ship's engines throbbed, and the bow swung
180 degrees, heading south at flank speed.

Jack reached into Gamasi's blood-soaked jacket and
removed the velvet holder containing the triangle.

The Israeli captain said, "As I told you, Mr. Raines,
fifteen minutes can be a lifetime."

CHAPTER FORTY-NINE

△

The tension in Gabriella's suite was palpable and excruciating. The men smoked, drank coffee, and maintained silence while she concentrated on deciphering the third triangle. She jotted down Hebrew letters and transposed them into English while constantly reviewing the cuneiform inscriptions on the preceding triangles, making certain of the sequential flow.

Jack thought about the irony of their situation: Barzani, Sorenson, and he—three hard cases, immobilized—totally dependent on the expertise of this Italian woman bent over a gold triangle inscribed three thousand years ago by a Hebrew priest.

The general sat in a leather chair, sipping coffee and staring intently at Gabriella.

Sorenson lounged against the wall, but his hands flexed nervously, and his cold blue eyes seemed unnaturally bright, almost feverish.

The doctor had congratulated Jack on the successful acquisition of Gamasi's triangle, at the same time admonishing him for taking the risk. The expression of

concern for Jack's safety underscored Sorenson's chilling schizophrenia.

A distant church bell tolled from the hills of Nazareth. Jack walked out onto the small balcony and
watched the fishermen casting their morning nets into
the placid waters of Galilee. Beyond the sea, a huge
dust cloud rose from a column of Israeli tank transport-
ers climbing up the severe ridges of the Golan Heights.

He turned back at the sudden sound of Gabriella's
chair being shoved away from her desk. She was on
her feet, heading toward a cork board attached to the
wall.

They crowded around her as she pinned three cards
to the board. She wiped the perspiration from her face
and proceeded to recite the block-lettered words:

Card One

"Ishtar, mistress of war. Queen of joy. Cobra of
dread. Vigilant goddess of the temple. I follow
your eyes. Forty cubits below the altar. Close to
the east wall is the entrance to Reshef's tomb, and
there is the passage . . .

Card Two

". . . to the north wall and the sealed door of the
royal armory. At the innermost room is the pillared hall. There is the false door to Ishtar's chamber of sorcery. Bronze steps lead to a stone passage.
At its end is a portal bearing the mark of Reshef.

Card Three

"Enter this place into the gold chamber. There you
will find the cobra goddess Ishtar. Her ruby eyes
will reveal the place where I, Ithamar, messenger
of the great prophet, placed the tablet of Moses."

Barzani made arrangements for a twenty-four-hour
shift, and all departments were alerted. An unspoken
but strongly felt excitement gripped the entire crew.

Shortly after noon those on the principal team disappeared into the darkness of the tell and descended

silently down through the eerie semidarkness, stratum after stratum, their senses assaulted by the damp, stale air and the sickening, acrid odor rising up from the fleshy residue of decaying rats.

At a depth of sixty feet they entered the rubble-strewn chamber where Gabriella had fallen. A trace of jasmine still sweetened the musky air. The walls had been braced with heavy beams, and the water level in the stratum below had been pumped out permitting the engineers to set a series of support struts. The team could now move about without fear of the floor's collapsing.

Following the directions of the first triangle, Barzani's soldiers hacked away at the eastern wall, their pickaxes rising and falling rhythmically. After twenty minutes a passageway was cleared, and they proceeded along a low limestone corridor. Gabriella crouched behind an Israeli soldier who carried a powerful battery-charged Sun Gun. The others were strung out behind her in single file.

The temperature in the tunnel varied sharply; pockets of hot air hissed from hidden gaps in the sweating walls. They halted at a point approximated by the directions set forth in the second triangle. The soldiers played their lights slowly over the walls, trying to locate the sealed door that would lead them to the royal armory.

It was Sorenson who first detected the red carnelian seals bearing a profile image of a bearded warrior. Gabriella pushed her way through the group and studied the seals. The wax impressions ran intermittently along two fine cracks in the limestone wall, outlining a portal three feet wide and seven feet high.

Barzani signaled to his men and motioned the others to step back to permit the soldiers room enough to swing their pickaxes. The soldiers set down their plastic face shields and proceeded to hack away at the portal. Stone chips flew in random directions. The soldiers grunted and cursed. The immediate area grew hot from the intense heat thrown by the Sun Guns. After ten minutes one of the picks broke through the wall, and a stream of warm, fetid air hissed into the passageway.

The soldiers quickly cleared the rubble and Gabriella led the way into the adjacent chamber. The lights illuminated the walls of the ancient Canaanite armory; bronze spears, shields, pieces of chariots, bows, arrows, and clay warrior masks were strewn about the chamber. The east wall was decorated in vivid colors depicting battle scenes of Canaanite armies locked in fierce combat with Hittite legions.

"We have to find the innermost room in this chamber," Gabriella explained, "the pillared hall described in the second triangle."

The group separated into twos and threes. Their lights darted and flared in the darkness, as if a swarm of fireflies had invaded the chamber. They wandered aimlessly through a series of small storage rooms. One group would exit only to bump into another group entering. Their plight reminded Jack of trying to get through a maze at an amusement park. By sheer persistence and constant tracking and retracking, they finally converged in a small bronze chamber flush to the west wall. They had found the "innermost room" and noticed an aperture at the base of the rear wall.

"Let me," Sorenson said.

He flattened out, squeezed through the opening, and disappeared. After a moment he called to them, "Come ahead!"

They found themselves in a cavernous chamber supported by black basalt columns.

"This has to be the pillared hall," Gabriella said. "Somewhere in or off this hall is a false door leading to Ishtar's chamber of magic."

Their breaths vaporized in the cold, damp air as they searched all four sides of the inner cavern and its tributary chambers.

Two hours passed. The sound of dripping water was like the ticking of a clock. It was as if some pagan god taunted them, drop by drop, with the futility of their search. People cursed, bumping into one another in the dark. Others stumbled over the rocks. Tempers grew short. Nerves frayed. A feeling of claustrophobia and frustration pervaded the dark chamber. They were hungry and thirsty. Their canteens had long since been drained.

Barzani was about to call a halt when Gabriella's voice echoed through the columned hallway: "Over here! Bring the lights!"

She was standing between two basalt columns at the north end of the chamber, her flashlight trained on a slab of stone that was oddly black against the limestone wall. She ran the palm of her hand over the blackened section. It was streaked with a layer of sootlike dirt.

"This piece of wall was fired," she explained.

"But there are no seals indicating a door," Sorenson said.

"The wax seals would have melted," she replied. "The Romans captured Megiddo from Judah in 60 B.C. They may have fired the door, destroying the seals."

Barzani issued an order in Hebrew. The soldiers stepped forward and swung their axes against the blackened oblong section. The chamber filled with the ringing sound of steel on stone. A section of the wall finally gave way just above the base line. It was followed instantly by a whistling rush of air escaping from an inner room.

One by one they wriggled through the irregular opening. The walls were adorned with friezes depicting strange animals, pagan godheads, suns, moons, and bizarre astrological signs. A huge coiled serpent made of lapis lazuli mosaics ran the length of the east wall.

"This is the sorcery chamber of Ishtar," Gabriella said. "According to the last triangle, we should find steps leading to a passageway."

"We've been down here for five hours," Barzani said, and glanced at Gabriella. "Should we take a break?"

"I can't speak for everyone, but I'd like to continue."

"I agree," Sorenson said.

"What about you, Jack?" Barzani asked.

"Let's keep going."

*   *   *

They spread out through the chamber, their lights appearing and disappearing as they searched out every crevice and tributary. Time became amorphous, dream-like.

A young soldier suddenly shouted from the rear of the chamber, *"Madregot!"*

They rushed to his side and saw a bronze staircase gleaming in the harsh beam of the Sun Gun.

No one spoke. The discovery of the staircase precluded any comment; it confirmed the sequential accuracy of the final triangle.

After descending the winding stairs, they entered a low, dark tunnel. Crouching down, they moved along the corridor for sixty feet before halting in front of a bronze portal decorated with the face of the Canaanite war god Reshef. The portal was five feet high and three feet wide and framed on both sides with timber slats.

"Everyone back!" Barzani shouted.

He grabbed a pickax from a soldier and swung it against the timber, splitting the wood on contact; a gap immediately appeared between the timber frame and the bronze portal.

The general examined the breach, wiped some perspiration from his face, and said something in Hebrew to one of his men. The soldier stepped forward and hooked the curved end of the pick into the gap between the wooden beam and the bronze portal.

The general and the soldier each took a firm hold on the ax handle and shoved their weight behind it, trying to separate the bronze facing from its wooden frame. The veins in their necks swelled, and their feet sank into the earth. As they continued to widen the separation, a wrenching, creaking sound echoed through the tunnel. Barzani and the soldier repositioned themselves against the wedge and fell forward as the bronze portal grudgingly separated from its wooden frame.

They entered a vast solid gold chamber and stood in awed silence at the sight that lay before them. In the center of the chamber, a heart-stopping, superbly sculpted gold statue of Ishtar rose fifteen feet from a base of coiled serpents.

Her face was a perfect oval, high cheekbones angled gracefully down to a straight nose and a set of slightly parted lips. Her eyes were inset by ruby pupils reflecting a sinister sensuality. Her hands cupped her breasts, offering them to snake heads curving up from her waist.

Gabriella's voice thickened with excitement. "You remember that cabalistic prophet," she said to the general, "that old man in Jerusalem. His room was decorated with the figure of Ishtar. He said she was in Megiddo, still possessed of great powers."

The general nodded, then shook his head in wonderment. "I've been on every important archaeological site in this country. I've explored caves and wadis in the hills and deserts, even underwater, but never have I seen anything to equal this."

Sorenson's hand flexed nervously, and he said, "There's no denying this is a magnificent sculpture. But how do her eyes reveal the location of the tablet?"

"I don't know," Gabriella replied. "That portion of the triangle is open to interpretation."

"Do you remember the exact words?" Jack asked.

Gabriella nodded. " 'Her ruby eyes will reveal the place where I, Ithamar, messenger of the great prophet, placed the tablet of Moses.' "

Jack stared up at the pupils of Ishtar and said, "Eyes can't express anything without light."

"Yes, but it says 'reveal,' " Gabriella replied.

"The tablet may be hidden behind her eyes," Sorenson suggested.

"No," Gabriella said. "Look at the dimension of her skull. There is no room for a tablet."

Jack picked up the Sun Gun and directed its beam into the eyes of Ishtar. They glowed with an eerie blood-red luminosity.

"My God," Gabriella whispered, "the light makes her seem alive."

"It's an illusion that doesn't help us," Sorenson replied tensely.

"Perhaps it does . . ." she said reflectively. "In upper Egypt, at Thebes, the sun god Hapotet was positioned so that a beam of sunlight struck his face at high noon. The Egyptians believed he left the outer world and returned to life when the sun struck his eyes."

"Maybe we can create a similar light," Jack suggested.

"How?" Barzani asked.

"Get some ladders in here," Jack replied. "Place a battery of Sun Guns at an elevated position and direct the light into her eyes."

"It's worth trying," Gabriella said. "When light is projected from a pair of closely set points, the beams bisect and come together at a certain focal length."

"That's precisely how human eyes work," Sorenson added. "The idol's eyes may be positioned to receive light and project a beam to a point on"—he turned and indicated the gold wall opposite the statue—"that wall."

"Well," Barzani said, "we have no other explanations and certainly no other options."

The general issued a stream of orders to his crew, and four men left on the double.

Ishtar, goddess of life and death, peered seductively down at them as they waited. It was close to midnight when Barzani's men returned with collapsible steel ladders and a battery-operated pneumatic drill.

Gabriella directed the placement of the ladders at angles approximating the apex of the sun at noon. Two men carrying Sun Guns went up the ladders to a height of fourteen feet. They turned the lights on, narrowed the beams, and focused them into the eyes of the statue.

An absolute silence descended over them as they stared, mesmerized by the glowing ruby pupils.

"There! There it is!" Sorenson suddenly shouted.

Five feet up, on the opposite wall, a dark red light glowed on a brick-size spot. The soldiers walked quickly to the wall and fitted a thin steel blade into the pneumatic drill.

"Cut along the borders of the light," Barzani ordered.

The soldiers placed their protective plastic shields

down over their faces. The drill kicked on, and the scream of steel on gold reverberated off the walls.

Gold dust sprayed the soldiers as the fine flat edge of the blade bit through the borders of the glowing square. Once the cut had been completed Barzani took a rifle bayonet and prodded the facing loose.

"*Hachmad*," he said to a soldier, who handed him a flashlight. The general directed the light into the square cavity and peered inside.

Gabriella, soaked by a cold sweat, shivered. Jack and Sorenson stood on either side of her, their eyes riveted to the general.

His hand disappeared inside the cavity.

The gold chamber fell silent.

Barzani slowly withdrew his hand, turned, and handed Gabriella a clay tablet that measured eleven inches by four inches.

They stared at her in hypnotic fascination as she examined the single Hebrew letters inscribed in five vertical lines.

"What is it?" Sorenson finally asked.

"Hebrew numbers," she replied.

"Numbers?" Jack asked with astonishment.

"Yes. Numbers in odd series. This is a code of some kind." She glanced at them, and her eyes slowly widened in recall. "The Ithamar stone said that we could find the *path* to Yahweh's words. The cuneiform seemed to indicate the Hebrew word *derech*, meaning 'direction,' but I thought it was too literal a translation."

"Which means," Jack said, "Moses gave Ithamar a coded tablet *leading* to the last words of God."

Gabriella nodded. "He must have believed that if tomb thieves found a tablet inscribed with numbers, they would ignore it."

"So"—Barzani smiled—"what we have found is mankind's first theft insurance policy."

"I don't find any humor in this," Sorenson said tensely. "We're stymied."

"No, we're not," Gabriella replied emphatically. "The army cryptographers in Tel Aviv will decode it."

"How do you know that?" Sorenson asked.

"It worked for me in Rome. The Italian military cryptographer broke the Ebla cuneiform. This code has to be primitive and not nearly as complex."

"She's right," Barzani said. "All numbered codes work on the same principle: repetition of numbers equated to letters. Once you discover the repetitive number, the rest falls into place. Trust me." He smiled. "Yahweh's great prophet is no match for our cryptographers."

CHAPTER FIFTY

△

The remnants of their dinner rested atop a serving table close to the terrace doors. Jack swirled the brandy snifter and glanced off at the dark, brooding hills rising up from the eastern shore of the Sea of Galilee. Gabriella stared at him thoughtfully, aware that he had been preoccupied and troubled since their return to the hotel.

He turned from the view and indicated the serving cart. "Don't they pick these damn things up?"

"It was almost two A.M. when we returned," she said. "They did us a favor by opening the kitchen."

"I suppose so." He sighed.

"What's wrong?"

"I phoned Jenny a while ago. She started to cry. Her math teacher embarrassed her in front of the class."

"What did you say?"

Jack shrugged and got to his feet. "What could I say? I told her those things happen, not to worry about it, and I'll be home soon. It's nothing serious, but I felt so damn inadequate."

Gabriella rose and stood beside him. "I don't know if this helps, but when my mother died, I went through a

323

similar phase. I transferred all my childhood problems to my father."

"How did he cope with it?"

"He was kind and loving but totally honest. He said no one could replace my mother and I would have to learn how to resolve my own problems. He did everything he could to encourage me to be independent. At first I thought he was simply trying to justify his absence. In those days he was often on tour with the orchestra. But as I got older, the wisdom of his advice became apparent. I gradually learned to depend on myself.

"But don't misunderstand, when something happened that I couldn't handle, he was always there, and knowing that made a big difference." She paused. "That's why you can't continue to take these risks. Barzani told me about your escapade in Lebanon. You're lucky to be alive."

"Listen, if Pancho Villa didn't get me, what chance did the Syrians have?"

"Who's Pancho Villa?"

"A Mexican bandit or patriot, depending on whose side you were on."

"Be serious, Jack. It's time you stopped placing yourself in jeopardy."

"I hadn't planned on being shot at. Gamasi seemed to have it all in hand."

"Barzani said he died in your arms."

"More or less."

"Who ordered the attack?"

"Syrian intelligence. They were on to Gamasi every step of the way. From their point of view, the seaborne attack was perfect: Gamasi, me, the triangle, and an Israeli spy ship all in one package. If not for a capricious moon and a crack crew, they would have succeeded. It was one hell of a fire fight for a while."

"You were lucky."

"I've always been lucky with bullets. It's knives that do me in."

"You have a responsibility to your daughter. Perhaps you should call it a case and go home. The men responsible for the killings are dead, and nothing you can do will bring Laura back."

"It isn't Laura that concerns me. It's you."

"Why? I'm perfectly safe."

"For the moment. Listen, I've met some hard cases in my time, but the good doctor is all by himself."

He turned back to the view and drained the brandy. "Sorenson's got a hell of a repertoire. All the way back to his days in the OSS. He's chilled a lot of people. He tampers with the soul of man in the name of patriotism. He builds an underground chamber for himself in the name of tranquillity. He meticulously stages his own death—freezing a cadaver, mutilating it. Missing nothing. He kills five people. All in the name of vengeance and self-preservation. He's got the same mad-eyed look that Hamilton had. When Barzani found that tablet, Sorenson's hands were flexing as if they needed a throat."

"I'm cold," she said. "Let's go inside."

Jack walked up to the night table and glanced at the three triangles, marveling at the perfect match of the three-thousand-year-old geometric figures.

"What do you intend to do with these?" he asked.

"I haven't thought about it. They were discovered at Ebla. So, technically, they belong to Syria."

"Who knows that besides Gamasi?"

"No one."

"Then you're free to exhibit them. All the former owners are dead."

"Except Sorenson."

"He's legally dead. Besides, I don't think the good doctor has any further interest in them. If I were you, I would give them to Ettinger, put them on display at the Metropolitan, courtesy of Rome University." He paused. "By the way, don't you think Sabitini should be here now? I mean, we're getting pretty close."

"I phoned him earlier. He was thrilled at the news of the tablet. But it's not possible for him to leave Rome."

"Why not?"

"He's fighting the semiannual battle with the administration for money. They keep cutting our budget." She shrugged. "Apparently the history of mankind is not as relevant as business management."

"Well, the exhibition rights to those triangles should produce some revenue for the university."

She sat down on the Styrofoam sofa, crossed her legs, and tossed her hair. "The irony of seeing those triangles together is incredible. I never thought they would surface and never dreamed that all along they were in the hands of my Ebla colleagues."

He stared at her with a curious intensity, as if he were X-raying her thoughts. The portent of her words had suddenly stirred the layers of doubt shrouding his perception of the case.

"What is it?" she asked, mystified by his abrupt change of attitude.

He walked slowly up to her and asked, "Do you remember when you first mentioned the existence of the triangles to Sorenson?"

"It was just after Laura's death. He returned my call and I asked him if he would help finance the Megiddo dig. I told him we had uncovered the stone of Ithamar. That its text indicated the possible existence of a Moses tablet inscribed with the last words of God and that three missing triangles contained the clues to the location of that tablet."

"How did he respond? Was he surprised? Excited?"

"No. Not at all. He told me that his wife had been shot to death, that he was bereaved and couldn't think about anything else."

"Did he tell you he had the triangle?"

"Of course not."

"Do you remember when you told Hamilton of the Ithamar stone and the missing triangles?"

"Yes." She nodded. "It was later that same day."

"What was his reaction?"

"He practically leaped through the phone."

"This is vital, Gabriella. Try to remember exactly what Hamilton said."

"He asked me if I had spoken to anyone else about

the triangle. I told him of my conversation with Sorenson, and he seemed to hesitate for a moment. Then he urged me to forget about Sorenson, and said that he, Hamilton, would provide a significant portion of the required funds."

"How did you respond?"

"Truthfully. I said my only obligation was to pursue the Megiddo dig, and if he were serious, I would respect his wishes. He thanked me profusely, and a few weeks later Claudon showed up in Rome with the money."

Jack rose and paced for a moment, feeling the exhilaration that accompanied a major break in a complex case. He turned to Gabriella. "You're absolutely certain that you informed both men of the triangle's importance *after* Laura's death?"

"Without question."

"But only Hamilton seemed genuinely excited at the news?"

"Yes."

Suddenly it all fell into place. He knew why Sorenson had overpaid Claudon for the triangle, and he knew the true purpose of Sorenson's trip to Damascus in July. He knew who had caused Laura's murder. He knew everything. But there was no place to go with it. Not yet.

"Why is all this so important?" she asked.

He crossed to the sofa, took her arms, and raised her to her feet. "Just promise me one thing. Don't ever permit yourself to be alone with Sorenson. Whatever happens, no matter what the circumstances are, make damn sure that you're not alone with him."

Her eyes were fearful, and she asked, "But why?"

"I can't tell you. The less you know, the better. Just listen to me." His arms went around her. "I don't want anything to happen to you." He kissed her ear and whispered, "After all, I wouldn't want to be alone in Venice, not in February."

CHAPTER FIFTY-ONE

△

The young Israeli captain operated the cryptographic computer with childlike glee.

He had just fed the entire Hebrew alphabet into the computer. A photostat of the numbered tablet rested on the shelf in front of him. The tablet itself had been sent to the curator of antiquities in Jerusalem.

"This is a welcome relief from my usual work," the captain said enthusiastically to Gabriella. "It's a privilege to decode a message written by the great prophet himself. Cryptography is as old as human writing. The prophet Jeremiah used a code word for Babylon, and that same coded system was later used by Julius Caesar and Napoleon."

He studied the photographic reproduction of the tablet. "Fortunately the numbers on this tablet run from one to twenty-two matching the number of the letters in the Hebrew alphabet. This makes the task infinitely easier."

Barzani spoke to the young captain, who answered him respectfully. The officer smiled at Gabriella. "The general is impatient. I'll speed things up by using a code override. We must assume Moses mentions Yahweh and himself in this code."

He fed the numbered text into the computer, and in a matter of seconds a stream of Hebrew characters flashed across the display screen in an irregular pattern. "Ah, now we'll see."

Almost immediately, a single line of six Hebrew numbers appeared, and below each number was a Hebrew letter running right to left.

The officer rubbed his hands in triumph. "You see, with precise instruction these computers will automatically encipher an illogical sequence."

"What does it say?" Sorenson asked.

The captain pressed a red key, and the display screen flashed two separate lines of six English numerals and letters:

$$10 - 1 - 8 - 20 - 3 - 8$$
$$Y \quad A \quad H \quad W \quad E \quad H$$

The young captain chuckled as if fascinated with his mastery of a marvelous toy. "Now I'll ask the computer to determine the name of Moses." In less than ten seconds, two lines of five numbers and letters appeared first in Hebrew, then in English.

$$9 - 11 - 21 - 3 - 21$$
$$M \quad O \quad S \quad E \quad S$$

"Okay, the computer has deciphered eight of twenty-two numbers. We have achieved close to one third of the puzzle. Now we'll see about the missing two thirds."

His fingers flew over the keys with the deftness and assurance of a concert pianist.

The screen displayed odd groupings of numbers and letters. The captain quickly scanned the information, his mind racing ahead to still another set of formations.

They watched him in silent admiration, caught up in what now appeared to be an intellectual contest between human and machine, as if a verdict of superior intelligence hung in the balance.

The captain's brow was furrowed with deep lines of concentration, and his fingers moved over the keys in a mysterious, final sequential combination. The machine answered, displaying the lines of Hebrew letters and numbers.

The captain leaned back, stretched his arms, swiveled around in his chair, and addressed Barzani. "Ah, General, if only my usual work were so simple." He paused and glanced at the others. "We now have a coherent text. I'll put those two lines into English without the corresponding numbers. After all, you're not interested in cryptographic science." He pressed the red key, and the Hebrew letters disappeared, instantly replaced by an English sentence that read: *"On the eastern shore of the Sea of Salt."*

The captain continued hitting the enciphered code key, and the full message followed. *"Close by Zohar, in the land of Moab, at the base of Mount Nebo, is the chamber of eternity. At the crypt below the east wall is my sepulcher. There did I place the papyrus in a bronze vessel. And on that papyrus, in my hand, did I, Moses, son of Amram, set down the last words of Yahweh."*

The captain pressed a key activating an automatic printout and handed the readout to Gabriella. "Perhaps now you will find the last words of Yahweh." He smiled. "And hopefully they will not be in code."

Barzani drove them through the maze of streets that honeycombed the military center. It was as if the streets had been paved in a hurried, random attempt to accommodate the rapid growth of buildings.

The jeep pulled up to a yellow stucco building, and they entered the base cafeteria. They sat at a large table, sipping thick, sweet Turkish coffee.

Jack lit a cigarillo and addressed Barzani. "That was one hell of a man on that console."

"You have to be nothing less than a genius to be assigned to cryptosystems."

"The translation confirms Deuteronomy's description

of Moses' death," Gabriella explained. "A cave at Nebo. Just across the Dead Sea, in Moab."

"From which he got his final glimpse of this land of milk and honey," Barzani said sarcastically.

"Maybe in those days it was," Jack remarked.

"No, it's always been a killing ground."

Sorenson drummed his fingertips nervously against the tabletop and said, "The Deuteronomy description and locale of Moses' death is a supportive factor. But finding that cave may be a different matter."

"Not really," the general said. "The Bedouins hold that cave in reverence. It is located at the southern base of Mount Nebo. But the cave itself is nothing more than an entrance to a geological nightmare. According to the Bedouins, Mount Nebo is a labyrinth honeycombed with tunnels and shafts and guarded by the spirit of Aba-Musa, Arabic for Moses."

"Why hasn't it been explored?" Gabriella asked.

"To what purpose? Finding the bones of a skeleton would mean nothing. These caves were historically used to bury the dead. Besides, until this moment, no one knew of the existence of a God scroll—or had clues to its whereabouts. And certainly the Jordanians have no interest in authenticating the Old Testament."

"What the hell have the Jordanians got to do with this?" Sorenson asked.

"Mount Nebo is in Jordan," Barzani replied.

Gabriella brushed a fly from her face and said, "Perhaps we can obtain permission from the Jordanian authorities."

"Not a chance," the general replied. "They will have nothing whatsoever to do with an Israeli-based archaeological team."

"But we're not Israelis," she protested.

"To them, you may as well be. They will know that what you are seeking at Nebo refers to Hebrew history. The Jordanians do not even respect our right to exist as a state, much less our historic roots to this land. We have an armed truce with Jordan, but neither country recognizes the other."

"Perhaps if Professor Sabitini made a formal request to the Jordanian ambassador in Rome," she suggested.

"He can make a formal request, and several months from now they will respond negatively. I know it's difficult for foreigners to perceive, but no Arab nation will aid you in a quest that proves the Old Testament is not legend."

"But," she said, "if they knew there was a lost word of God . . ."

"You had your experience in Syria. The mere fact of an idiom resembling ancient Hebrew surfaced on those tablets and you were expelled. You're free to act as you wish, but I can't help you in Jordan."

The table fell silent. The clatter of dishes and sounds of conversation around them reverberated off the cafeteria walls.

Sorenson took out a pack of English Oval cigarettes and offered one to Barzani.

"Tell me, General, what is the distance from the closest point in Israel to Mount Nebo?"

"The boundary is measured by the northern curve of the Dead Sea. I would say it's no more than thirty kilometers."

"Is it heavily patrolled?"

"No. We've had no terrorist incursions from Jordan, and we have launched no missions against them." He paused and puffed the strong English cigarette. "But there are patrols of Jordanian border police. The Dead Sea shoreline follows an ancient caravan track. As a matter of fact, Bedouin tribes who live in our Negev Desert still cross into Jordan, smuggling and trading in hashish. The Jordanian police leave them pretty much alone. Why do you ask?"

"Because we've come too damn far to permit a vague frontier and ancient enmities to stop us now." Sorenson leaned forward and in a low conspiratorial tone said, "I suggest we cross at night and take our chances."

"Who's *we*?" Jack asked.

"You, me, and Gabriella, of course."

"Without any protection?"

"Well, what's the downside risk? Let's examine it.

Assume we're stopped by Jordanian border police. We apologize for getting lost. We produce our passports. They send us back across the border. They're not going to execute us as Israeli spies."

"Suppose you're caught on the return portion," Barzani said. "You're crossing back into Israel in possession of ancient artifacts. The sentence for stealing national treasures in the kingdom of Jordan is twenty years."

"That wouldn't apply in our case," Sorenson persisted.

"Don't argue with me, Doctor!" Barzani replied angrily. "You will find yourselves locked in some medieval dungeon, demanding to see your respective consul generals."

"I understand your concern," Gabriella answered soothingly. "But they couldn't prove we found that scroll in the cave at Mount Nebo."

"The Jordanian authorities are not required to prove anything. It's not a democracy. It's a kingdom, an absolute one-man dictatorship."

"Well, it's a risk I'm prepared to take," Sorenson stated.

"I agree," Gabriella said.

Barzani glanced at Jack. "You, my friend, are a professional. It's up to you. If you decide to try to cross, I'll help you in a limited way. Remember, my authority ends on the western edge of the Dead Sea."

There was a moment of contemplative silence, and all eyes turned to Jack. He swallowed some coffee and quietly asked Barzani, "You say that area is lightly patrolled?"

"Relatively speaking, yes."

Jack rubbed the stubble on his cheek. "Christ, I don't know." He paused. "What do you think our chances are?"

"To cross at night undetected is possible with certain arrangements, but you would have to locate Moses' sepulcher and that bronze vessel before dawn. You'd have to be well on your way back before sunrise."

Sorenson quickly said, "Fine. We'll set a time limit. If

we haven't succeeded by, say, four A.M., we give it up and return under cover of darkness."

They watched Barzani brush a fly from the lip of his coffee cup. He stared at them one by one, then sighed heavily. "You know the risks. I'll do what I can to help you."

He took out a pen, spread his napkin, and drew a rough map. The sketch depicted two landmasses separated by a narrow loop. He penciled a series of dashes into the loop indicating water and outlined a mountain on the eastern side of the water and wrote "Mount Nebo." He then drew a Star of David on the opposite side of the water. "We will be stationed here. I'll supply you with a jeep, equipped with a two-way radio tuned to a receiver on an armored personnel carrier. I'll be in that vehicle waiting for you. You will be crossing under a full moon. But if you trail a band of Bedouins, you can pass as tourists who engaged Bedouin guides and mistakenly strayed into Jordan."

"You mean use the Bedouins as a cover?" Sorenson asked.

Barzani nodded. "The border police often follow but rarely stop them."

"How do we arrange that?"

"It's not difficult. There is a Bedouin sheikh, an old and trusted friend. He can organize a small caravan and escort you to Mount Nebo. Then you're on your own. The Bedouins will continue south to Aqaba, the Jordanian seaport where they pick up hashish from the Sudan."

Sorenson's fingertips drummed nervously against the table for a moment. "I'm not questioning your intent, General, but I dislike the idea of Bedouin cover."

"Why is that, Doctor?"

"Suppose the Bedouins deposit us at Nebo, then contact the Jordanian police."

"What would motivate them to do that?"

"Gain favor with the Jordanian authorities."

"Don't confuse your corrupt Anglo-Saxon practices with the ways of Bedouins. They are a people who live by tribal codes of honor burned into them by five thousand years of survival in an environment that would destroy the best of men. They possess a primitive nobility and seek favors from no one. They do not betray friends."

"I have to bow to your knowledge," Sorenson said amicably.

"All right. I'll provide all the necessary equipment and maps."

"What about weapons?" Sorenson asked.

"Absolutely not," Barzani replied. "That's the last thing you want to take into Jordan."

"But I don't see how—"

"For chrissake, Martin!" Jack interrupted. "The general is sticking his neck out for us! This is his turf!"

Sorenson smiled and in a honey-laced voice said, "Why the sudden anger, Jack? My question was a logical one. After all, crossing the desert at night unarmed is not the safest of propositions."

"No one's forcing you to go," Jack replied testily.

There was a beat of tense silence before Gabriella rose and asked Barzani, "Where shall we assemble?"

"Right here at ten P.M. I'll arrange quarters. You'd better get some sleep. You'll be crossing shortly after midnight."

CHAPTER FIFTY-TWO

⚠

A luminous pale moon painted surreal shadows across the desert and beyond to the dark hills of Jordan. They were camped at the western edge of the Dead Sea. A light wind whipped the sand against an armored personnel carrier. Two soldiers sat atop the vehicle, smoking and chatting.

Gabriella and Sorenson studied a topographical map and checked positions with an Israeli officer. Jack lounged against the jeep, watching Barzani use his hands to make a point with the Bedouin chief.

The sheikh's tribesmen sat astride their camels, waiting patiently for the negotiation to conclude. They were dark, sinuous, and in the moonlight their impassive black eyes seemed to reflect the wisdom of the ages.

Barzani grasped the old sheikh's hand and shouted to Jack, "Come! Bring the others!"

The general poured some wine into the cupped palms of the old man. "By drinking the wine from his hands, we consecrate our agreement with him," Barzani explained.

They each in turn sipped the sweet red wine from

the old man's brown palms. The sheikh then poured wine into Barzani's cupped palms and drank from the general's hand.

"*Allah inshallah*," he said in a low, raspy voice.

"*Allah akbar*," Barzani replied.

The old chief kissed Barzani on both cheeks, turned abruptly, and climbed aboard the lead camel. He hit the animal twice. It brayed in protest but began to move. The line of fifteen camels and Bedouins started east toward the curving shore of the Dead Sea.

Jack got behind the wheel of the jeep. Gabriella sat beside him, and Sorenson occupied the rear seat. The vehicle was packed with a battery-operated Sun Gun, powerful flashlights, ropes, climbing axes, a first-aid kit, and thermos jugs of hot coffee.

"You know how to operate the radio?" Barzani asked.

Jack nodded. "Depress this button to send, and hit this switch to receive."

"Okay." Barzani sighed. "Now remember, just follow the caravan, don't attempt to pass. When you get close to Mount Nebo, the sheikh will show you the cave entrance. If you run into a Jordanian patrol, tell them you hired the Bedouins to show you the ruins of Zohar. Produce your passports. They'll search you. Be civil, and say no more. The old man will confirm your story. Chances are you will be escorted back to our side of the sea."

"Got it," Jack said.

"But"—Barzani sighed and leaned into the jeep—"if you find that scroll and get stopped on the way back . . ." He shrugged and straightened up. "Good luck."

The camels loped along with surprising speed, and the wind flared the black robes of the Bedouins. The caravan hugged the north shore of the Dead Sea.

"My God, look at that!" Gabriella exclaimed. Columns of crystallized salt looking strangely human loomed up out of the black waters like white phantoms guarding the ancient sea.

"One of those salt columns is Lot's wife," Sorenson said. "She made the mistake of looking back."

"That legend may be fact," Gabriella replied. "Recent archaeological evidence places Sodom and Gomorrah at the southern edge of the Dead Sea."

Jack remained silent, his thoughts shifting between past and present. He had perceived the truth too late. He was out of his jurisdiction, and a confrontation with Sorenson would be senseless. Besides, they would need each other before this night was over. Jack's scalp tingled as he thought about the history of the man seated just behind him. Sorenson was a predator. The deadliest kind: genius crossed with madness and no conscience.

They bumped along the rocky desert floor in the dusty wake of the caravan. The jagged face of Mount Nebo rose above the desert like a great stone altar. A pair of nighthawks flew off their high perch on the cliff face and glided gracefully over the desert, seeking a nocturnal lizard or scorpion. From a distant wadi an eerie cry carried on the wind.

"What the hell is that?" Sorenson asked nervously.

"Jackals," Gabriella replied.

The Bedouin chief wheeled his camel around and trotted down the line of tribesmen toward the jeep. He reined to a stop and pointed toward Mount Nebo. "*Jabal nabi Musa.*"

"The mountain of the prophet, Moses," Gabriella translated.

The sheikh's coal black eyes shone through slits in his headdress. He leaned down and cupped his mouth against the wind. "*Madchal abrashia Musa garib. Giddan muzlim.*"

"He says the entrance to Moses' cathedral is near. But very dark."

"*Yahdia yati!*" the chief ordered.

"He wants us to follow him."

The sheikh whipped and spurred his braying camel into a fast gallop. Jack gunned the jeep, following him toward the base of Mount Nebo.

The night air was cold, pure, and intoxicating. The

wind cracked and whipped through the mountain crevices, carrying with it the eerie wail of jackals. As they approached Mount Nebo, the sheikh slowed his camel to a walk, and Jack geared down, steering carefully around fallen rocks.

The sheikh halted, hit his camel, and shouted, *"Asfal! Asfal!"* The beast brayed in protest but obediently folded its legs and assumed a sitting position.

The sheikh dismounted and motioned them to a narrow opening between two boulders. *"Moutanazh nouna!"*

"He says to park in there," Gabriella translated.

Jack downshifted and, steering carefully, brought the jeep to a jolting stop between the boulders.

The chief watched them collect their equipment and shouted, *"Saria! Saria!"*

"What's he saying?" Jack asked.

"Hurry up," Gabriella replied.

The sheikh led them to a jagged outcropping that formed a deep alleylike wedge. He pointed into the dark opening and issued a stream of Arabic.

"He says it's the entrance," Gabriella explained. "But its tunnels and chambers are protected by evil spirits."

Directing their flashlights into the dark crevice, they noticed the narrow ledge angling sharply up from the desert floor into the mouth of the cave.

"Hawaa la gayid," the sheikh said.

"What is it now?" Sorenson asked impatiently.

"I'm not sure. The Bedouin dialect is not pure Arabic, but I think he said, 'The air inside is not good, difficult to breathe.' "

The wind moaned, and the camels brayed from the line of waiting tribesmen. The lead camel driver called something out to the chief, who glanced up at the curious halo surrounding the moon. *"Roubama khamsin,"* he murmured.

"He thinks there will be a sandstorm," Gabriella said.

"That would be a break," Sorenson replied. "Cover us coming back."

"If you've ever seen a full-fledged sandstorm, don't

count on going anywhere," Gabriella cautioned. "Compasses go crazy; day turns into night."

"Let's not worry about it now," Jack said. "Thank the chief and wish him well."

Gabriella kissed the old man on both cheeks and said, *"Shikran habibi. Gayid har."*

"Sigaia tabqh." The sheikh smiled.

"He wants tobacco, cigarettes."

Sorenson pressed a pack of cigarettes into the old man's hand.

"Shikran," the chief replied in gratitude.

The sand swirled as the old man cupped his hands around a flaming wooden match and lit the cigarette. The smoke rushed out of his nostrils in two fine streams. He touched Gabriella's hair and smiled. *"Yagtaa yuti shama ashqar. Gayid haz."*

"He wants a piece of my hair," she explained. "Blond hair is good fortune."

Sorenson slipped a hunting knife out of its sheath and, raising the tips of her hair, quickly sliced a few strands and offered them to the chief, but the old man shook his head. *"Imraa."*

"He will accept it only from me," Gabriella said.

She gave the blond strands to the sheikh. He turned and held them up to his tribesmen. *"Gayid!"*

"Gayid!" they responded.

The old man remounted his camel, spurred the animal up to the head of the column, and waved back to them. *"Salam alakum!"*

The Bedouin caravan slowly moved out, following a southern track, their billowing black shadows gliding ominously across the shifting sea of sand.

CHAPTER FIFTY-THREE

$\triangle$

They started up the jagged ledge with Sorenson leading the way. The ledge rose gradually but precipi-
tously. A single misstep meant a deadly fall to the
sharp-edged rocks below. Halfway up the escarpment
Sorenson's flashlight illuminated a four-foot break in
the ledge.

The doctor hugged the wall and turned to them.
"We're all capable of jumping this break. Concentrate
on the other side, and don't look down."

He tucked his flashlight into his pack, took a deep
breath, crouched slightly, and leaped over the gap. He
landed easily on the other side.

Gabriella moved to the lip of the break, crossed herself, and jumped. Her left foot landed on the far side,
but her right foot fell short. Sorenson's hand sprang
out, grabbing her and pulling her to safety. Jack was
amazed at the speed and dexterity of the doctor's
reflexes.

A flurry of wind whipped around the curved section
of the wall. Jack clutched a protruding stone above his
head. "Wait for the wind!" Sorenson shouted.

Jack pressed himself to the wall. The gusting wind died as suddenly as it arose. He released his handhold, crouched, and leaped across the gap. He landed on the far side with room to spare.

"That seems to be the worst of it," Sorenson said. "Just hug the wall and follow me."

Their progress was excruciatingly slow. They clung tenaciously to the outcroppings, seeking secure handholds to maintain their precarious balance. Sixty-five feet above the desert floor the ledge disappeared into the mouth of the cave. Sorenson switched from his flashlight to the powerful Sun Gun, directing the beam into the dark recesses of the cave. The air was cold and thin, causing their breaths to come in short gasps.

They proceeded into the narrow passage and followed its twists and turns, almost unaware of its subtle rise. The sounds of their boots and labored breathing filled the void of silence. At odd moments the ceiling dropped severely, forcing them to crouch. Their bodies were chilled by perspiration from the exertion of the climb and the thin air.

The walls gradually angled toward an adjacent tunnel.

"What do you think?" Sorenson asked Gabriella.

"Let's take it. We should see a crypt, or skeletons, or some sign of a burial chamber. There must be a reason it's called the cave of eternity."

Entering the tunnel, they were instantly assaulted by an overwhelming stench of ammonia. Their lights illuminated thousands of bats, their wings stirring fitfully as they clung upside down to the ceiling.

"Cave bats," Gabriella said. "The ammonia is the residual odor of their urine. They're not dangerous."

"The stench of ammonia can be fatal," Sorenson cautioned.

"This thin air doesn't help," Jack said. "We should have brought portable oxygen units."

Their boots crunched over the fallen stones and fossilized bat droppings. The tunnel narrowed, and the ceiling dropped abruptly. Crouching down, they moved forward and struggled up the subtle angle of incline.

Sorenson stopped and gasped for breath; his light beam bounced off a solid wall.

"Goddammit!" he exclaimed. "Another dead end."

"It's two thirty-five," Jack cautioned. "We've got three hours left to sunrise."

Gabriella moved past the men and knelt beside a large boulder lodged against the base of the wall.

"What is it?" Sorenson asked.

"There's a draft of warm air coming from behind this boulder," she said, "which indicates another tunnel or passage."

They put their shoulders to the flat side of the granite, their boots digging into the earthen floor for leverage. They strained and heaved, grunting and cursing. The boulder moved slightly off its flat base, and the balance of its weight began to shift in their favor. "Come on. Shove!" Sorenson gasped. "Another few inches."

They pressed against the boulder, and with a loud rumble the huge stone tipped off its purchase and toppled over. Sorenson's Sun Gun illuminated a body-size opening at the base of the wall.

"The boulder was set deliberately," Gabriella explained. "A blocking device."

"That warm air smells like death," Jack said.

"Let's hope so," Sorenson replied. "We may have found the crypt."

One by one they crawled inside the opening. The cavernous chamber was studded with mounds of bleached grinning skulls, some without jawbones, others with struts of shoulder bones.

Gabriella stood beside a shallow depression containing a skeleton still partially covered by a tattered, decomposed fabric. A cluster of bronze jars, coins, and lapis lazuli jewelry were strewn in and around this shallow grave. "These are the remains of Midianite slaves and servants buried along with their masters."

"What period?" Sorenson asked.

"Mosaic. Thirteen hundred to twelve hundred B.C."

"How do you know they were slaves?" Jack asked.

"By the dye colors of these wrappings. Yellow, blue, and red were common dye colors; purple was the color of royalty and high priests. We can assume that somewhere close by is a royal crypt."

"We'll never make it by sunrise," Jack cautioned.

"The hell with that," Sorenson snapped. "If you're nervous, leave."

Jack flashed his light beam into Sorenson's face and smiled. "You'd be lost without me, Martin."

Sorenson's eyes glittered dangerously in the light. "Get that goddamn light out of my eyes."

"Please! Stop it!" Gabriella said, grabbing Jack's hand, forcing his flashlight down. "We still have time if we work together."

They picked their way warily past the mounds of skulls and skeletons. Straining against the incline, they pushed ahead, gasping in the oxygen-starved air.

Twenty minutes later the stone hall veered abruptly left, forming a narrow crevice. Their lights fell upon a skeleton in a sitting position. Bits of fabric clung to its bones; across its lap lay a spear and a bronze shield. In the shield's center was the Star of David and five Hebrew letters.

Gabriella examined the bronze inscription. "This is the remains of a sentry, an officer, a warrior of the Hebrew tribe of Naphtali," she said. "He may have been part of a burial detail left behind by Joshua to guard Moses' tomb."

"Let's keep going!" Sorenson said tensely.

They squeezed through the crevice and found themselves in a limestone passageway. There were no bats, no skeletons, no visible signs of animal or human life. Their legs wobbled, and they felt intoxicated by the lack of oxygen.

Sorenson's light illuminated an alcove that seemed to have been carved out of the rear wall. He cautioned them to wait and disappeared inside. They heard sounds of stumbling, followed by loud, angry expletives.

Jack was about to enter the alcove when Sorenson emerged, his pants torn, and his cheek cut.

"The floor drops almost forty-five degrees." He gasped. "I grabbed a goddamn ledge at the last second. There's a remnant of steps worn down by dripping water. Place yourself sideways, watch your footing, and use the wall for balance."

Clutching at handholds, they barely managed to maintain their balance down the steep incline. Panting for breath, they entered a cool cavern lined with porous clay walls. In the center of the chamber, a bronze coffin gleamed in the light of Sorenson's Sun Gun.

They moved trancelike across the earthen floor and stared in silent wonder at the purple-robed skeleton inside the coffin. A large oval-shaped basket rested at the foot of the skeleton. The only sound was the coarse whisper of sand being sucked down through small crevices in the floor.

Gabriella gently lifted the amber-colored basket. It had been woven together with palm fronds and was sealed at the top with a carnelian red wax. Turning it to the light, she clearly saw three Hebrew letters.

In a hushed voice she said, "The letters are *MSM*, biblical Hebrew consonants that spell 'Moses.' Let me have your knife, Martin."

Her breath was barely audible as she edged the blade under the seal. A gust of wind moaned through the chamber, and the floor trembled.

"What is that?" Jack asked.

"Mountains like this, interlaced with caverns and tunnels, react like old mine shafts," Gabriella explained. "Crypts, chambers, tunnels can collapse without warning."

She continued to loosen the seal and with a final twist of the blade removed it intact and slipped it into her pocket. She placed her palms against the oval sides of the basket, exerting a pulling pressure. The basket sprang open, revealing a beautifully crafted bronze jug.

They stared at it speechlessly for a moment, each of them sensing the presence of an omniscient supernatural force.

"Go ahead, pick it up," Sorenson said hoarsely.

She lifted the bronze vessel and held it up to their lights. The twin lions of Judah were carved into its flared sides. She depressed the jug handle, opening the circular lid. They held their breaths as she reached inside and carefully removed a cylindrical papyrus bound by strips of worn purple cloth.

"Put it back!" Sorenson shouted, and reached for the papyrus.

Jack grabbed his arm. "Take it easy, Martin!"

The doctor's eyes were wild, and his voice was shrill. "The air! The scroll will evaporate!"

Gabriella shook her head and in a calm, reassuring voice said, "Papyrus is made out of reed and is impervious to air. They made boats out of papyrus in Egypt. Trust me, Martin."

Sorenson stared at her, his breath coming in short gasps. "You're absolutely right. Forgive me."

She moved to a flat-topped rock and, exercising exquisite care, unrolled the yellowed papyrus. The scroll measured eight and a half inches across and fourteen inches in length and was inscribed in flowing cursive characters.

"Pure biblical Hebrew," she said in a hushed voice.

She took out a marking pen and searched her pockets for a piece of paper.

"Use the reverse side of this," Jack said, handing her a topographical map.

Gabriella bent over the scroll and studied its opening lines.

"Can you read it?" Sorenson asked tensely.

She nodded. "The sentences appear to be logical and"—she paused—"uncoded."

She began to write in block-lettered English, glancing in quick intervals from the scroll to her developing translation.

At the place of the waters in Meribah-Kadesh Yahweh's voice commanded me, "Moses, son of Amram, assemble the tribes and say unto them, 'Listen now to the last words of the Lord thy God.'"

The men watched, transfixed, the danger of passing time forgotten.

I listened to God's words. And he did burn them into my soul. And there they remained. And in my torment I committed the sin of doubt. For the meaning of the Lord's text was fearful to me. And I did withhold Yahweh's words from the people. And the Lord did punish me for this transgression. And in repentance on this last day I dispatched Ithamar with a stone tablet to be placed in Megiddo. I granted unto Ithamar that his days would know peace in our ancient kingdom of Ebla. I looked into the future world and saw there my words would be found by the righteous and those of pure heart. Therefore, do I now in this cave of eternity, in the pagan land of Moab, in my dying hours herein inscribe the last words of Yahweh to be preserved into the midnight of time.

Gabriella placed the pen down and wiped the beads of perspiration from her face. She flexed her right hand, took a deep breath, and bent over the papyrus, studying the Hebrew script. After a moment of intense concentration she glanced at them and in a soft, reverent voice said, "What follows are the words of Yahweh." She rubbed her sweaty palm against her thigh, gripped the pen firmly, and began to write:

It has come to pass that I, the Lord thy God, failed thee. For out of love I bestowed upon man the power of mind and choice above all other living things. But this blessing has caused him to be imperfect and carries with it the seeds of his own destruction. From the time of Adam, this creature whom I created in my own image and likeness has perverted this gift of intelligence. He sacrifices spirit in the pursuit of matter. His wisdom has turned to cunning. He heeds not my commandments and in fear of his transgressions seeks redemption through burnt offerings and the ritual prayers of priests.

She paused and again flexed her right hand. There was a whispered rush of seeping sand, and she resumed writing.

Make them to know that priests cannot absolve their transgressions. Mortal man cannot grant mortal man salvation in my name. And say this unto the priests: Though they cloak themselves in purple raiments and stand upon splendorous altars, they have no power but to teach my law. They cannot heal man or redeem his sins. The redemption of man is reflected in the mirror of his own soul, for in that sacred place do I dwell and no other. Not in your temples, or shrines, or tabernacles, for only in the mirror of man's soul will he see the truth of his life. And though he is become an imperfect creature, still does he possess the power of choice. And in the goodness of that choice lies his salvation—and the resurrection of my love.

The clay walls trembled, and funnels of dust devils swirled across the floor.

Gabriella carefully rerolled the scroll and placed it back inside the bronze jar. She then folded the map with its English translation and tucked it in her breast pocket. Her eyes shone brightly as if they were illuminated from an inner source.

"We now know why the great prophet withheld the last word of God," she said. "Moses led those former slaves through the wilderness for forty years, and only through priestly power did they finally accept the concept of one God. In that time the priests had the power of life and death. It must have been inconceivable to Moses that those primitive tribes would adhere to God's laws if the choice were theirs to make."

She started for the palm frond basket, but Sorenson picked it up and casually said, "I'll take the jar."

Jack quickly placed himself between Sorenson and Gabriella. "She found it. She translated it. She'll carry it."

"Suppose we're stopped by Jordanian police," Sorenson replied. "You want them to find it in her possession?"

"Physical possession of that jar is irrelevant," Jack said quietly. "They'll grab us all anyway."

"If he wants to carry it," Gabriella interjected, "let him have it."

"Just hold it!" Jack snapped at her.

"What are you afraid of?" Sorenson asked.

"I'm not afraid of anything. Just let's have some ground rules up front. Gabriella is going to put that scroll right into Barzani's hands."

Two dust devils suddenly whirled up, spouting sand over Sorenson's boots.

"You're wrong, Jack. If we manage to get back without any trouble, we've got to tell Barzani we failed. We found nothing."

Gabriella stared at Sorenson with growing apprehension. "Why would we lie about it?"

"The state of Israel is not going to acknowledge this scroll," Sorenson replied calmly. "You think these Orthodox rabbis are anxious to know that their great and powerful God, Yahweh, not only failed man but declared his priests to be powerless? These words will never see the light of day. But I have the means and connections to ensure its exhibition."

"Those rights are already spoken for," Jack replied.

Sorenson shook his head, and his voice was traced with anger. "Don't quarrel with me. I know what I'm talking about. There are organized forces that have the capability to destroy this scroll and prevent its public exposure. I've spent the last years of my life scientifically stealing the soul of man." He paused, and his voice assumed a messianic tone. "You have to understand that bringing to light the last word of God is my redemption."

"You don't want redemption," Jack said. "You want immortality. The same way Hamilton did."

Sorenson's eyes flicked between Jack and Gabriella. His hands flexed rapidly, and beads of sweat dotted his upper lip. "Don't equate my motives with Hamilton."

"Why not?" Jack asked calmly. "You and Hamilton were practically clones. It's too bad you killed him. You two could have done business."

"I never do business with assassins."

"You've spent the best part of your life doing business with assassins," Jack replied. "*You* made the deal with the Syrians. The same deal you claimed Hamilton made. Claudon sold you a lot more than the triangle; he told you what that triangle truly represented. That's why you paid him an additional hundred and fifty thousand, and a few weeks later, in early July you went to Damascus and met with Syrian intelligence and made your deal with them."

"I paid a quarter of a million for that triangle because I thought it was a bargain at that price." He wiped the sweat from his lip. "I went to Damascus in the cause of science and enlightenment. I urged the Syrians to re-open the Ebla site."

"You couldn't have cared less about science and enlightenment. You wanted the tablet for yourself, so you went into business with the Syrians. You needed their help and approval. But your greed got in the way of your intellect. You misjudged the Syrian mentality. Once you gave them the game and the players, all they had to do was come after you."

"I misjudged nothing. I was betrayed by Hamilton!"

"You betrayed yourself! Hamilton had nothing to do with the Syrians. He never understood the true value of the triangle until *after* Laura was killed! It was only after Gabriella phoned him in late September that Hamilton perceived the triangle's intrinsic worth. That's when he offered to finance the Megiddo dig."

"Emory knew about the triangle before Laura's death!"

"Emory's interest was innocent. He may have told Hamilton that you purchased an interesting artifact, but nothing more because he didn't know any more. Hamilton was still frightened of the Syrians long after Laura was killed. That's why he sent Claudon to Rome to meet with Gabriella. You were the only one who understood what was really at stake, and from the moment you made the Syrian deal, Laura was in jeopardy. You might as well have pulled the trigger."

"I avenged her death!" Sorenson screamed. "All alone!"

His voice echoed eerily through the chamber. Gabriella watched them circling like two predators sizing each other up.

"It won't work," Jack replied calmly. "You set the Syrians in motion and caused Laura's death. And if Jenny had been home that morning, they'd have killed her, too."

"You sanctimonious son of a bitch!" Sorenson's eyes blazed with madness. "Where were you when the chips were down? I was out there alone. I put my life on the line!"

"You placed the lives of innocent people on the line. You made a mistake, Martin, a fatal mistake. But your ego won't permit you to face up to the truth. You assumed the role of the avenging angel, and in your distorted logic murder became an act of contrition."

The wind moaned through the chamber, and swirls of sand disappeared into the network of tiny crevices in the earthen floor.

Sorenson's jaw muscles jumped, and his face glistened with beads of sweat. "I saved your life!" he shouted.

Jack shook his head. "It wasn't me you were protecting. It was Gabriella, and only because you needed her."

A dangerous smile appeared on Sorenson's face. "What does it matter now?" His voice was flat and deadly. "I have the God scroll."

He slipped the eight-inch hunting knife out of its sheath and started toward them. Jack simultaneously hurled his body into Sorenson. They fell grappling in the sand.

Sorenson tried to free his right arm, to gain leverage with his knife hand. Rolling in the dirt, they tore at each other, each seeking an opening.

Sorenson jabbed his elbow into Jack's throat, and his right hand came down with the knife. Jack rolled, and the blade whipped across his face, missing his throat and slashing into his shoulder. Instantly, he felt the warm flow of blood seeping down his arm.

Sorenson placed his knee on Jack's chest and raised the knife high above his head. Jack scooped up handfuls of dirt and tossed it into Sorenson's face.

Sorenson choked and fell back. Jack threw a jolting left jab into his solar plexus. The doctor grunted in pain but maintained his grip on the knife. He jammed his knee into Jack's groin and then grabbed his hair. He yanked Jack's head up and pressed the point of the blade just behind his ear.

Gabriella raised her flashlight with both hands and smashed it into the back of Sorenson's head. He toppled over. Blood seeped from his head and ran down both sides of his face. He shook his head, struggled to his feet, and lurched toward her. Jack tried desperately to rise, but he was paralyzed by the pain in his groin. Sorenson hit Gabriella once. She dropped to the floor, her cheek cut, tears coursing down her face.

Sorenson then started toward Jack, the knife poised in his hand. His eyes were feverish and he licked at the blood running down his face into his mouth. The floor trembled, and a sudden cracking sound reverberated off the walls.

Sorenson screamed and fell out of sight.

Jack crawled to the spot where the earth had opened and peered into the dark abyss. He shouted the doctor's name, but all that came back was the echo of his own voice.

He glanced at Gabriella, who sat on her haunches, her eyes trancelike, a large purple swelling on her cheek, a trickle of blood running down to her throat.

Jack retrieved the Sun Gun and crawled back to the edge of the pit. Gabriella moved beside him. He switched on the light and directed its beam into the pit. They peered into the deep hole and gasped in horror.

Sorenson was flat on his back, his dead eyes wide

open in terror. The pointed head of a spear protruded from an oozing red hole in his belly.

Jack turned the focus knob, widening the light beam.

"My God . . ." Gabriella whispered.

Close to Sorenson's skewered body, the grotesque face of the devil-god Pazuzu grinned at the doctor's bloody corpse.

CHAPTER FIFTY-FOUR

△

Two hours later they emerged from the mouth of the cave and squinted against the rising sun. The desert stretched before them, and in the distance, on the western horizon, a glistening blue smudge marked the Dead Sea. An ominous stillness pervaded the timeless landscape.

In the light of day the stone ledge curving down to the desert floor appeared to be less forbidding. Nevertheless, Jack set a slow, deliberate pace, stopping occasionally to gain secure handholds and instructing Gabriella to imitate his actions.

They reached the break and jumped across it. The ledge widened, and they descended to the desert floor without mishap.

They picked their way through the fallen rocks surrounding the base of Mount Nebo and felt a surge of relief at the sight of the twin boulders sheltering the jeep.

Jack got behind the wheel. Gabriella sat alongside, holding the bronze jar in her lap. He inserted the ignition key and smiled. "Say a prayer." He turned the key, depressed the accelerator, and the four-cylinder engine kicked instantly into life.

His eyes swept the purple mountains to the east. If a Jordanian border patrol spotted their dust cloud, it would come after them from out of those mountain passes.

The granite peaks to their right glowed deep amber in the yellow sunlight, and to the south a vast sea of high dunes rose and fell into infinity. A hot wind blew against the windshield, depositing insects that instantly turned into small, wet blobs.

"There's a pack of cigarettes in the glove compartment," Jack shouted over the roar of the motor. "Light one for me."

She handed him the glowing cigarette. He took it with his left hand and steered with his right. His left shoulder throbbed painfully from the knife wound.

Gabriella noticed beads of sweat oozing from his forehead and running down his cheeks. His eyes periodically darted to the rearview mirror.

They traveled in silence, moving inexorably toward the distant blur of the Dead Sea. She studied him intently—the hard set of his jaw and the dead, flat look of his eyes.

"What is it?" she asked.

"Nothing."

She placed the bronze vessel on the floorboard and moved closer to him, her arm circling his shoulder.

"Tell me."

"Hell, I don't know. I can't get those words out of my mind. God's words. They keep turning over."

He glanced off to the south and noticed great sprays of sand blowing off the crests of the dunes. He downshifted as the terrain grew rocky. "I'm not sure we have the right to reveal them."

She withdrew her arm and stared at him curiously. "Why not?"

"How do you tell people they were created flawed and imperfect and that priests have no power to absolve or forgive, that churches, temples, shrines have no meaning?"

"Where in the text is that stated?"

"The meaning seems very clear to me. 'Look into the mirror of your own soul, for in no other place do I dwell. Mortal man cannot grant absolution to mortal man.' The essence of that text robs mankind of hope."

"Hope of what?"

"Any ultimate salvation."

The force of the wind increased with sudden velocity, and the yellow sunlight perceptibly diminished.

"Fine," she said. "That's your opinion, and I respect it."

"But you don't agree?"

"No. Quite the opposite. It restores hope. 'In the goodness of man's choice lies salvation and the restoration of my love.' The essence of the full text strips away the hypocrisy of religion and man's misuse of intelligence. If those words had been revealed three thousand years ago, we might not be looking at each other over nuclear warheads."

"So you have no moral problems with it?"

"Not at all. Discovery is its own morality. Anything that enlightens man is moral."

A surge of hot wind whipped clouds of sand against the windshield. Jack's eyes narrowed to slits against the blowing sand.

Gabriella suddenly gasped and pointed south. "Look!"

Jack glanced off to the left, and his eyes widened in horror. The entire desert floor had risen, sucked skyward, forming a towering concave wave of sand. The crest soared thousands of feet skyward, blotting out the sun.

The great column of sand seemed to be frozen in place, collecting its energy like a vast army massing for an assault on a distant enemy. They watched it in fearful silence.

Then it moved.

Jack cut the ignition, braked, and set the gearshift in reverse. A blistering wind whipped their clothes, and sand particles stung their faces. Their eyes were riveted on the mountainous black wave roaring toward them.

Jack shouted over the wind, "Get on that radio! We've got to be in frequency range of Barzani!"

He took the bronze jar and, struggling against the wind, fought his way around to the passenger side of the jeep. Gabriella shouted Hebrew words repeatedly into the speaker.

The colossal funnel of sand swept over them, obliterating the sun, turning day into night. Jack grabbed Gabriella and dragged her under the jeep. They flattened out, belly down. He held the bronze jar in his hands and they buried their heads in the sand.

Their eyes were clenched shut. The jeep shuddered violently above them. The sand split their skin. Tiny blood spots dotted their faces and arms. Life and death merged as they clung together, gasping at the dust-caked air, trapped by a howling demonic force that seemed to have risen out of hell itself.

The grip of terror distorted their perception of time. Each second was a lifetime, each minute an eternity.

Finally, the diminishing roar of wind signaled that the vortex of the wave had passed. A dim ray of sunlight angled across the jeep. Jack raised his face and glanced to his right; fifty yards off the wave of sand howled in the darkness. He crawled out from under the jeep, still holding the bronze vessel.

The wind instantly pinned him against the tire.

Gabriella wriggled out from under the jeep, and he pulled her to him. They sat in the half-light, watching the great wave of sand whirling in place, gathering its force.

Their eardrums were clogged by the roaring funnel. Its outer circles buffeted them like ripples curling out of an explosive force. Their lips were cracked, their throats scratchy and parched, their eyes slitted against the blowing sand.

They stared at the monstrous phenomenon in awed disbelief. The desert floor trembled, and the yellow sunlight disappeared.

A dark finger of wind emerged from the whirling funnel and struck them with stunning force. It held them fast for a moment, then drew back with a frightening roar. The suction pulled the jar out of Jack's hand.

Gabriella screamed and bolted after the bronze vessel. Jack hurled himself through the clouds of sand and, running full out, managed to tackle her at the very perimeter of the whirlwind.

He covered her body with his own. She beat against his chest and clawed at his face. She tried to bite his wrists and screamed, "You let it go! You let it go!"

He fought her off, pinning her arms to the sand.

The towering column moved, spiraling east toward Mount Nebo. The wind slowly died. The yellow sunlight reappeared. He helped her to her feet.

She panted for breath, and tears coursed down her swollen, blood-flecked face. "You let it go, didn't you?" she gasped.

"The scroll said that they of 'pure heart' would find the last word of God. Well, none of us qualified. I wanted vengeance. Sorenson wanted immortality. You wanted the pride of discovery. We weren't meant to have it."

"Just tell me," she said, catching her breath, "did the wind take it or did you let it go?"

Jack glanced off at the tidal wave of swirling sand. "I don't know." He sighed and looked at her. "The truth is I don't want to know."

And in that frozen second of time, in the glaring sunlight, his eyes reminded her of Bedouins' eyes and seemed to reflect a timeless wisdom. She stared at him and remembered the words of God: *Only in the mirror of man's soul will he see the truth of his life.* And if he had let the jar go, perhaps that was his truth; and she could never hate him for that.

He gently brushed some sand from her cheek and said, "Maybe we found something more important, something we'll never lose."

She nodded almost imperceptibly. His arm circled her shoulders, and they walked slowly back to the jeep. He gunned the motor and, following the wide curve of the Dead Sea, sped west toward Israel.

*   *   *

The bronze jar skimmed across the desert floor, carried on a cushion of wind, swept along by the great column of sand—back toward the shadow of Mount Nebo, back into the midnight of time. . . .

ABOUT THE AUTHOR

STEVE SHAGAN is the author of the novel and award-winning screenplay *Save the Tiger*, which won the Writers Guild Award as best original screen drama of 1973. His second novel, *City of Angels*, was the basis for the Paramount movie *Hustle*. In 1976, he received his second Academy Award nomination for his screenplay of *Voyage of the Damned*. His most recent novels were the smash best sellers *The Formula* and *The Circle*.